About the Author

Judith Pratt's experiences – actor, director, professor, fundraiser, and freelance writer – inspire her novels, stories and plays. Most recently, her stories were published in "The Gateway Review," "Fifth Di," and "Modern Magic" magazines. They have also appeared online in "Fiction Junkies," "Stars and Staffs Magazine," "Golden Walkman podcasts," "Hags Fire," and "Synkroniciti Magazine." Her novel, "Siljeea Magic" was indie-published in 2019. In 2019, her play "Maize" was selected for the Louisiana State University SciArts Prize. Her play "Losing It" was published in Best Ten-Minute Plays of 2020. She lives in Ithaca, NY, with her husband and three cockatiels. www.judithpratt.com

The Skill

Judith Pratt

The Skill

Vanguard Press

VANGUARD PAPERBACK

© Copyright 2024
Judith Pratt

The right of Judith Pratt to be identified as author of
this work has been asserted by her in accordance with the
Copyright, Designs and Patents Act 1988.

All Rights Reserved

No reproduction, copy or transmission of this publication
may be made without written permission.
No paragraph of this publication may be reproduced,
copied or transmitted save with the written permission of the publisher, or in
accordance with the provisions
of the Copyright Act 1956 (as amended).

Any person who commits any unauthorised act in relation to
this publication may be liable to criminal
prosecution and civil claims for damages.

A CIP catalogue record for this title is
available from the British Library.

ISBN 978 1 80016 841 1

This is a work of fiction. Names, characters, businesses, places, events and incidents are either the product of the author's imagination or used in a fictitious manner. Any resemblance to actual persons, living or dead, or actual events is purely coincidental.

Vanguard Press is an imprint of
Pegasus Elliot Mackenzie Publishers Ltd.
www.pegasuspublishers.com

First Published in 2024

Vanguard Press
Sheraton House Castle Park
Cambridge England

Printed & Bound in Great Britain

Dedication

For the Saturday Writers' Group.

Acknowledgements

Thanks to Tom Bruce, Elaine Meyers, and Kathy Morris.

ONE: CASEY

Standing on the faded yellow-brown linoleum floor of her great aunt's huge kitchen, Casey breathed in rosemary, lemon polish, and silence.

"Aunt Cill?" she called. "It's Casey. I'm here."

No answer.

Then the house took a deep breath.

Houses don't breathe, but Annoying Voice thought this one did. Annoying Voice always popped into Casey's head when she felt something unusual was happening.

When she was a kid and Annoying Voice showed up, Casey would repeat its statements out loud. "I don't think that maple tree feels well," she'd say. Or "We shouldn't play on the Rock today, it's mad at us."

"Oh yeah," her brother Duncan would say, "That tree needs therapy!" or "Right, and the front steps hate us too!"

As a result, Casey had named the thing Annoying Voice and spent the next fifteen years ignoring it. Now and then she wondered if Annoying Voice meant she needed therapy, but she couldn't face explaining it to anyone, even a kindly psychologist.

If you hadn't believed Jake's ideas about business, Annoying Voice whispered, you wouldn't be bankrupt.

"Aunt Cill!"

"No need to yell."

Casey jumped, dropping her suitcase with a thunk. Behind her, Great Aunt Cill closed the door to the back stairs. The house had been built in the days of live-in servants. They used the back stairs to get to the kitchen from their attic bedrooms. Somehow, her great aunt had negotiated the steep flight so quietly, Casey didn't hear her. How could someone that old move so silently?

"There you are, Priscilla. You made good time," said Aunt Cill. "Your room's all ready. Better take that case up the front stairs; not so steep, more places to rest," and she led the way to the front hall.

Tall and lanky, Great Aunt Cill took her mop of gray frizz to Hazel the Hairdresser two or three times a year, without perceptible results. When Casey was a child, her aunt would give her a bony hug once on her arrival and again when the family left after their summertime visit. But now, Casey realized that adults don't get bony hugs. Not a problem. Being called by her full name, Priscilla, was a problem, although she'd just have to deal with it.

When eleven-year-old Casey had announced she hated her name, her father explained. "We named you Priscilla because we hope that Great Aunt Cill might will her land to you if we named you for her. Developers would pay a lot for it."

"That's gross," Casey had responded, with all the arrogance of her youth. As soon as she got to college, she introduced herself as Casey.

Once again she told herself that spending a month here was a good idea, even if her aunt called her Priscilla. Staying here would give her time to breathe, to forget Jake, to find a job, to get out of debt from their bankruptcy. Then she could finally live up to her parents' expectations, get a position with a real company and prove she was a worthy member of her successful family.

Annoying Voice disliked the whole notion of becoming successful, but Casey had worked hard to tune out those complaints.

For the first eighteen summers of her life, her family had visited Great Aunt Cill every July. They'd drive from their Boston suburb to a tiny Maine town, then up the long driveway to the old house and its surrounding acres of trees. As a child, Casey had believed the forest was magical. Now, at almost twenty-five years old, she knew better. But exploring the forest would keep her from obsessing about Jake. He'd left her for a sweet and dainty girl named, of course, Melissa. Casey felt gangly and awkward every time she thought of that girl.

Now, her great aunt led Casey past the big mahogany dining table, polished to a glow, through the dark wood archway into the living room with its ancient, squashy furniture, into the cavernous front hall, up the curved staircase with the blue and white Chinese vase on a little shelf above the first landing. Casey did put her suitcase down there for a moment in order to bring some feeling back into her fingers.

Aunt Cill waited in the doorway to the back bedroom. "Your bed's all made. Towels right on top. I put in a shower in the back hall, you probably saw it when you came in. I know you young girls are always washing your hair. I won't have a shower up here. Baths are better for you. Dinner at six, like always."

"Thank you, Aunt Cill," Casey said dutifully. "I'll wash up and come set the table."

"That's my good girl," said her aunt, as if Casey were still eight years old, still learning that in Aunt Cill's house you had chores and did them without complaint. She felt the clumsy childishness of those days, when she was a suburban rich kid stunned by a big house and tight rules.

Hunting out her comb, Casey tried to get the knots out of her curls. They tangled on the least pretext, such as from the wind blowing through the gas station when she filled the tank in Albany, or because of the friction of the backrest when she napped in a rest stop, stupefied by the long dull drive from Rochester.

Once she'd combed out the knots, she tried to tame the resulting frizz, then gave up. Red hair was okay, but she always thought her nose was too beaky, her skin too pink, and her eyes too small, even if they were a nice hazel color. Besides, she was even taller and lankier than Aunt Cill.

Acres of forest surrounded the house. Aunt Cill owned five miles in every direction.

Casey spent a moment gazing out the back window at the trees. Tomorrow, she told them, I'll visit you tomorrow.

An old barn stood at the forest's edge. Casey remembered how she and her sister T.J. would spend rainy days exploring it, finding strange tools and scurrying mice. Today, the rain that had chased her through downstate Maine had stopped, and a cool breeze blew away the clouds.

The trees next to the barn had odd shapes. No, they were sculptures, tall, curving wood sculptures, blending in with the trees. Annoying Voice said they were protecting the forest.

A man stood in front of the barn, washing something in a metal bucket, using a dark green hose. Casey couldn't see much of his face, only a brush of dark sideburns and a wide back under a ragged white T-shirt bisected by a braid of black hair. Annoying Voice told her he was worried. Casey told Annoying Voice not to be silly, adding, 'if you're so smart, tell me what he's doing here!'

Annoying Voice didn't answer.

Grabbing a towel, she crossed the hall to the bathroom for a wash.

When Casey was little, crossing the narrow upstairs hall scared her to death. She was sure she would trip and fall down the long, curving, precipitous front stairs. But she had always loved the bathroom, with its huge claw-foot tub, tiny black and white tiles, and old pedestal sink. As she washed her hands and face, she thought: 'Nothing changes in this house, only me.'

No depressing thoughts, dammit, she told herself, and headed downstairs to set the table.

Dinner was fish, fresh green peas, and baked potato. The ocean lay ten miles away, and her aunt believed in eating plain fish. Casey's older brother Duncan hated that inevitable and boring fish. Now he only ate in New York City's fanciest restaurants, where the plates of culinary miracles looked like works of art.

"I'm glad to see you have someone helping you with the yard," Casey said, buttering her potato lavishly. After Jake left, she'd given up on dieting, given up on trying to be beautiful for men. Besides, she could never resist real butter.

"He mows for me," her aunt said. "Watches out for the trees. Helps him with his rent."

"Rent?"

"He and Eddie Kerr made a nice big apartment upstairs in the old barn. The young man is some kind of artist. Likes the north light. Very quiet, no trouble at all."

To Aunt Cill, "young man" could mean anyone from twenty to fifty. Casey hoped he was at least fifty. "Did he make those sculptures next to the barn?"

"Yup," said her aunt. "You wash the dishes, I'll dry 'em."

Swallowing her questions, Casey picked up a dishtowel. She could still hear her aunt snapping "Silence is golden," or "Children should be seen and not heard." In that kind of mood, Aunt Cill might just decide that Casey should go live somewhere else. Not until I visit the forest, Casey told herself.

Dishes done, they headed out to sit on the front porch, to enjoy the June evening. But the quiet hummed in her ears. Casey remembered how she, Duncan, and her sister T.J. would argue, yell, and roll down the sloping front lawn, getting grass stains on their shirts. She remembered her parents sitting on the porch, visiting with friends, drinking wine, chatting. Now it was only Casey and Aunt Cill, who was reading a book. *Great Expectations*, the title said. Casey had vague memories of trying to read Dickens and falling asleep.

She tried to check e-mails on her phone, and to write to her Rochester friends to say that she'd arrived; but out here, in the middle of nowhere, the signal had disappeared. Lost without her phone, Casey found herself gazing longingly down the long grassy hill into the woods beyond.

When she had told her parents she planned to stay with Aunt Cill for the summer, they'd been pleased. "She shouldn't live way out there by herself," Dad said. "Let us know if she needs help."

The last time Casey's family had visited, the summer before she went to college, her parents had suggested that Aunt Cill move to a nice assisted living place in a nearby town.

"Nope," said Aunt Cill.

Casey's parents never took no for an answer, so they started in talking about the wonders of Shady Acres. Aunt Cill simply left, went into her room, locked the door, and didn't come out for the rest of their visit.

Eight years later, Aunt Cill definitely didn't need Shady Acres. Making dinner, she had charged around the kitchen just the way Casey remembered. While they ate, her aunt had announced Casey's tasks—vacuum weekly, dust daily, do all the shopping and errands. Who had been doing the errands? The man she saw from her window, the "some kind of artist," or Aunt Cill? Casey had opened her mouth to ask, then shut it again. Questioning the old lady never ended well. She'd learned that by the time she was eight years old.

Now, as Casey stared at the darkening trees, the man she'd seen by the barn came out of the south woods, his T-shirt pale in the dusk. He was squarely built, with a muscular chest and arms, and walked like a young man—confident, powerful.

"Is that the man who takes care of your yard?" The question came out of her mouth before Casey knew it.

Aunt Cill frowned and looked up from her book. "Ayup, the Pelotte boy. He likes to walk around the place in the evening, stretch his legs." The old lady stood up. "It's my bedtime. I'm up early. I know you youngsters like to sleep late. You'll just have to make your own breakfast." And off she went, trotting up the staircase, her steps astonishingly light for a woman her age.

Although Casey had no idea of her age. Her aunt never changed. She looked the same as Casey remembered her from eight years ago. Even Aunt Cill's clothes were the same: wide, loose slacks that reminded Casey of 1930s movie fashions, topped by slightly less old-fashioned shirts. Tonight, the shirt was a muted blue, with short sleeves and a narrow collar.

Alone, Casey watched moths trying to get through the screen to the porch light. The silence kept hissing in her ears.

Climbing the steep staircase to her room, she pulled a small sketchbook out of the bottom of her suitcase, along with her little bag of pencils. While going through the things in the Rochester apartment, Casey had discovered her old sketchbooks. Ignoring the drawings in them, she had stuffed them into her suitcase, along with the bag of drawing pencils, sharpener, and erasers she had stowed away with the sketchbooks.

Back on the porch, with the yellow porch light attracting soft brownish moths, she sketched them, then drew the heavy old wicker rocking chair Aunt Cill had vacated, drew the dark line of trees silhouetted against the full moon. She hadn't drawn anything for several years—ever since starting the business that failed. Sketching had then felt like a waste of time, as she obsessed about how to find customers before their money ran out. Now she realized how much she had missed drawing. It helped her to think.

When the hissing quiet finally got too much for her, Casey headed for her bedroom. The sheets on her bed had been dried outside. They smelled like wind and new beginnings.

Despite the wonderful sheets, Casey discovered that early to bed did not mean early to sleep. As the business had failed, her insomnia had prospered. She would lie in bed for hours, mentally going over the figures, worrying about how to get more customers, wishing that optimistic Jake would share that worry. Now, she brooded over how she'd failed her family.

Growing up, she'd hated her parents' preoccupation with business success. Instead of choosing a school in Boston, she broke tradition and went to college in Rochester NY. She stayed there because of Jake and their web design business, planning on a happily-ever-after. Then WebLicious went broke, and Jake left her. Now Casey had three maxed-out credit cards and no idea how to pay them off—or how to pay her share of the WebLicious creditors. She had sold everything she could. It didn't bring much, but every dollar helped to pay off her debt.

When she'd finally found the courage to tell her parents that the business she and Jake had created was bankrupt, her father said, "You should have got more experience before starting a new venture. If you'd worked for a real company for a few years, you might still have a working business."

Trying not to cry, Casey could only nod at the phone. Her mother had tried to smooth things over, but Casey knew her dad was right. Her parents had a successful accounting business. They had given all three of their children, love, advice, and a good life. Casey's sister and brother would be lawyers. But she had thrown away all her advantages. She was the family failure. Her insomnia grew worse.

Tonight, she tried all the relaxation and breathing exercises she knew, did a few gentle yoga postures, turned on the white noise app on her phone. But her mind itched and obsessed over the need to find a job, get out of debt, prove herself. Sometime after one a.m., she gave up.

Maybe a drink would help. She tiptoed barefoot down the curving stairs, through the archway, into the dining room, where her parents used to make drinks at the heavy mahogany sideboard. A silk-shaded lamp stood nearby. Turning it on, she crouched down to open the lower door of the sideboard. It stuck. She jiggled it carefully, quietly, but it popped open so fast that Casey sat down hard on her butt. She tried not to breathe while listening for Aunt Cill. All she heard were tree frogs chirping. Okay.

The cabinet held an unopened bottle of red wine, an almost empty vodka bottle—Casey hated vodka—and a bunch of brown bottles with corks. Picking up one of them, she sniffed at the cork and was overwhelmed by a pungent, astringent, eye-watering odor, unlike any liquor she'd ever met. It made her sneeze. Afraid she'd disturb Aunt Cill; she held her nose and almost blew her ears off.

Thoroughly awakened by her abortive sneeze, she gave up on the liquor cabinet. Opening the wine might annoy Aunt Cill. Besides, Casey thought, I'd probably drink it all. Maybe I should take a walk.

Back upstairs, she pulled on some sweats over her T-shirt nightgown, grabbed her sandals, barefooted her way down the stairs, out the open front door to the porch, and down the long porch stairs, where she sat to put on her sandals.

The grass smelled like childhood memories. All around her, the forest hummed. We missed you, it said.

Without a flashlight, Casey couldn't explore the woods in the dark. She'd fall over roots and rocks. Still, she walked toward the trees closest to the house, and put her hand on the ridged bark. I'll be there soon, she told it. *"Soon,"* echoed the tree.

Casey lay down on the grass near the maple. The sheer numbers of stars out here overwhelmed her. She found the Milky Way, the Big Dipper, and Cassiopeia. Sleep and dreams ran together.

Deep in the forest, she built the kind of wonderful house that only exists in dreams. Trees grew out of some of the rooms, while other rooms perched high among the branches. Many of the walls were made of green leaves or dark pine needles, but a few of them were white. White as painters' canvases. On those walls, Casey created pictures she'd never imagined, forest paintings. No painting out, no giving up. Everything came out of her brush perfectly.

TWO: RINNE

The idea of marrying Gavin made Rinne's stomach roil and her heart bang with panic.

Before Gran had insisted she get married, Rinne Gilley had planned to stay on Halloran Island forever. The Island floats in the Atlantic Ocean, several miles from the coast of Maine. Her family had lived there for a hundred and fifty years.

As a child, Rinne loved to lie on the long grass under the pine trees, staring at the swaying branches until she was joyously dizzy. She loved to spend hours with her older sister Sarah, watching the wind and surf off Lookout Ledge, their dark hair mingling in the sea breeze.

Then Sarah ran away.

The summer after she graduated from high school, Sarah went out with some friends on their yacht, and never came back. Instead, she sent a letter, writing that she planned to travel. "I'll be back someday," the letter concluded.

Their dad, Brian, spent hours going up and down the coast on his lobster boat. He never found Sarah.

"Now *you* have to marry Gavin," Gran told Rinne.

Sarah and Gavin were meant for one another. Their children would keep the family's Skill strong for the next generation. Without the Skill, life on the Island would be impossible.

When Sarah ran away, everyone was surprised, except Rinne. She knew Sarah was too beautiful to stay on the Island. But Rinne didn't plan to marry anyone, let alone Gavin.

However, Gran's word was law in the Gilley family—unless Great Gran disagreed—so Rinne simply nodded. Nodding was always easier than arguing. And no one argued with Gran; or Great Gran. Besides, Rinne had three more years of high school before the marriage would take place; three years to figure out how to find her sister Sarah. Three years to avoid the marriage.

Gavin was handsome enough, six feet tall and burly, with brown curls, strong shoulders, and pale skin sunburned by days on the fishing boat. Most girls found Gavin's ocean-blue eyes and easy grin irresistible. Rinne did not. They had grown up together, and as an annoying big brother—he was actually some kind of third or fourth cousin—Gavin wasn't so bad. As a husband—well, Rinne hated the idea.

Hate it or not, two days later, on a Saturday, Gavin came to visit, wearing a clean plaid shirt and clean jeans, instead of his usual grimy sweatshirt and fish-encrusted pants. Rinne saw him coming through the back yard, past the vegetable garden and the chicken house. He sauntered along like a man who knows all the girls love him.

Rinne considered escaping out the front door. But Gran, sitting at the scarred wooden kitchen table with a cup of tea, said, "Here comes that boy. You'd better go and meet him."

Nodding obediently, although she did not feel obedient, Rinne opened the screen door.

"Hey, Gavin," she said.

He asked her to go for a walk, something he'd never done in her whole fifteen years. Rinne unenthusiastically agreed. They walked through the Gilley yard, Rinne taking two steps for every one of Gavin's. She hated being so short.

She found herself hoping that Elsie, the grumpy nanny goat, would butt Gavin. Elsie often took a dislike to someone and chased them out of the yard. But today, she'd climbed to the top of the chicken house to survey her domain.

"I figure you know what I'm gonna say," Gavin muttered. Rinne didn't answer.

After a pause, he said, "I'd rather marry you than Sarah. She never thought I was good enough for her."

"No one here was good enough for her," Rinne said.

In silence, they walked up the rocky hill to the pine grove. Panicked adrenaline made Rinne shaky. She couldn't do this. She had to do this.

"Can we wait a year after I graduate?" she asked. "I promise I won't run away like Sarah did. I'd like a little time before—before we settle down."

"Okay with me," Gavin said. "But you'll have to convince Gran."

Gran was not convinced. "You and Gavin must have children as soon as possible," she said. "Without Sarah, we don't have enough young folk with the Skill. Plan for a wedding right after you graduate."

Rinne's mother nodded in agreement. Between them, they had settled Rinne's life for her.

But Rinne did not want to be like her parents, whose arguments often kept her awake at night. She and Sarah shared a room under the sloping roof of their house, and the stairs funneled the arguments right into their bedroom.

Their mother had always been difficult. Her name, Maris, meant "ocean," and it described her perfectly. For days, she'd be peacefully lapping around the corners of the house, preparing meals, canning tomatoes, hanging clothes out to dry in the soft salt breeze. But Rinne learned very young when a storm was brewing in her mother, whose temper appeared as randomly as the Island weather. So, when six-year-old Rinne spilled her glass of milk, Maris would say, "Be more careful dear," and mop it up. But the next day, if little Rinne came in ten minutes late for her dinner chores, Maris would storm that Rinne was the most impossible child on the Island. Being the most impossible among six kids—Rinne, Sarah, and their four sort-of-cousins—shouldn't have been so bad, but Maris in a bad temper could blow all the sense out of Rinne.

Sometimes, when they were supposed to be asleep, young Sarah and Rinne would hear yelling downstairs. Sarah would put the pillow over her head and ignore the noise. But one night, when Rinne was about twelve, she crept down the stairs to listen, to find out what the arguing meant.

"... not going out fishing with you again," came her mother's voice. "You're the worst fisherman in Maine. It's useless, having me along!"

"What do you think pays for everything in this house? If I couldn't catch fish and lobsters, the kids would go naked, and the roof would fall in!"

"I don't care! I'm not going!"

"We'll see what your mother has to say about that!" Brian yelled.

"To hell with her. Marrying you ruined my life. Her grandchild with the Skill should be enough for her!"

"You planning to run off to the mainland? You won't last a day over there!"

"I'm planning to live my own life here. Take Sarah with you if you think you need someone with the Skill. It won't help you find any lobsters, but I don't give a damn!"

The whole thing made young Rinne feel awful. Did her aunts and uncles argue like this? Was that what it meant to be grown up and married? She'd heard about the Skill all her life. Her mother had it. Sarah had it even more strongly, although Gran said that was still too young to learn how to use it. Their cousins didn't have it, but it had never mattered to any of them. Well, they were called "cousins," the way the family spoke of "Aunt Darina and Uncle Bill," and "Aunt Cathy and Uncle Neil," even though they were only second - or third - removed cousins. Rinne could never keep the relationships clear in her head. They acted like aunts and uncles and cousins, which was enough for her.

The cousins played Capture the Flag together, or built huts out of driftwood. Sometimes they argued, but they never screamed at each other the way her parents did. Despite the screaming, her mother still went out on the lobster boat whenever bad weather threatened.

"If they hate each other so much, how could they have had children?" Rinne asked Sarah, after an especially long night of screaming.

"You don't have to like someone to have sex with him," Sarah said loftily. She now went across the bay to Gorham Harbor to high school, and treated twelve-year-old Rinne like a silly child.

Rinne made disgusted noises. Sarah just laughed.

Now, three years later, Rinne had to find Sarah, find out why she left, and then figure out how not to marry Gavin.

THREE: RIORDAN

If his girlfriend kept calling, Dan would never finish the sculpture. Cill would be angry. Not that she'd yell or anything, only purse her lips, frown, and say nothing, very loudly. So, Dan ignored the ringing phone and kept sanding.

At least Alix had finally learned that cell phones didn't work way out here in Cill's forest. For the first month he'd lived there, she'd call his cell, then complain he never answered. She was always on her cell phone. At first, Dan had found it endearing. But out here, he was happy his phone didn't work.

Cill had hired him at the end of the summer almost three years ago. It took him until October to dig out the old barn attic and turn it into an apartment, complete with a studio where he could work on the sculptures Cill wanted.

But when the apartment was finished, Alix refused to move. "I can't live way out there," she said, and when Dan mentioned that she'd agreed it was a good idea, she veiled her lovely face in her hair and wept. He had never been able to withstand her tears, so he said he'd just try it for the winter. A few months later, Alix invited her band's drummer to live in their apartment. "Only as roommates," she told him. He nodded as if he believed her, and stayed in his new apartment on Woodward Lane.

Dan had met Cill Woodward at a craft fair in Blake Harbor, Maine, where he sold wooden cutting boards, decorative wood bowls with carved covers, and big salad bowls.

Between customers, he'd sand his work. Sanding, if you do it right, takes time, and Alix didn't want him getting wood dust all over their apartment. That summer, Dan had been working the craft fair circuit all over New England. He liked the Blake Harbor craft fair because the apartment he shared with Alix, in Greenville, was only a few miles away.

Every craft fair has at least two woodworkers like him, but what brought people to his booth was the five-foot-high sculpture he'd carved out of oak, creating a flowing, twisting form that folks came to look at, and touch. Some said it looked like wind. Others thought it was inspired by the ocean. Then they'd feel that they should at least check out Dan's other wares. Sometimes they'd even buy.

Dan was sanding away when something made him look up. A tall, angular old woman with a mop of gray curls stood next to the tall carving. Then she walked all around it. Finally, she put one hand on it and closed her eyes. "Great," thought Dan, "a crazy lady."

Her eyes snapped open, catching him staring at her. "You make this?" she asked.

"Yup."

"What's the price?"

The carving had taken him two winters, in between working as a finish carpenter for a construction company, turning bowls to sell in the summer, and going to see Alix sing in her band. He'd loved making the sculpture, even though he knew he'd never sell it.

"A thousand dollars?" It was a nice round number.

"You got more of those things?"

"No," he said. "Takes a long time to make one."

"Oak." She patted it. "I'll take it Can you make these in other wood? Pine? Maple?"

"Maple is hard to carve, takes extra time," he said. "And I'd have to find the right piece."

He didn't mention the six logs under the bed in the apartment. Alix hated them. But she left her clothes all over the place, not to mention stinking up the bathroom with hair spray and perfume and God knows what, so she couldn't complain; much. After all, Alix was beautiful—long wavy blond hair, long legs, a heart-shaped face, a perfect figure. Everyone said she and Dan made a gorgeous couple. Lately, Dan hadn't been sure about that. He didn't like living in an apartment. He wanted a house, and a yard, and maybe a patch of woods. Alix wanted to move to Boston and become a famous singer.

"I'm Cill Woodward," said the old lady, sticking out a veined hand.

Wiping off the sawdust on his jeans, Dan shook hands. "Riordan Pelotte," he said.

Riordan sounded exotic, intriguing people into purchasing his wares. It was a family name, handed down through an Irish great-grandfather. "Pelotte" came from his French-Abenaki father. Dan's father had been proud of his Native American heritage. He wore his black hair long, tied with a string, or braided. Dan did the same.

As Cill shook his hand, someone came to look at the bowls. If one person is looking, other people always figure there might be something good. Cill Woodward clearly knew that. She picked up a cutting board and winked at Dan.

After the fair closed for the day, she returned and invited him to supper at Ed's Eats, where fishermen sat at the counter drinking coffee and eating fat gooey sandwiches. Somehow, the old lady managed to learn all about what he did in the winter and the farm he grew up on. He told her about snowshoeing around the family woodlot as a kid, and trying to get Alix to go camping. But hair spray and camping don't mix.

Dan went back to his van to sleep, wondering how the old lady had induced him to talk so much.

The next day, she showed up again, handed him $1,000 in cash, and asked if he delivered. Of course, he said yes. She gave him directions to Woodward Lane. It was the longest "Lane" Dan ever encountered. Two miles of it, surrounded by forest. He'd started wondering if it was all some kind of strange joke when the house finally appeared on his left, its gray shingles and dark roof rising above an expanse of ragged grass.

The old lady wanted the carving placed just so, in her back yard, out by what she called the barn. It probably was a barn once, but now it held an ancient station wagon and a hundred years' worth of clutter.

"I've been thinking about turning the barn attic into an apartment," she said, offhandedly. "Could put in a picture window facing north. You hungry?"

Over tuna fish sandwiches, on bread that tasted homemade, she offered him a job. She needed someone to mow the lawn and walk through her woods, doing what she called "keeping an eye on 'em."

"Got acres of trees," she told him. "I can't get through them quick enough now. Not so young as I used to be."

Dan loved the idea, but worried about convincing Alix. He asked for a week to think it over.

"Call me in a week," said Cill Woodward.

As he drove his ancient van back to Greenville, Dan considered how to get Alix to agree.

"I can work on my sculptures out there," he explained to her, carefully. "No more sawdust in the living room or slabs of wood under the bed." To his amazement, Alix thought that was great. Then he discovered that her band had set up a tour of New England for the winter, and that she was completely obsessed with planning it.

Now, Dan was living in the best apartment he'd ever had, with a studio, a view of the woods, and time to work on his own carving. He made several more sculptures and, with Cill directing, set them up along the north woods. He plowed the snow, mowed the lawn, planted the vegetable garden, and learned what to look for when walking the miles of trails through Cill's woods.

At first, Cill came with him. "Keep an eye on those birch trees," she'd say. "They can get nervous." Right. Dan figured she meant they fell over easily. Or "Read up on brown spot, and tell me if you see anything at all wrong with these pine trees." Dan collected some books about trees and read them in the evenings. Early every morning, he'd walk a section of the woods. Then, over homemade muffins, scrambled eggs, or oatmeal, he'd report to Cill about what he had seen in the forest. Then he'd work on his sculpture, then walk through the next chunk of woods. It was a great life, although it did get a little lonely.

In September, after the drummer from Alix's band went off on a tour, Dan drove an hour to Greenville every week for a visit. They still had great sex, although Alix kept insisting that she would never live out in the woods with some strange old lady.

Dan finished more sculptures, which Cill wanted on the edge of the south forest. She seemed to think they'd protect her trees. Dan sometimes thought she was right, that his sculptures had something unusual about them—he didn't let himself think of it as 'magic.' Other times, Dan thought Cill had odd ideas about her forest.

He was working on a fourth sculpture when Casey Todd arrived.

In sixty years or so, Dan figured, she would look like her aunt. Just as tall and lanky, Casey had a short mop of reddish curls, freckles, and hazel eyes that looked green if she wore a green T-shirt. Her pointed nose gave character to her otherwise ordinary face. Now, Cill said, he needed to teach Casey what he had learned about the forest. He hoped Casey wouldn't take over his work. He had grown to love the forest.

FOUR: THE FOREST

A sharp sunbeam caught Casey right in the eye. The stars had put her to sleep on the lawn. But she felt good. Everything seemed possible. All she needed was a shower.

Aunt Cill wasn't on the porch or in the living room, thank heavens. Casey did not want to have to explain why she hadn't slept in her bed. Upstairs, she gathered her towels and shampoo, ready for the new shower room that had been installed on the "back porch". The porch was fully enclosed and crammed with ancient rubber boots, even more ancient barn coats, and frayed scarves. Wearing her ratty terrycloth bathrobe, Casey trotted down the front stairs, planning to say good morning to her aunt. But in the archway to the dining room, she skidded to a stop. Aunt Cill sat at the table with the Pelotte boy. Both of them looked up.

"Good morning, Priscilla," said Aunt Cill. "This is Riodan Pelotte, who lives in my barn."

"Dan," said the man, standing up and smiling at Casey.

"Casey." Aunt Cill might call her Priscilla, but no one else should. "Sorry, I'm heading for the shower. I didn't know anyone was here." She edged toward the kitchen door, escaping as fast as possible. The man was about her age, with big shoulders, long black hair tied back with string, golden brown skin, and high cheekbones. Okay, he wasn't much taller than Casey. As if that helped, with that smile and those shoulders. Still, she told herself, his face was too round to match those heart-throb muscles.

In the new shower stall, rubbing shampoo into her hair, all she could think of was avoiding this Riordan person. She thanked heavens and old houses for the back stairs.

Respectably dressed in good jeans and a green T-shirt, she snuck down the back stairs and peered from the kitchen into the dining room, as if she were still ten years old. Dan was sketching something on a sheet of paper with Aunt Cill looking over his shoulder, both of them frowning in concentration. Casey ducked back into the kitchen, figuring she'd get some toast and coffee and take it outside. Out the *back* door, so she didn't have to see Riordan.

"Priscilla, bring us the coffee pot, if you don't mind," her aunt called. "Cream for Riordan."

Aren't old ladies supposed go deaf? Casey wondered. She'd been as quiet as possible. Aunt Cill must have hearing like a bat.

Bringing in the coffee, Casey said, all on one breath. "I'll take mine on to the porch; it's a beautiful day."

"Nope," said her aunt. "Join us. I want you to go with Riordan and learn about my forest. Each day he checks a different section. Today, you'll go with him."

Realizing her mouth was hanging open, Casey closed it, breathed in and out, and said, "Okay." Then, when her aunt frowned, she said, "Yes, Aunt Cill, I'll need to change my shoes." She wiggled a sandaled foot, in case the old lady thought she was stalling; which she was.

Casey had looked forward to walking through the forest, but had planned to do it alone. She did not want to be forced into spending time with another gorgeous man, so soon after Jake. Riordan wasn't wearing a wedding ring. She hadn't seen anyone else living in the barn apartment, although they—he or she—might be away. Maybe he was gay. Whatever. She decided to ignore him.

Escaping to her room, she dug out her sneakers, and an old shirt and jeans she had used for cleaning out her Rochester apartment. City living didn't give you the right wardrobe for hiking in the forest. Especially because Jake had hated hiking, even in the manicured parks of Rochester. Returning down the steep stairs, she found Riordan and her aunt in the kitchen, stowing a backpack with several collapsible water bottles, and some of those brown bottles like the ones that had made Casey sneeze.

Riordan led her out the back door, then past the barn, where a trail led northwest through the woods. Following his broad back, she couldn't decide whether his braid was sexy or silly. The path widened, so they could walk side by side.

"This is the only old-growth forest I've ever seen," Riordan said. "The Maine Forest Service would love it, but for some reason, Cill refuses to talk to them. Instead, I'm supposed to check the trees for pests." He grinned ruefully. "I've had to learn a lot, and I'm nothing close to an expert. Look at that," he added, waving at a tree on their left. "It's a cherry tree. It shouldn't survive this far north."

The tree was at least forty feet high, with a trunk almost two feet wide. Casey went over and put her hands on the bark, which was gray, with thin black horizontal stripes.

"I thought cherry trees were small," she said. "This is beautiful." The tree purred under her touch, like she had always imagined her house plants did.

"This is the kind of cherry they make fancy furniture out of," said Riordan. The tree stopped purring. "Not that Cill would allow such a thing."

The tree purred again. I must miss my house plants, Casey thought. Here I am imagining trees purr.

To distract herself, she asked about the size of the forest.

"It's not quite a perfect rectangle of about 3,000 acres," Dan replied. "According to the forest service, there's a 5,000-acre old-growth forest in Maine, and a bunch of small ones, so this is special. And don't ask me why your aunt won't register this with the forest service; I have no idea."

They continued along the trail. Riordan waved to their left. "That's mostly white and red pine," he said. "Look for streams of resin on the trunk from the brown spruce beetle, or waxy white stuff from red pine scale."

They circled the trees. No resin. No waxy white stuff. They kept walking, with Riordan making forays off the trail to check on a particular tree, each time explaining what he was looking for, or commenting that a particular tree hadn't been doing well.

'This will be fine,' Casey thought. 'He only wants to tell me all about trees'.

But she found it hard to pay attention. All around her, the forest hummed. Each kind of tree had a different tone. Her Rochester house plants had hummed, so the purring trees weren't too surprising. But she could feel their roots under her feet, conversing. No, she was imagining that, because she had once read about how trees communicate. Besides, she had walked in the forested parks of Rochester several times, but had never felt those trees communicating.

"Earth to Priscilla," Riordan said.

Casey discovered she was standing still in the middle of the path, like an airhead.

She blinked. "Um," she said. "Casey. Priscilla is my aunt."

"She'll quiz you about the trees. You need to pay attention."

"Yes sir," said Casey.

"Hey, it was only a friendly warning. Do what you want." He strode off, leaving her to scurry after him.

"Riordan," she called. He paused, turned.

She couldn't tell him that she thought trees were communicating. "I'm sorry. I used to wander this forest as a child. I was remembering."

He smiled at her. "Call me Dan," he said. "I only use Riordan when I'm selling my wood carvings."

Wood carvings. They lined the edge of the woods on the north and south. Casey had seen them. They felt like part of the forest, beautiful curving tree trunks.

"Oh," she said. "Those are yours?"

"Yup. It's a long story. Right now, I'm supposed to be explaining about Cill's forest." He turned and kept walking. Casey followed him obediently.

A beautiful stand of hemlock trees appeared on the right, downhill from the curving path. Riordan—Dan—slid down the slope to check on them.

"Look for white stuff on the twigs," he said. "It's called woolly adelgid."

'It could take hours to hunt through all those trees,' Casey thought; but she could feel something was wrong. She plunged through the soft, fragrant branches, and found a tree that was whining like an unhappy puppy. Yes, there were several twigs with white stuff between the needles.

"Here!" she said.

Dan appeared beside her. "How the hell did you find it so fast?" he asked.

"I just, um, saw it," said Casey, lamely.

He shrugged out of the backpack, pulled out a brown bottle, and dabbed the contents on the affected places. Both of them went over the rest of the tree carefully, but found no more white stuff.

"Drat," said Dan. "We'll have to check all of them now. I'll come back tomorrow with lots of Cill's adelgid potion."

Casey nearly blurted out that the rest of the hemlocks were fine, but decided that he wouldn't believe her. She didn't believe it herself.

Next, they came to a healthy patch of elm trees. Casey stared at them, astonished. "I thought they all died of Dutch elm disease years ago."

Dan grinned. "Not these. If they don't die of disease, elm trees can live for two hundred years."

While he poked around for beetles or fungus, Casey stroked the deeply ridged bark, and stared up into the branches. She wanted to put her arms around the huge trunk, but didn't. Annoying Voice said the tree didn't want to be hugged. Oh, right, she was projecting her own concerns about looking stupid onto a tree.

The path turned sharply to the right. Dan pointed to their left. "Up there is Blackwood Road. It runs along the harbor. Lots of big fancy houses along there. It's the north boundary of Cill's forest."

Casey was breathing in the Christmas scent of balsam fir well before they came to a stand of several dozen giant trees. Some showed areas of resin on their bumpy gray bark. Casey stared at them.; but the trees murmured contentedly.

"Those are the older trees," Dan said. "Resin isn't a problem for them. Not like resin on a pine tree. We have to look for moth larvae from the eastern spruce budworm."

Patiently, he walked through the aromatic grove. Casey followed, although she knew that all the trees were perfectly happy. Or did she? All this must be some kind of reaction, like her insomnia, to the stress of losing Jake and their business. She understood house plants. She knew very little about trees.

The trail came out a little north of Aunt Cill's huge vegetable garden, which lay between the house and the driveway.

"Tomorrow we'll go through the east woods," Dan said. "Ash, beech, butternut, birch. But first, we report to Cill."

Casey sat and listened as Dan reported on the woolly adelgid, and the health of all the other trees. When he finished, Aunt Cill fixed Casey with her bright glower.

"What did you think?" she asked.

"There's a lot to learn," she said. She did not add "And I might be hallucinating."

FIVE: RINNE'S SKILL

Getting Rinne and her five cousins over to the mainland for elementary school was too hard during a Maine winter, so Halloran Island children were always home-schooled until they entered Gorham Harbor High School.

Aunt Darina taught them English and history. Aunt Cathy taught math and science. Rinne's mother Maris taught writing until the day that she held up one of nine-year-old Rinne's exercises.

"This is not acceptable," she said to the class, which was made up of the oldest cousin Nola, a younger cousin Liam, and Gavin, along with Sarah and Rinne. "This writing is not worthy of a five-year-old."

No one spoke, but Nola smiled in a nasty way. Rinne stood up, took the sheet of paper from her mother, and walked, coatless, out the back door into a rainstorm, heading for her Aunt Darina's house.

Aunt Darina was kneading bread when Rinne stomped into her kitchen, dripping water everywhere, and stuck the soggy essay in front of her aunt's nose.

"I won't study with her!" Rinne yelled. "I hate her!" And she burst into tears.

Aunt Darina went to see Maris. As a result, the two women didn't talk to each other at all for about a month. Then Maris stopped trying to teach, and Aunt Darina took it over.

Away from her mother's anger, Rinne didn't mind writing practice, although she preferred the math lessons with Aunt Cathy. Darina, however, was always Rinne's favorite aunt. She and Uncle Bill laughed a lot. Unlike the thin, dark-haired Gilley family, Darina was round, with fluffy blonde hair. When teaching, she told stupid jokes to help the kids remember things—like "what do you call a dinosaur with a big vocabulary? A thesaurus!" Rinne thought that was hilarious. Sarah did not. She said it was a childish joke.

One morning, after twelve-year-old Rinne had her sleep wrecked for the third night in a row because her parents were arguing, she stayed at the table when Aunt Darina said, "Okay, enough school for today. Go run around!" and everyone else dashed out the door.

"What's up, Rinne?" her aunt asked. "You seem tired today."

Rinne said she hadn't slept very well.

"What's going on? You're too young to have trouble sleeping." Aunt Darina brought out some ginger cookies, then poured a glass of milk for Rinne and a cup of coffee for herself.

"Um," said Rinne, discovering she wasn't interested in cookies. "Sometimes my parents argue."

Her aunt nodded. "Married folks do that. It's part of being married."

Rinne took a deep breath and sighed it away. "How come my parents got married?"

"Well. I guess you're old enough. You know that your mum, and Sarah, have the Skill?"

"It's something to do with wind and water."

"That's right. Your gran and great gran wanted your folks to marry, because they both come from families with the Skill. Even though Cathy's son Gavin doesn't, he should be able to pass it on, if he and Sarah get married."

"I don't want the Skill," Rinne said. "Not if I have to marry someone I argue with all the time."

Aunt Darina rose and put her empty coffee cup in the sink. "Your mom has always had a temper," she said. "But she's not going anywhere. Neither is your dad." For a moment, she stared out the kitchen window at the rain, while Rinne discovered she'd forgotten her coat. Then Aunt Darina said, "I have to make sure Seaside Cottage hasn't sprung a leak from all this rain. Want to come along?"

Rinne did. Aunt Darina put on her yellow sou'wester against the rain, and gave Rinne one that her son Liam had grown out of. They climbed into the old Jeep and bounced across the Island.

Unlike Rinne's father and her Uncle Neil, Aunt Darina and Uncle Bill didn't fish. Instead, they took care of Seaside Cottage, a summer home on the north end of Halloran Island. In the 1890s, an improvident Halloran had sold the land to some wealthy folks. Wealthy folks had lived there ever since. Over the years, the summer "cottage" grew into a mansion.

Rinne had never been there before, although she had been told wonderful stories about how these rich people lived. Rinne grew up with such stories the way most children grow up with fairy tales.

The huge front room of the cottage, as big as her own house, with the white-sheeted furniture floating in the rainy light, seemed full of ghosts.

While Aunt Darina trotted around looking for leaks, Rinne wandered through the house, finding a kitchen full of huge silver appliances, a room with a big desk and a glass case full of books, and a dining room that could seat a dozen people. The Gilley house had ancient, frayed braided rugs, dark chintz curtains that didn't show the dirt, and barely enough room for its five occupants.

"What do you think?" Rinne jumped; the rain had blurred the sound of Aunt Darina's feet. "Quite a place, isn't it?"

"How many people live here?"

Her aunt laughed. "Only two. But they have a lot of visitors in the summertime."

Rinne had been thinking about visiting the house with Aunt Darina in the summertime, but the phrase "a lot of visitors" changed her mind. She only liked people one or two at a time.

Aunt Darina must have talked to Maris again, because after that, Rinne never heard her parents argue, and her mom and dad still went out together on the Sary, the family fishing boat. Meanwhile, Rinne and Sarah did their homework, fed the chickens and the goat, helped with the cooking and weeded the vegetable garden, all as usual.

Over the next few years, the oldest cousin, Nola, went off to high school on the mainland, followed by Gavin and then Sarah. That left Liam, who spent most of his time on his uncle's fishing boat, and the youngest cousin, Chloe, who only wanted to sew dolls' clothes. Rinne didn't want to sit around, and she hated to sew. She'd rather go fishing, but only women who had Skill with wind did that. Pretending she wasn't lonely; she wandered the Island. In a deep cleft in the rocks, overlooking endless ocean on the east side of the Island, she spent most of her time if not taken up with chores or homework.

There, she discovered how to play with the waves.

Rinne's mom had never tried to teach Rinne how to control the waves. No one seemed to need Rinne to have a Skill. But she loved watching the waves. She even liked to wash dishes, feeling the water being drawn from the well that served all three Island families, letting it splash over her hands as she rinsed the plates.

Without Sarah, without the boys to play Capture the Flag with them, Rinne sat in her corner on Lookout Ledge and watched the ocean, enjoying the endless swell breaking over the rocks into creamy foam. In Aunt Cathy's class, Rinne had learned that the human body was mostly water. She could feel her blood moving in rhythm to the surf. Without thinking, she reached out as if to hold the ocean in her hand, like a purring cat; and the waves flattened and calmed.

Rinne tingled all over. The waves slowed down exactly as she imagined, flowing among the rocks as if they had been oiled. She stared at them, thrilled and amazed. She had the Skill! It was like being part of the water, imagining where it should go. It opened something inside her, an indescribable feeling that she didn't know she was missing until now.

What would the surf look like if it curled instead of splashing, making ringlets like Sarah's? And the waves became ringlets, dark water beneath, white frothing curls above.

"I have the Skill!" she shouted, running into the yard where her mother was digging up carrots. "I flattened the waves!"

Her mother kept digging. "Only for water?" she said. "That's easy enough. Come help me get the rest of the carrots up."

After that, Rinne played with the waves in secret.

SIX: THE ROCK

Four days later, Casey had now learned about the ash, beech, and birch trees in the east forest, and the swamp maple, sugar maple, and white oak in the south forest. After every trip, her aunt grilled her about her experience, but never seemed satisfied. Alone in her room, Casey would mutter the list of trees, recalling each in careful detail.

If she learned about the forest, maybe Aunt Cill would like her better. Although she did recall her father telling a joke about the old New Englander who said to his wife. "Martha, when I think about how much you've meant to me all these years, it's all I can do to keep from tellin' you so." Maybe Aunt Cill was like that.

After her lesson in forests and trees, and after lunch, Dan would go to his studio, or back to the forest, and her aunt would sit, watching the forest, and reading. Some days she'd sit in a crunchy wicker chair on the far end of the porch, where she could see the marsh area in the south woods and the birch trees on the hill that made up the east woods. Other days she'd go out behind the house, sitting in one of her old, lovely, and uncomfortable Adirondack chairs with a view of the north woods.

Aunt Cill couldn't oversee the Rock from any of her chairs, and she never asked Dan to check there. The stone outcrop loomed above the house on the west, with only a few cedar trees growing on its broad back. To the north, tall fir trees grew, smelling like balsam and comfort. To the south, white oak trees lifted their fluffy June leaves almost as high as the Rock.

Up here, Casey could forget her problems and hide from Aunt Cill's frown. Up here, scents of dusty grass and warm stone brought childhood memories of building secret hideouts.

'That's what I need,' thought Casey, 'a secret hideout.'

She sat in the niche where she and her sister once created fantastic landscapes and stories. Casey felt too old for fantasy, but the Rock was a good, solid-underneath-you place for thinking. A little grass grew in the niche, making a seat where you could look down at the trees of Thayer Park, which lay on the other side of the Rock. Or just gaze at the sky. Instead of the sky, however, Casey watched an odd green-gray leaf flutter down—and up—and down. Not a leaf, a green-gray butterfly floating among the cedar and sumac trees. She'd never seen a butterfly that color. A few green Luna moths lived in Maine, but they didn't come out in the daytime. This butterfly was as big as a Luna, although it didn't have tails.

The gentle flutter of leaves became a wind so sudden, it pulled the air from Casey's lungs. It felt like the time she'd ignored her parents and stepped outside their house to feel Hurricane Noel. Before her skinny ten-year-old body could blow away, her dad had grabbed her, hauled her inside, and yelled at her for being so stupid.

This wind bent the cedar and sumac trees almost flat. It howled through the forest below the Rock, oak and maple trees thrashing like they were in a hurricane. But the sky stayed blue, and Casey's red curls stayed flat with sweaty summer heat.

It made no sense. And the green-gray butterfly kept floating, as untouched by the strange wind as she was.

A loud crack made Casey jump. In the forest below where she stood, the branch of an enormous oak tree split painfully, the gashed wood showing white in the bright sunlight. She stared at the broken branch.

When she was a child, the oak was *her* tree. Hers to climb when her energetic family and cranky aunt got too much for her. Now it was broken. Like her life. She wanted to howl with misery.

Then something did howl. Not the wind. It sounded almost human, but it was probably a coyote. If Maine had coyotes.

'Coyotes sound like people sometimes,' Casey thought. 'Don't they?'

As quickly as it started, the hurricane disappeared. So did the howling. Must have been an animal scared by the wind; the wind she didn't feel.

Maybe it was some kind of weird downdraft thing. Casey recalled reading about them, where an ordinary storm would become a mini-tornado, taking down a patch of trees or sometimes a house. Except, this time, there was no storm. Not even a cloud.

Right, she thought, it's another hallucination.

"No, it's not," said Annoying Voice. She ignored it.

Instead, she headed down the east side of the Rock—the only side that wasn't too steep, or too covered with briars, to climb. A winding path led to the downhill side of the house, where Aunt Cill could see everything from the windows, or from the screened-in porch.

The path was overgrown with white-flowered hobblebush loops, which grabbed at Casey's legs. Stumbling, she tottered a few steps into the trees, and there was her oak tree with the broken branch. The low branch she used to grab first when climbing had broken, snapped off completely, dying among the underbrush. Poor tree. Putting both hands on the ridged gray trunk, leaning her head against it, Casey breathed in the sharp scent of the broken wood. And found herself crying.

All the tears she had given up shedding when everything fell apart, she now shed for the broken oak tree, holding onto its rough bark and weeping.

'I'm as broken as my oak tree,' she thought.

And then, "Get a grip, girl, you're crying over a stupid tree!"

Blowing her nose on a squashed tissue she found in her pocket, she leaned against the oak for a moment, before striding through the dead leaves, back to the path. Behind her, the oak tree began to grow a small twig from the stump of the broken branch. But Casey, now off the path and onto the lawn, didn't see it.

SEVEN: PLANNING

After Sarah ran away, Rinne's parents argued even more often. Clearly, marrying because Gran or Great Gran wanted them to had not worked well for Brian and Maris Gilley. Rinne did not want to live her life arguing with her husband. If she married Gavin, that's what would happen. Even now, he wanted to tell her the right way to coil ropes on her father's fishing boat, the Sary.

"I've been doing this all my life," she told him, irritated. "When did you become the expert?"

"I was only trying to help," Gavin said, smiling seductively.

"Then you can swab the deck," Rinne said. "That would be helping."

"Having one of *those* days?" Gavin asked.

Rinne could not believe what he'd said. "Tell you what, Mr. Expert," she said. "You finish it up yourself."

Handing him the soggy rope, she jumped onto the dock and ran up the hill. Instead of going into the house, where Maris would find chores for her to do, she kept going, through the pine grove, all the way to her niche on Lookout Ledge, where she sat and played with the waves.

Later, her father asked why she'd left Gavin to do all the work. Her explanation made him frown.

"Boys will be boys," he said. "Don't walk off the job again."

Rinne didn't argue. She went back to work on the Sary, ignoring Gavin when he told how to do things.

"You didn't get that spot clean," he'd say, as Rinne hosed off the deck, or "That's not the best way to stow the lobster pots." She simply acted like he wasn't there.

It didn't take long for him to lose his temper. "I'm talking to you!" he said loudly, grabbing Rinne's arm.

Rinne dropped the hose, where it sprayed randomly, and stood still. Gavin's grip on her arm tightened.

"Why are you ignoring me! What is your problem!" he yelled.

"Lovers quarrel?" Rinne's father appeared from behind the cabin. He leaned over and shut off the hose nozzle. "Not while working. Kiss and make up, and get back to work." And he stood there grinning.

Gavin let go of Rinne's arm, grabbed her, and kissed her, complete with his tongue in her mouth. By now, her senior year in high school, she had gone out with a few boys who also kissed her, but didn't stick their slimy tongue down her throat. When Gavin finally let go, she wanted to wipe her mouth, but he was grinning at her like something wonderful had happened.

"Now get to work," said her dad.

She didn't argue. She finished hosing off the deck and made plans.

Rinne was a good planner. In fact, in her high school, she had become the go to student for anything that required great organizational skills. It began back in the spring of her freshman year, when one of Gorham High School's best athletes injured his knee.

"Oh my God," Rinne's friend Alison Carr said dramatically. "The basketball team is so screwed!" Blonde and voluptuous, Alison had already been cast in the school's annual musical.

Helena Williams, who made up the third member of their group, tossed her brown curls and said, "You are such a drama queen."

"You don't think it's awful? What will happen to Mark? If he can't play basketball, the team will lose to Ellisville!" Ellisville was the hated rival of every Gorham High School team.

"His family can't afford knee surgery," said Helena flatly. "His career is over."

Helena knew all about Mark's family, because she was going out with a junior who was also on the basketball team. Like Alison, she lived in Gorham Harbor. Unlike Alison, she knew most of the guys in her class, having gone out with all of them during junior high school.

"We can raise money for the surgery," Rinne said.

Her friends stared at her. "How can we raise so much money?" Alison demanded. "We're just kids!"

Two months later, Rinne and her friends presented the Goodman family with a check for three thousand dollars. Under Rinne's direction, the freshman and sophomore classes washed cars, sold cakes, and created a successful crowdfunding campaign. The school was so impressed with this, they came up with the rest of the cost of repairing Mark's torn cartilage. And Rinne began her career as the organization woman.

Alison asked her to do the publicity for the musical, which attracted the largest audience the high school theater department had ever seen.

The next year, Alison talked her into stage managing the show. In her junior year, Rinne raised money for their school trip to Boston, and became president of the school's marketing and entrepreneurship club.

None of this made any sense to her family. "You have work to do here," her mother complained. "You can't keep staying late at school!"

Rinne sighed, and kept staying late. In high school, she'd learned that most people didn't live the way her family did. Rinne's father and her Uncle Neil fished; her mother and Aunt Cathy planted gardens, canned vegetables, raised chickens, milked goats and made cheese. The only computer on the Island was at Aunt Darina's. All the kids had to share it for their home-school work.

Now, in her senior year, Rinne made new plans. She got her homework done as quickly as possible so she could spend time in the school library, hunting for a job on their computers, and with their newspapers. With a job, she'd have time and money to find Sarah and bring her back to the Island. With her strong Skill, Sarah was the one who should marry Gavin, or at least help Rinne to avoid it. Besides, Rinne missed Sarah.

So far, however, Rinne had only found fast food or waitressing jobs, all in Gorham Harbor. If she stayed in Gorham Harbor, her father might try to make her return to the Island. Which was one step away from being stuck with Gavin for the rest of her life.

She had promised Gavin she wouldn't run away. But getting a job wasn't as simple as disappearing the way Sarah had. After all, Rinne would tell her parents where she was. Once she got there.

Worrying about all this, she almost missed the online advertisement. "Clerk wanted for the fascinating Puffin Feather Shoppe in Wabanaki Port. Customer service, stock maintenance. Open mind, open heart."

'I have an open mind,' Rinne thought. But she wasn't sure about having an open heart.

She spent the next two study halls composing an application letter for the job, which she mailed after school on her way back to the ferry. She had to stay up late finishing her homework, but she didn't care.

A week later, her father said, "You have a letter. Who's writing to you?"

"A school friend," Rinne lied. When she was safe in the attic bedroom she once shared with her sister, she ripped the letter open.

It asked her to come to the Puffin Feather for an interview. Wabanaki Port was fifteen miles from Gorham Harbor. How the hell would she get there?

When she told Helena and Alison about her problem, Helena said, "I'll drive you! I would love to work in the Harbor Hotel there!" Not that she had applied for the job or anything.

Helena lived for the moment, and enjoyed every single one of them. Her father was an officer at the local bank and loved to spoil his only daughter, which included giving her a red Chevy Nova as soon as she got her license. Rinne made plans to stay overnight with Helena on a Friday, so they could go to Wabanaki Port on Saturday morning.

"You're staying overnight again?" Rinne's mother asked her. "You're never home. Who's going to do the chores?"

"Sarah spent half of her senior year staying overnight in Gorham Harbor," Rinne said.

"You aren't Sarah. You'll come home tonight."

Rinne didn't argue, but she didn't come home either. She stayed with Helena. The next morning, they drove to Wabanaki Port.

It was smaller than Gorham Harbor, but the town had made itself into a tourist spot, with a big hotel and a bunch of little stores where tourists could wander and spend money. Rinne found the Puffin Feather Shop in an old clapboard house on Main Street. The sign showed a fat puffin gazing cutely at the feather it had plucked, which became the "I" in "Puffin".

The proprietor, Tavish Fortunato, was medium tall, and slender, with light brown skin and gorgeous brown eyes. And he wore the most beautiful shirt Rinne had ever seen on a man, a muted green and gold plaid, which made the usual flannel shirts worn by her father and cousins look even skuzzier. Rinne wore the dark red blouse she planned to wear for her graduation, because it looked good with her straight dark hair and brown eyes. But next to Mr. Fortunato, she felt as dowdy as she'd ever felt next to her beautiful sister.

"Tavish," he told her. "Mr. Fortunato is my father. Who doesn't speak to me." He laughed, as if it was a big joke. "I need someone who can lift and unpack boxes, as well as work the cash register. Your resume is great; you'll keep me organized if anyone can. How strong are you?"

Rinne said she was pretty strong. Work on the Island was unrelenting; helping on her father's lobster boat, keeping the garden alive on the sandy soil, sweeping the endless grit out of their small house. Tavish took her into the stockroom and asked her to lift a few boxes, which she did easily.

A bell rang. "Customer," said Tavish. "See what you can do."

The customer wore new, perfectly pressed L.L. Bean clothes, and wanted to know more about the artist who had created the lighthouse paintings hanging on the shop walls. Tavish silently handed Rinne a brochure about the artist. Rinne made the sale and got the job.

Helena, of course, found a job at the Harbor Hotel simply by walking in and asking for it. Her friend led a charmed life, which sometimes annoyed Rinne. But when Helena suggested sharing an apartment, Rinne agreed. She'd been worrying about how to afford a place on her own.

When Rinne returned after her trip, Maris was furious. "You said you'd come home! What were you doing? Out partying all night?"

"No," said Rinne. That was all she said. After Maris yelled herself into exhaustion, Rinne went out to clean the henhouse.

With her usual luck, Helena found a great apartment in a fairly new, brown-shingled building on a back street. Rinne hadn't seen it. She didn't dare take another overnight trip; but the day after they graduated from high school, Rinne and Helena moved to Wabanaki Port.

The move was easier than Rinne had thought it might be. Only Maris came to her graduation. At Sarah's graduation, the entire family had shown up, from Great Gran to little Chloe. But Rinne didn't mind. She didn't want to deal with all of them. After the ceremony, she told her mother that she wanted to stay in Gorham for some graduation parties.

"I packed a suitcase for it," Rinne said.

"We need you at home."

"Sarah stayed all week before and after graduation."

"You aren't Sarah."

"There's a party tonight. People are expecting me."

Maris sighed theatrically. "Fine. But be home tomorrow."

Rinne didn't respond. And she didn't come home the next day. Instead, she and Helena moved to Wabanaki Port. Helena's red Chevy was so crammed with her clothes, along with a microwave, hair dryer, curling iron, blender, and a box of stuffed animals, Rinne barely fitted into the front seat.

'Thank heavens the apartment is furnished,' Rinne thought. Otherwise, they'd be towing a trailer with Helena's canopy bed and antique bureau in it.

Helena chattered away about how amazing it would be to work at Harbor Hotel and meet people from all over; how she'd already met a cute guy who worked at the desk, and about how much fun they'd have living in their very own apartment. Rinne stared out the window, only half listening. Helena reminded her, painfully, of Sarah. Especially the times they spent spinning fantasies of where they would travel when they grew up.

"I'm going to California," Sarah had announced one cool sunny day, when she was twelve and Rinne almost ten. A northerly wind stirred the tops of the pines, but didn't reach their nest in the golden needles underneath the trees.

"Yeah, and you're gonna be a movie star," Rinne responded. She adopted a teasing voice, but secretly she believed that Sarah could be a movie star, or anything else she wanted.

"Maybe." Sarah sat up to finger comb her dark curls, which were ruffled from lying flat to stare up at the sky between the dark green branches.

"We have to stay on the Island," Rinne said. "You know that. You have the Skill."

"Don't you ever want to have any *fun*?" Sarah asked.

Rinne didn't answer. She couldn't imagine anything better than living on the Island, learning more about the wind and the water, helping her dad clean up his boat after a successful fishing trip.

But now she'd be living in Wabanaki Port, where the water lay quiet under the fishing boats, not needing anyone's Skill to calm the waves.

Calling home to tell her parents about her new job scared Rinne just as much as she knew the ringing phone would frighten them, so she sent them a letter. On The Island, phone calls often meant trouble—such as her dad or uncle's fishing boats had broken down, or that a nor'easter was on the way.

"Dear Mum and Dad," the letter said. "I've taken a job at the Puffin Feather in Wabanaki Port. I want to keep looking for Sarah. Once I find her, I'll come back home. Love, Rinne." She included the number of her new cell phone.

Her parents didn't answer. Or call.

However, about a week after Rinne began her new job, her father came to the Puffin Feather. Among the tourists, who were wandering the town in their L.L. Bean and Izod shirts, Brian stood out in his best baggy jeans, faded plaid shirt, and ancient blue necktie. Rinne, who stood at the cash register selling a set of earrings shaped like puffins, saw her father crossing the street toward the shop. Luckily, Tavish then asked her to clean up the rumpled pile of T-shirts at the back of the store while he helped a young couple who were intrigued by a lobster trap coffee table. Rinne was glad to get away for a moment, to get ready to see her dad, but when he came into the shop, she could hear every word he said.

Brian interrupted Tavish and the customer. "I'm Rinne's father," he announced. "We need my daughter at home." Brian wasn't tall, but his shoulders were wide, and he wore his heavy boots, which he only changed for weddings, funerals, and high school graduations. The young couple stared at him.

"No, you don't," said Rinne, dropping the T-shirts and joining them. "You need me to find Sarah."

"I looked for her everywhere," her father said. "So did the police." He glared at Tavish.

"You can talk with your dad in the office," Tavish said smoothly, and turned to the young couple. "This will be an heirloom," he told them, gesturing theatrically at the lobster pot coffee table. "No one will have anything like it."

Rinne led her father up the staircase to the office, which looked out over the street and the harbor. Meanwhile, the young couple were asking Tavish if that man was a "real fisherman."

Before her father could start, Rinne said, "I can't be Sarah for you. The best I can do is find her."

Brian shook his head. "You can't stay here. The mainland people stole Sarah from us. They'll steal you, too."

"Stole her? She ran away!"

"If we hadn't let her work with those rich folks, she'd still be here."

Rinne glared at her father. "In high school, Sarah spent all her time flirting with boys, going to parties, and spending every weekend in town. You let her do that. Don't blame the mainland people!" She discovered she was yelling. Her father's sunburned face turned redder.

"I'm sorry," Rinne said softly. "It's only that... I guess I've always..." She didn't want to say she'd always been jealous of her sister, even while adoring her beauty, popularity, and importance to the Island.

Brian breathed loudly through his nose. "Whatever happened, it's water under the bridge. We need you at home."

"You have Gran," said Rinne. "She's still strong. I'm going to find Sarah."

"I hunted for her. The police hunted for her. What can you do?"

"I can hunt for her on the internet, here at the library."

"You can do that on the Island."

"With Aunt Darina's computer? It crashes every time I get on a useful website!"

"We could get another one."

"If you can convince Great Gran," Rinne said, knowing the old lady hated the idea of another computer.

"That cellish phone is bad enough," Great Gran said. And what she said was law.

"Come home and marry Gavin. You're the..." her father stopped.

"I'm the best you've got," said Rinne. Her father turned even redder. "I'm of age now. I'm staying here."

"You're coming home," Brian said, and grabbed Rinne by the arm.

"You gonna kidnap me? I'll scream. All the nice tourist people will panic and call the police!"

Brian let go of her as if he'd been burned. Before he could say anything else, Rinne ran out of the office, down the stairs, and into the stockroom, where she locked the door and unpacked a shipment of puffin figurines that didn't need unpacking.

Half an hour later, Tavish joined her there. "Your father threatened to shut me down," he said. "Told me he'd make sure none of his friends shopped here."

"None of his friends would be seen dead in here."

He raised a perfect eyebrow at her. "Is that why you applied for this job?"

Rinne stared at him in surprise, and he laughed. But Rinne didn't feel like laughing. Her family, her cousins, her beloved Island, were now lost to her.

EIGHT: SEEING THINGS

Escaping alone to the forest or the Rock kept Casey from brooding.

'I'm brooding too much,' she told herself. 'Time to get on with it. Why let some stupid guy who couldn't run his stupid business ruin my life?'

In the mornings, she had to walk the forest with Dan and learn more about tree diseases than she wanted to. Then the two of them had to report to Aunt Cill—who still wanted something from Casey that made no sense.

"Riordan says you found a hemlock with woolly adelgid very quickly," Aunt Cill said.

"Beginner's luck," Casey said.

Her aunt said, "Hmpf."

Then Aunt Cill asked why Casey had a bunch of weeds in her room.

"Weeds?"

"In pots. Plants belong outside."

Casey knit her brows. "They're African violets. They don't grow in Maine. They're tropical. I had lots of houseplants in my apartment in Rochester. These were the only plants I could keep."

"They don't belong in the house."

"May I put them on the porch?"

"Welp," said Aunt Cill, with a sharp nod. Casey took it as a "yes."

She wanted to say "if you don't want me here. tell me," but she needed to have a job before she confronted her aunt. Instead, she brought her babies down to the big porch, putting them in a shady back corner where Aunt Cill couldn't see them from her usual chair.

The violets had helped Casey cope with losing the rest of her jungle. As everything fell apart, she would hide under her ficus tree and big hanging Swedish ivy and listen to them hum. Only her African violets were left. No one wanted them. Even her friend Robin, who had a houseful of plants, wouldn't take them.

"They're impossible!" Robin said. "I've killed three of them. You're the only one I know who can manage their fragile little souls!"

Once she had the violets comfortable, Casey returned to visiting the places she'd loved as a kid. One was in the forest north of the house, where pine trees grew two hundred feet high, with trunks over six feet around. In one spot, a giant pine had fallen after a long life, leaving a small, sunlit gap where ferns and baby pines grew.

Another ancient pine tree bordered this tiny field. When she was in her teens and frustrated with her family, Casey used to bring her journal to this spot and write about her horrible teenage life. Now she brought her sketchbook, hoping it would help her ignore those unsettling feelings about the forest.

Leaning against the pine's wide trunk, Casey gazed into the sunlit area, where a few orange and black butterflies danced around a honeysuckle bush. She breathed in the cozy, restful scent of the ferns covering the ground. She sketched the ferns, then tried to draw the butterflies, but, being butterflies, they wouldn't stay still long enough for her to capture them on paper. The quiet smell of pine and fern, the way images grew under her fingers, soothed her unquiet mind.

Something moved in the ferny undergrowth. Too big for a squirrel, and too slow. Maybe a coyote. She remembered the howl she'd heard on the day of the strange wind. Warily sliding up the tree trunk into a standing position, she then realized that running would probably excite the animal into chasing her. So, she stood still and tried to disappear into the bark, hoping the coyote, or whatever it was, wouldn't be interested in her.

But it was not a coyote. The head was too long, unusually long, almost as long as the low, furry, green-gray body. And it didn't trot like a coyote; it flowed over the ground, snake fashion. The ferns hid its legs, but there seemed to be too many of them. It flowed right up to Casey, sniffed at her feet, then looked at her with sad yellow eyes, mouth open, showing an overlong tongue and too many sharp teeth. Frozen, fingers digging into the pine bark, Casey found herself staring back, feeling like the thing wanted to tell her something. Then it slid past her into the trees.

For a long time, she remained motionless. Would it come back? What was it trying to tell her? Had she dreamed it? But she could see the track the thing had made through the undergrowth.

A catbird meowed, and then the rest of the birds began to chirp and rustle. Only then did Casey realize they had been silent while whatever it was crossed the clearing. Panic caught up with her and she ran, back through the big trees to the trail, running until she burst into the back yard, panting with fear.

Then she slowed to a stroll, hoping Aunt Cill or Dan hadn't seen her dashing around like a crazy woman.

She tried to convince herself that she must have fallen asleep in the clearing and dreamed about the coyote-snake thing. The way it slunk low to the ground, the sadness in its eyes, mirrored her own feelings about her failures. She'd been sketching the green shadows, and the thing was grayish green--greenish among the grass, shadow gray as it disappeared into the trees. She could have fallen asleep while sketching and had a nightmare.

For a few days after that, however, Casey tried to avoid the woods, except for her trips with Dan. But it didn't last long. Without her forest fix, she felt unsettled and cranky. Going to town and hunting for jobs in the library—where she could actually get an internet connection—didn't help.

So, on an especially beautiful day, she went to another favorite spot. This lay in the east woods, where there was a magical grove of birches rising from a bed of ferns. The birches clustered on a small hill, surrounded by ash and beech trees. The silvery trunks of beech were smaller than the pine trees in the north forest, but their roots reached out across the ferns like long gray fingers. White paper birch trees don't live as many years as other trees, but some of these were a foot around. Others lay among the ferns, peeling white trunks rotting into the earth.

Casey loved how the birch grove, and its surrounding beech trees, glowed silver-white in the sun. Wandering through the woods, breathing in the scent of crushed ferns under her feet, she always felt that a world with places like this couldn't be so bad.

But today, she was antsy and restless. What the heck was wrong? Frustrated, she wandered around the birches. The green-gray butterfly appeared, finding something interesting in the ferns. Its wings had brighter green spots around the edges. As Casey watched, it fluttered away, toward the south.

Then Annoying Voice told her she should be in the south woods—which Aunt Cill was guarding today from a chair in the middle of the porch. At least, it felt like the old lady was on guard against something.

"Aunt Cill is watching the south woods," Casey said aloud to Annoying Voice. 'Great, I'm talking to myself,' she thought.

Immediately she heard the same cry, or howl, she'd heard before that strange wind appeared up on the Rock. It reminded her of the coyote-snake thing. She worried that another sudden wind might appear. Maybe that was why Annoying Voice wanted her in the south woods.

Irrationally wanting to avoid Aunt Cill's watchful glare, she had an idea. Making her way downhill to a section of Woodward Lane where a curve hid the road from the house, Casey ran across the lane like a guilty rabbit, then edged along the brush on the downhill side. Below her lay a swampy area, full of cattails, which flowed into a little pond where frogs sang every spring.

From there, Casey could steal undetected into the south woods. As she moved away from the soggy ground, scrubbing the mud off her boots whenever she found a handy log, she came to a grove of sugar maple. Aunt Cill used to tap these trees, Casey recalled. Her parents would exclaim over having as much real maple syrup as they wanted for their pancakes. They even suggested that Aunt Cill could sell it. That did not go over well.

Casey wondered if Aunt Cill still tapped the trees, or if Dan did it for her, or if the long cooking down of the pale sap was too much work for either of them.

The tops of the maples started swaying, then thrashed around like they were in the middle of a hurricane. Casey stared up at them. The wind didn't touch her. Like the first time, up on the Rock.

She did not want another tree to get hurt by this impossible wind. Putting her hands on the closest tree trunks, she yelled, idiotically, "Hey, stop that!"

The wind did not stop. She could see it moving toward the west, toward the Rock. She followed the wind, always keeping at least one hand on an endangered tree trunk. Hand over hand, patting each tree gently, she made her way toward the Rock. As she touched each tree, she felt its strength, the sap moving upward, pulling water and food from the earth.

"Be strong," she whispered.

As suddenly as the wind had started, it stopped, leaving Casey feeling bewildered and a little silly. Be strong, what kind of cosmic hippie crap was that? To get away from feeling like an idiot, she kept walking, picking up the trail as she came to a group of basswood trees, continuing to the white oaks below the Rock.

The scar on her oak tree, where the first strange wind had broken off a branch, was now scabbed over with gray bark and growing a new twig. The twig was already two feet long.

"Good for you," said Annoying Voice

"I'm seeing things," Casey told herself.

"No, you're not," said Annoying Voice.

Heading back to the house, Casey considered asking Aunt Cill or Dan if they'd ever seen anything like these winds, but decided Aunt Cill would sniff in disgust, and Dan would think Casey had gone crazy. She didn't consider telling either of them about the branch that grew so quickly. Trees don't grow that fast—although, Casey kept telling herself, everything grew fast in June.

No. If the branch grew, then the forest did communicate, and the sudden wind was real, and the coyote-snake thing was not a dream.

NINE: A JOB OFFER

The next morning, while Casey sat on the porch steps to drink her coffee and plan her day, Annoying Voice kept dinging at her about downdrafts, telling her that her experience with the non-wind on the Rock and in the south woods should be taken seriously.

With no internet signal on Woodward Lane, Casey now drove the ten miles to Blake Harbor and the town library every few days. There, she could hunt for jobs online, e-mail friends, look at cute animals on Facebook, and ignore oddly verdant oak trees. Today, she decided to research downdrafts and other peculiar winds.

After lunch, when Riordan had retreated to his studio, Aunt Cill headed for the kitchen to concoct something smelling pungent and sneezy, which she then decanted into one of her many brown bottles.

"I'm going to the library," Casey told her aunt. "Can I pick up anything at the store?"

"Grocery list on the fridge," her aunt said. "Get the fish at Manny's down to the harbor."

Aunt Cill always said that. Casey knew only Manny's would do for fish. The grocery store lay far from the harbor, way out on the highway that ran south, toward Greenville. The grocery list was long, so Casey's library time would be short.

Not even a longer time would have done much for her today. Microbursts, she discovered, could account for odd winds, but they required some kind of thunderstorm activity, especially here on the east coast. The weather websites showed absolutely no thunderstorms in the area on either of the days she'd experienced the odd downdrafts, or winds, or whatever they were. Then she looked up green-gray butterflies. Some lived in India, some in Colorado, some in Florida, but none looked like the butterfly she'd seen. Her butterfly did have wide eye-like spots, one on each wing, but no green butterfly online matched it.

Giving up on research, Casey checked her e-mail. And found one from Susan that made everything harder.

Susan and Casey had been best friends since college. After college, Susan took over the coffee shop where she had worked her way through school. When Jake left, and Casey couldn't find a job or an apartment, Susan had pulled her out of her misery.

The misery had worsened when any apartments Casey could afford were too dark for her beloved plants, and her overdue credit cards didn't convince apartment managers to trust her. Job hunting was slow, because her only real experience was with WebLicious.

One interviewer said, "You have never worked in a team environment, have you?"

He sounded like her father, who had said, "I told you that your business was undercapitalized. I told you that you should have worked somewhere for longer before starting WebLicious."

The should-haves ate at Casey. Should have listened to dad. Shouldn't have moved in with Jake so quickly. Should have understood he no longer cared about her. She sold their furniture. She slept on the floor of their apartment in her old sleeping bag. She ignored her e-mail.

It was harder to ignore the zealous ringing of her cell phone. It was Susan. Susan dragged her out for lunch, and told her to take some time off.

"You can always come be a barista for me," she had said.

But now Susan's fiancé had taken a job in Chicago. They were planning a big wedding in Buffalo in August, and then they'd be off to the Midwest.

Somehow Casey had always thought of Susan's shop as a backup plan. Besides, getting to Buffalo, getting the kind of wedding present she wanted for Susan, would cost money.

Slamming her computer shut, Casey gave up on any job hunting and headed for the grocery store.

The big chain grocery on Route One sold perfectly good fish, of course, but Casey obediently bought only the things on the list—things like flour, sugar, butter, hamburger, vinegar, and a bunch of spices—before heading for Manny's Fish Market.

She drove back past the library, admiring the big old houses on the Greenville Road, circled the Common with its obligatory white church, and turned right on Harbor Road. That was the center of Blake Harbor, lined with touristy stores selling aprons with puffins embroidered on them, or pictures of lighthouses. There was an old-fashioned hardware store with wooden floors, along with a tiny grocery, good only for milk, emergency candles, and the kind of packaged snacks Aunt Cill wouldn't have in her house. Manny's Fish Market lay across the street from the harbor, close to where the fishing boats docked.

Manny, a gregarious soul, had discovered that Casey was staying with Miz Woodward, and always greeted her by name. Which, to Manny, was not "Casey".

"Miz Priscilla!" he said today, "Got some nice scrod in from Uncle Sal this noon! Your auntie Cill will love it!"

While he wrapped it up, the man behind her said, "Excuse me, but are you Cill Woodward's niece? I've known her all my life."

Many people in the town knew Aunt Cill. The library staff always asked Casey to say hello to her aunt, although as far as Casey knew, Aunt Cill rarely left her house. Dan had done the errands, until Casey showed up and inherited the grocery and fish shopping.

With his chiseled face, tanned skin, athletic build, and graying temples, the man who spoke to her could have posed for an advertisement featuring a successful businessman. He introduced himself as Joe Burnside, and asked how her aunt was doing.

"She's fine," she told him. "I'm Casey Todd. Cill is my great aunt. I'm staying with her while I'm between jobs."

"What kind of work do you do?" he asked. "Manny, I'd like two pounds of the scrod; your Uncle Sal always brings in the best."

"I'm a graphic designer." She named the company she'd interned for—he didn't have to know how much she'd hated working there. "Most recently, a friend and I started a web design business in Rochester, New York, but it didn't do as well as we'd hoped."

"Startups are difficult," he said, paying for his fish. "I have to get this fish home, but I'd like to find out more about your work. Are you available for lunch tomorrow?"

This was too good to be true. Casey didn't care. She told him she was free, and they planned to meet at a nearby restaurant—an expensive one, but you have to spend money to make money, Casey told herself. Her fourth credit card still worked.

"Give my best to your aunt," Mr. Burnside said, with practiced geniality. As they left the store, Casey noticed, without surprise, that he drove a Porsche.

At supper—at Aunt Cill's, the evening meal was always supper, not dinner—Casey told her about Mr. Burnside.

"That man?" Her tone was sharp; her eyes snapped.

"He might be able to find me a job."

"A job, a job, always a job," Aunt Cill said.

"Well, I only planned to stay here for a month, Aunt Cill. I'm in debt because a friend and I had a business that failed. I have to get a job."

Aunt Cill pursed her lips, then said nothing else for the rest of the evening. Casey washed the dishes and cleaned the kitchen thoroughly, hoping it might help the situation. But her aunt simply sat in her big chair with her lips pursed.

The next day, Casey put on her best summertime dress, a dark green print that made her eyes look green, took a curling iron to her hair—"iron" being the operative word in taming her frizz—and even put on makeup.

Aunt Cill was back in the kitchen with her smelly potions. When Casey, on her way to the back door, mentioned she was going out for lunch, her aunt only snorted.

The restaurant was right on the bay. Of course, Joe Burnside rated a table next to the window, where they could enjoy the view. With him was a woman who radiated seduction, with huge dark eyes and wavy blonde hair, her curves highlighted by a red brocade dress more suited to a country club dance than lunchtime.

"This is my wife Zora," said Burnside. "Honey, this is Cill Woodward's niece Casey." Zora's polished blonde curls looked like they had recently come from an expensive salon, and her makeup was perfect. Patting down her own frizzy curls, Casey wondered if her lipstick was the wrong color.

Around Zora's neck, on a gold chain, hung a lovely piece of art, two golden, interlocking spirals. Trying to be social and polite, Casey admired it.

"Oh, where did we get this, Joseph? Was it Paris, or Rome?" She had an indefinable accent; not French, maybe Italian, although that didn't seem right either.

Joe didn't know. "My wife collects jewelry," he told Casey, "instead of art."

"This *is* art," Zora said, pouting sweetly. Annoying Voice announced the woman had ulterior motives. Casey told it to go away. She had to be polite.

Burnside ordered for them. The waiter treated him like royalty.

"It's been too long since I've seen your aunt," Joe told Casey. "She's an institution in our town. I remember when she'd drive her old Buick station wagon to town for supplies. It had wooden sides, a real antique. Now and then, she'd come into my uncle's store, where I worked as a kid. I was scared to wait on her, but later we became friends."

Casey wondered how anyone could become friends with her cranky aunt, but didn't ask. Although she had eaten in a few fancy restaurants, she'd never learned to enjoy a meal like this one, with the food arranged like a work of art—more art than food—but she didn't want to eat much. She was too focused on making a good impression and getting a job.

As the meal progressed, Burnside talked about Burnside & Company, which dealt in fine leather goods, and about marketing, during which Casey kept her mouth firmly shut, since he didn't know as much as he thought he did. But then, the guys in charge were always like that. At least this guy was charming.

Over coffee, Burnside said, "So, Casey, what are your career goals?"

'Get a job I can stand and pay off my debts,' she thought, but came up with something suitably fuzzy and aspirational about working collaboratively in an environment where she could use her graphic design skills in service of a company's marketing goals. The bullshit came out of her mouth while she tried not to listen to herself.

Burnside exchanged glances with his wife, who gave an infinitesimal nod; a nod Casey would have missed, except for the sixth-sense-annoying-voice saying Zora was dangerous. Which was silly, because Zora spent the meal smiling, fiddling with her necklace, and being beautiful.

"We might have something for you," Burnside said. "Can you send me a resume?"

Casey had actually brought one with her, and gave it to him, with amusing complaints about the lack of network at her aunt's house that kept her from e-mailing it. He insisted on paying for lunch and she thanked him in what she hoped was a graceful manner. He said he'd call her, or perhaps stop by and visit her aunt.

Casey stayed numb until her old Jetta was heading up her aunt's long driveway.

Then she yelled, "WOOO!"

Aunt Cill did not yell Wooo.

TEN: MR. AND MRS. BURNSIDE

"You want to go work for That Man?" Aunt Cill demanded when Casey told her about the job offer.

Along with Dan, they were sitting at the dining room table eating breakfast while birds chirped their dawn chorus.

"If he has a job for me," she said. "Do you know anything bad about him? He thinks you're great."

Her aunt pursed up her lips. She was the only person Casey knew who did it, and she did it all the time.

"He'd sell his own mother," she said.

"I looked up Burnside Company before our lunch yesterday," Casey told her aunt. "Not only their website, but everything else written about them. I didn't find anything bad. He grew up in Greenville. He says he knows you."

"You wouldn't find anything bad. He's too clever." Aunt Cill picked up her coffee cup. "You do as you like. You always have." She snorted. "Keeping weeds on the porch." And she marched out to the kitchen.

'If she thinks I'm so awful,' thought Casey, 'why did she agree to have me come here?' Of course, she didn't ask. She couldn't get into an argument with her aunt before she even had this job.

"Ready to go?" Dan asked her. He had kept his head down, spooning up oatmeal while Casey tried to deal with Aunt Cill.

Not sure whether she liked that or not, Casey said "yup," and followed him out the back door to check out the east forest.

Three days later, Burnside called and invited Casey to dinner at his house. Aunt Cill answered the phone, listened, said nothing, and yelled "Priscilla!" Casey, who was out on the porch checking on her African violets, jumped up and ran into the hall, worried that she'd done something else to irritate her aunt.

"For you," said Aunt Cill, handing Casey the phone—an ancient black thing from about 1959. With a dial, not buttons. Aunt Cill marched back into the kitchen.

"Joe Burnside here," said the phone. "We'd like to invite you to dinner at our house on White's Point on Thursday. I've got a few ideas I'd like to run by you."

"Thank you," Casey said. "I'd love that."

"Terrific. Come about six. Only me and my wife. Nothing fancy. You need directions?"

Casey said she had a GPS and only needed the address.

"How's your aunt doing?" Burnside asked. "She seems a little deaf."

"Well, she's kind of eccentric," Casey murmured. She did not mention how much Aunt Cill hated him.

For the dinner, Casey wore her best russet dress with her gold necklace and earrings. As she headed out the door, Aunt Cill called, "If he asks you if I want to sell the south woods, the answer is still NO."

"That woman is a master of non-communication," Casey grumbled to herself as she climbed into the Jetta. "Dropping comments like that when she knows I'll be late if I ask for explanations. Why would someone in the expensive leather goods business want to buy the south woods?"

Dismissing the question, Casey drove down the long driveway, turned left into town, then left again at the harbor. As she drove along the shore on Blackwood Road, she ran into a deep fog rolling in from the ocean. She had to slow down to a crawl, worrying that she would be late, or miss the turn, even with the GPS talking to her.

Luckily, White Point Road sported a couple of stone towers on either side of it, topped with bright lantern-shaped lights gleaming through the mist. The Burnside mansion took up most of a rocky headland, called White's Point, thrusting itself out past Blake Harbor into the ocean. Turning into the gravel driveway, Casey came to a tall ironwork fence. Its gate was open. Her headlights picked out the edges of what appeared to be neatly landscaped lawns on either side.

As she parked the car, Joe Burnside himself opened the door. She'd half-expected an English butler.

"Come in, come in, I see you didn't get lost in the fog," he said jovially.

The hallway was a large as Aunt Cill's dining room; the living room could have doubled as a basketball court. The place even smelled wealthy, of floor polish and expensive perfume. According to Manny, Burnside had had the house completely redone from the original nineteenth century summer residence.

"They say it's real nice inside," Manny had said. "Not that I'd ever been invited there. Wouldn't know what knife to eat my peas with!"

Looking like a fashion model, Zora posed at the end of the hallway. She wore white silk palazzo pants, with a deep blue shirt setting off her golden scroll necklace. "Welcome to our home," she said. "We will have aperitifs in the sitting room."

The sitting room—Casey would have called it the living room—was only half a basketball court in size. The aperitifs were tiny, vermouth and something as indefinable as Zora's accent. A small brown woman served the drinks, along with delicately artistic canapés. Nibbling carefully, all Casey could taste was something fish-like. The brown woman didn't look Portuguese, like Manny. Casey wondered where she came from.

A wind came up, blowing the fog away. Dinner was served in a dining room where a wall of windows gave a spectacular view of the ocean. Waves crashed on the rocks far beneath them, as the small brown woman brought in the food. The plates of perfect fish and artistically shredded vegetables reminded Casey of the place they'd had lunch. The Burnsides probably had a professional chef on their staff.

Joe talked about how he'd bought and restored the house, explaining all the improvements he'd thought up, and how he had to hire builders from Boston.

Zora smiled. "These curtains," she said, waving a slender arm at the white linen panels fluttering expensively in the ocean breeze, "we hunted and hunted, didn't we Joseph, to find the perfect ones."

Casey wasn't sure what made them more perfect than other upscale drapes, but she didn't ask.

In trendy European style, they had salad after the meal; then little crackers with a spicy spread; then tiny tarts.

'Rochester was never like this,' Casey thought, smiling until her face felt stiff.

"We will have coffee in the study," Zora announced, leading them to a book-lined room where all the books were organized by color.

Fat leather chairs surrounded a small gas fire. The brown woman served coffee from a silver pot. When Casey thanked the woman for the coffee, both Burnsides stared straight ahead.

'Oh,' thought Casey, 'this is like Upstairs Downstairs. You're supposed to ignore the servants.'

"Well now," Joe announced. "I told my marketing folks at Burnside Leathers all about you. They're as enthusiastic as I am. What I have in mind is a corporate liaison with the stores carrying our high-end products. You have experience and an understanding of the marketing process. What do you think?" He beamed at her.

Casey tried to smile back. 'I'm a graphic designer,' she thought. 'I know nothing about liaison work except that you have to charm people.'

Annoying Voice said, "You would hate a job where you had to charm people."

'You can make money as a corporate liaison,' she told Annoying Voice. And right now, money was the most important thing. Make it, get out of debt. The Todd family did not have unpayable debts.

She asked Joe to tell her more about how he envisioned the job.

"We need someone to build a closer relationship between our main company and the stores. Visit the stores, talk with them about how our product is doing, solve any problems that might arise."

"It sounds both challenging and exciting," she said. Joe didn't seem to mind the smarmy cliché. He probably lived on them.

Joe went on to tell her more about Burnside Leathers, how he'd taken his grandfather's company into the twenty-first century, how they sold to small stores in well-to-do areas. Somewhere a clock chimed eleven musical strokes.

"You've given me a lot to think about," Casey said, rising as gracefully as she could manage. Zora's every move was choreographed to perfection. Next to her Casey felt like a baby giraffe. "May I have a day to consider your wonderful offer?"

"Of course, of course," Joe said. "I always sleep on big decisions."

Casey said everything she was supposed to—praised their hospitality, would call soon, thank you so much for a lovely evening. Joe walked her to her car, which felt grubby and out of place in the meticulously graveled driveway.

What with the aperitif, the wine, and the liqueur served with the coffee, Casey had to turn the car's air conditioning on full blast to stay awake. Once back at Woodward Lane, she fell asleep before she could even begin to consider Burnside's offer.

She dreamed of Zora's necklace. It laced itself around green trees, which turned brown as the golden strands tightened. Then the necklace wound itself into her hair, heading for her neck to strangle her. When she woke up, she was all tangled in the bed sheet, and felt groggy. Her phone said 10:02 in the morning. She stumbled down the back stairs into a cold shower, which she hoped would wake her up.

Aunt Cill was already out on the porch with her book, supervising her forest. Casey had missed her assignment to walk the forest with Dan. That was fine. She didn't want to go back into the forest. Either it made her hallucinate, or something strange lived there.

'I've gotta get out of here,' Casey thought. 'This place is making me crazy.'

Carrying her third cup of coffee and going out the back door to avoid her aunt, Casey wandered past the barn and along the edge of the north woods. As she walked, Annoying Voice kept intruding, announcing the offer was too good, that the man wanted something from her.

"Don't be stupid," she told Annoying Voice. "He has Zora, what would he want with me?" Anyway, she thought, I could work for him for a year or so, pay off my debts, then go back to graphic design.

Then all thoughts of the job skittered away. Two new sculptures stood along the woods growing behind the back yard. She'd seen them from her bedroom window, or while coming out of the trails in the north or south woods, but had never been this close to them.

Each sculpture was at least six feet high, in rich brown wood, the grain flowing like water. Each one was different, each one miraculous. Stepping forward, she ran her hand down the nearest one. A spark leaped to her fingers, as if the sculpture wasn't wood, but a live, furry animal.

"You like them?" Dan appeared soundlessly, making Casey jump.

"Yeah," she said, inadequately.

"Magic sculptures," said Annoying Voice.

It was easy to ignore Annoying Voice when Dan smiled at her. Taking a deep breath, Casey tried to relax, telling herself that she'd felt the same way about Jake when she first met him. And he knew how irresistible she found him. No more, she'd promised herself, no more.

"I'm sorry I missed our appointment this morning. Last night I was out late."

"No problem," he said. He had a wide mouth, a beautifully shaped nose, and dark eyes that seemed to see into her soul. Probably he was staring at her own beaky nose, not her soul.

Casey folded her arms to keep Dan from turning her inside out.

"I never told you—I'm glad you're living here. Helping my aunt. My parents worry about her."

Dan considered her. "Why didn't you stay when she wanted you to?"

Until he asked her, Casey had completely forgotten what had happened, but it all came back into her head like it never left. When she was seventeen, Aunt Cill had asked her to come and help her keep the forest strong.

"You've ignored everything I tried to teach you," she had said, "but I still need you here."

None of it had made sense to Casey. She didn't *want* it to make sense. She wanted to go to art school. She wanted to be part of her energetic, successful family; T.J. on the honor roll in high school, Duncan at MIT, her parents with their profitable business.

"She asked me to live with her instead of going to college. No kid would say yes to that." Casey told Dan, then frowned at him. "Is that why she's so—why she doesn't seem to like me? Then why did she take me in?"

"I don't know," he said. "Not my business. Sorry I mentioned it. Maybe you should ask your aunt."

"Yeah, thanks," said Casey as she continued around the west side of the house, and up the stairs to the porch.

Her aunt still sat there, reading a book with a faded green cover, *My Summer in a Garden*.

"That looks interesting," Casey said, nodding at the book.

"It is," said Aunt Cill.

"I've been offered a job," Casey said.

"That's good," said her aunt, still reading.

"It's with Joe Burnside's company in Portland. I've been here a month. I thought it was time I found work."

"With that man?"

"Why do you hate him so much," Casey asked. "Is there something I should know? Like I said, I read everything I could find about the company. It looks great."

Her aunt slammed her book shut and stalked away into the kitchen.

Casey wanted to scream. Too furious to listen to Annoying Voice insisting that it was a bad idea, she went inside and called Joe Burnside.

*

Dan felt ridiculously pleased that Casey liked his sculptures. They liked her, too, he thought, then sighed. Spending so much time with Cill was giving him strange ideas. Too strange to share with a niece who Cill apparently disliked. And why was he still thinking about her more than a week after she admired his work?

Deeply breathing in the fresh morning air, mostly to wake himself up, he circled the house, listening to the few birds who still sang at dawn. Today was his day for the south woods, which began at the bottom of the hill. For the second time, Casey hadn't appeared at breakfast, ready to go with him. He missed her.

First, he checked on the tall carvings, which Cill had asked him to put along the edge of the south woods. Running his hands along their sides, he felt all was well with the trees. Feelings, however, weren't enough. He had to check them carefully. Following a narrow path, he entered the swampy area, where a little creek tangled itself up in the buttonbushes, cattails, and blackflies. Cill hated commercial bug repellent, so she made her own. It kept the blackflies away, which nothing else did, although Dan discovered it made him smell pungently sweet, like the array of cosmetics that Alix used.

Everything looked fine; no insect or fungus infestations, only lots of green healthy leaves. On beautiful days like this, he loved his job. Sometimes he even wondered if he should train to be a forest ranger. Although they mostly had to tell people about the beauties of the woods, and Dan would rather enjoy those beauties without a crowd of tourists. Besides, with such a job, he would have no time for carving.

By noon, he was sitting at Cill's dining room table as usual, ready to give his report. Normally, she arrived first, but today she wasn't there. Dan went into the kitchen to look for her and get some of her freshly-squeezed lemonade.

Cill and Casey stood there, silent, glaring at each other.

Casey had a suitcase. When she saw him, she said, "Goodbye, Aunt Cill. I'll call you when I get to Portland."

Cill said nothing, so Casey turned and went out through the back hall. Dan heard the Jetta start up.

In silence, Dan poured his coffee, found a homemade blueberry muffin, and headed back to the dining room. After about five minutes, Cill joined him.

"Report," she said.

So he did. "Swamp alders are doing well. The young tamarack tree off to the eastern edge doing well after losing a few branches. Everything is doing well." More silence.

"Priscilla got a job with that Burnside man," she said.

Dan nodded. Life with a grumpy mother taught him that sometimes only a nod is safe.

"She'll regret it. She never would listen to me." Cill marched back into the kitchen, where she banged pots around.

'I'll miss Casey,' Dan thought. 'Even though I never got to know her.'

ELEVEN: CHANGE

When Rinne was fourteen, her world changed.

She should have known that when Great Gran died, life would be different. She just didn't know how bad it would become.

Rinne knew Great Gran was old. Very old. Still, for all of Rinne's life, her great grandmother had spent every day in her big brown armchair, looking out the wide bay window which faced the Island's little harbor, watching the wind, the sky, and the sea. The house revolved around her. Rinne and Sarah would bring her wonderfully twisty pieces of driftwood, or lucky stones with stripes all the way around them. Their mother and Aunt Cathy would consult Great Gran about hens that weren't laying, or new ways to cook the inevitable fish. Their father and Uncle Neil would tell her about legends of great lobster-hunters.

Then, one day in early winter, Great Gran stayed in bed, and her chair stayed empty. For several weeks, her daughter, Rinne's Gran Aileen, spent every day with Great Gran, reading to her, holding her hand, or sitting quietly. Work continued as usual. Brian went out on his lobster boat; Rinne milked the goat; Sarah collected the few eggs. They traded off cleaning the henhouse. Hens didn't like winter, so they didn't lay many eggs, but the henhouse still needed to be cleaned. Sarah and Rinne did their homework. They helped their mother cook dinner. But Maris went about with a preoccupied frown, like she was listening for something.

One day a wind came up, a gale. It didn't rain, which was odd, but the wind howled all day, keeping Brian from fishing and Maris from spading over the garden for winter; keeping Sarah and Rinne from getting to school on the mainland. The four of them sat in the front room, listening to the waves pound on the rocks, not talking. Great Gran died at midnight.

It was Rinne's first experience of death, with losing someone she loved. She felt like a piece of the Island had broken off, floating away on the waves, disappearing out to sea. The family mourned, but Great Gran's death was expected; she had been part of life on the Island.

Nobody, however, expected that Sarah would run away the next summer; Rinne's big sister Sarah, the beautiful one, the special one, the one who would keep their Island strong for generations to come.

When she graduated from high school, Sarah had insisted on being allowed to spend the whole week before graduation in Gorham Harbor, staying with her friend Hannah and going to parties. As always, her parents let her go.

With Sarah away, Rinne's work doubled. Their mother was always working; gardening, cooking, preserving food, cleaning up the sand and kelp that Brian tracked in. Today, Rinne was helping Maris turn over the garden soil, in preparation for planting the seedlings growing on every sunny window in their house. Rinne had always loved getting out of school so she could spend summer on the Island, wandering the rocky shores, playing with the waves. As a child, she had believed that life on the Island would never change. She'd always have time to lie on the rocks, or under the pine trees. But when Sarah wasn't around to help with the endless work of the Gilley household, Rinne never had time for herself.

"Let Sarah have her fun," Maris said, turning over another spade full of dirt. "She'll have to take her place soon enough."

Breaking up the sandy clods with her hoe, Rinne wondered what she and her mother would wear to the graduation ceremony. Although Sarah's beauty came from her mother, Maris had never cared about clothes. Today, working in the garden, she wore ancient baggy jeans, a stained gray sweatshirt too worn out for fishing, and a straw hat that once belonged to Great Gran. She owned two dresses, one black, for winter and funerals, and one printed, for summer. The printed dress made her look like one of those old-time hippies. As far as Rinne knew, no packages containing new dresses had arrived on the ferry, except for Sarah's graduation dress.

At the graduation, her mother wore her hippie dress, and her father wore his all-purpose black suit, made festive with a red tie. He still looked like a lobsterman—like he'd be more comfortable in suspenders or a sou'-wester—but so did a lot of the other fathers. Rinne wore her best school clothes, a navy-blue skirt with a tight white top, a hand-me-down from Sarah. On Sarah, the top was sexy; on Rinne, it was merely a T-shirt.

Everyone from the Island came to Sarah's graduation. Aunt Cathy wore a new dress because her son Gavin was graduating too. He and his father had big plans for their lobstering partnership. Aunt Darina always had new dresses, because she could sew beautifully, and because she learned about the newest styles from her work at Seaview Cottage. Surrounded by her aunts, uncles, and cousins, Rinne tried to keep her excited littlest cousin Chloe from running up and down the aisle.

Marching music poured through the speakers, bringing in rows of students in bright blue caps and gowns, blue as the ocean on a sunny day.

"There's Gavin. Hi, Gavin!" Chloe called, waving wildly.

He grinned at her, giving her a special thumbs-up. But Sarah, behind him, gazed straight ahead, ignoring the smiles and waves of her family, even ignoring Aunt Darina's flashing camera.

After the endless ceremony, however, when Evan Zacharias finally received his diploma, Sarah did come to see her family, laughing and hugging, posing for pictures. Then she took off for a party with her friends.

Everyone expected Sarah and Gavin would marry right after graduation, but Sarah didn't want to have the wedding immediately.

"Let me have one more summer," she begged her parents, who sighed and gave in.

They always gave in to Sarah. Rinne understood why they did, because Sarah's Skill was so strong, but it still bothered her.

Sarah went to work full time at Seaview Cottage, helping Aunt Darina in the kitchen, serving drinks and canapés at the endless parties that the owners, Mr. and Mrs. Bresky, held for their endless friends.

"They want to pretend they're just folks," Aunt Darina explained one day, "but they want to have servants. It's kind of a fine line. You gotta be responsive, but not submissive."

Much later, Rinne would use this advice when waiting on customers at the Puffin Feather.

Sarah was brilliant at negotiating the fine line. And she loved working for rich people.

Aunt Darina couldn't say enough good things about her niece. "Mr. and Mrs. Bresky think Sarah walks on water," she told Brian and Maris, while Rinne peeled potatoes for dinner and eavesdropped. "She's so pretty, she charms all the guests. She helps the women with their hairdos; she brings the men iced tea or beer when they come back from sailing. I don't know what I did without her."

What the family didn't know, until too late, was how often Sarah was invited to go out sailing with the rich men and women, and how often Aunt Darina and the Bresky's let her go.

On a hot Friday in late August, Sarah went sailing with Alice and Marc Vauclain, who were staying at Seaview Cottage. That evening, the Vauclains called the Bresky house to say that they were staying the weekend with some friends in Bar Harbor, but would bring Sarah back on Monday.

On Monday afternoon, Aunt Darina called Maris. The only phone calls the Gilley household ever received came from Brian if the boat developed a problem and he had to stay in Gorham Harbor. But a hurricane was roaring up the coast, so he was home. When the phone rang, everyone froze. By unspoken agreement, Brian answered.

He listened, turned as pale as his reddish tan would allow, said, "Okay," and hung up.

"What happened?" asked Maris.

"Sarah didn't come back with those Vauclains. They think she ran off with some young man who was visiting the same folks they were," Brian said. "Darina is on her way over."

"Ran off?" asked Maris. "She can't run off! We need her here!"

Aunt Darina arrived, breathless and apologetic. "Mr. and Mrs. Vauclain took such a liking to Sarah, we thought she deserved a weekend off, we had no idea that she might—I mean, she knows the Island needs her!"

"How do you know she ran off? Maybe those people are lying!" Brian yelled. "She could have been kidnapped!"

Rinne huddled in a corner, not believing Sarah could run away, yet knowing she would.

"She left a note," Aunt Darina said. "She only wrote she was going to visit a friend. But those Vauclain people didn't know anyone in Bar Harbor except some kid who owned a catboat there, he'd got friendly with them and they thought it was nice for Sarah to have someone her age come over to the yacht. The boy disappeared too. The police are looking for both of them."

"A catboat," Brian said. "Hate those little foolish sailboats. Could anything have happened to it?"

"Coast Guard hunted, didn't find any flotsam," said Aunt Darina. "And it was dead calm all weekend."

"Storm's on the way," Brian said.

"Not here yet. Even a city kid wouldn't stay out all night in a catboat."

The police came to the Island to ask questions. "Any reason your daughter might run away?" they asked Brian and Maris.

"No reason," Maris said. "She loves the Island."

They asked Rinne the same question, and Rinne lied, just as her mother had. She knew that Sarah wanted to be a movie star, or a princess; anything but the wife of a fisherman.

Brian thought that the boy with the catboat might do something awful to Sarah, so he didn't leave the problem to the police. For a month, he chugged up and down the Maine coast in his lobster boat, carrying Sarah's graduation photo, asking everyone he knew, and many people he didn't, if they'd seen her. He asked the lobstermen, the workers in the boatyards, folks in coffee shops, and people who ran summer cruises for tourists. No one had seen Sarah.

On a bright day in mid-September, Brian came back from the mainland with the mail - a letter and two bills. He held the letter as if it would explode, or crush his fingers like an unpegged lobster.

The envelope was postmarked Portland. The writing was Sarah's.

"Dear Mum and Dad," she wrote. "Don't worry about me, I'm fine, but I need some time away. I'm going to travel. I'll be back someday. Love, Sarah."

Brian read it and handed it to Maris. She read it, then dropped it on the kitchen table like it had dirtied her hands. Rinne picked it up and read it. Then they all sat and stared at each other.

"I'll go back to Portland tomorrow," Brian said, finally.

First, however, he brought the letter to the police, who told him that finding runaways wasn't their job. In Portland, Brian found the catboat, and the young man who belonged to it. His name was Ethan. He said he'd thought Sarah was in love with him, but she'd left him after a month for some rich kid she met at a bar. He didn't know the guy's name. He never wanted to see Sarah again.

Rinne, however, wanted nothing more than to find her sister, so she didn't have to take on the impossible task of replacing Sarah and her Skill; so, she could avoid having to marry Gavin.

TWELVE: WORKING AT BURNSIDE CO.

Casey's new job, at The Burnside Co. office in Portland Maine, was located in a business park out on the northwest edge of the city. It turned out to be a strange place to work.

Although Casey was making more than she ever had, she had almost nothing to do. As soon as she had arrived, she went to meetings with the marketing staff, which comprised two writers, two designers, and Topher Pederick, the sleek marketing manager in charge of all five of them. Topher wore artfully tousled and bleached hair, with his long thin legs covered by designer jeans. He smiled constantly, but his brown eyes remained narrowly focused.

At his suggestion, Casey visited several stores in Portland, where Burnside's sold upscale leather handbags, briefcases, and wallets, along with leather slipcases for computer tablets. The price tags astonished her. What kind of people could buy this stuff? Although the store managers were a bit bewildered by her presence, they gave her their sales and marketing reports to read. The stores weren't crowded, but their cash registers were usually busy. People clearly loved the Burnside Leathers, despite the price tags.

Joe Burnside had indicated that Casey would serve as a marketing liaison with the stores, but after she had read every marketing report, boiled them down to an executive summary, and sent them to Topher, she heard nothing back from him.

The writers and designers created all the marketing materials, and didn't need her help, or her research. Topher was supposed to meet with her weekly, but most of the time something came up.

"Sorry, have to make a phone call," he'd say. Or "Got to get to Boston by four; let's reschedule." Casey felt useless.

Okay, she decided, maybe she was supposed to learn the business on her own. She read everything she could find about Burnside Co. She found a file full of old marketing plans and read all of them. She visited the stores again, and carefully looked over all the merchandise. She checked out how other stores marketed their goods. Portland was full of fancy boutiques selling everything from clothing to caviar, and jewelry to Jacuzzis.

Portland also offered a wonderful store that sold artist's materials. After spending a Saturday morning combing through their enticing wares, however, Casey never returned. Spending money on pastels and sketchpads wasn't in her budget, although she did purchase a set of inexpensive colored drawing pencils. Not the good ones. She had to bank her paychecks to get back on her financial feet; and to pay rent.

Joe Burnside had found Casey a sublet in a very nice apartment building; a place fully furnished in impeccable taste. She hardly dared cook or eat anything there for fear she'd get crumbs on the rug or chicken juice on the counter.

The only interesting thing about the place was its tiny balcony, which was mostly taken up with a huge ficus tree. The tree she'd owned in the Rochester apartment was almost eight feet tall; she'd sold it for a hundred dollars. This tree's silvery trunk was at least ten feet tall. Its slender leaves rustled companionably when she sat on the balcony to drink her morning coffee. It didn't hum; Casey thought the tree probably needed to get to know her. Back in Rochester, every time she'd purchased a new houseplant, it had needed time to get used to her.

The view from the balcony wasn't great. Even though it faced south, the apartment was on the back side of the building, so she looked at the alley, a dumpster, and part of a four-story office complex. But Casey liked being outside. Especially because she kept dreaming about Zora's necklace. It would tangle her feet as she did a presentation, pull down all the clothes in her closet, or strangle her until she woke up gasping. Then she'd go out on the balcony and listen to the ficus leaves talking to the night wind.

When Casey had moved into her first apartment in Rochester—a building surrounded by other buildings, and pavement—she missed trees. Houseplants might be a substitute, she thought. She bought a philodendron, then a spider plant, then a ficus tree. When she moved in with Jake, he thought her plants were funny and cute—until they couldn't see out of their windows because every single one was crowded with plants. Then his teasing grew a little mean.

'I should have known then,' Casey thought, 'that he would leave. I always figure things out too late.'

At this new job, Casey was prepared for another uncommunicative boss like Laurel, her internship boss in Rochester. Laurel would announce, "We need graphics for this article." No matter how many questions Casey would ask, she never learned more—only that questions irritated Laurel. After Casey had pored over the article three times and made a dozen sketches, Laurel would say, "But the graphic ought to be red and white," like somehow Casey should have read her mind.

But Topher was a new kind of boss, one who didn't seem to have anything for Casey to do. At the end of her first month, she finally found the nerve to ask him what was going on.

"I don't have very much work," she said, as diplomatically as possible. "I'm happy to pitch in anywhere I'm needed."

"You're doing great," he told her. "Keep up the good work." Then his cell phone rang and the meeting was over.

*

Nearly a month after Casey left, Alix visited Dan. She even stayed overnight.

"This place is so *quaint*," she said, of the barn apartment. "Ms. Woodward should put more apartments up here. She's certainly has the space."

Dan tried to explain that Cill Woodward would never do such a thing, but Alix had other things on her mind, and he was happy to oblige. They didn't always get along—except in bed.

In the morning, she wrinkled her nose at the apartment's smell of wood chips.

"You still carving?" she asked. He showed her his studio, where the current tall sculpture was in process. It was his best yet; strong and powerful. It would make a good Guardian for the trees.

"I guess I'm glad the thing isn't in our apartment," Alix said. "But it's beautiful. What will you do with it?"

"Cill wants them along the forest." He pointed out the studio window, where two of his sculptures guarded the northern edge of the woods.

Alix laughed. "She pays you for these?"

Dan nodded.

"What a great gig! What else can you sell the old lady?"

Dan said the apartment and the job were enough. Alix laughed again.

She left the next afternoon because she had a gig that night, but he hoped that maybe the relationship would work after all. She liked his art. She was beautiful and charming.

Early the next morning, Dan headed out to walk the eastern woods. But as he crossed the yard, something caught his eye.

Down the hill, the south woods lay wrecked. Trees toppled, shrubs flattened, leaves already turning brown. Like a tornado had hit. His sculptures still stood, with a few trees surviving behind them.

But last night, there'd hardly been a breeze. In fact, Dan turned on the fan in the bedroom so he and Alix wouldn't suffocate. It hadn't even rained.

To hell with the east woods. Dan tore down the hill. The path into the south woods had disappeared under a giant pine tree, which had snapped like a stick. Climbing over it, he surveyed the damage for a moment; then crunched through splinters, zigzagging around fallen branches. A huge swath of the forest lay toppled over.

Cill needed to know about this. Now. Dan dashed back up the hill, tore up the porch steps, paused on the porch to catch his breath, ran inside. At this time of morning, Cill was always in the kitchen, making coffee and oatmeal, or apple bread, or scrambled eggs.

But she wasn't in the kitchen. She was sitting in her big green chair, eyes closed. The chair gave her a view of the west woods, through a window next to the fireplace, and the south woods, through a window opening onto the porch.

"Cill?" Dan said.

"I know," she said, eyes still closed.

"What can I do for you? Did you have breakfast?"

She turned her head side to side. "No".

"You have to eat something. At least drink some water."

Again the head turn. "No".

"I can't imagine what happened. It doesn't make sense."

She whispered something. Dan leaned in to hear better.

"Get Priscilla," she whispered.

THIRTEEN: WIND

On a Monday morning, Casey awakened to her cell phone ringing.

"Wha?" she muttered, rolling over to look at the time. Seven a.m. Casey was not a morning person. Neither were the people at Burnside Co. Especially not on a Monday.

"Casey? It's Dan. Are you up?"

"I am now," she said irritably. That man probably gets up at five a.m. every day.

"It's your aunt."

That woke her right up. "Is she okay? What happened?"

"I think she's been up all night. She's downstairs in her big chair, won't eat anything," Dan said. "There's more. Trees are down all through the south woods. It's so bad, you can see the wreckage from the porch."

"Was there a storm?"

"Not even a breeze. Your aunt said to get you."

What the hell does she think I can do, Casey wanted to ask. But if Aunt Cill were sick—her parents had asked her to be sure the old lady was okay. And now Casey was miles away in Portland, at a job where she had nothing to do.

Annoying Voice pointed out that if Casey had been with her aunt, maybe she could have stopped the wind. "You stopped it the first time," it said.

"And how did I do it?" she asked it. No answer.

"Casey? You there?"

"Yeah, sorry, I was thinking. You're four hours from here. I'll pack, call work, and be there by two o'clock."

No one at Burnside got to work until nine or ten o'clock. Casey put the coffeemaker on, then took a fast shower. With no idea about how long she'd have to be away, she stuffed all her clothes, sketchbooks, and drawing pencils into her suitcase. By then the clock said 8:30. She decided to clean up the place, in case she couldn't come back right away.

"Or at all," said Annoying Voice.

She tried not to listen to it. Or to think about strange winds and downdrafts.

Throwing the towels and sheets into the washing machine—this apartment had everything—Casey ran the vacuum around the clean carpet. She'd spent most of her time out on the tiny porch, and in July there wasn't any rain or snow to track in. At ten a.m., with the sheets in the dryer, she called Topher to explain.

"How long will you be gone?" he asked. "We have a big project coming up."

"I don't know. My great aunt isn't young."

"Can't another member of your family deal with it?"

"I'm the closest," she told him. Why the hell did he care? She wasn't doing any work anyway. "I'll call you as soon as I know anything."

"We have a meeting about the new project tomorrow. You can put off your trip until then."

"My aunt is sick," she said. "I have to be there. I'll stay in touch."

"You haven't accrued enough personal time for a trip like this."

"Topher, you may not have any family, but I do, and this is important. If you have to dock my pay, then do it."

"Of course I have family. But I keep my priorities straight."

"So do I," Casey said. "I'll keep you informed." And she clicked off, wondering why she was suddenly so essential. What had gotten into the man?

She folded the sheets and towels, put them in the rose-scented linen closet, picked up her suitcase, and headed for the door.

On the way to the apartment building's garage and her car, Casey stopped in the manager's office to let them know she would be away for at least two weeks. While explaining this to Nora, the secretary, the manager came out of his office and listened. Mr. Vachon was a stocky man of about fifty, with a polished bald head and a strong Maine accent.

"I'm so sorry to hear about your aunt," he said. "But if you plan to be away for some time, I should check the apartment before you leave."

"I vacuumed, cleaned the bathrooms, and washed the sheets and towels," Casey told him. "Once I get my aunt cared for, I can come back and deal with any problem."

"Sorry, but it's company policy for me to check it. Take a seat here. Nora will get you some coffee, and I'll be right back."

He was gone for a full hour.

"Looking good," he said. "But you did leave a couple of items in the fridge. You might want to take them with you."

Casey expected him to hand her the two bottles of seltzer she now remembered leaving in there, but no, she had to remove them herself.

Controlling her irritation, she rang for the elevator, marched down the hall to her apartment, fetched the seltzer, stuffed it in the plastic shopping bag, which Nora had kindly offered her, brought it down stairs, said goodbye to Nora and to Mr. Vachon with freezing politeness, and took the elevator to the parking garage.

The Jetta had half a tank of gas, which would get Casey to a cheaper gas station outside of the Portland gas gougers. Loading her suitcase in the back, she drove to the gate, slid her parking permit in the slot, and—the gate did not open. Two more tries, no luck. Before Casey could go hunting for an attendant, he showed up.

"Sorry, Ma'am," he said. "There's some difficulty with your pass. I'll have to call the manager. Please back up so other people can get out."

"I'll wait here," Casey snapped.

"But…"

"This is not my problem. Get it sorted out. I'll wait."

By the time he returned, a Subaru had pulled up behind her.

"The manager is on his way. Please move your car."

This had gone beyond irritating to completely strange. Annoying Voice thought so too. Both of them lost their temper.

"I'll wait," Casey said. Then she rolled up her windows, locked the car, turned off the engine, and sat there. Behind her, the Subaru honked. Then a Ford truck showed up behind the Subaru.

The attendant yelled something, but with the windows shut and two cars honking, Casey couldn't hear him. Besides, she was considering what it would do to her car if she ran it through the wooden barrier.

After a full six minutes—she timed it—and a fourth car honking in the line, the attendant clomped over to his booth, glared at Casey, and popped the gate open. Turning the key, Casey slammed the car into gear and stomped on the accelerator.

Once headed for I-95, she worried that whoever was behind all the strange delays might have called the cops or something. But she got to the first service plaza, near Lewiston, without seeing any flashing lights in her rearview mirror. From the plaza, she called Dan to tell him she'd be late.

"Your friend Joe Burnside has been here," he said.

"Not my friend." Casey had been thinking about the delays, about how Topher abruptly decided she was an essential employee, and about Joe Burnside.

"He'd heard your aunt wasn't feeling well," Dan continued. "The only person I told about her illness is my friend Alix, and she wouldn't know Burnside from a hole in the wall. He was horrified at the damage to the south woods, and asked Cill if he'd like him to take it off her hands."

Annoying Voice dropped the puzzle pieces together with a thunk. Why had Joe Burnside given her this job where she wasn't needed? Why did it take so long for the manager to check the apartment? And why was there such a problem getting out of the parking garage?

Annoying Voice was nuts. Joe Burnside was a respectable man. Wasn't he?

All Casey said was, "I hope she told him where to put his offer."

Dan laughed. "Just about. Then she did her crazy lady imitation, shrieking at him to get out, yelling at me to *throw* him out. He advised me to put her in a home, and gave me the number of a good one to call."

"Did you—?"

"Hell no. She's still sitting with her eyes closed, but I convinced her to drink some tea."

Pushing the speed limit as much as she dared—the last thing she needed was being slowed down by getting a speeding ticket—Casey arrived at Aunt Cill's house a little after three p.m. Dan came out to meet her.

"How is she?" she asked, climbing stiffly out of the driver's seat.

"The same. Come around front so you can see what happened."

What had happened was even stranger than the antics of Mr. Vachon and the parking attendant. The south woods looked like a hurricane blew through them. Broken trees were scattered like a spillage of giant toothpicks. But Dan swore there had been no storm; no wind at all in fact. Nothing that would topple maple trees like they were twigs. At least Casey's oak tree had survived. It seemed to be surveying the wreckage with horror. Or else she was projecting her own horror onto the tree.

"Your sculptures seem to have protected some of the trees," Casey said. Putting her hand on one of them, she felt the snap of energy.

Annoying Voice told her the sculptures were powerful. Casey told Annoying Voice that they weren't powerful enough.

When they returned to the living room, Great Aunt Cill sat in her big green armchair, eyes closed. The armchair had always been in the front corner of the room, with a good view of everything that went on. Her aunt had aged overnight. How old was she, anyway? Great Aunt, she should be about the age of Casey's grandmothers. But one of those grandmothers lived in Arizona where she could golf every day, and the other one lived in Boston so she could go to the museums and the theater. Neither one needed any help from an indigent grandchild. Great Aunt Cill should be a sister to one of them, but now she looked centuries older than they were.

'Which side of the family did she come from?' Casey asked herself. She had no idea. Her parents had never cared about family genealogy; their own accomplishments were enough for them.

Giving up on the question, and figuring that the old lady wouldn't appreciate a sweet bedside manner, Casey simply marched up to her and asked, "You okay, Aunt Cill? What's going on?"

"You have to fix my trees," Aunt Cill said, and closed her eyes.

"How do I do that?" But Aunt Cill didn't answer.

'Fine,' thought Casey. 'Business as usual.'

FOURTEEN: TEAMWORK

"I need coffee and explanations," she told Dan, and headed to the kitchen.

"Not sure I have any explanations," he said, following her. "But I made more coffee."

Casey poured herself coffee into the biggest mug she could find. It had a bright red lobster on it, so Aunt Cill never used it. Dan had smaller green mug with no pictures.

"Okay," said Casey. "How do we even begin to figure out what happened?"

"No idea. We have trees that look like they were hit by a tornado, but there wasn't even a breeze." Dan looked down at his coffee. "Did you see some of the area behind the sculptures is okay?"

Casey nodded. "Aunt Cill wanted them for a reason."

"And the trees falling made your aunt collapse."

"Let me tell you about something else that is strange," Casey said, and she explained how Topher suddenly decided she was an essential team member, and how long it took her to get away from her apartment. "I could only figure that Burnside was behind all of it. I found myself wondering— yeah, I know how weird it sounds—but did this happen so Aunt Cill would sell Burnside the south woods?"

"I don't think she can. No matter what happens."

"Why?"

Dan looked away. "I'm not sure. It doesn't make sense."

"None of this makes sense. All ideas welcome. Even stupid ones."

He shook his head. "All I know is how much she needs the forest. That's why I have to walk around all of it, every week, to make sure everything is okay. That's why she wanted my sculptures. Somehow, they protected the trees. She has fallen just like the south woods."

Casey decided she needed toast. It might help her to think. Getting out the homemade bread, slicing it, putting it into a toaster that was so old it shouldn't work at all, getting butter out of the refrigerator, finding homemade rose hip jelly, might help.

Meanwhile, Dan disappeared into the living room and returned to say, "She's the same."

"I'd like to go up on the Rock to see what happened to the south woods from there," Casey said, through toast crumbs. "Will you come with me?"

"Sure."

Dropping her dishes into the sink, Casey headed back to her car to collect her water bottle, sketchbook and drawing pencils, along with a backpack to stow them in. She had discovered she did her best thinking while sketching. Too bad she hadn't realized that when she was worrying about the fate of WebLicious.

Dan waited while she filled the water bottle at the sink.

"You know, it could be dangerous, if the wind comes back."

Casey made finger quotes. "It doesn't touch me."

He followed her down the porch stairs. "You don't know that."

Marching across the lawn, with Dan striding beside her, she told him about her experience on the Rock; how the not-wind tore a branch off her big oak tree, then flattened all the bushes around her without touching a hair on her head. She even told him about the branch growing back, although she still wasn't sure she could believe her eyes.

"You never mentioned that!"

Casey headed into the tree-lined path leading to the Rock. "There's been a lot of not-mentioning going on around here."

Negotiating the path and climbing the Rock left no energy for a chat. But when they reached the top, Dan grabbed her arm, so she was forced to turn and face him.

"It's important!" he said. "You should have told us!" Then he let her go, frowning at his hand like it had operated without him.

"Sure I should. Because you told me everything. You and Aunt Cill. Made me feel like part of the team. Let me know that something odd was happening here, something I had no way of even believing, let alone figuring out."

"She didn't tell me anything either! All she said was 'take care of my woods'."

"Didn't you ever wonder why she wanted that? Or wanted your sculptures?"

Dan took a few steps away, considered a small cedar tree carefully, then looked at the sky. "She was paying me. I didn't want to—make waves."

He may be hot, but he's a wimp, Casey thought. "Money fixes everything for you."

"I had no money! In between carving, I worked as a finish carpenter on houses. Cill gave me a studio and time to carve."

"Must be nice."

Dan turned around sharply, but all he said was, "Did you really see the branch break? And fixed it?"

The man didn't know how to argue. Casey decided he wasn't worth yelling at. She took him to the south edge of the Rock and pointed out the oak tree's new branch, with its spring-green leaves sprouting in late July.

"I figured I probably dreamed it. Or I was going crazy. Why would I tell anyone about it?"

Dan regarded the tree in silence. Finally, he said, "Can you re-grow all those trees? Like you did with this one?"

From here, Casey could see the destruction in the south woods, the twisting, curving paths of downed trees. Giant trees that had withstood years of hurricanes and nor'easters.

"I don't know," she said.

She'd hugged the oak tree, but hugging every single tree in the south forest was impossible. How many trees could she hug in one day? Besides, she had no idea if the oak tree responded because she loved it, or because she could actually make trees grow.

"It would take a long time to get around to all those trees," she added. "Especially because I have no idea what I'm doing. Why the hell couldn't Aunt Cill tell me why she needs the woods?"

"Maybe she didn't think anyone would believe her."

Casey gave him a small razzberry, which made him laugh. But she was still considering the wreckage. "There's something odd about how the trees blew down," she said.

"No kidding!"

"No, there's some kind of pattern. Maybe if I sketch it, I can figure it out."

Pulling out her sketchbook, Casey drew the lines of destruction, hoping that whatever nagged at the back of her mind would show itself. The lines began right after her oak tree, then fanned out across the woods, curling slightly. It reminded her of something, but she could not figure out what. Understanding the pattern was harder because Dan's tall, sinuous sculptures had protected the trees for several yards behind them.

Dan watched her sketch for a few minutes, then paced around, staring at the fallen trees.

At last, Casey stopped frowning at her sketches and said, "I have some kind of idea, but it's—well, let's go down and look more closely."

Where they stood, on the south side of the Rock, it was too steep to climb down, so once again she crossed to the eastern path, jogged across the lawn, and faced the destruction of the south woods. Dan followed her like a big protective dog.

Casey climbed over a pine tree fallen across the path, getting pine sap on her fingers and jeans. She remembered when she used to get it in her hair when she climbed this very tree. To remove the sap, her mother would plaster mayonnaise into her hair, which had the added advantage of taming Casey's wild curls, even though she smelled like a tuna-mayo sandwich.

On the other side of the pine, the destruction stretched away like a winding road. She followed the splinters and broken trunks as they curved along. The damage was shaped like a spiral, just like she'd sketched it from the Rock.

Pulling the sketchbook out her backpack, she considered the patterns she'd drawn. The back of her mind came to the front.

"Zora's necklace," she said.

"Who?"

"Joe Burnside wants these woods. His wife, Zora, has a necklace with the same pattern as the lines of destroyed trees."

She showed Dan the page of the sketchbook where she had drawn the necklace the morning after she dreamed of it. Two interlocked gold spirals, hanging on a gold chain. She explained the dream, while worrying that Dan would think she was delusional. Which he did.

"You think she waved her necklace at the trees, and they fell down?"

"Look at it! The trees fell in the exact same shape as the necklace!"

"What is she, a witch or something?"

"Once you eliminate the impossible," she began.

Dan finished the quote. "Whatever remains, however improbable, must be the truth."

"Sherlock Holmes, right?"

"Probably."

Casey snorted, Dan grinned, and they both laughed shakily. "It's hard to believe," he said.

"Try believing this," said Casey, and she told him about the not-coyote thing. "I thought I'd been dreaming, but could see its track through the ferns. Besides, the wind showed up a second time." She told him about that, too. "Maybe I'm just crazy," she added.

Dan was staring at a fallen oak tree. "Maybe. Let me see your drawing again."

She handed him the sketchbook. He held the necklace drawing up toward the fallen trees. "All I have to do is look at the way these trees fell in a spiral shape to decide *I'm* the crazy one. But they're too real."

He began paging through the sketchbook.

"Hey," Casey said. "You weren't supposed to look at everything, only the necklace."

"You're an artist," he said.

"Graphic designer."

He flipped through the pages, looking at her sketch of one of her sculptures, then the drawing of the old toaster, and finally the sketch of how the front stairs appeared from a child's eye view.

"That one is amazing," he said. "The angles of the staircase—how did you get those? They're terrific."

"It's what they looked like to me when I was about seven."

The man who made those magical sculptures liked her art. The *gorgeous* man who made those sculptures liked her art. Casey tried to ignore the weakness in her knees and the heat in her insides. No more gorgeous men, she told herself. Jake was enough. Next man in my life has to look ordinary. Maybe even ugly. Or, worse, dull.

Dan turned the sketchbook pages back to the spiral drawings. "Do you think the Burnsides know that destroying the forest would make your aunt sick?"

"I don't know," she said.

He sat down on a fallen trunk. "I don't think Cill can live without the forest," he said softly.

Somehow, it made sense to Casey. At least, Annoying Voice thought it made sense. Still, she asked Dan why.

"Yeah, it sounds pretty strange," he said. "But why else would she hire me to walk the forest? She told me she used to do it, but was too old to spend all day there. I'm her eyes and ears. When she saw the first sculpture I made, she wanted dozens of them, all around the edges of the forest. Now I think it might be some kind of barrier against—" He stopped, giving Casey a wry look. "Maybe I should have put *all* of them along the south forest. They did seem to block some of the wind. Only it's not fast work—I have to find the right piece of wood, and then figure out, well..."

"What it wants to do," she finished.

"Of course you'd understand that." Okay, he had a great smile. Which he probably used on every woman he met. The smile disappeared. "But she did want some on the north side of the house. Where they did no good."

"We can move them all here." Casey remembered the spark jumping from her fingers when she touched one of Dan's sculptures. "At least we'll be doing something." She blew out a breath. "I shouldn't have taken that job. But how was I to know about Burnside? My aunt never tells me anything."

Dan sighed too. "This morning, when she told me to get you, I think she hoped you might be able to help, but wouldn't ask. She made me call, instead. Maybe it's because you took the job with Burnside. Or maybe it's because you turned her down when she asked you to live here."

"I was seventeen years old, dammit! And did she say, 'Priscilla, you love the forest, and I can teach you how to take care of it?' No, she acted like I was an irritating brat. Which I probably was when I was ten years old, but at seventeen I might have understood."

"You're still irritating," Dan teased. "But so is she. She's been here alone for so long she doesn't know how to ask for help."

"She asked *you*."

'I'm jealous,' Casey thought. She was jealous. She hated that.

"Only to walk the forest and explain what I found."

"I think it's time *I* explained a few things to her," Casey growled, grabbing the sketchbook and heading back to the house.

Once again, she didn't bother breaking it gently; she simply marched into the living room. She didn't worry about getting splinters and pine sap on the rug, strode over to Aunt Cill in her chair, and said, "Zora Burnside is wrecking your forest. Her necklace has the same pattern as the destruction. We have to get it away from her."

Aunt Cill opened her eyes. "Is that a fact?" she said.

"Yes!"

Then Casey explained how the not-wind didn't touch her; how she'd dreamed about the necklace; how the curves of the downed trees mirrored the necklace. "You told me Joe Burnside wants to buy your south forest. This is his way of forcing you to sell."

During all this, Aunt Cill sat up a little, listening attentively. But did she say, "that's amazing? or "how can a necklace blow down trees?" No; she pinned Casey with her eyes.

"You took a job with that man."

"Before I figured out what was going on."

"You didn't *want* to know anything. You wouldn't come and live here."

"I was a kid! My whole family believed in logic, in numbers. Me wanting to be an artist instead of a lawyer made my parents crazy. And the only reason they didn't insist I come home now, instead of staying here, is because they thought you needed a keeper!"

Aunt Cill pursed up her lips. "Jim and Linda have always been fools."

"Maybe, but they're the only parents I've got!"

Dan moved in between them. "Cill, do you think Casey is right? Could Zora use her necklace to wreck the forest?"

"How do I know?" Aunt Cill lay back and closed her eyes.

Patience, Casey told herself. "The only way to find out is to get the thing away from her," she said.

"Steal it?" Dan asked.

A plan dawned. Annoying Voice was earning its keep. "We could invite them here for dinner," she said slowly. "Pretend you're thinking about selling to Burnside. We could put something in the wine to make them sleep."

"Poisoning people could be dangerous," Dan said.

Aunt Cill opened one eye. "That's not a problem. But they wake up, the necklace is gone, then what?"

"It would have to be all of us, all of us asleep. Then Dan could come steal the necklace."

"Nonsense!" snapped her aunt. "They'll know we stole it. We'll all end up in jail."

"You got a better idea?" That was not the proper way to speak to one's great aunt, but the woman was pissing Casey off. Aunt Cill glared. Casey glared back.

"I know someone who could make a replica," Dan said, in a placating voice. "Although it might be expensive. Even if Zora noticed, what would she say? You stole my voodoo necklace? No lawyer would take the case. As long as whatever we give them doesn't kill them."

Aunt Cill climbed out of her chair. "It won't," she said. "But the forest will still be dead."

"If I'm right, she won't be able to kill the rest of it," said Casey.

"That's not enough."

'Okay,' Casey thought, 'if I believe in Zora's magic necklace, I can believe in all the other strange happenings. Maybe I can find a way help the forest regenerate, like I made the oak tree grow.' But she had no idea how to do it for acres of wreckage. And she wasn't going to tell her aunt about the oak tree until she could figure out *how* she'd made it grow.

"Of course, Zora could keep blowing it down," Casey said defensively. "But it's up to you."

"We don't know she's blowing it down," Dan said.

"It's a test! If the necklace is gone, and the wind never comes back, we'll know it's her!"

Aunt Cill stared at Casey, the cold stare that had always terrified her as a child. Then Cill staggered a little, pursed her lips at Dan's helping arm, and sat down again.

"How much will your friend charge to make a replica?" she demanded

"I'll ask him," said Dan.

Aunt Cill nodded. "I have something we could put in the wine."

FIFTEEN: CHARMING ZORA

Before they could even consider how to doctor the wine, however, Casey wanted to see Zora's necklace again. Dan's friend would need drawings to even give them a price. The next morning, after hating the idea for about an hour, Casey called Joe Burnside to apologize for having to leave the job he gave her, and to explain her aunt was not well. Then she had to listen while he told her all about the wonderful nursing home in Greenville, pretending to take his advice.

She did not, however, want to visit the Burnside mansion and ask to see Zora. Too obvious.

So, she drove into Blake Harbor to buy fish from Manny. Manny loved to gossip, and might tell Casey what Zora did all day. Then she could "accidentally" run into her.

While Manny wrapped up the scrod, Casey said she'd been working for Joe in Portland, but came home because her aunt was sick, that she had talked to Joe, but forgot to ask after Zora, and how was she doing?

At first, Manny was too worried about Aunt Cill to think about Zora. "Never heard of Miz Woodward getting sick," he said. "But she is getting up there. When I was a kid, helping my dad in this store, she'd come buy fish. Very particular about her fish."

Casey asked again about Zora. Manny said she was doing fine.

"Such a beautiful lady, and she spends every Wednesday at Carrie's Changes, getting her hair and nails done. Ever seen those nails? Long and shiny, clearly the woman never has to work. Why she needs anything from Carrie when she's already the prettiest woman in six counties I'll never know. But Joe can afford it. You'd think he'd stay home more, with such a gorgeous wife, but he's always off somewhere on business. That big house must get kind of lonely."

Then Casey had to hear all about Carrie and how she'd started her beauty shop when her no-good husband left her. If another customer hadn't come in, she might have been there for hours. Manny did love to talk. But Casey had her information.

Back at Woodward House, she and Dan ate the fish. Aunt Cill would only nibble some toast and sip tea.

"What if Zora doesn't go to the beauty shop tomorrow?" Dan asked. "What if she isn't wearing the necklace?"

"Then I'll hire a detective to follow her around until she does wear it," Casey snapped, exasperated.

To her astonishment, Dan didn't snap back at her. Instead, he laughed. "You're right, it's the only plan we have right now. We can always hire a detective later!"

So, the next day, Wednesday, Casey arrived when Carrie's opened at ten a.m., planning to wait for Zora.

Casey on a bench reading; wandered up and down the street; pulled out her phone and pretended to be on a long call. Feeling like she was in a spy movie, she worried that she might have to dither there all day. What if Zora had a four p.m. appointment? So, Casey had brought along a thermos of coffee, a bottle of water, some of Aunt Cill's oatmeal cookies, and a hunk of cheese so strong, it made her nose itch. The cheese came from a fancy grocery store in the harbor. Aunt Cill thought the store was overpriced and full of tourists. Except, she said, it was the only place that sold decent cheese.

At one p.m., a golden BMW sedan parked near the shop, and Zora stepped out.

After giving her ten minutes, Casey headed to Carrie's. Her plan was to make an appointment for a haircut, and get a look at Zora's necklace while she did. If Zora was wearing the necklace.

"We can take you in just a few minutes, honey, if you got time now," said the woman behind the counter. "Kimmy had a cancellation." The woman had lacquered black hair and thick makeup.

Hoping her own hair wouldn't end up glued together, Casey sat down to wait in a chrome chair with a pink leather seat, gazing at the black and silver wallpaper. In Rochester, she'd had her hair cut in an inexpensive artsy place with brick walls, where the proprietor believed in organically sourced shampoo. Carrie's shop smelled like hairspray.

When Kimmy appeared, she wore nicely shagged hair and no makeup. Casey felt better. Maybe her hair wouldn't be glued together after all.

When she discovered her chair was right next to Zora's, and that Zora was wearing the necklace, she felt much more than better.

"Casey!" Zora said. Her blonde hair was encased in curlers, and her long nails were being painted a dusty pink. "How nice to see you! Where did you hear about Carrie's? She is the best."

Casey explained how Manny had told her about Carrie, and they laughed about how much Manny liked to talk.

"How's your auntie? Joseph told me that she wasn't feeling well."

Casey said Aunt Cill was a little better, but she was still worried about her, because the old lady refused to go to a doctor.

Zora waved her finished pink nails to dry them. "All my physicians are in Boston. That's the best city for doctors. But I hear young doctor Pompeo isn't bad."

While Kimmy clipped away at Casey's hair, Zora chatted about her trips to Boston, and where she bought her clothes. Casey made listening noises and eyed Zora's necklace, checking details. A pair of interlocking spirals of heavy gold had tiny links that kept them on a necklace of gold links. The spirals faced each other, as if they were conversing, maybe about how to blow down trees in twin spirals.

Casey needed a photo. Meanwhile, another stylist began removing Zora's curlers, combing and spraying and combing,

"Is this short enough?" Kimmy asked. Casey hadn't been paying attention to her own hair. Now she considered herself in the big mirror. Her frizzy curls looked softer and much more organized, framing her wide face becomingly.

"It's great," she said, as the other stylist whisked off Zora's covering smock.

"Everyone here is the best!" Zora announced, primping.

"Let's take a picture of us!" said Casey, hoping that her girlishness didn't sound as fake as it felt.

Getting a clearer view of the necklace was worth acting like an idiot. But Zora said that a picture was a so-lovely idea. Casey pulled out her phone. Putting her face close to Zora's blonde curls, she made sure some of the photos showed the necklace clearly.

"Would you ever be free for lunch?" she asked. "Now that I'm back living with my aunt, I'd like to get out now and then."

Zora jumped on the idea with enthusiasm. Casey hoped it wasn't because she planned to somehow blow down the rest of the south woods while they were off having lunch. They agreed to meet the next Monday. The more Casey could see of the necklace, the better.

Back in her Jetta, with one of the best haircuts she'd ever had in her life, Casey looked at the photos on her phone, didn't like them, and decided to sketch the necklace, from memory and from every point of view.

Now all they needed to do was get a replica, manage to change the real necklace for the fake, and re-grow the south woods.

SIXTEEN: VALERIE

To survive in Wabanaki Port, where the Puffin Feather was located, Rinne had to learn new skills.

She could plant a garden, cook a meal for ten people, and pilot her father's lobster boat. But she couldn't drive a car, or, at first, even find her way around the little town. Halloran Island had one dirt road, leading from the family houses to Seaview Cottage. In high school, Rinne had spent most of her time at the school. When she went anywhere else, Alison or Helena went with her, guiding her as they walked the winding streets of Gorham Harbor, having their parents drive them for shopping or visits, or, once her friends had their licenses, taking Rinne around in their own cars. In Wabanaki Port, it took Rinne a month before the curving streets made sense.

With her fourth paycheck, Rinne found a secondhand laptop through a friend of Tavish. The apartment she shared with Helena actually had Wi-Fi. Now she could hunt for Sarah without always going to the library.

Sharing a small apartment with Helena gave her claustrophobia. Not only did Helena strew her belongings everywhere, but she also filled the apartment bathroom with an astonishing array of beauty products, along with a curling iron, a blow dryer, and a razor to keep her legs smooth. After they had lived there only a week, the bathroom smelled like an overwhelming mélange of perfume and hair spray. It reminded Rinne of her sister, making her feel even smaller and plainer

At home, Rinne's family spent a lot of their time outside their little house. Brian on his boat, Maris in the garden, Rinne and Sarah running around the Island or, later, in school. Now Rinne looked for ways to escape the cluttered apartment whenever she could.

Helena was the complete party girl. She worked as a receptionist at the Wabanaki Harbor Hotel, and loved it. "You meet all kinds of people," she told Rinne. "When the hotel has events, I help the caterers. They have wonderful parties there!"

Inspired by these events, and the caterers, Helena started hosting parties at their tiny apartment. Rinne couldn't imagine how Helena knew so many people after only three months in Wabanaki Port. She spent the first party hiding in the kitchen, making fancy canapés from recipes Helena had cadged from the hotel.

After that happened a few times, Helena told Rinne she needed help. "You gotta be more social," she said. "Come out with me. You can't spend your whole life at the library or glued to that ancient laptop of yours."

"Sure I can," Rinne said, but Helena didn't listen. "First, you need a makeover!" she announced.

"How's it gonna help?" Rinne asked. "Lipstick is not going to make me like parties."

"You organized our prom! It was fantastic!"

"Yeah, but I didn't like going to it. Too many people."

"Trust me. It'll be fun."

Because it was pouring with rain, and tomorrow was her day off, Rinne didn't want to have to listen to Helena go on and on. Once she got an idea into her head, Helena never shut up, so Rinne said okay. Delighted, Helena painted Rinne's fingernails a pale pink, then applied eyeliner, eye shadow and mascara. Rinne balked at any foundation or rouge, so Helena worked Rinne's straight dark hair with her curling iron, then hunted out a push-up bra and a red, skin-tight top, to go with Rinne's best black pants.

"Check it out," Helena said, pushing Rinne toward a full-length mirror. The only full-length mirror on the Island had been a gift to Sarah when she graduated from high school. Rinne had always ignored it, instead using the tiny mirror in the bathroom to make sure her hair was combed, and her shirt was clean.

Now Sarah stared back at Rinne from the mirror. With her dark hair in curls, wearing makeup, she looked like her sister. To find Sarah, she would need to go to the kind of places Sarah loved. That meant learning how to wear nail polish and go to parties. And bars.

"You okay?" Helena asked. "You look gorgeous; don't be so surprised, it's the real you! Come on, let's go to the Big Cat tonight. They have a terrific band. You know how to dance, you danced at our prom."

"Not well."

"Then it's time to learn!"

The band at the Big Cat was loud. Helena knew everyone. She yelled introductions to Rinne; then disappeared into a wall of gyrating dancers. So much for learning how to dance. Rinne perched on a bar stool, nursing a gin and tonic, trying to remember the image of herself from the mirror. But she still felt like the efficient and ordinary girl she had always been. Sarah would have loved this place. Makeover or not, Rinne could never be anything like Sarah.

"C'mon, pretty lady, less dance!" A drunken guy with pale brown hair grabbed her arm, pulling her off the bar stool.

"No thank you!" Rinne yelled over the pulsating band. But the guy kept pulling her. Tugged off her stool, Rinne stumbled, then planted her feet. "NO!" she yelled, like she was telling Biff, the mutt who guarded the Island's chickens, not to bark at the rich Mrs. Bresky.

The guy lost his balance; staggered, then went down on the beer-slimed floor. A woman drew back the booted foot. She had tripped the drunk. He glared up at her, cursing inventively if slushily, then climbed to his feet, fists out.

"Hey, Bart!" the woman called. "Get rid of this jerk!"

A guy came around the bar and put a hand on the drunk guy's shoulder, saying, "Come on, buddy, let's take a walk."

"That bitch tripped me!"

"Why would she do that?" Bart asked. The guy stared up at him. Bart was at least six-three, with shoulders to match.

"Fu'en bitch," the guy said, but shambled off with Bart.

"You okay?" asked Rinne's rescuer. "That guy is a known asshole. I can introduce you to a few men who aren't." The woman had a wide brown face and a wave of short brown hair. She was taller than Rinne, and bigger, not with fat, but with muscle. And she had a wonderful grin below a snub nose and blue eyes. The grin faded. "You look a little creeped out. Wanna get some air?"

'Air would be okay, but some peace and quiet would be better,' thought Rinne, and followed as the woman led her to a side door, out into the chilly September night. The cold air felt wonderful. It smelled of hamburgers and wood smoke.

"I'm Val," said the woman. "You come here often?" And she laughed at the silly joke.

"Rinne. Two Ns. No. Um. Thanks." Rinne felt more than usually small, and unusually tongue-tied. "I, um, I came here with a friend. Roommate. First time. In a place like this." She also felt shaky but tried not to show it. On the Island, she'd always been strong and tough. On the Island, the only jerk she had to deal with was Gavin, and she could handle him. Usually.

"Kind of jumping in at the deep end," Val said. "You might start with someplace quieter, like Sam's Pub."

"Helena said she comes here a lot."

"Helena. Tall, blonde, party girl?"

Rinne nodded.

"This is my cousin's place," Val explained. "He's too cheap to hire a bouncer, even though he needs one. Bart's supposed to bartend *and* bounce. Doing both at once is impossible. I come by when I can, to help out, so I get to know the regulars."

"I should go find Helena," Rinne said. She needed to sit down before her legs betrayed her. She hated noise and arguments. Val took her arm, led her inside. "Sit here," she said. "I'll go find Miss Helena."

Rinne sat at a small table at the end of the bar. Bart appeared, put a glass in front of her, disappeared. Rinne smelled it gingerly. Water. She drank it all.

"Val says you're not feeling good," said Helena, appearing from the growing crowd. "I'll drive you home."

Hating to feel like a dork and a wimp, but hating the crowded bar more, Rinne said, "Yeah. Thanks."

But Sarah would have loved the noise and the dancing. If Rinne were going to find her sister, she'd have to learn to handle places like the Big Cat.

The morning after her disastrous visit to the bar, Rinne woke to a comfortingly misty day, with the foghorns echoing gently across the harbor. On the Island, days like this often meant her dad stayed home, with Rinne helping him to fix things around the house, and to clean up the boat. Even now, she loved foggy days, especially when, like today, they coincided with her day off. Staying comfortable in her pajamas, she made coffee and sat by the apartment's small window to drink it, watching the fog turning the ordinary street into mystery.

Last night, after delivering Rinne to their apartment, Helena had returned to the Big Cat. Today, at about two o'clock in the afternoon, she staggered out of her bedroom, hungover and cranky. By then, Rinne had changed into jeans and a sweater, and was chopping onions and mushrooms for spaghetti.

"Oh God you're not *cooking*," moaned Helena, clutching her second cup of strong coffee.

"I'm only getting things ready. I'll wait until you feel better to cook," Rinne said cheerfully. Helena mumbled something, and took her coffee back to bed. Rinne kept chopping.

Then Helena's phone rang. "Tell 'em to go to hell," Helena called.

Rinne sighed and dug her roommate's phone out from under her coat, where Helena had dropped both of them at some early morning hour.

"Hello," Rinne said, wondering which of Helena's boyfriends this might be.

"Hi, this is Val Costa. From last night? Is Rinne there?"

"This is Rinne. Helena isn't up to answering the phone."

Val laughed. "I figured. I got her number from Bart. Just wanted to see how you're feeling today."

"Fine, I'm fine. Sorry to be such a wimp. Thanks for, um, looking out for me."

"No problem. Glad to hear you're okay."

"Hey," Rinne found herself saying. "I'm cooking spaghetti tonight. Would you like to come have dinner?" To her amazement and panic, Val said yes.

Rinne spent the rest of the day dusting, picking up the shoes and coats Helena always left around, and making bread. Around five, the shower whooshed; then Helena wandered in, wearing her flowered kimono, combing out her wet hair.

"What the hell is all this domesticity?" she demanded.

"Val called. I invited her over for dinner."

"Didn't think she was your type."

"My type? She kept some drunken asshole from hitting on me. Least I could do is invite her to dinner."

"Is *that* what was wrong with you? Jeez, if I had a dollar for every time a drunken asshole hit on me, I wouldn't have to live in this crummy apartment!" And Helena disappeared to spend an hour getting dressed, while Rinne finished cooking. Helena would think she was an antisocial idiot.

"But I am an antisocial idiot," she told the lettuce she was washing. In high school, she had done the background work—the planning, the organizing. Others, like Helena, ran around charming people into helping with whatever project Rinne had dreamed up.

When the doorbell rang, Helena appeared, in zebra striped leggings and a black top, which left nothing to the imagination. Rinne, who had put on a clean shirt and her good jeans because her other clothes were covered with sauce and flour, almost asked if Helena was going out again even though she had to work tomorrow, but bit her tongue.

"Smells great," Helena said, as Rinne buzzed Val in.

Val also wore jeans, a jean jacket, and black boots; Rinne vaguely remembered the boot that had tripped the blond jerk was brown. The woman must have a collection of boots for all occasions.

"Hope you like wine," Val said, handing Rinne a bottle. "Hey, Helena, how you doing?"

"Great, now my hangover's gone!" Helena said. "Your cousin makes strong drinks!"

Four or five of those drinks would definitely be too strong, but Rinne decided not to mention it.

At dinner, Helena asked Val about her three brothers and the bartender Bart, then moved on to several of the Big Cat regulars. She wanted to know if any of them had girlfriends. Val answered patiently. Bart was seeing a social worker, her brother Sandy was engaged, brother Matt was married, and her youngest brother, Carl, was a flake. She didn't know whether any of the bar's regulars had girlfriends.

When Helena finally ran down, Val asked Rinne what she did.

"Tavish!" Val exclaimed, when Rinne told her about the Puffin Feather. "He's a piece of work, he gives all the church ladies something to talk about! Hey, I have been wondering, is your dad Brian Gilley?"

Rinne said he was.

"I've heard a lot about him," Val said. "One of the best lobstermen on the coast. My dad and uncles can't figure out how he does it with that old-fashioned trawler of his. My family are Costa Fisheries."

Rinne had seen the sign on the harbor and admired their fleet of three trawlers. She spent a lot of time at the docks. It helped her not to feel so homesick.

"I do the books for the business," Val explained. "I research new gear, talk to the buyers. Yeah, some days I'd rather be out on the ocean, but I'm good at this stuff, and selling fish is a complicated business now."

Rinne wanted to know all about the new gear Val researched. After she and Val had been talking Maine fisheries for half an hour, Helena said, "I'm going out, see you later."

Rinne didn't even care that Helena was in full pouting mode. Maybe Val could take her back to the Big Cat and keep idiots away while Rinne learned how to act like Sarah.

On her next day off, Rinne visited the Costa offices with Val. The offices inhabited a square, tar-shingled building near the harbor. The first floor was full of nets, lobster traps, and ancient sonar and other electronic equipment. Val wrinkled her nose at the mess.

"Dad always says he's going to fix or sell his junk. I keep telling him that he should use it to reinforce the sea wall!"

The second floor included a conference room with a table, five chairs, and a view of the harbor, along with a couple of smaller rooms. One held Val's neatly organized desk and computer; the others had desks piled with dusty papers.

"Dad hates the office," Val said. "But he insists on having a desk anyway. So my brothers have to have them too."

The tour ended with coffee in Val's apartment, which was on the building's third floor.

"I pay rent, so I don't have to live completely in my family's pocket," Val explained The apartment had a big living-kitchen area, with an old brown couch, which looked like you could lose yourself in it, and windows with a view of the harbor.

They went down to the dock, where Val introduced Rinne to her father.

"You're Brian Gilley's kid?" said Ferdie Costa, holding Rinne's hand in his both of his. They were rough and strong, like her father's. "He can catch lobsters anywhere," Mr. Costa continued. "How's he _do_ that?"

Rinne mumbled something about experience and luck. You didn't tell anyone about the family's Skill.

Ferdie was taller than Val and twice as big around. He wore yellow fisherman's overalls and a flannel shirt, like Rinne's father. While he gave Rinne a tour of one of his trawlers, she breathed deeply of the smell of brine and fish and oil. She missed working with her father.

"We don't do much lobstering," Val explained. "Not like your dad. We mostly catch sole and plaice, and shrimp or scallops in the winter."

The Costa trawler sported the latest in electronic equipment—net sounders, catch sensors, symmetry sensors, tension sensors. Rinne's head spun as she tried to understand all the terms. Brian and her Uncle Neil made do with GPS and a hydraulic hauler for the lobster pots.

Val and her father laughed. "If we could catch lobsters like they do, we wouldn't need all these geegaws either," Ferdie said. "You come down here any time. A Gilley will bring us luck!"

"I'd love to," Rinne said. "I miss working on my dad's boat."

A few weeks later, when the Costa trawlers came into port, Val invited Rinne to help the fishermen hose things down. They both got filthy, Rinne went home happy, and pleased to be invited to the next trawler cleaning. At first, the work made her homesickness worse, but after a couple of cleanup sessions, she felt both comfortable and comforted. Val and her brothers made dumb jokes, yelled at each other, had water fights with the hose, and were nothing like the serious Islanders.

After a couple of months of trawler cleaning, Val asked Rinne if she'd like to work for Costa Fisheries, saying, "I could use some help in the office."

Rinne shook her head.

"What?" said Val. "You keep doing that, shutting your mouth over something. No, you don't have to tell me," she added. "Sorry. It's just--it worries me when you worry."

Rinne had never had a friend like Val. She could never talk with Sarah, or Helena, the way she could with Val. She'd never had anyone say something like "it worries me when you worry," and mean it.

"It's complicated," Rinne said finally. "But—about three years ago, my sister ran away. She was supposed to marry our cousin Gavin and, um, carry on the family tradition. Business. Without her, I'm supposed to do that. But I can't. I can't marry Gavin, even though I'd like to spend my life on the Island."

"Seems like marrying would be the way to spend your life there," Val said.

"It's like Gavin is my brother. A brother I don't even like very much. Marrying him feels... wrong. I can't be Sarah. If I worked for you, my dad would find a way to get at me through you, because he knows everyone in the fishing business. He'd find a way to bring me home."

"My dad would never do anything to hurt you," Val said.

"Someone else might. Or do something to hurt his business. But none of my dad's friends shop at the Puffin." Val snorted a laugh, and Rinne had to laugh too, at the image of a bunch of fishermen buying unicorn statues or puffin potholders. "Anyway, he can't do anything while I work at the Puffin. And I can keep looking for Sarah."

"Wow," said Val. "I guess families can sometimes be the pits." Rinne nodded.

"But maybe I can help you find your sister," Val added.

"She loved places like the Big Cat," said Rinne. "That's why I wanted to go there. But I hated it. I'm not like Sarah."

"They aren't my favorite places either," said Val. "But I don't hate them. And my cousin Rick, who owns it, knows all the bartenders from here to Portland. Do you have a picture of your sister? Rick can show it around."

Rinne did. She also had pictures of the guy Sarah ran away with for the first time, and the boy she'd met in Portland. Sarah had left both guys behind, and neither one had any idea where she'd gone. The police had given their photos to Brian, but when he couldn't find Sarah, he left the photos on the kitchen table, and Rinne picked them up. She had already posted their photos, and photos of Sarah, on various social media sites, but no one had responded, except for the usual trolls.

"I'll send them around," Val said. "And I'll get Rick to send them, too."

Now Rinne spent most of her days off with Val--working on the Costa trawlers, hiking along the rocky coastline, and talking. She spent less and less time on the computer hunting for her sister.

One day in mid-November, unseasonably sunny weather tempted Val and Rinne to hike farther than usual, up and down the worn granite, under spice-scented fir trees, along stony beaches where the waves rattled the pebbles. Finally, they sat down on a high ledge to drink water, eat granola bars, and watch the ocean splashing below, whitecaps accenting its gleaming back. The sun warmed the rock. Val lay back and closed her eyes, gave a faint snore.

After a long rainy week, cooped up in the shop or the apartment, the sharp clear air went to Rinne's head. The waves called to her. No one else was around; no hiking tourists, no fishing trawlers.

While Sarah had required lessons for her important Skill, Rinne was allowed to simply grow into hers, although sometimes she'd ask her Gran questions, and sometimes Gran would answer them. Mostly, Rinne played with the waves off Lookout Ledge. When she'd turned fourteen, her mother had decided it was okay for Rinne to go out with her father and keep the ocean calm for him. But since coming to Wabanaki Port, she hadn't practiced at all. Working for Tavish, helping out with the Costa trawlers, and hiking with Val took up all Rinne' time.

Now, playing with the waves felt wonderful. First, she calmed them; then encouraged them. She loved to get them to curl into fantastic shapes.

"Do you see that!" Val was awake. "Those waves! They're all curling in the same direction! Look!"

Rinne jumped. "Where?" she managed to ask.

Val shook her head. "They're gone now. You didn't see it?"

"I was watching a shearwater fly by," Rinne said lamely.

"I never saw anything like it. It looked like that Japanese painting you see on notecards and stuff, you know, the one with the curled wave. Only all these waves curled, not just one. Reminds me of some flat clouds I saw one time when I was out with my dad. He even knew what they were called, lenticular." Val peered down at the rocks, where the waves tumbled and frothed. "I'll see if Dad or Uncle Jack knows of some kind of rock formation, something that would make the currents do that. Except those waves have disappeared. If it was a rock formation they should have stuck around. You sure you didn't see them?"

Rinne decided that she wouldn't play with waves again unless she was miles away from anyone. Even Val.

SEVENTEEN: THE NECKLACE

Dan was working in his studio when he heard a tentative knock at his door. Heading down the hallway, he found Casey standing on the stairs, holding out her phone and some sketches.

"I saw Zora, got a photo and made some sketches," she said. "You can send them to your friend, see what it might cost."

He reached for the drawings and Casey's phone. She seemed unwilling to leave the landing. "These sketches are great. But the photo is a little blurry."

"We're having lunch. I'll try for another selfie." And she turned to leave.

Discovering that he wanted to keep Casey there, Dan said, "Come in a moment. Do you think we could purchase a chain? It doesn't look all that special."

Casey turned back and stood in his doorway. "I think that would work. It's the spirals on the charm that do it, I'm pretty sure."

"I was about to take a break, have some coffee," Dan said.

For a moment, he thought she'd run away again, but then she nodded, saying, "Sure. Thanks." And she stepped over his threshold. Her curls were shorter. Dan wondered if they'd be as soft to touch as they looked. He told himself that he belonged to Alix, and busied himself with making coffee.

Turning on the coffee machine, his back to Casey, Dan said, "Your aunt is just the same; no worse, no better. At least she listened to your idea about the necklace."

"Do you think I'm nuts? I mean, it's only a crazy theory."

He turned around to face her. She was perched on the edge of his fat blue couch, which he'd rescued from a junk store. Cleaned up, with new legs, it looked pretty good.

"God no, Casey," he said. "I saw what happened to those woods on a perfectly calm night. I saw what happened to Cill because of it. Yeah, we're into the Twilight Zone, but there's no other explanation for all this."

She nodded. "I have to come up with some way to fix the forest," she said. "But I have no idea what to do."

"You'll figure it out," Dan said reflexively; then he realized he believed she would.

"Looks like the coffee's done," she said.

While they drank, they reviewed the sketches, then Casey sent her photos to Dan's phone. "I'll head to town right now, send these on to Wyatt," he said.

"My lunch with Zora isn't until Monday. I can get more pictures then."

"He can probably give us a ballpark figure from the sketches alone. They're really good."

She actually blushed, standing up to hide it. "Thanks for the coffee," she said.

Dan's college friend Wyatt made jewelry in Gloucester, Massachusetts. Based on Casey's sketches, Wyatt gave Dan a price that made him blink. Cill may have thought she had the money to make a copy of Zora's charm, but this price could be too much for her.

Wyatt misunderstood Dan's shocked pause at the price. "Just for you, man," he said. "Got someone special to give it to?"

Dan laughed, letting Wyatt believe what he wanted to believe, trying not to think about Alix, instead thinking how the necklace would suit Casey better. 'She doesn't even wear jewelry,' he told himself. 'What is <u>with</u> you'?

When Cill heard the cost, she said, "Why can't <u>you</u> do it?"

She still spent all her time napping in her chair, instead of cooking, making potions, and running up and down the stairs. She would only eat tea and toast. When she was awake, however, she was as formidable as ever.

"Making jewelry is complicated," Dan told her. "It's completely different from making a wood sculpture. But you're right, it is awfully expensive. Maybe we need to think of another way to stop Zora from blowing down any more trees."

Cill pursed her lips, then nodded. "My trees are worth it," she said. "Go ahead. But I've got some old stuff, might be gold. Maybe your friend could melt it down, give us a better price."

With her directions, Dan and Casey rummaged in her bureau drawers, then took on the attic.

They sneezed their way through old trunks, mahogany chests, and a beautiful bird's-eye maple table. "She should sell some of these things on E-Bay," Dan said. "And why is this gorgeous table up in the attic?"

"*You* want to try and persuade her to sell any of this?" Casey asked, and Dan shook his head so ruefully, it made her laugh. They collected a double handful of gold jewelry to show to Cill, after rejecting other items as too good to melt down.

"Look at the detail on this brooch," Dan marveled, fingering its intricate whorls. "It's wonderful!"

Casey found a ring with faded names inside and a readable date: 1801. "We have to keep this," she said. "It's probably from a great-great-great grandparent!"

Once again, Casey wondered how Aunt Cill was related to her parents.

But when they told Cill about the ring, she announced that she didn't give a darn about any old jewelry.

"They must be heirlooms!" Casey said. "You could sell some of the furniture instead, if you need money for the charm!"

Her aunt pursed her lips. "My father made all the furniture," she announced, in a tone that stopped all discussion.

"Let's see if my friend will buy any of the jewelry we chose," Dan said peaceably.

Wyatt was interested. "Probably can't use it for your charm," he said. "But I do buy old gold. Send it on. It'll give you a little break on the price."

After Casey and Dan had chosen pieces of Cill's jewelry for Wyatt, Dan had another idea. "I know every antique store and flea market in the area. Maybe we can find a few more things, get the price down more."

Making sure Cill had her book about gardens, a glass of water, and a plate of crackers and cheese, Dan and Casey spent a day prowling antique and junk stores, digging into dusty corners and grimy boxes, gathering enough odd bits of gold to make a larger difference in the cost of the necklace. It was fun. Alix hated flea markets, and only liked the clean fancy antique stores, where everything was overpriced. But Casey loved the grubby markets and "junque" stores. Every now and then, she would tap Dan on the shoulder and point at a particularly wacky piece—a painting of cute cats, or a chair from what she called "the crouch-and-spring era" of furniture. With its squat legs and short back, the chair did look like it was about to spring up, dumping its occupant. They laughed together.

"Look at the price on this!" Casey called, patting a birds-eye maple table. "Aunt Cill could sell everything in her house and make a billion dollars! Like that would ever happen," she added. Then she found a box of tools and rummaged around until she found some stuff useful for making jewelry, even though neither of them knew how.

"If I can fix the forest, maybe I can learn to use these!" she said. She had a smudge of dust on her face. Dan loved the way it looked, so he didn't mention it.

Spending so much time with Casey was not a good idea. After all, he'd been with Alix for five years. Getting involved with another woman felt wrong to him. So, when he returned from their day in antique and junk stores, Dan called Alix, who told him she'd hired a new bass player who was absolutely wonderful. All he got out of the call was that Alix had another non-boyfriend, and a realization he's rather talk to Casey.

Cill seemed to be better. She ate more, and one day Dan found her climbing the stairs.

When he objected, she said, "I stink. Get Priscilla. I need a bath." After that, she settled down on her big bed.

Dan worried, but there was nothing he could do. Yet.

EIGHTEEN: DAN'S SCULPTURES

Casey's lunch with Zora was both tasty and uncomfortable. Zora took her to a cute and expensive place downtown, with the obligatory lighthouse-and-sailboat décor, but Casey was surprised at how good the food was. They ate lobster bisque and had a nice Riesling wine. While Casey was still sipping her first glass, Zora was well into her second, and became very talkative.

"I love, what do you call our house, White's Point? It isn't white. But sometimes the wind is white, not the color, but the feel, you understand. Joe is so often away; the wind keeps me company."

'I bet it does,' Casey thought. 'Sounds like my crazy theory is right.'

"It's called White's Point because the White Family built your house in about 1900," she told Zora.

"Perhaps, but it is now the Burnside house. Burnside Point. Joe complains about the name. 'I own this house,' he says, 'it must have my name on it.' Men are like that. Joe came from nothing, as I did, and he wants all to know of his success."

Casey said the townspeople certainly knew of his success, and that Joe had been so kind to get her a job, and how sorry she was to have to leave it.

"Your aunt, she is very old, yes? Joe thinks she needs better care. If she sells to him some of her land, she will be able to afford the care."

Stifling a desire to throw her wine in Zora's face, Casey said with a smile that she tried not to turn into gritted teeth. "You're very generous, but my aunt won't even talk about leaving her house. You know how old ladies are." To change the subject, she went into girly raptures about Carrie's haircut. "It's the best one I ever had," she told Zora.

"Always I go there. Joe tells me to go to Portland or Boston, and I say, am I not beautiful enough from Carrie? It makes him laugh, but he knows I am right."

Zora was delighted to pose for a few more selfies, then insisted on paying for lunch. "You have no job, only caring for your aunt," she said. "When you go back to work for Joe, you will take me to lunch in Portland." She embraced Casey in a cloud of expensive perfume, waved goodbye, and gracefully entered her gold BMW.

Once Casey was back home, she went into the north woods and rolled around in the dead leaves to get rid of the perfume smell. Then she took a shower.

Dan sent the new selfie pictures to his friend Wyatt, who said they were exactly what he needed, and that he'd begin working immediately.

Now they had to wait.

That night, Casey dreamed. She sat on a shattered log in the woods, sketching; hobblebush, rabbits, mushrooms—except the bushes looked like rabbits and the mushrooms spiraled like the necklace. The spirals wound around her hands until she couldn't sketch at all. "I'm sorry," she told the broken forest, which seemed to be crying softly to itself.

She woke up unusually early, and discovered that Aunt Cill wanted to stay in bed. "I'm perfectly fine!" she snapped. "Overdid it, that's all. Too much excitement." Casey accepted the lie; her aunt accepted a cup of tea and shooed Casey out the door.

But she found herself too jumpy to eat much. The dream kept coming back into her mind. She'd spent too much time on the darn necklace. She had to do something about the broken trees. Leaving half her toast uneaten, she stowed her sketchbook, pencils and some water in her backpack, along with her aunt's homemade mosquito repellant. Sitting on a fallen tree was sure to bring out clouds of mosquitoes and blackflies.

It did, but her fingers sketched so busily, she could ignore all the little bugs flittering around her face. She sketched all kinds of plants. Plants she didn't recognize, although as they emerged from her pencil each one looked familiar. Trees she did recognize, oak, maple, beech. Only a sore arm and a stiff neck stopped her. Pulling each sheet off the sketchbook, she placed them all along the first curve of flattened trees—under branches, in bushes, in splintered tree trunks. Casey had no idea why she did it; her hands had decided it for themselves.

Then she saw a green-gray bird perched on a splintered tree trunk. At first, Casey thought it was an owl which, for some reason, was awake in the daytime. But the owl's face looked almost human, with a beak that could have been a nose, and yellow eyes much narrower than any owl would have. As she stared at it, the thing climbed down the tree trunk, headfirst like a nuthatch, until its eyes were level with Casey's.

And it winked at her. Not a slow owl-like wink, but quickly, like a sly human wink. The bird was the exact same green-gray as the dog-coyote she'd seen, or dreamed, sliding among the ferns. And the butterfly; the one she'd seen on the Rock, a month ago.

"What do you want?" she asked aloud, surprised to hear the sound of her voice after spending a long morning listening to nothing but squirrels rustling and a wood thrush trilling.

For a moment, the bird stretched out sideways from the broken tree trunk. Then, with a sudden flap of wings, it landed on Casey's shoulder. She jumped in surprise, then froze. Would it bite?

The bird nibbled her hair, gently bit her ear, and flew away.

"It likes you," said Annoying Voice. "The dog-coyote wasn't sure, but the bird likes you."

"Who's next," Casey asked aloud. "The Cheshire Cat?"

She couldn't think about peculiar green-gray animals. She had to fix the broken forest. She had no idea why sticking a bunch of sketches among the trees seemed essential. *I could have walked around hugging the stumps,* she thought. *Maybe they'd grow like my oak tree.*

Back at the house, she climbed in the shower to wash off the bug spray and wood chips. When she came down the back stairs into the kitchen, towel around her hair, T-shirt clinging damply, Dan was waiting.

"Where the hell have you been? Cill was worried about you!"

"Sketching the splinters. Leaving the sketches there."

"Leaving them there? Will that help?"

"I don't know. It felt like the right thing to do. We should put more of your sculptures there, too, take them from the north edge of the forest."

"What if the north woods blows down too?"

"Joe is after the south woods," Casey pointed out. "The wind will be there."

"You think the sculptures might help the woods grow back?"

Casey thought about how Dan's sculptures sent sparks into her hands but couldn't bring herself to talk about it. She had enough trouble believing that she could make trees grow.

"I have no idea what I'm doing," she said, lamely "But I have to do something."

"*We* have to do something," said Dan. "But first, we need lunch."

He made tuna sandwiches while Casey, thinking about biting bugs and nibbling birds, put on a long-sleeved shirt and tied a scarf around her hair. Having left most of her breakfast uneaten, she wolfed down two sandwiches, an apple, and three of Aunt Cill's giant raisin-oatmeal cookies, along with about a gallon of iced tea. Her aunt froze the cookies in little packages, and these were the last of them. Aunt Cill never used a recipe, so Casey decided to hunt one up online and make some more. But Annoying Voice told her to fix the forest so Aunt Cill could make cookies again.

Outside, along the north edge of the forest, they stared at the sculptures. Moving them would be difficult.

"You can't drag them," Casey said. "They won't like it."

She expected Dan to laugh at her, but he only nodded. "There's an old lawn cart in the garage," he said. "We can balance them on it."

Wheeling the cart and sculpture down the hill was difficult. Dan pushed while Casey steadied the carving, trying to ignore the energy that it sent through her fingers. Then they reloaded the wagon with a second sculpture, and a third, with attendant cursing.

Getting each six-foot tall slab of wood into place took both of them. Sweat dripping into their eyes, they tripped over broken branches, unable to fend off the blackflies and no-see-ums that flittered around them despite the bug repellant. Somehow, Casey knew exactly where each of the three sculptures should be planted—one among fallen trees, two more spaced widely along the edge of the downed forest. It took more sweating. With her fingers buzzing every time she touched a sculpture, she was grateful for the extra energy.

"Remind me never to help you to hang pictures," Dan said, after they had set out the last sculpture and stopped to rest and wipe their sweaty faces.

Casey grinned at him, feeling suddenly, foolishly happy. "Once this is over, I should have a show of my alleged art. You can help me hang the pictures."

"Good idea," he said, quite seriously.

She punched his arm, as if he were her brother Duncan. "Don't tempt me!"

He opened his mouth, shut it, then said, "We could use more sculptures. But it'll take time to carve them."

Casey closed her eyes and inhaled the forest. "It's broken," said Annoying Voice.

'I know,' she told it. 'I'm doing the best I can.'

Dan wheeled the cart back up the lawn, while Casey walked beside him and brooded. Would the sculptures help at all?

At the back door, she stopped. "Thanks," she said.

"You're welcome. But it's a problem for both of us to solve." He reached out and picked a leaf from her hair, stepping in close. Then he kissed her lightly. On the lips.

"See you tomorrow morning," he said. Giving her that smile he added, "It's not soon enough." And he wheeled the old cart back into the barn.

Casey floated up the back stairs like a lovesick teenager.

Then she looked in the mirror. Her face was bright pink, her hair flying in all directions. Jake had once given her sweet kisses. Dan could be another Jake. He kisses all the girls, Casey told herself. Don't fall for it.

NINETEEN: THANKSGIVING

Between December and March, Tavish always closed the Puffin Feather. He spent the winter with friends in New York City, buying new items for the store, then met other friends in Key West, where he worked on his tan.

"I can pay you to check on the store once a week," Tavish told Rinne. "Make sure the furnace is working and nothing leaks. And check it after a storm. I hope you'll do it, and come back next summer so I won't have to train some gum-chewing airhead."

Rinne thanked him, but said she'd have to find something that paid more. At a place that her father couldn't boycott.

"I have some ideas," Tavish said.

So Rinne found herself with a job checking on four big "cottages" along the coast. She considered asking Aunt Darina for tips, but decided against it. She still wanted to avoid her family. To get to the cottages, Rinne had to buy a car, but she'd been saving money for it in case she eventually found Sarah somewhere and needed to get her home. Val had asked her brothers to help find a good used car. They discovered a green Nissan, which had belonged to a little old man whose family wouldn't let him drive anymore. Rinne purchased it.

She did have a learner's permit, but she needed someone with a license to teach her how to drive on Wabanaki streets. Rinne could drive her uncle's Jeep and pilot the Sary, but on the ocean and on the Island, all she needed to worry about was the wind, the tide and the rocks, not hundreds of other jeeps or boats trying to hit her.

Val laughed at Rinne's first driving lesson. "It's not a fishing trawler. You're not the only boat in this ocean!"

Their driving lessons included a trip out to Route One, where Rinne dodged trucks and tourists, and a drive on the back streets of Wabanaki Port, where she had some harrowing adventures in parallel parking. Finally, Val declared Rinne was ready for the test.

The day Rinne got her license, Val bought her dinner at the Harbor Restaurant. For the occasion, Rinne wore her maroon skirt and a fancy new top. Tavish had picked out the shirt for her. It was white, with a deep V neck and maroon embroidery. It felt like silk, but Tavish said it was rayon. He'd seen it in another of the tourist shops, which was called Ocean One, and insisted on purchasing it for Rinne.

"You gotta learn how to dress, girl," he told her. "These are the perfect colors for that dark hair and white skin of yours. Don't worry, my friend Katie gave me a discount."

Val wore a dress. "I didn't know you even owned a dress!" Rinne said.

"It's for special occasions," said Val. "I bought it for my grandmother's seventy-fifth birthday. She hates girls in slacks." The dress showed off Val's figure and made her eyes even bluer.

"You mean I rate up there with your grandmother?"

"At least!"

They drank wine and laughed all evening. Afterward, Rinne couldn't remember ever being so happy. She wasn't thinking about chores she was shirking, or her mother's temper, or boring history homework, or finding Sarah. Just plain happy. Because she was with Val.

But the worry returned. As Thanksgiving approached, Rinne knew her family would find some way to keep her home if she went there for the holiday. Even though she missed her father and Aunt Darina, she decided to stay in Wabanaki Port instead.

"You can't be alone all day," Val told her. "Come have Thanksgiving with us. There are a lot of Costas, and we can be loud, but I'll protect you!"

Rinne protested at first, then realized Helena would be with her family in Gorham Harbor, and that staying alone on Thanksgiving would be too depressing.

"Don't rattle around by yourself after the party," Val said, when Rinne agreed to have Thanksgiving with the Costas. "The party will go late. Stay overnight at my place." So Rinne packed clean underwear and her toothbrush.

"My whole fam damily will be there," Val told her, "along with the deckhands and everyone's friends. I know you hate loud parties. If it's too much, let me know, and I'll take you back to my place."

"Well, I know your brothers and father," Rinne said. "And I don't think any of them will hit on me, like that guy in the Big Cat!"

Still, on the night of the party, Rinne tried not to flinch from the noisy crowd. Before the party, Val had given her a rundown of her family: three brothers, two aunt/uncle pairs, and six cousins. Only two of the cousins were female, and both of them were married. So was Val's brother Matt. Her brother Sandy had a girlfriend, but brother Carl didn't.

"He plays the field," Val said. "He's the crazy one; Matt is the serious one, and Sandy is somewhere in the middle—only a little bit crazy!"

The married cousins and brother Matt brought their babies and toddlers to the party. Cousin Rick had invited several people who worked at the Big Cat. Most of the men who worked on the Costa fleet were there, with their wives and children. When Rinne arrived, a bunch of leggy kids were dashing up and down the stairs, while dozens of people talked and laughed. Torrents of sound rattled in Rinne's ears.

Val's dad pushed through the crowd. "Rinne!" he yelled, enveloping her in his beefy arms. "Come meet the gang!" He towed her from cousin to aunt to uncle, introducing her as "my best deckhand!" Before Rinne's head was too full of Martys and Lilys and Hannahs and Jacks, Val's mother took over.

"Ferdie," she said, "give the poor kid a rest. Come on into the kitchen, Rinne honey, it's quieter in there."

Although it was slightly quieter, the kitchen seemed full of women, until Rinne managed to separate them into Kathy, who was one of Val's sisters-in-law, and Alice, one of her aunts. And Val, who was under the kitchen table playing with a boy of about three. He had a little plastic tugboat and was making tugboat noises. Val was being a storm.

"Bbbbbbbbbbb," said the boy.

"Whooooo!" said Val, pretending she was a nor'easter. "Hi Rinne, I'd recognize those feet anywhere. Come meet my godson Luke!"

"Boat!" said Luke.

After the boat survived the storm created by Val and Rinne, Luke's mother scooped him up to be washed, and everyone gathered around two immense tables, one in the living room, one in the adjacent dining room. Each table was loaded down with a huge turkey, along with bowls of stuffing, cranberry sauce, mashed potatoes, and a bean dish called jagacinda, which came from a great grandmother who had immigrated from Cape Verde in Portugal with her fisherman husband. Val explained to Rinne that the Costa family was very proud of their interesting ancestor, which was why her father was named Fernando.

Everyone talked at once, but Rinne felt comfortable simply listening and laughing. Luke sat next to her on a high chair. They discussed boats—he boasted about his own toy fleet—and Rinne helped him manage his turkey. Luke's mother smiled at Rinne over the boy's brown curls. "You must have small brothers!" she said.

"Cousins," said Rinne, missing Chloe.

Eventually, the children were taken home to bed, and the torrent of sound became gentle waves. People scattered around the house in small groups. Rinne found herself eating mince pie and discussing sustainable fishing with Val, one of her brothers and a couple of her cousins.

"Lookit that snow," said one of the cousins.

"Better get home before we hafta camp on the floor," said someone else.

"We've got lots of blankets," Val's mother said. Looking at her watch, Rinne was amazed to find it was almost midnight.

"Hope it wasn't too much party for you," Val said, as they headed for her old blue truck. The flurries had stopped, but the east wind made Rinne tuck her chin into her parka.

"I liked it," she said. "I had a great time." But she was almost asleep before Val had put the sheets onto the couch.

In the morning, the sun came out, pretending that it was still October instead of almost December.

"You don't have work until tomorrow," Val said, as Rinne came out of the bathroom, fully dressed. "You could stay another night."

"I need to—I don't know, I'd like to be quiet for a while," said Rinne.

She needed more than quiet. She needed to figure out how she felt about Val.

On her laptop, Rinne had found a picture of two women in wedding dresses; and a picture of a woman in a wedding dress and a woman in a suit. The first pair were standing under a flowered arch; the second pair on a pebbly beach. She found pictures of old women holding hands. She understood why she'd hadn't dated very much in high school. It just didn't interest her.

Val was her best friend. She did not want to mess it up. Still, Val had never mentioned a boyfriend. And they never talked about boyfriends. Wasn't that what you did with a best girlfriend? Helena talked about men all the time—who she was seeing, who she'd rather go out with than the man she was seeing, trying to decide among two or three guys. So did Tavish, who made no secret of being gay. Was Val gay, Rinne wondered. Am I?

How was she going to meet Val like nothing had happened? Not that anything had happened, except inside Rinne's head. Or heart. Or other places.

TWENTY: GREEN PAINT

Dan brooded about Casey. He'd never been the kind of guy who had two women at once. And he and Alix had been together almost five years—although Alix would tour New England with her band in the winter, and he'd tour craft fairs in the summer, so it's not like they spent much time as a couple. Still, only because Casey had flying red curls and dirt on her nose was no reason to kiss her. He told himself that Casey was fierce and determined, that she'd run over him like his mother and sister always tried to do, that he and Alix would make their relationship work.

The next morning, Cill was still in bed. Casey, up unusually early for her, paced the kitchen, acting like Dan was nothing but the hired help. '

'I shouldn't have kissed her,' he thought.

"I brought Aunt Cill tea and toast," Casey said. "I told her we were working on the forest. She said it wasn't enough." Plunking down at the table, she put her face in her hands.

Not sure what to do, Dan poured himself some coffee and sat down across from her.

"Nothing else has fallen," he said. "I was up early and checked the south forest; then I went up on the Rock to search for other problems. No more wind."

"No more wind for *now*. I wish your friend would hurry up with the necklace. Anyway, we still have to fix the broken places in the forest. The sculptures are--" and she stopped.

'Weird?' thought Dan. 'Useless?'

"They're wonderful, but they aren't enough. Neither are my drawings."

Casey paced the kitchen, then paced into the dining room, where she stared out the window at the west woods, then into the living room, where she stared out the south window at the south woods. She stared so long, Dan came to look over her shoulder, worrying he might see that more trees had fallen. All he saw was green lawn and green leaves. The surviving tree trunks were wound with wild grape and woodbine, creating dozens of different shades of green, glowing in the summer sunlight.

"Green," Casey said, turning so quickly that Dan had to step back—although he discovered he didn't want to move away from her. So much for his non-kissing resolutions. "Do you have any green paint?" Her eyes were wide, unseeing. "Maybe there's some in the barn; the house shutters are green, maybe there's some left." She dashed for the back door. Dan ran after her.

"I still have my oil paints," he called as she ran toward the barn. By the time he caught up with her, Casey was digging through the boxes of stuff he and Ed Kerr had hauled out of the attic when they built the studio.

"I'll look for my oil paints!" he told her. But she kept digging.

Realizing there was no talking to her, Dan climbed the stairs, jogged down the hall to his studio, and hunted up his paints, finding them in an old tackle box. After testing one to make sure they were still good, he wiped the paint off his fingers; then carried them back down the hall, through his living area, and down the stairs.

Half-hidden in a pile of junk, Casey blinked at him as he held out the box.

"Oil paint," Dan said. "Plenty of green. This stuff lasts forever if you treat it right."

She pushed boxes aside and grabbed the tackle box out of his hands. "Something to paint," she said. "Wood."

"I got a lot of that," he said, leading the way back up the stairs and into his studio.

It was littered with bits of wood Dan had carved from his sculptures. He collected them, while Casey dug through the paints, pulling out all the green. Viridian, olive, emerald, chromium oxide, all the greens Dan remembered from art school. When he handed her the wood, she picked up a tube of paint, then stopped.

"Brushes," she said.

He found some brushes and an old palette. 'Good thing I never throw away art materials,' he thought. 'If it can make art, I keep it. Otherwise, I travel light.'

She grabbed one of the bits of wood. She painted vines—woodbine, wild grape, bittersweet, wild clematis, honeysuckle. She picked up another chunk of wood and painted little trees—maple, pine, oak, ash, beech. She painted like she was possessed by a green demon.

Dan tried to work on his current sculpture, but had to keep stopping to find her more pieces of wood. After two hours, he added a water bottle, which she picked up with paint-covered hands, drank from, went back to painting. After four hours, Dan went to his kitchen to make peanut butter sandwiches—which she inhaled while he tried not to worry about the amount of green paint she was ingesting. Eventually he ran out of wood in the studio. Leaving her with what he hoped were enough chunks to keep her going, he headed for the woodpile to chop up some more. There, he discovered only some pieces were right, the same way he knew the right wood for his sculptures. He brought up three armfuls of small chunks of wood.

After six hours, Casey dropped her brush in the middle of painting a tendril of deep green ivy, and fainted.

Dan picked her up and got her to a chair.

His trestle table was covered with painted wood—irregular chunks, bits of fireplace logs, offcuts, a hundred of them, more, all with trees and vines painted on them in cobalt green, light green, greens Casey had combined in ways he'd never imagined.

"Did I do that?" Her voice sounded hoarse and unused.

Dan knelt beside her. "Are you okay? You fainted."

"I did? I never fainted in my whole life." She stared at the heap of painted wood.

"Where did all the wood come from?"

"I brought them. Good thing I never throw anything out. Although I'll have to work hard to refill the woodpile by fall."

Her clothes had green blotches everywhere. She picked at them.

"You're green all over," he told her. "It's particularly nice in your red hair."

"I'm not usually—I mean I never did anything like that. Paint like a crazy person, I mean."

"There's always a first time. Sometimes the sculptures take me that way. Although I don't forget how to talk. Or eat."

"This better work," she said, and fell asleep in the chair.

*

Waking up, Casey wasn't sure where she was. Her old apartment bedroom? No, the window was too big. Aunt Cill's house? No, the room was too small. Then she remembered. Painting and painting, green and green and green. She must be in Dan's bedroom.

Sitting up, muscles aching, Casey was glad to see that, although she wasn't wearing shoes, she was otherwise fully dressed, in green-splotched T-shirt and jeans. Having Dan undress her would have been too embarrassing. She was lying in an old-fashioned spool bed, which used to be in her brother Duncan's room at Aunt Cill's. She remembered how she liked to run her fingers along its curving spindles. Vaguely recalling a bathroom somewhere, she staggered out to search for it.

After using the facilities, Casey dared to look in the mirror. Hair all on end, with green paint scattered through it. A smear of green on her cheek complimented the bags under her eyes. Staring at herself, she wondered what on earth had possessed her.

Annoying Voice answered her right away. "The forest, and Aunt Cill."

"But Aunt Cill was in bed," Casey told it.

Annoying Voice didn't listen. Instead, it announced that she must get her creations into the south woods *now*.

Flinging open the bathroom door, she almost crashed into Dan.

"Want a shower?" he asked, handing her a towel, T-shirt, and sweat pants.

"We have to get those things into the woods!" she said, incoherently.

"Aunt Cill is doing better," he soothed. "She ate some soup last night, and this morning she ate two pieces of toast with jelly along with her tea. Then she insisted I bring her another pillow so she could sit up. She asked for you, so I had to explain what you'd created. She said you've always been too enthusiastic."

'Maybe when I was ten,' Casey thought, 'but I've been asleep since then. Well, since I went to college and didn't study art. I've been ignoring what I actually wanted.'

"Thanks for taking care of me," she said, uncomfortably. "I probably got paint on your sheets."

"Wouldn't be the first time." He gave her a bottle of turpentine and some rags. "Get cleaned up while I make breakfast. Then we'll head for the south woods."

She managed to get the paint off her arms, and most of the paint out of her hair, although a few green strands eluded her. A hot shower helped her sore muscles, as well as getting rid of the worst of the turpentine smell. Although she and Dan were about the same height, his pants were too long and the T-shirt kind of baggy. However, the smell of coffee and bacon brought Casey out of the bathroom without worrying too much about how she looked. What with the green hair, it was pretty hopeless anyway. Besides, she felt hollow with hunger. Her nose was happy to replace turpentine stink with the aroma of fresh coffee.

The hall opened directly into a room with the comfortable blue sofa she remembered from her previous visit. Now she noticed a bookcase populated with tattered paperbacks and a few big art books, and a small kitchen divided from the rest of the room by a long counter. Everything was clean and uncluttered. She must have gone through this room on her way to paint everything green, and she'd been there on the day she and Dan shared coffee, but only now could she take it all in.

He'd made pancakes too, good ones. "You're a great cook," Casey told him between mouthfuls.

"Pancakes and tuna fish sandwiches," he said. "Pretty soon I'll be on the Iron Chef."

"I've wondered," she said. "I mean, you don't have to tell me. But how did you meet Aunt Cill?"

"At a craft fair," he said, refilling her plate. "I'd been doing the circuit for a couple of summers, selling cutting boards and turned wooden stuff like bowls. I always dragged one of those wood sculptures along to fairs because it intrigued people enough to come see what else I'd made. Aunt Cill marched right up to me and said, 'How much for that sculpture?' I'd never imagined anyone would want it, so I had no idea what to charge. Then she asked me to make more of them. When I told her how much time it would take, she offered me this studio." He grinned. "Only it wasn't built yet. So Ed Kerr and I worked on it together."

That's why the walls in the living area were a pale orangey-gold, and the bedroom ceiling a deep blue. Ed Kerr would have painted everything white. Casey often met Ed at Manny's; he was one of the many people who wanted to know how Aunt Cill was doing. He was a stolid, salt-of-the-earth, totally unimaginative guy. Nothing like Dan.

After Casey ate enough for two people, they gathered up her creations in a couple of big plastic tubs Dan used for hauling wood for his sculptures, maneuvered them down the stairs and balanced them in the old lawn cart. It was only eight a.m., but the steamy heat made Casey want to head right back into the shower.

"They're predicting thunderstorms," Dan said, as they trundled down the hill. He pushed the cart; Casey steadied the tubs. She hardly heard him; she was already thinking about where each bit of wood should be placed.

A few tendrils of green wound around each one of Dan's sculptures, but the dying leaves on the splintered tree trunks made everything look dead. It took them hours to place the green blocks of wood. Somehow Casey knew where each one should go: this one next to a sculpture, this one under a fallen pine tree, others scattered along the curving path of destruction. She was too absorbed to notice much except the correct spots for her painted wood, until thunder rolled, much closer than she expected. Working so hard, neither one had watched the weather. Black clouds roiled above them, and a wind blew through the trees.

Dan froze. "Is that a real storm or one of those weird winds?"

Casey paused with her hands on piece of wood with green vines on it. "Look at the clouds," she said. "The other winds came from a clear blue sky. It's a real storm. Let me get this one placed and we can go in."

She'd finally found the right spot for the wood when lightning flashed, striking a tall spruce tree that had survived the wind with a terrifying blaze of light and ear-splitting crack. Diving for cover, she smashed into Dan as he dove for the same patch of brush. They rolled together just as the rain poured down, soaking both of them immediately. Lightning flashed again, and Dan moved protectively over Casey.

He smelled like fresh wood chips, maple syrup, and laundry soap. He felt like hard muscle and safety. She discovered she had wrapped her arms and legs around him. As her relationship with Jake had collapsed, Casey had stopped herself from feeling this kind of heat. Now it overwhelmed her.

Blinking rain out of her eyes, she looked up at him.

"You okay?" he asked.

Unable to speak, she nodded.

They kissed. His mouth was soft, his tongue warm, melting Casey into the ground. His hands moved under her shirt, then along her leg.

The rain slowed to a steady rhythm. Dan's kisses moved to her neck. She moaned.

"Hey?" he said.

"Yes," she said.

It was wonderful and complicated, trying to get rid of soggy shirts and rain-slick jeans, all the while kissing, giggling, kissing again. Twigs poked into their naked backs. Neither of them cared.

When Casey came to, the rain had stopped, and sun slanted through the tangle of green above her. Tangle of green? Turning her head, she could see Dan, lying on his back, with green shoots, vines, and tendrils winding all around him.

Sitting up, Casey felt the pull of vines on her arms, felt them snap as she moved.

New growth was everywhere. The bushes they sheltered under had grown a foot. A small sapling sprouted between Casey's feet. Woodbine, baby cat-briar too young to have thorns, wild grape, more saplings, created a bower of green all around them. Casey could feel the saplings digging into the earth, curling out, reaching for the light, searching for the air.

"What the hell?" Dan sat up beside her, picking partridge berry vines off his arms.

"It worked," she said.

He felt around in the undergrowth. "Do you think this stuff ate our clothes?"

By judicious digging they found most of them, although an enthusiastic honeysuckle vine had carried Casey's T-shirt part way up a nearby sapling. Dan's pants hung from another sapling, and he removed a caterpillar from one shoe while she removed a garden spider from a leg of her sweatpants.

"There's lots of new growth, but it's strongest around us," Dan said, gazing about. "How did those saplings grow so fast?" He had his jeans back on, but nothing else. To stop herself from touching his muscled back, Casey gazed with him. Beyond the shadbush patch where they had fallen, the bright green faded away into the brown of broken trees.

"Well," she said drily. "Now we know how to get Aunt Cill's forest to grow."

Dan began laughing and couldn't stop. Casey joined him. They lay in the green and howled.

Then they held hands all the way back through the south woods, up the wet grass on the hillside, around the house to the back door. Dan picked a partridge berry out of her hair, and kissed her.

This time she didn't float like a teenager. Instead, she simply basked in the glow, not worrying about anything except for the wonderful now.

*

When Casey got out of the shower, Aunt Cill was in the kitchen making a late lunch; slicing bread and tomatoes as bacon sizzled in her huge iron frying pan.

"You must be feeling better," said Casey.

"Looks like it. You kids must have done something to help my trees."

"Yup," said Casey. She could be as cryptic as her aunt.

Aunt Cill forked the bacon onto a plate of paper towels, poured herself some iced tea, and sat down at the kitchen table.

"What did you do?" she asked.

Casey poured her own tea and tried to think of a way not to answer the question. Then she wondered why she didn't want to answer. Being as close-mouthed-stubborn as her aunt didn't seem like a good reason. But it was hard to explain.

Fortunately, the back door slammed, and Dan charged into the kitchen, damp from his shower, wearing fresh clothes.

"Bacon!" he said. "You're feeling better, Cill! Casey's plan worked!"

"And what was that plan?"

Dan plunked down at the table and told Aunt Cill, in awful detail, all about Casey's paintings, how they placed the painted wood all around the forest, how she arranged his sculptures, how the thunderstorm came, and the trees grew. Casey, who busied herself serving sandwiches, held her breath at that part, but Dan only shot her a grin, left out their lovemaking, and kept talking.

When he finished the tale, and started on his lunch there was a long pause. Then Aunt Cill said, "Painted wood?" Her tone made it sound like the stupidest thing she'd ever heard.

"I know," Dan said, still cheerful and excited. "But it worked."

"That's not how you do it," the old lady said. She stood up to put her dishes in the sink.

"How *do* you do it?" Casey asked.

"You need to learn that," said her aunt, and stamped up the back stairs.

For a moment, Casey sat frozen. Then she grabbed her glass of iced tea and threw it across the room. It exploded against the wall.

"SHIT!" she yelled.

"Hey," said Dan.

But Casey ran out the back door, slamming the screen as hard as she could, and kept running straight across the driveway into the birch woods. She kept running until she felt sick and had to stop. Then she cried.

Sitting under a birch tree, wiping her nose with some leaves because she didn't have any tissues, Casey realized that poor Dan was caught between two furious women. She gave a slightly hysterical laugh, and slowly walked back to the house. Dan met her outside the door.

"You okay?"

"She may be impossible, but I don't want her to die," Casey said, as if they'd been talking it over calmly. "We still have to get the copy of the necklace, so we can stop Zora from blowing things down."

"Right," said Dan.

To his astonishment, Casey laughed. "Poor Riordan!" she said. "Caught between two crazy ladies! I'm sorry for running off. Is Aunt Cill okay? Can you go check on her?"

"Are *you* okay?" he asked gently.

"I'm fine," Casey said, and started doing the dishes.

TWENTY-ONE: THE DINNER PARTY

When sending the photographs of the necklace, Dan hinted again to Wyatt the importance of the necklace. Of course, Wyatt thought it was for Alix, so he dropped a couple of other projects to finish the necklace for his old buddy. Meanwhile, Casey prowled jewelry stores, looking for the perfect chain.

Two days after she found the chain, in a tiny store down toward Portland, the package arrived from Wyatt. Dan and Casey carefully compared it to the sketches and the pictures.

"It looks good to me," Dan said. "But you've seen it live and in person."

Casey frowned over the lovely little charm for a long time. "I think it will work," she said finally.

Now it was time to invite the Burnsides for dinner, so the necklace could be replaced. Casey still wondered if it would work or if her idea was even crazier than her wood-painting escapade. But now they were committed.

Cill and Casey had never discussed their differences. Instead, they both acted like nothing had happened.

"I just can't," Casey told Dan when he asked her if she'd talked with her aunt. "If I can figure out how I make things grow—" Dan grinned at her; she rolled her eyes at him. "That won't work all the time! Anyway, once I understand what I'm doing, I'll talk with her about it. Meanwhile, we have to keep the forest safe from those weird winds."

Dan managed to convince Aunt Cill that, because it was her house, she should be the one to invite the Burnsides to dinner, although both he and Casey hung around while she made the call at the old landline phone in the living room, fearful she'd let Joe know exactly what she thought of him.

"Shoo," Aunt Cill told them. "Stop hovering." Casey disappeared upstairs; Dan sat on the back step and worried. After a long five minutes, they each snuck back into the living room.

"I behaved very nicely," Aunt Cill told them. "I did not call that man any names. In fact, I lied myself blue. They're coming Friday night."

Three days to prepare. Casey cleaned, polished silver, ironed table linens, dug out the Meissen china that must have belonged to Aunt Cill's grandmother. Once they had the necklace, once she'd figured out how to make the south woods grow back completely, she had a lot of questions for her aunt.

Cill was much better, but not yet back to her old self. She still spent a lot of time in the green armchair, and didn't seem up to cooking dinner for the guests. But she did insist on having blueberry pie. Dan volunteered to make the crust. His mother had taught him to make pie, because he loved it, and she got tired of having him eat it all so quickly. Cill watched from a chair at the kitchen table; then jumped up and snatched the rolling pin away from Dan.

"Bang it around like that, it'll be tough as shoe leather," she complained.

Dan knew he hadn't been banging the dough around, but gave in and let Cill, roll out the pastry. Casey went to set the table with the good silver and white embroidered tablecloth while Dan made sure Cill didn't fall over with her vigorous pie-making. The old lady still had to sit down often—something she'd never done before.

Once the pie was safely in the oven, Aunt Cill sat at the kitchen table to direct their efforts while Dan and Casey prepared the dinner: fresh salmon, fresh peas cooked with morels Dan had found in the north forest, a salad with arugula—Cill announced she'd just as soon eat lawnmower clippings—and the pie.

"Get it out of that oven before it burns up!" she snapped, seconds before Dan's watch timer went off.

Now it was wine-doctoring time. Somewhere, Cill had found a syringe. Dan and Casey looked at it, looked at each other, and tacitly decided not to ask why she had it. They watched while she drew a couple of teaspoons of liquid out of one of her brown bottles, then stuck the syringe through the cork and into the wine.

Then it was time for Dan to fade into the background, to hide upstairs, ready to come down the back stairs once the wine had put everyone to sleep, and change the real necklace for the fake one.

Joe and Zora arrived fashionably late. While they waited, Casey worked hard to calm Cill down.

"In my day, we arrived on time," she fumed.

The Burnsides loved the house, although Joe ostentatiously ignored the new growth in the south forest. "It's just like I remember it," he said, gazing around the living room. "I was here once with my father when I was a boy. Do you remember, Cill?"

Aunt Cill nodded. "I do," she said. "You were a very polite little boy."

They sat on the front porch for drinks; not fancy aperitifs like the Burnsides had given Casey, but cocktails. Aunt Cill, Casey discovered, liked Manhattans—whiskey, vermouth, bitters that turned them purple.

"Been years since I've had one of these," Joe said appreciatively.

Zora wrinkled her lovely nose and sipped daintily. As usual, her blond hair was perfect. Although her white brocade dress belonged at a much fancier party, it was as perfect as her hair.

"So you're finally thinking of selling those woods," Joe said, gazing at them like he was already seeing a housing development popping up.

"Welp, I'm not getting any younger," Aunt Cill told him, playing the frail old lady.

Casey tried not to giggle, remembering how vigorously her aunt had rolled out the pastry for two pies.

"What'll you give me for that land?" Aunt Cill asked Joe.

When he mentioned a stupidly low number, Casey forgot about giggling and had to purse her lips like Aunt Cill so she wouldn't tell the man he was a cheap bastard. Aunt Cill pretended to consider the offer, telling a long pointless story about her father's ability in business, playing the dotty old lady until Casey again had to swallow her laughter.

Then they went inside to dinner. "Priscilla bought the wine," Aunt Cill said. "Joey, will you open it for us?"

They toasted Aunt Cill's returning health. They ate salmon.

"Morels!" exclaimed Zora. "Where did you find them?"

"They grow in the south forest," Aunt Cill told her. A complete lie; they came from the northern part. But Joe only grinned, and poured more wine for everyone.

"This is marvelous," he told them. "Glad to see Casey understands good wine."

Actually, she didn't; she simply took the advice of the nice woman at the wine store. She didn't mention that.

For some time, Joe told them all about wine. Then things became a little hazy for Casey. Zora's eyes closed. Aunt Cill was leaning back in her chair. That felt like a good idea, so Casey leaned back too.

"Zora? Zora!" Slapping noises. Opening her eyes a crack, Casey saw Joe kneeling beside his wife.

Aunt Cill snored gently.

"I'm sorry, I spaced out for a minute," Casey said, muzzily. "Hey, is Zora okay?"

"We all fell asleep! I woke up and all of you were out cold! I can't wake Zora!"

Wetting a napkin from the crystal pitcher of water, Casey patted Zora's face. Her necklace hung there as usual. Had Dan made the switch?

"I'm perfectly fine, just closed my eyes for a moment," Aunt Cill announced. "What on earth are you doing, Priscilla?"

"She won't wake up!" said Joe, panic in his voice. "We all fell asleep! It must have been the damned wine!"

"Does she usually drink a lot of wine?" Cill asked kindly. Casey felt a nervous laugh bubbling up. She reached her foot under the table to poke her aunt.

Joe waved his Rolex at them. "We lost almost an hour," he yelled. "I'm having this wine tested! Call 911!"

Fortunately, Zora began to toss and mutter, finally opening her eyes. While her husband soothed and explained, Casey turned to Aunt Cill, horrified. What would they find if the wine was tested? Aunt Cill shook her head, smiling serenely.

"I fell asleep," Zora said faintly. "I am so sorry, Miss Woodward." Blond curls fell over her eyes.

"We all fell asleep," Joe said. "I'm taking you to the emergency room. And I'm taking the wine! I'll have it tested!"

"Now, now, now," said Aunt Cill. "We are all perfectly fine. Casey, go put the coffee on."

But Zora was asleep again.

"I'm not drinking any of your coffee!" snapped Joe. "Get me a bag for the wine right now!"

Casey went to the kitchen, turned on the old percolator, and found a bag for the wine. Aunt Cill didn't like plastic bags--instead, she used her antique sewing machine to stitch scraps into bags. The one Casey found had red flowers on it.

Joe picked up his sleeping wife. "Bring it" he ordered, as Casey proffered the flowered bag with the wine bottle inside. And he strode through the kitchen, out the back door, and toward his car. Trotting after him, Casey opened doors, handed Joe the flowered bag, watched the Porsche roar down the lane, then headed for the barn.

Dan met her part way, holding up the golden spirals of the real necklace.

"Any pie left?" he asked.

"We never got to the dessert," Casey told him.

While they all sat around the dining room table drinking coffee and eating pie, Aunt Cill assured them it would be impossible for anyone to find the stuff she put in the wine. "It'll only seem like more wine," she told them.

Casey and Dan had to help her to bed, but on the way, she said "Good work, children."

TWENTY-TWO: A STORM

Rinne still had no luck in finding her sister. Val's cousin Rick sent Sarah's picture around to friends all along the Maine coast, friends who owned places like his Big Cat Bar. But no one had seen Sarah.

"Don't worry," Val said. "Rick asked his buddies to send the pictures to *their* buddies. By now, they should have made their way to Boston and the South Shore; maybe even as far as Cape Cod."

But Rinne had gone back to hunting Sarah on every social media site. She spent hours scrutinizing images of women named Sarah. Her picture of her sister, with "Have you seen this woman?" written on it, drew a lot of disgusting trolls. Gritting her teeth, Rinne dug through them all, every day. She located some inexpensive picture-matching software, but couldn't use it on the library computers, and her cheap laptop didn't have enough memory to run it.

"Put it on the office computer and work there," Val said. "I could use the company." The Costa boats were now preparing for the scallop season, and Val was negotiating with buyers.

"I don't want to be in the way," Rinne began.

But Val said, "Of course you will. You'll be a total pain. That's why I asked you!"

Rinne had to laugh, but she wasn't sure it was a good idea spend the extra time with Valerie, even though she <u>wanted </u>to spend all her time with Valerie. The latter wish won out, and Rinne agreed to use Val's office computer. She installed the software and hunted for images matching Sarah's graduation picture. Working so close to Val was both wonderful and frustrating.

"This search will take you forever," Val said.

"It's better than nothing," Rinne told her. "And I can't sit and wait."

To make things more difficult, her father stopped by the Puffin Feather every few weeks, telling Rinne how the fishing was going badly without her help, which Rinne believed, and how much her mother missed her, which Rinne did not believe.

Then one day in mid-December, as Brian docked his fishing boat at Wabanaki Port, he discovered Rinne and Val helping to clean one of the Costa trawlers, the *Marisela*.

Brian strode toward them and stood glowering.

"Hi Dad," Rinne called down to him. "I didn't know you'd be here today."

"You're working for *them* now?" he asked, like Rinne had gone over to the dark side.

"Only helping out," Rinne said, climbing off the *Marisela* and waving toward Val. "This is my friend Val Costa. Val, this is my dad."

Brian snorted. "I hope you don't go out with those Costas when they fish," he said. "It's bad enough how you won't take on your responsibility to your own family."

Val leaned over the side of boat. "She just helps me clean the trawlers, Mr. Gilley."

"If you're not working for that limp-wristed boss of yours, I don't see why you can't come home."

"Excuse me?" Rinne said. "Tavish gave me two jobs and taught me everything about running a store."

"You call it work?" Brian said. "I asked you a question. Why won't you come home?"

Still steaming from her dad's insulting Tavish and Val, Rinne snapped. "Because I don't trust you to ever bring me back here! You'll find a way to make me marry Gavin, so I have to stay on the Island forever!"

For a telling moment, Brian hesitated. Then he said, "I'm not a jailer! Come home for Christmas. Your mother wants to see you."

The hesitation was enough for Rinne. "No," she said. "Can you finish up, Val? I'm taking a walk."

Leaving both of them, she left the dock and strode down Harbor Street. She wanted to go home. She didn't want to go home. Not being able to trust her own father felt awful.

Pulling up the hood of her grubby parka, she kept going until she was on the rocky shore that lined the harbor on the north. There, the frozen wind stopped her. She found a sheltered spot and huddled down to watch the surf.

Rinne had left her family in order to help them; in order to find Sarah. But now they had as much as left *her*. Clearly, they would try and force her to stay on the Island whether she wanted to or not. Of course, Val would come get her if she needed her, or she could manage to escape on the ferry. But how horrible to have to sneak away from her own family. She did want to visit. She missed the Island. But she did not want to live there. Or marry Gavin.

Families, as Val said, could be the pits.

Brooding, Rinne made the waves larger and larger until they pounded the shore like a nor'easter. When one of the waves rose so high they soaked her feet, she gave up and cried. The tears made her face even colder, so she finally headed back.

But she didn't want to see anyone. Not even Val. Especially not Val. Too tired and cold for the walk to her apartment—she only used her Nissan for trips to check on the cottages—she stopped at Warren's Diner, where the fishermen got their coffee and sandwiches. First checking to see if any of the Costa family or fishing crew were inside—they weren't—Rinne drank boiling coffee from a thick white mug until she was warm enough to head back to the apartment. Fortunately, Helena was still at work. Rinne took off her soggy parka, wet boots and damp socks, changed into sweats, and curled up in bed. When her cell phone rang, she ignored it.

"Hey, it's Val. Are you okay? Call me."

Rinne ignored the next two messages and a text; then got tired of listening to it ring and picked up.

"Rinne! Are you all right? You scared the shit out of me!"

"I'm fine, Val. I needed to walk."

"Where are you? It's freezing out there! I can come and get you."

"Back at the apartment. I'm okay, Val, really." Having someone worry about her made Rinne want to cry again. She took deep breaths.

The front door slammed. "You here, Rinne?" Helena yelled. "Wanna go out to eat? I'm starving!"

"Crap," Rinne muttered. "Helena's back, Val. I gotta deal with her. See you soon." Clicking off the phone, she stepped into the living room.

As usual, Helena had tossed her coat on the sofa and was checking her hair in front of the mirror she'd hung by the front door.

"Hey, Helena," Rinne said. "I'm not feeling great; you go ahead."

Helena had to find out if Rinne had a bug that might be catching; had to talk endlessly about her day while changing clothes for a night out; had to ask three more times if Rinne would come with her. Finally, she was gone. Rinne fell onto the sofa and turned on the television. Nothing interested her. There was a huge knot in her chest, but she couldn't cry anymore. Eventually, she staggered into her bedroom and fell asleep.

In the morning, Rinne woke, starving, to a snowy day. While making up for missing supper by eating a giant omelet and four pieces of toast, she reviewed the weather app on her phone. It made her realize it was time to get out and check the four cottages and the shop before the snow was too deep. She was putting on her heavy boots—the light ones were still damp from their soaking yesterday—when her phone buzzed.

"Hey, it's Val. You going out to check your houses before the snow gets bad? I'll come with you. I'll be there in five." Before Rinne could object, Val clicked off.

Rinne couldn't decide if she wanted to see Val more than anything, or if she wanted to be alone all day. She collected her keys, put on the cleaner of her two parkas and a wool hat, found her heavy gloves, and went downstairs. In three minutes, Val's truck appeared. Rinne got in.

"Don't you have work to do?" Rinne asked. "I mean, thanks, but I don't want to..."

"Worrying about you driving in this crap, I won't get anything done."

"I can drive in snow." After the first snowfall, Val had showed Rinne how to brake through a skid, and how to get unstuck.

"I know you can, but your little old Nissan is not any kind of snow car. They're predicting eight inches by afternoon."

"Did the trawlers go out?"

"You know my dad; he'd go out in a hurricane if my mum didn't tie him down. Which she did. But while they were arguing, Carl went out. Got Alan to go along, you've met him, right? They're both idiots. Still, the wind shouldn't be bad until later on."

They checked the Puffin Feather first. The cellar, which only housed the furnace and a slop sink, which Tavish never used, was a little damp. Worried about what might happen when the snow eventually melted, Rinne found a stash of old towels, which she and Val placed strategically around the furnace. Then they drove to the south side of the harbor, where two of the four giant cottages lay. Val wandered through them in amazement, helping Rinne to check on windows, doors, and the furnace.

"This place would house a third-world country!" Val exclaimed. "And these people only live here in the summer!"

Rinne said she was used to it, from Seaview Cottage on the Island. "But I finally realized how much I'd hate to live like this, even if I were a zillionaire."

"What would you do if you were a zillionaire?"

"I'd use the money to buy a little boat, and a house far enough onshore so I wouldn't have to worry about storms."

"What would you do with the other billion dollars?"

"Hire detectives to find Sarah. Give some away, too."

"The Rinne Gilley Foundation for Old Fishermen!"

"And the Val Costa Foundation for Overworked Administrators!"

By the time they came up with the "Tavish Fortunato Fund for Cute Shoppe-keepers," they were both laughing so hard, they had to sit down on a linen-sheeted couch. But then Rinne stopped laughing.

"My father hates him," she said. "And I hate my father for being like that."

Val looked at her. "Your dad can't help it," she said. "He has no idea how mean it sounds. But he thinks Tavish took you away from him."

"He didn't."

"As Mark Twain said, 'Denial ain't just a river in Egypt'."

Rinne had never heard the phrase, and laughed again.

The other two cottages were on the north shore of the harbor, and the truck plowed its way through the snow. As she navigated the slippery street, Val asked Rinne to check the weather app.

"It's getting squally," Rinne reported.

When they reached the last cottage, perched high on a rocky ledge at the end of the point, the wind was worse than squally. Rinne was tying down a banging shutter when Val's phone buzzed.

"Out on Avery Point," she said. "Yeah, the wind has picked up like they said it would." Then she said "What?" in a tone that made Rinne turn around. Val's skin looked green in the stormy light. Whoever it was talked for a bit. "I'll get home as fast as I can," Val said, and clicked off.

"Carl is still out," she told Rinne, "His boat is wallowing. The wind is a lot worse than those weather idiots say it is. Coming from the northeast, but not a nor'easter, they say. Idiots. Dad has called the Coast Guard, but they're nowhere near Carl. We've gotta get back. Mom is worrying." And Val headed out the door onto the wrap-around porch.

Rinne ran after her. "Where is he?"

"Two miles off this point. Trying to make it in. Having engine trouble, he says." Val ran for her truck. Rinne stared out to sea. Two miles was farther than she'd ever been able to calm the ocean. But this was Val, and Val's brother.

"Come on!" Val yelled. "What are you doing?"

The porch was perfect; sheltered from the wind and flying snow, with a view directly toward Carl's position.

"Go ahead," Rinne said. "I'm gonna try something."

"What the hell can you try?" Val ran back up the stairs and took Rinne's arm. "You can't stay here all night."

Rinne took in a deep breath; let it out. "I might be able to calm the sea enough so Carl can get in."

Val stared at her.

"It's what my family does. It's why I want Sarah back. She's the only one, now that my Great Gran died and Gran is getting tired, Sarah is the only one who can handle wind. My mother can handle water, like me."

"This is nuts," Val said.

"Give me a few minutes. If I'm still nuts, we'll go back."

Rinne stepped away from Val, put her gloved hands on the porch railing, and felt the water. When she was a kid, she thought everyone could feel the water, the way it moved somewhere inside them. Gran briefly taught her how to focus the feeling—and explained to Rinne how only descendants of the original Amos Halloran, like them, were wind-workers or water-workers. "And not all of us," Gran had said. "Some are stronger than others. And not many of us have the wind Skill."

The surf stopped pounding on the rocks below and became a gentle wash. It wasn't easy, calming the water when the wind was so strong. Gradually, Rinne extended her reach. On her father's boat, she'd once calmed the surf for almost a mile, allowing Brian to land in a growing storm. Her face felt cold, as the frigid air dried her sweat. The water calmed for a mile. A mile and a half. Val said something but Rinne couldn't focus on anything but the water. Feeling it trying to get away from her, trying to answer the wind. Two miles. Vaguely, she felt her hands cramp on the porch railing. She leaned against it. The wind fought her, trying to whip the waves higher. Her knees gave way, but someone was holding her up. The sound of a motor rumbled into her consciousness. She connected to the sound, soothed the waves in front and behind the rumble. But she was losing them. She wasn't strong enough. The surf pounded on the rocks below. The rumble grew louder. She couldn't breathe.

"Rinne. Rinne, he's in the lee of the point. He made it. He made it. Rinne?"

TWENTY-THREE: ALIX

The day after the dinner party, Alix showed up. With a suitcase.

When Dan heard the car drive up, right after lunch, he went out to see who it was. Not many people would drive the two miles up Woodward Lane without a good reason.

Alix leaped gracefully out of her red hatchback and flung herself into his arms.

"I've been e-mailing you forever! Where have you been? The band broke up in Providence! It's been awful!"

Dan was sure he felt Casey watching; she would have gone to the back door out of the same curiosity to see the visitor. Damn.

"It's hard to get cell connection out here," he told Alix.

"I miss you so much!" she continued, clutching him close. "I know I've been so busy with gigs and everything I haven't had time to visit. What with everything falling apart, I really needed to see you!"

Dan had to get her out of there. "Come on," he told her, and led the way to the barn and up the stairs to his apartment.

Alix kept talking, telling him all about how the bass player hated the drummer, and how both of them quit. He couldn't get a word in. Not that he had any words.

What was he going to say? "I've slept with Casey, and I think she's the best thing that's ever happened to me?" Not unless he wanted a full Alix breakdown right in front of the Woodward kitchen window, with Cill and Casey watching.

As she talked, however, Dan understood what happened. She'd broken up with the drummer who was her "roommate," and started flirting with the bass player. When the latter relationship didn't work out, both players left the band. With no bass line, only guitar and keyboards, the band sounded terrible, even to themselves. They'd decided to take a break while hunting for a new drummer and bass player. A band breakup had happened once before, throwing Alix into Dan's arms until she found a new group and new gigs. He was tired of it.

Still talking, Alix tossed her purse into Dan's bedroom. "It's great to have some time off, you know? Even though we were really going places, ready for a big break, but I know we can get a much better sound with some new people. I told you all about it in an e-mail."

"Cill has been sick," he told her. "I haven't been able to get away to check my e-mail."

If he stayed here, he'd have to see about convincing Cill to allow Blake Harbor to put in a tower somewhere in the east woods, so cell phone reception wouldn't be so impossible.

"I'm starved," Alix said. "I was so excited to see you I only had coffee before I left."

Dan started making some peanut butter sandwiches. "I ate lunch already. But I don't have much time. We have to walk the south woods this afternoon."

"All you have is peanut butter? You need someone to take care of you."

"I usually eat with Cill and Casey."

He did have some beer in the fridge, and he opened two. This conversation needed beer. Alix swigged, then nibbled on her sandwich. "Won't the old lady let you take the afternoon off, just this once?"

"I don't want to. I need to check the trees today. The south woods have been in trouble, and I'm behind in my work."

She tilted her head at him, letting her blond curls hang along her shoulder. That was the first thing Dan had loved about her, her childish gesture. Why had he loved it? When did he stop?

"How do woods get in trouble?" she asked him sweetly

Knowing how information about tree fungus and woolly adelgids bored Alix, Dan certainly didn't want to try to explain strange magical winds.

"Trees get insect pests and stuff," he said. "And, uh, there was a—a derecho." Casey had once told him about them; she'd looked up strange winds when the oak tree limb blew down. "It's a sudden downdraft storm; took a lot of trees down. We need to make sure the new growth is strong."

"We?" Ice dripped off the word.

"Casey and me. She's learning about the woods from—from her aunt."

"Casey? That scrawny woman with the red hair?"

Dan said it was. He did not say he thought Casey was beautiful.

"Yo the Studio!" Casey yelled from the bottom of the stairs. "We have a visitor! It's Joe Burnside," she added, as Dan came down. "He's in some kind of frenzy. We need to—" and she stopped, because Alix joined him, twining an arm around his waist.

"Hi," she said. "I'm Alix."

Casey went perfectly still, like she was encased in gel. Then she smiled, with only her teeth, and said, "I'm Casey. Never mind, Dan, my aunt and I will handle him. Nice to meet you, Alix." And she left.

Dan realized Casey hadn't seen Alix from the kitchen door; it was only his bad conscience.

Without intending to, he followed Casey, with Alix in his wake.

"Who is Joe Burnside and why do you care?" Alix asked.

Burnside's Porsche sat sideways in the driveway, as if he'd slammed on the brakes without pausing to park. The man was now heading for the front steps. He never came to the back door; he was too important. Ignoring Alix's question Dan ran after him.

Cill called, "Hello, Joey. Come have some iced tea."

Dan ran faster, pounding up the steps right behind the furious businessman.

Burnside slammed the screen door in Dan's face. "My wife is in the hospital," he announced. "She won't wake up. The little hospital over in Greenville is hopeless, malpractice waiting to happen, so I got a doctor in from Boston. He has no idea what's wrong!"

"Oh dear," said Cill. "That's terrible."

"I had your dammed wine tested. Twice. All negative."

"Well, we're all fine, dear," Cill said, in a grandmotherly voice Dan didn't recognize. "It can't be the wine."

"Whatever it was, it happened to my wife here, in this house," Burnside growled. "I want to have the whole house tested. It could be radon; it could be a gas leak. *Something* put us all to sleep and made my wife sick!"

"I'm so sorry to hear Zora is ill," Aunt Cill said, sounding as if she were at an old-fashioned tea party. "Anything we can do to help? Can I offer you a glass of iced tea? Some cookies?"

"I do not want any of your tea or any of your damned cookies!" he shouted. "I'll be back this afternoon with people to test this place for radon. Or mold. God knows what kind of crap is in your attic or cellar!"

Alix cuddled up behind Dan. "Who is this man?" she whispered.

Before he could answer, Burnside brushed past them, slamming the screen door again, as he strode toward his car. As he crossed the yard, his head jerked around to the south. For a moment he froze, staring at the newly green forest. The saplings were well on their way to being trees. Burnside shook his head, jumped into his Porsche, and roared away.

Casey had disappeared.

"Hello Alix," Cill said, still in her irritatingly sweet old voice. "We haven't seen you here for some time. How is your band doing?"

Alix explained the loss of the drummer and bass player while Dan stood there feeling like an idiot.

"Dear me," quavered Cill. "Will you be staying for a little while? I hope you won't be bored. I keep Riordan quite busy. Perhaps you might help me around the house while Riordan works. I'm not as young as I used to be."

"Um," said Alix, with a pleading look at Dan. "I don't know."

His head was too full of Casey, not to mention Burnside, to respond.

"What will Burnside find?" Dan asked Cill. "I want to be here when Burnside's men come. You'll have them prowling in the cellar and all over your house. I don't trust them."

"Well, now, I haven't been down cellar for years," lied the newly ancient Cill. Dan knew for a fact that she kept the ingredients for her potions down there, running up and down the creaky stairs like a girl.

"I hope it's not too much of a mess down there. Danny, you need to check on the east woods. Perhaps Alix could help me down the cellar stairs."

"Danny?" She never called him 'Danny'."

Just then he heard Casey's car start up, and found his head turning toward it.

Cill said, "Yes, I asked Casey to do a few errands for me."

Another lie, Dan was certain. Casey was angry with him. She might not come back. He rubbed his face to clear his head.

There was no way he'd leave Alix to handle Cill while the old lady was in this mood.

"I'll check the trees once we take a look at your cellar," he said.

"That's very nice of you, dear," said Cill. Taking Dan's arm, she tottered into the kitchen, Alix following slowly. Both of them had to help Cill down the cellar stairs—the ones she usually took at a trot.

'This is an act', thought Dan, 'she was never this wobbly, except when the south woods blew down.'

The cellar smelled of ancient dirt and damp stone. Cill poked around, tsking and tutting and asking Dan and Alix to move huge old barrels of God knows what from one side of the cellar to another. Although some sections of the floor were still dirt, the main area, where Cill kept her potions, was concrete. Dan frowned at the shelf of brown bottles. Would Burnside's men think they were poison? Or would they assume the bottles were as innocent as the jars of tomatoes Cill canned every year?

Cill made sure her helpers had to dive into all the dusty, cobwebby corners, where Alix squeaked and cursed as webs caught in her hair and dirt leaked into her trendy shoes.

"Thank you so much," Cill gushed, as they emerged into the bright kitchen. "I feel so much better about having all those men down there with their radar."

"Radon," said Alix. "Where's the powder room?"

While she was combing webs out of her hair, Dan hissed, "What are you doing? Radar, for crap's sake? *Radar?*"

Cill gave him a grin that made her seem about twelve. "Now we'll have some nice tea," she said, filling the old copper teakettle and lighting the burner.

Alix reappeared. "Hot tea in August?" she hissed in Dan's ear.

Having no idea what Cill was up to, he didn't answer. She couldn't possibly want Alix to help her with anything.

While they sat at the kitchen table with their hot tea, Cill nattered on. "I grew up in this house," she told Alix confidingly. "My papa was very strict. Young people today don't know what it was like, having to wear foundation garments and serve tea." She started a lengthy story about the tea parties her mother used to give. Trying to make it all go away, Dan glazed over, only kept awake by Alix kicking him under the table.

"How can you stand it?" she asked when they finally escaped. "That old lady should be in a home!"

Dan explained his work meant spending most of his time in the woods or the vegetable garden. "But we always eat together," he added. "She's actually a good cook, and enjoys feeding me. It's part of the job. You and I can have breakfast together, but lunch and supper we'll have to have in the house."

'I'm getting as shameless as Cill,' he thought.

"She can't make you do that!" Alix snapped. "I need a shower; I feel like I have spiders crawling all over me!" Even after her shower, Alix remained itchy and upset. "There's nothing to eat here," she said. "I can't stand having dinner with a crazy old woman." After rejecting scrambled eggs or grilled cheese, she said "Let's go to Nates."

Nate's was a bar out on the Greenville Road, where Alix's band, now styled Alix and the Vortex, sometimes played when it wasn't touring. Dan thought it might be easier to break up with her away from his studio, but as they drove, he still couldn't find the words. Sometimes, he realized, I revert to the confused, incoherent farm boy of many years ago.

His dad loved farming. So did Dan. But his mom hated farming. Vocally. As a result, his dad spent more and more time out in the fields or woods. If Dan went with him, mom got furious; if Dan stayed with her, she told him at length what a good-for-nothing his dad was. Dan learned to keep his mouth shut. As a result, he attracted women like Alix, who required endless patience and good listening skills.

Sitting at the heavily shellacked bar table, watching Alix flirt with the bartender while she ordered another drink, Dan figured it out. When he first met Alix, when she was singing here, he enjoyed spending time drinking and laughing with friends. When Alix chose him rather than all the other men who wanted her, he was amazed and in love. But almost two years of walking the forests for Cill Woodward had changed him. Maybe Cill changed him. Whatever, he'd rather hike through the woods like he used to do with his dad than spend time in noisy bars. No, he realized, he hadn't changed, he'd gone back to who he once was. Alix had stayed the same.

Instead of finding the words to explain all this to Alix, to say he wanted to break up, Dan got wasted. Hammered, sloshed, tanked, wrecked. Or, to use the term the old sailors of Blake Harbor once used, three sheets to the wind. Alix was also bombed, but managed to drive them home without hitting anything. They giggled their way up the stairs to the studio. Alix was trying to take off his clothes when Dan passed out on the couch.

He woke up to the smell of frying eggs, which destroyed his already queasy stomach. Two years of a single beer before bed didn't prepare him for the kind of drunken evening he and Alix used to do all the time.

"The eggs will get cold," she called, as Dan lurched into the bathroom and turned on the shower.

When he came out, Alix was sitting on the couch, finishing toast and fried eggs. "Feeling better?" she asked. "You used to be able to drink me under the table!"

"No longer my idea of fun," he said, pouring coffee.

She lay back on the couch, stretching seductively. "Then let's find another kind of fun," she said.

"Look, Alix…," he began, but then his landline rang.

"Riordan? Cill. Tomorrow we're going to Greenville. Casey will visit Zora in the hospital. I need you to drive me to my lawyer's."

Dan said, "Okay," and hung up.

"Who was that?" Alix asked. "Why don't you use your cell?"

Dan put down the phone. "Cill. I have to drive her to Greenville tomorrow. Like I keep telling you, cell phones don't work out here."

Alix made a pouting face, which used to charm Dan, but now, to his surprise, it irritated him. He found himself thinking that Casey never pouted. She yelled. Or she froze up. He couldn't get the picture of her chilly smile out of his head.

"I can't stay here all alone," Alix said. "I might as well go back to Greenville."

"You'll like it better there," he said. "I'm not around much during the day."

"What do you mean?"

"I really like it out here. You know how I always wanted a house in the woods. This is—this is the right place for me. And Cill needs me." At least until Casey could take over, with her magical ability to make things grow.

"It's a phase you're going through," Alix told him, with a dangerous glitter in her eyes. "Like when you moved from Portland to Greenville, or when you began making those giant sculptures."

"I still make the giant sculptures," he said. "We want different things, Alix. You're the one who should live in Portland, where you could get a lot more gigs."

"Are you trying to get rid of me so you can hang out with that lanky redhead?"

Dan didn't know what to say or how to say it. "I like it out here," he repeated lamely.

"Maybe you're in love with the old bat!" And she burst into tears.

He knew Alix wanted him to take her into his arms, soothe away her tears like he had always done. He didn't want to do what he had always done.

"You don't like it here," he said. "You need to be where you can do your music."

"I thought you'd get over this," she cried. "If you love me, you'll come back to Greenville!"

"Do you love *me* enough to stay here?"

"Not when you're like this!" Alix fled into the bedroom, where she sobbed while throwing things into her suitcase. And Dan sat without speaking, like he used to do when his mother lost her temper.

As she drove away, he stood staring after her little Honda, feeling nothing. Then he gathered his gear and went to check on Cill's north woods.

*

Naturally, Casey thought as she drove down Woodward Lane, naturally he had a girlfriend. A beautiful girlfriend, with a perfect nose and beautiful hair. A girlfriend who only came up to his shoulder. Just as high as my heart, popped into her head from somewhere.

Casey banged her hands on the steering wheel and cursed, almost driving into the swampy area that ran along Woodward Lane. Maybe she should live in the swamp with the frogs and salamanders.

At the end of the lane, Casey stopped, with no idea where to go. All she'd thought of was getting out of there, so she didn't have to watch Alix twining herself around Dan. She considered her options. Not around the Common to the left, with its Blake Harbor shops, where everyone knew

Aunt Cill. Not straight ahead to Greenville, where Dan's beautiful woman lived.

'If I knew her address, I could set her place on fire,' Casey thought, 'but then I'd end up in jail. Which might be drier than living in the swamp.'

It was all too much like Jake. While they struggled with the business, he'd tell her about this sweet young woman who worked at the Rello company. Silly little thing didn't have good winter boots, Jake laughed, because she'd come here from Arizona or Arkansas or someplace. He'd talked about how funny and cute she was. She sounded like a total wimp to Casey, who ignored his stories, too preoccupied with keeping WebLicious going to realize what was happening. Only after Jake left did Casey remember that the girl was tiny and beautiful, only with dark curls and brown eyes instead of golden curls and long legs. All happening again, this time because Casey was so focused on getting the south woods to grow, and stealing the necklace, she didn't pay enough attention to Dan.

And why do men need so much damn attention, anyway?

Instead of going downtown, she turned right, onto Pond Street, which curved around to the west. She passed the entrance to Thayer State Park, drove through the tiny town of Jefferson; then all the way to Orland. There, she sat in her car, gazing at the way the white steeple of the church was reflected in the pond. Why did it have to be a beautifully sunny day? A thunderstorm would have suited her mood much better. Or fog. Fog would be perfect.

'I probably fell into Dan's arms because I was all crazy with whatever made the trees grow,' thought Casey. 'I can do something worth doing, or I can have a boyfriend. One or the other.'

To hell with him.

Pulling a small sketchbook out of her purse, along with her thick bag of pencils and erasers, Casey drew the reflection of the church spire, while the light slowly moved toward the west.

She couldn't leave Aunt Cill, at least not until the forest had regrown. Once it was done, she'd go and bunk with T.J. at her college. Or go back to Rochester and work as a barista for her friend Susan's coffee shop. But she'd hate to leave the forest. And if the ability to grow stuff stuck around, she could never explain it to her sister. Or brother. Or parents. Or even to Susan.

Somehow, she'd have to manage life at Woodward House for the rest of the summer, until the forest completely re-grew. She'd mostly ignored Dan for the first month she lived with Aunt Cill. She could do it again. Besides, they had to deal with Joe and Zora and whatever he might try next. Biting her lip, Casey turned the car around and headed home. Behind her, the westering sun flashed into her mirrors, trying to blind her. She stopped to put on her sunglasses.

Even though Casey was late for supper, Aunt Cill didn't scold her; only asked her to set the table and cut up the cucumbers fresh from the garden. Dan must have picked them, but he was nowhere to be found. Casey couldn't decide whether it was a good thing or it meant that he and the blonde were going at it.

Once Casey and her aunt were sitting at the kitchen table eating hamburgers, along with cucumbers and tomatoes in vinegar, Aunt Cill said Zora was in some kind of coma, and Joe was furious.

"Joey sent three or four men to hunt for radon and mold," Aunt Cill concluded. "All they found were a few cobwebs."

"You don't have any cobwebs," Casey said. She herself had dusted and vacuumed.

"Oh, there are some left down cellar and up attic. Nice and hot up in the attic, too. The youngest Whipple boy checked it out. He managed to stay polite, though. All those Whipples are polite."

"What did those Whipples think about your bottles of potions down cellar?"

Cill grinned. "All they saw was my tomatoes. Gave the boys some to take home."

Casey didn't even blink. It was only one more strange thing in a summer full of them.

Cill brought over a plate of oatmeal raisin cookies. Brooding, Casey ate two without tasting them.

"Aunt Cill," she said, finally. "We can't let Zora die."

"We can't give her back her necklace, either. Maybe Joey is forcing her to blow down our woods, or maybe it's her idea. Either way, we can't take the chance."

"She must need her necklace the way you need the forest."

Aunt Cill shook her head. "If we give it back, the whole thing will start over again."

They sat and frowned at their iced tea, unable to think of a way out of this problem. Casey didn't want to destroy their brief moment of friendliness to suggest any possibilities that her aunt could glower into impossibilities.

The sound of a fast car broke the silence. Casey stood up to look out the kitchen window, where Joe Burnside's Porsche came to a sliding stop.

"Zora," she said. "I hope nothing's happened to her," and ran out the back door.

"How is she?" she called to Joe. "Is anything wrong?"

Without a word, Joe simply handed Casey an envelope made of thick, heavy paper, stomped back to his auto, and zoomed off. Typed on the envelope were the words "Priscilla Woodward." The typing made small indents in the thick paper.

Casey brought the envelope to Aunt Cill, who ripped it open with her butter knife. "He always was a brat," she announced, after reading the papers inside. "Got himself an impressive Boston lawyer to sue us for Zora's illness. Stupid; he can't prove anything. Can't imagine what he thinks he's doing."

Taking the creamily expensive paper, Casey skimmed it. "He'll keep you in court until you run out of money. He doesn't have to care what he spends."

This time when Aunt Cill pursed her lips, her eyes danced above them. "Two can play at that game," she said. "I'll make an appointment with my own lawyer in Greenville. Zora's in the hospital there, Priscilla, so you can visit her while I see young Adams. See if you can figure out what ails her." She marched off to her fat old-fashioned phone, while Casey stared at the letter.

'Aunt Cill had a lawyer? What did she mean by "two can play at that game"? Would Burnside even let her see Zora?' Casey thought.

Still depressed about Dan's desertion, Casey ate another cookie. 'Aunt Cill seems happy with me now,' she thought, 'but the old lady still won't tell me how to fix the forest.'

'Well,' Casey realized, 'I don't plan to walk the woods with Dan any more, and that will make Aunt Cill mad at me all over again.'

TWENTY-FOUR: BRIARS

Along with her arrangements with her lawyer, Aunt Cill had also hatched a plan for Casey to visit Zora. But Casey didn't think it would work, and that night her insomnia returned full blast. She worried about how she'd ever learn to re-grow a forest the correct way. She imagined all the new growth in the south woods turning brown and dying. She worried about Dan. He was probably interested in Casey because he loved Aunt Cill. Did he think Casey was somehow supposed to succeed her aunt to take care of the woods? Was that why he made love to her, so he could stay here? Or maybe it was some kind of magic left over from how she made the south woods grow back. Whatever it was, she could never compete with someone as pretty as the horrible Alix.

Casey finally fell asleep around two a.m. and didn't wake up until almost ten.

"Well, sleeping beauty, glad you could join us," Aunt Cill announced. She and Dan sat at the dining room table as usual, discussing the state of the forest. "Get your coffee and get in here."

Somehow Casey thought, I have to make this work. Pretend I'm meeting Dan for the first time. Or something like that.

Bringing coffee and some leftover fruit salad into the dining room, Casey sat down and waited, while Dan told Aunt Cill the hemlocks were doing fine, and the balsam fir was spreading nicely. Casey wanted to add that the birch trees in the east woods were unhappy about something—they were, she'd noticed it while walking out there—but she kept her mouth shut. What does "unhappy" mean, Aunt Cill would ask. Having no idea what it meant, Casey couldn't face her aunt's disgust at her ignorance. She might have some kind of Skill for growing trees, but it hadn't affected her problems with her great aunt, who too often didn't think Casey could do anything right.

The Greenville Hospital was an hour away. Dan drove, with Aunt Cill sitting in front to give him directions. Casey sat in the back and fretted. They dropped Casey at the hospital before heading for the lawyer's office.

The receptionist told Casey where to find Zora Burnside's room. Of course, she would have a private room. Rather than checking at the nurses' station and being told no, Casey decided to walk in like she belonged there, hoping Joe Burnside wasn't around.

He wasn't. A chunky older woman, in nurse's scrubs, sat by the bed reading a mystery novel.

"Hi," Casey said. "I'm Casey Todd, a friend of Zora's. I brought her these. How is she?"

The nurse took the bunch of black-eyed Susan's, chicory, and Queen-Anne's lace that Casey picked from the edges of Aunt Cill's woods.

"How nice," she said. "Real flowers, not those hothouse things. I'll get a vase." The 'hothouse things', a huge bouquet of red roses and white lilies, sat on the windowsill, clearly a gift from Joe. The nurse trotted out, holding the wildflowers.

Zora lay flat in her hospital bed, eyes closed, an IV tube in one arm. She might only have been sleeping, although her pale skin looked slightly greenish. Quickly, before the nurse could return, Casey reached in her jeans pocket, pulled out the little box holding the real necklace, and opened it. She put the gold spiral on Zora's forehead, immediately covering it with her hand, as if she were patting Zora's head in concern. All according to Aunt Cill's plan.

Zora sighed deeply, opened her eyes, tried to speak. With her free hand, Casey picked up a cup of water and held it to Zora's dry lips.

"Where am I?" The obvious question almost made Casey laugh out loud.

"In the hospital. I have an important question to ask you."

"Where's Joseph?"

"He'll be here soon," Casey lied, hoping it was a lie. "Why did you wreck Cill Woodward's forest?"

Huge wary brown eyes focused on Casey. "What do you mean?"

"Was it your idea, or your husband's?"

"Where is he?"

Casey lifted her hand from Zora's forehead, lifting the gold charm with it.

"No," she whispered. The huge eyes closed. Casey stuffed the charm back in her pocket right as the nurse came in with the flowers in a plastic vase.

"I do wish she could see these," said the nurse. "Where did you get them?"

"My aunt's garden." Not quite true. Aunt Cill only believed in growing vegetables. Wildflowers, however, flourished around the edges of the vegetable garden.

"How is Zora doing? Have they figured out what's wrong?"

The nurse shook her head. "Poor Mr. Burnside. He hired me to sit with her all the time. Of course, the hospital nurses can't possibly do that. I make sure her IV is okay—nutrients and water are important, because she can't eat. But her breathing is fine. Mr. Burnside is in Boston, finding some specialists. Maybe they can figure out what's wrong with his wife."

The nurse's nametag said Deschanes. She had light brown skin and dark curly hair with a few gray streaks.

"Do you get breaks, Ms. Deschanes?" Casey asked. "I'd be glad to sit with her a little while. I miss her. We used to go shopping together and have lunch." She tried to look woebegone.

"Well now, I don't see why not. I just changed her IV, and I wouldn't mind a cup of coffee. If anything happens, go out to the nurses' desk, they'll handle it. Not that anything will happen. Can I get you anything?"

Casey said no thank you and held her breath until the nurse was gone. What luck that Joe Burnside was off in Boston. Pulling out the necklace charm, she laid it on Zora's forehead again. This time, the huge eyes glared at her.

"What are you doing to me?"

"Did you know that destroying Cill Woodward's forest might destroy her? Kind of like destroying your charm hurts you?"

Zora grabbed Casey's wrist, but wasn't strong enough to move the hand from her head or grab the necklace.

"You took it," she whispered. "How did you know?"

"Whose idea was it to blow down our woods?"

"If I tell you, will you give it back to me?"

"We can't trust you," Casey said. "Your husband has filed a lawsuit against Cill Woodward, saying she hurt you. He can't prove anything, but he can bankrupt her."

"I can stop him. He'll do anything for me. He'd always do anything for me." Now the dark eyes narrowed like a stalking cat, making Casey wonder how much Joe Burnside had to do with the windstorm, and how much of it was Zora's idea.

"I'll have to ask my aunt," Casey said, and lifted the charm from Zora's forehead.

Returning after her coffee break, Nurse Deschanes was sympathetic to Casey's unhappiness about her friend.

"Come back any time, honey," the nurse said. "You never know what people in a coma understand. Not that this is exactly a coma. But you might do her good."

Casey thanked her. When she was outside the hospital, she called Dan's cell phone. Although he was the last person she wanted to speak to, it was the only way to contact her aunt, to let them know they should come get her.

"I'm ready any time" she said tersely. "I'll be outside."

"Okay," Dan said. "We'll be about fifteen minutes. How did it—" but Casey cut the call. She did not want to talk to him.

Dan and her aunt picked her up twenty minutes later, during which time Casey walked most of the way around the hospital to burn off her nerves.

As they drove back to Woodward House, Casey recounted her visit to Zora. "Even if it was Joe's idea, I don't think Zora minded blowing down the south woods," she concluded.

Aunt Cill nodded. "Needed to be sure it was that necklace doodad."

"What did your lawyer say?"

"He'll file this thing and that thing, charge me some money. I think he's tough enough to handle Joey. His dad wasn't much, but young Charles favors his grandfather. A bulldog."

"We can't trust her with the necklace, but I don't want to let her die," Casey said from the back seat. In front of her, Dan nodded.

"You think she'll die?" Aunt Cill asked.

"Would you have died, if we hadn't stopped them from killing the forest?"

"I'm old," said Aunt Cill. "Zora might live a long while yet."

"How old are you?" Sitting in the back seat, having just tortured Zora and lied to the nice nurse, Casey wasn't feeling tactful.

"One hundred and fifty."

She said it completely seriously. Dan's head swiveled around to stare at Cill; then snapped back to the road. He thought she was serious, too. No wonder she was so cranky. Poor old lady was losing it.

"I need to rest," Aunt Cill said. "I'll close my eyes for a moment. Let me know when we're back in Blake Harbor. We need to get some fish for dinner."

That night, Casey couldn't sleep. 'Aunt Cill could be as old as ninety,' she thought. 'Although she doesn't seem to have changed much in the eight years since I've seen her. Great aunt--she should be my grandmother's sister. Except that Grammie Todd never talks about her. Neither does my Nana. What is Aunt Cill's relationship to my family? Maybe I call her "great aunt" when she's only a family friend. But why did we visit her every summer? Because my father wanted her land? Why would she give it to him if she wasn't related to him or to her mother?'

Annoying Voice whispered. "There is more to it than you understand."

Casey turned the white noise up on her phone, put her head under the covers, and finally slept.

*

Even after the short time they'd been in Greenville, Dan noticed how the new trees in the south forest had grown another four feet. Ferns, ground pine, and partridge berry covered everything beneath them. Wild grape wound around Dan's sculptures. Casey's little green blocks of wood had completely disappeared.

Cill said it looked good. 'She managed not to actually say that Casey was a wonder; too much Maine in her,' thought Dan. 'Darn dour New Englanders.' Besides, the old lady was already on to the next task.

She ordered Casey and Dan to walk the border between the South Woods and Seybourne Park, where families gathered for picnics and Frisbee-throwing.

"We didn't want a fence put up between our forest and the park," Aunt Cill explained. "Instead, we encouraged a lot of horse-briar, maybe you call it cat-briar; anyway, it now makes a hedge all along the border with the town park. Lately, Riordan tells me, some of it has died off. Priscilla, I hope you can figure out how to do something about it without painting anything. It should be within your ability."

Casey bit her lip and nodded. "I'll go there in the morning," she said, and headed for her room.

The next morning, Casey was gone even before Dan came to breakfast. She'd left a note on the kitchen table, dated six a.m. "I'd rather do this alone," it said. "Be back for lunch."

With her mouth tightened in disgust, Cill showed it to Dan.

"She shouldn't do this without someone watching," the old lady said. "First time alone, you need a watcher to make sure you come back."

"Um," said Dan. "Maybe you should go. Casey doesn't want me around."

"Too far for me," Cill said tersely. "She'll get over it."

So, after breakfast, Dan headed for the spot where the south woods bordered on Seybourne Park. Walking through the new, bright green growth, he found himself remembering Casey's long back and soft curls. He walked faster.

At first, he couldn't even see the park through the screen of new pine saplings, shadbush, and tall ferns. But as he walked, full-grown oaks replaced the pine saplings, and the understory faded back. Now he could see the park, its large trees surrounded by nicely mowed lawn. Along the border with Cill's woods, cat-briar and wild raspberries made an impenetrable barrier. Dan headed for the section he'd discovered that had become thin and skimpy—maybe because of too much shade, maybe because some rowdy kids had forced their way through.

He found Casey sitting with her back against an oak tree. The hedge had regrown, and the briars now crept around Casey's feet and crawled up her arm.

"Casey," he said, squeezing her cold fingers. "Casey!"

The hazel eyes opened, gazed at him as if he were another sapling, then blinked back into reality.

"Guess it worked," she said.

Dan started pulling briars off her shirt and out of her hair.

"I can do it!" she snapped, so he backed off. She walked along the barrier inspecting it, ignoring Dan, who followed her, trying not to think about how she had looked with green tendrils winding across her breasts.

"Looks okay," she said, and strode off toward the house as fast as the undergrowth allowed her. Dan followed more slowly, although running seemed like a good idea to him.

As they neared the house, they could see Cill standing on the porch, watching them. Casey headed toward the back door. Dan sighed, and climbed the front steps to the porch.

"What happened?" Cill asked. After Dan made his report, she nodded several times, then said, "You haven't had any time to work on your sculpture. The woods will be okay for the rest of the day. Where's Priscilla. Priscilla!"

Casey came out to the porch, carrying a glass of iced tea. "Yes, Aunt Cill?"

"You did well. You may go to town to do whatever you do with that computer. I'll give you a grocery list."

"Yes, Aunt Cill."

"Sounds like work," Dan said, trying to warm up the frozen atmosphere. "How about doing some sketching?"

She nodded like he was a friendly but uninteresting stranger. "I'll bring my sketchbook."

*

Casey didn't tell her aunt, or Dan, what had happened while she was re-growing the hedge. The work wasn't as hard as re-growing the forest. She'd considered the task all the way to the broken hedge, and realized that putting her paintings all around the flattened forest had been a way of putting *herself* all around it. Therefore, she needed to put herself into growing the hedge.

She walked along the place where the hedge showed gaps, imagining how she would paint a flourishing tangle of cat-briar and wild raspberry. Carefully, avoiding the thorns, she took hold of one of the wide, heart-shaped cat-briar leaves. It felt tired and unhappy.

'No, I'm *not* projecting into it,' she thought. 'I can do this.' Turning away, she breathed in the scent of dry oak leaves, crushed ferns, pine tree spice, knowing it would make her smile. It did. Then she put her hand on another cat-briar leaf.

Tired and unhappy.

"Why?" she asked it.

Images of trampling feet. Images of sharp knives. Someone trying to take the hedge down. Kids. She could almost see them, imagined them talking about the crazy old lady who grew briars to keep everyone out.

'At least,' Casey thought, 'I don't have to figure out anything about soil quality or access to water.' Trying to radiate comfort to the abused vines, she concentrated on images of long tendrils, wide green leaves, and sharp, protective thorns.

The briars began to grow.

After half an hour of work, she found herself sweaty and tired. Her images faded out, and the growth stopped. Before finishing the job, she sat and rested, listening to a vireo chirp and whistle.

'I'm done with this,' she thought. 'Aunt Cill doesn't like me; Dan has his bimbo. They can deal with Zora—she's Aunt Cill's problem, not mine.'

After the bankruptcy, she had avoided her parents' offers of help, but now she decided to call them and ask them to lend her money for a cheap apartment back in Rochester. She had to get away from her parents, her brother and sister, Aunt Cill and Dan. She'd go back to Rochester, take the cheapest apartment she could find, go job hunting. Susan still owned the coffee shop. Maybe Casey could work as a barista there until she found something. Or in a grocery store. Anything to get away.

Focused on planning her escape from Woodward House, she didn't immediately notice when another green-gray thing slipped through the undergrowth to stand beside her. This one looked human—about four feet high, covered in gray-green fur, with a wide human face. Snub nose, some sparse greenish hair on its round head, and long yellow eyes.

"You do well," it said. "You are now the Guardian."

"Thanks," Casey said, "but no thanks. I'm moving back to Rochester."

The thing glared. "You are the Guardian!" it said loudly.

Casey could hear the capital letter that began the title.

"You have Aunt Cill. I'm sick of her and her secrets and her ordering me around."

The small person transformed into the coyote-snake beast, which growled and showed its long, pointed teeth.

"Go ahead," said Casey. "Some real teeth will feel better than being chewed up by life."

When the thing took her arm in its teeth, she was too angry to reconsider. Instead, she kicked it, hard. It gave a howl more confused than pained and let her go.

"You got any useful advice about this Guardian thing, fine!" she yelled. "Otherwise, leave me alone!"

In a tumble of foggy gray-green, the human version of whatever-this-thing-was returned. "You are strong and fierce," it said, approvingly. "You will make a good Guardian." It slipped behind a sapling and disappeared.

Casey sat down against the tree. Was she hallucinating because of her insomnia, or because of Dan? Ignoring the trail where something coyote-shaped had disturbed the undergrowth, ignoring the bruise on her arm from fantasized teeth, she closed her eyes and finished re-growing the briars. When Dan appeared, she got away from him as quickly as possible.

TWENTY-FIVE: SURPRISES

Rinne didn't know what to say to Great Gran. You weren't supposed to use your Skill to help anyone but family. No one else could know about it.

"It was Val," she explained. Great Gran was frowning at her. Great Gran was dead. Rinne must be dead, too. "I did it for Val," she told Great Gran. "Val is family. I did it for Val."

"I'm here, Rinne, I'm here."

She was lying in bed, a wide, comfortable bed. Had she been sick? She felt softly wonderful, like she might have been sick, but was fine now. Val was talking to her. This was Val's bedroom, in her apartment over the boat shop. She was in Val's double bed, the spindle bed, which once belonged to Val's grandmother. The room was dim. A sliver of light from the half-open door was the only illumination. Val was sitting beside her on the bed.

"Val," Rinne said.

"I'm here, sweetheart, I'm here."

Val was crying. Rinne had never seen Val cry.

"I'm okay," Rinne said. She remembered how she'd calmed more ocean than she'd ever done before, how tired she'd been. "I'm okay," she said again, because Val was blowing her nose and trying to smile through her tears. "How did you get me here?"

"You fainted on the porch of Curlew House. I hauled you into the car. I wanted to take you to the hospital, but didn't think I'd get through the snow to Gorham Harbor. How do you feel?"

Rinne sat up. Her mouth felt sticky. "Can I have some water?"

"Lie down. I'll get you some."

A clock on the bedside table glowed three forty-five a.m. Rinne discovered she was wearing her flannel shirt and her underpants. Val must have undressed her. She didn't know how to feel about that.

When Val brought the water, Rinne drank thirstily.

"How do you feel?" Val asked again.

"Fine. Hungry. What are you doing up at this hour?"

"You scared the shit out of me," said Val. "I've been sitting and watching you breathe. I kept thinking I should have tried for the hospital. I thought about calling Dr. Crothers, but what would I tell him? That you calmed half the bay and then passed out? Anyway, the storm was too bad to even get to his office. If you hadn't woken up soon, I would have called him."

"Is Carl okay?"

Val laughed a little. "Couldn't figure out what was happening with the weather. First it's all but a nor'easter, then it goes dead calm, then the surf picks up again but by then, he's in the lee of Avery Point, headed for the dock. If he survives Dad reaming him out for being so stupid, he'll be fine."

"We can't tell my dad any of this. He'll do worse than ream me out. We're only supposed to use our Skill for family. For *Island* family," Rinne added.

"I won't tell. I still don't believe it, and I saw it happen. The waves just stopped, like it was a foggy spring day instead of a winter storm. But you can't do that again. I was afraid it had killed you." Val pulled her chair up close, leaning her arms on the bed.

"I used to do it all the time on Dad's boat. I'd calm the waves around him. It was easy. It was going two miles out that exhausted me. I'm fine now. Only hungry." Rinne discovered Val was holding her hands, both her hands. Her insides turned over.

Val let her go.

"I'm hungry too; I couldn't eat any supper. How about a grilled cheese sandwich? You can wear some of my sweatpants. You need to keep warm."

The sweatpants were too big for her, but they smelled like Val; salt, her shampoo, something indefinably Val. Rinne wanted to help cook, but Val told her to lie on the sofa and rest. Once they had eaten, Rinne felt sleepy again. It was now five-thirty a.m., two hours before her usual rising time. She yawned.

"You need to go back to bed," Val said.

"So do you, if you were up all night."

"I'm okay," Val said, and yawned.

Rinne said she could sleep on the sofa, but Val wouldn't hear of it.

"I'm still worried about you. Come on, get into bed. I'll sleep in the chair."

"You'll get an awful crick in your neck," Rinne said, following Val into the bedroom. "Lie down next to me. I don't snore." She couldn't believe she'd actually suggested that, but Val nodded, and curled up on the bed, and was asleep immediately. For almost half an hour, Rinne remained awake, listening to Val breathe, thinking she wanted to stay like this forever.

When Rinne woke up again, the bedside clock said nine seventeen, and Val was still asleep. Rinne carefully slid out of bed and went hunting for the coffeemaker. Once the coffee was brewing, she found her backpack on the floor and dug through it for her phone. Helena had texted her.

"Staying in hotel tonite rm w Jacuzzi!" Worrying about Helena was silly. She always landed on her feet, and believed everyone else did, too.

But Rinne texted back. "Snowbound @ Vals."

Val's living room window showed a distant view of the harbor. Rinne pulled back the curtains and blinked against the bright sun reflecting off the snow, which was beginning to melt. Maine weather: first it tried to kill you, then it pretended the storm had never happened.

Val came out of the bedroom. Her short hair stuck up everywhere, making her look like a crazed porcupine. Rinne laughed.

"I smell coffee. What's so funny?"

"Nothing. I love your hair."

Val gave her a cheerful razzberry, poured herself some coffee, and sat down at her little pine table to drink it. Rinne joined her with a fresh cup of coffee and a glass of cranberry juice.

After eating grilled cheese at four a.m., neither of them wanted breakfast, although Rinne drank two cups of coffee and three glasses of juice. Val called her parents. The Costa fleet was fine, although Carl was grounded forever. Then she pulled out her laptop to check on work, while Rinne took a shower. Because her own clothes were full of salt spray and sweat, she put on one of Val's sweatshirts to go with Val's sweatpants— secretly breathing in Val scent before pulling it over her head.

"I should check on the Puffin Feather, at least," Rinne said, toweling her hair. "And get some clothes."

"You should rest. Maybe see Dr. Crothers."

"Val, I was only tired. Like I'd run a marathon or something. You worry too much!"

"Okay, okay. Let me shower, and I'll take you home."

Rinne did feel like she'd run a marathon. She stretched out her sore muscles; then curled up on the sofa.

"Yeah, you're fine," Val said, sitting next to her. "You're asleep again." She smelled like the soap from her shower.

Still half asleep, Rinne sat up, finding that Val was closer than she'd thought. For one intense moment, they looked at each other. Then Val kissed her.

Val kissed lightly, tentatively, but Rinne did not feel tentative. She grabbed hold of Val and kissed back, thoroughly. When they came up for air, Rinne buried her face in Val's neck.

"Oh Rinnlet," said Val.

"Rinnlet?" Rinne didn't know if she wanted to laugh or object.

"Only because you're smaller than me. I always think of you that way. Because I didn't dare tell you that I love you."

"I didn't either," said Rinne. And they kissed again.

In high school, Rinne had gone out with a couple of guys and experienced some of the usual back seat groping. Making love with Val was nothing like that. First of all, Rinne liked the way Val smelled, like the ocean, salty and sweet.

"Fishy," Val said, and laughed.

Val laughed often as they made love, in surprise and delight. No one in the movies Rinne had watched with the groping guys, or with Helena and Alison, ever laughed when they made love. In movies, lovemaking was like a dance. In reality, it was complicated, disorganized, and amazing.

As they lay together afterwards, Rinne said, "I was going to go home," and laughed.

"This is your home," Val said. "If you want to."

"I spend most of my time here," said Rinne. "But…"

"But?"

"What will people think?"

"What do they think about your living with Helena? Anyway, my family knows I'm a lesbian. Carl figured it out first, and didn't see any problem. Don't tell the others, but he's my favorite brother! When I was at the community college, I had my first girlfriend—don't look at me like that, it only lasted a couple of years. I was practicing for you. Anyway, I felt like I wanted to tell my mother, and she said, 'I thought so,' like she'd figured it out before I did, and it was no big deal."

Lying on her back, Rinne blinked at the ceiling. Her family would think it was a huge deal, especially because she was supposed to marry Gavin and produce children who could work the wind or the water. She couldn't possibly tell them about Val.

"I know," said Val. She rolled over and got Rinne a tissue. "We'll figure it out."

Figuring it out meant that Rinne had to tell Helena she wanted to move to Val's apartment. To her surprise, Helena didn't ask why.

"I was thinking of moving in with Ryan. Now he can move here!" That surprised Rinne even more. She had never imagined that Helena would stick with one boyfriend.

'Maybe Helena's luck was rubbing off on me,' Rinne thought.

Living with Val was like making love with her—complicated, sometimes difficult, but always wonderful. On her weekly phone call with Tavish, Rinne told him her address had changed; that she was living with Val. He gave a whoop that blew Rinne's ear off.

"You go girl!" he said. "Took you long enough."

"Was it so obvious?" Would everyone in town know what was going on?

"Only to me, darling, only to me. May you both be very happy. And don't worry about the Puffin's cellar; it always gets a little wet in the winter. I forgot the dehumidifier died last year. Go get another one; put it on the card."

One sunny, cold weekend, Val and Rinne hiked along the rocky shore, and Rinne showed Val how she could make the waves do tricks.

"So that was you! I thought there was some kind of peculiar tide!" Val said. "Even though I saw you calm that storm, I still don't believe it!"

"That's why I have to find Sarah. She can do the same tricks with wind. It's how my dad does so well lobstering. My mom goes with him to keep the water steady. Sarah used to go with him on windy days." Rinne explained how her family had passed the abilities down through two centuries, and how Great Gran was an especially good wind-worker. "They think I should marry Gavin, hoping our children will have the same Skill."

"What are you, a prize cow? Keep this going long enough and none of your family will have any brains. Or teeth!" Rinne laughed, but Val only smiled. "If they want you to have your cousin's children, he can be a sperm donor. Like a stud horse."

"A what!" The idea of Gavin being a—Rinne couldn't imagine it. She began laughing and couldn't stop, which made Val laugh, until they were both breathless.

Growing up with the Gilley family on Halloran Island, Rinne had assumed her life would be the way it had always been. Leaving, hunting for Sarah, felt like the most revolutionary thing anyone ever did. Until Val, she had never told anyone about her life on the Island; not Alison, not Helena. After all, no one else could possibly understand, or believe, in the Gilley approach to life. Rinne felt like she was free-falling into another world. She felt both excited and terrified.

Using her face-recognition software, Rinne still hunted for Sarah now and then, although her panicky obsession had subsided. Besides, she now understood why Sarah had run away—from parents with their impossible expectations for her, from the claustrophobic little Island. Rinne felt like her life had expanded in all directions. She was finally herself, instead of just another Gilley. But she still wanted to at least talk to her sister. Maybe they could share their frustration with their family, and their guilt at leaving them. Besides, Rinne wanted to make sure Sarah was okay.

Sometimes Rick would call her to look at a blurry photo sent by one of his friends, but the photos were never Sarah. It didn't matter how blurry the photo; Rinne believed that she'd know Sarah when she saw her.

By early summer, however, Rinne was ready to give up. If Sarah didn't want to come back and be a prize cow, then maybe Rinne should leave her alone. She loved living with Val, she enjoyed working at the Puffin Feather. She couldn't imagine returning to the Island. Other boats managed without the Skill; her father would have to.

Unless something terrible had happened and Sarah needed her help. That thought would sometimes wake Rinne up in the middle of the night, or stop her dead while she was ringing up a set of lighthouse earrings at the Puffin. She finally became better at banishing the idea to the back of her mind, but it kept showing up whenever she wasn't paying attention. Maybe they hadn't always got along, but Rinne remembered all those confidences under the pine trees, watching the ocean on Lookout Point, sharing a bedroom and a life.

Then, in July, while Rinne was restocking the T-shirt shelves, Val's cousin Rick called from the Big Cat. "I think I might have found your sister," he told Rinne. "This time for real."

All her need to find Sarah exploded inside Rinne. She dashed over to the bar, not caring that she should have been opening the Curlew House. The other "cottages" were open, but the family who owned Curlew House were late this year.

"You go ahead," Tavish had told her. "I'll deal with the Curlew shack."

At the Big Cat, Rick opened his laptop and showed Rinne a newspaper article. The headline read, "Mr. and Mrs. Burnside host Hospital Fundraiser." In the black and white picture, Sarah stood smiling in a tight dark dress and high heels. Her hair seemed much too light—had she dyed it? Beside her was an older man in a tuxedo. Sarah's necklace caught the light. The wind-worker necklace.

"That's her," said Rinne. "That's Sarah." Her heart pounded.

"According to the article, her name is Zora Burnside," Rick said. "A guy I know who runs the fisherman's diner in Blake Harbor saw the article, recognized the Zora woman from Sarah's picture, and sent it to me." He eyed Rinne, who was staring blindly into space. "Here, sit down so you can read better."

"Joseph and Zora Burnside open their White's Point home to help the Greenville Hospital," the article said. "Joseph Burnside grew up in Greenville, and runs Burnside Leathers, selling high-end leather goods. He and Mrs. Burnside married in Europe and returned to live in Blake Harbor." The article went on to describe the house, the party attendees, and the amount of money raised for the hospital.

"Europe?" That made no sense to Rinne. How did Sarah get to Europe in only a few years? And why had she changed her name?

"Where's Blake Harbor?" she asked.

"I got work to do," said Rick. "Feel free to Google it."

*

"You can't go all by yourself," Val said. Blake Harbor was a two-hour drive to the south. "It's summer. Route 1 will be crawling with clueless tourists. Route 95 will be a parking lot."

"It's summer," Rinne told her. "You have a lot of lobster and fish to sell."

They argued about it, but Rinne was right, Val couldn't leave. The big cottages wanted fresh lobster and scrod, as did the Harbor Hotel. But that didn't stop Val from checking the route, checking Rinne's GPS, insisting her cousin Johnny look over Rinne's car, making sure Rinne get an AAA membership and earbuds for her cell phone. When Val wanted to help Rinne pack, however, Rinne said no, she understood how to put her underwear in a suitcase. She thought about saying, "You're not my mother," but Rinne's mother had never worried about her like Val did.

Val sat on their bed and watched Rinne fold underwear, jeans, and shirts into the cheap red duffle bag she'd bought on sale.

"This will be the first time we've been apart in almost a year," Val said, finally.

Rinne hadn't realized that. She'd been thinking about finding Sarah, wondering if she even wanted to find her sister now. After all, she had a job, she had Val. Her parents couldn't possibly force her to marry Gavin, or return to the Island. She stopped packing and sat down next to Val, putting an arm around her.

"I have to do this," she said. "After all this time looking, I need to talk to her, to find out why she left. If I can convince her to come back—well, my dad needs her help. Yeah," she added, as Val frowned, "my dad can be a jerk. But he's still my dad, and he can't compete with your family without Sarah's help. I'm not sure he can even make a living without Sarah's help."

"Or your help," said Val. "Not that I'd let you go back to the Island."

That night, they made love. In the morning, Rinne climbed into her green Nissan and headed for Blake Harbor.

TWENTY-SIX: IVY

After the briar re-growing and lunch Dan headed for his studio while Casey, armed with a laptop and grocery list, headed for Blake Harbor. She missed being with Dan. She refused to miss him. Okay, Alix seemed to be gone—for now. But Casey was not going to get involved with another Jake-type man, who preferred long-legged, beautiful blondes to bony, big-nosed redheads.

At the library, Casey wrote a note to her mother, asking if her parents might help with the Boston rent. Boston would be better than going back to Rochester, where she might run into Jake. Besides, it might be easier to find a job in a larger city. Although she knew people in Rochester. She couldn't make up her mind.

Instead of making up her mind, Casey spent some time researching how to become a freelance graphic designer, before reading the rest of her e-mail. Her friend Susan wrote more about her upcoming marriage.

"We plan to get pregnant as soon as possible," Susan wrote. "Are you ready to be Aunt Casey?"

Casey wrote, "You'll do all the work. I'll bring the kid presents. Congratulations!"

She didn't think she'd ever marry.

One of her long-shot applications received a response.

"Your resume is very interesting, although we don't have a position at the moment. If you are in Boston, let us know."

Doing some quick figuring, she decided that, in few days, the south woods and Aunt Cill would be in good enough shape so she could drive to Boston, ask her folks for help, find a job, find a place to live, pay off her debts. Leave the woods and their strange green-gray animal people.

By the time she'd canvassed all her e-mail and social media, her concentration disappeared, telling her it was well past time for lunch. She grabbed a sandwich at the cute little "shoppe" across the street, then drove to the grocery store.

Coming out into the long August twilight, with a shopping cart full of bags, she ran into Joe Burnside. He was getting out of his Porsche, which was parked right next to her old Jetta, making the latter appear even scuzzier.

Given the lawsuit and all, Casey just said, "Hi," and opened her trunk to load up the groceries.

Then everything went dark.

When she woke up, she was lying down in the back of an unfamiliar car. Her head hurt and she felt queasy. Sitting up made it worse. She quickly rolled down the window for air, hoping she wouldn't need it for anything else. The cool evening wind helped the nausea.

"Sorry I had to hit you," said Joe Burnside from the front seat. "There's a bottle of water in the seat pocket." He sounded as calm as if he were at a business meeting.

The Porsche. She was in Burnside's car. She felt around in the seat pockets, found the water, took a swig.

"Why did you have to hit me at all?" she asked, in the same reasonable tone he'd used.

"Your aunt made my wife sick," he explained. "I'll trade you for Zora's life."

An expensive-looking white silk scarf lay next to Casey on the gray leather seat. Pouring water on it, she wrapped the scarf around her aching head. It helped, especially when she hoped she might be wrecking the silk. Then she imagined everything she might say to Joe. "You're crazy," headed the list. But there was no sense in pissing him off more than he already was, no sense in letting him know what they actually did to Zora. Hunting around in the back seat, Casey discovered he must have taken both her purse and her cell phone. She closed her eyes against the headache, and cursed inwardly.

Joey—it helped to think of him like that—used a clicker to open and close the gate in the fence surrounding his house. He drove up the perfectly graveled driveway, and stopped at the front door.

"Can you walk?" he asked.

"I think so." And if she puked on his expensive oriental carpet, so much the better.

But she didn't. Taking her arm in a firm grip, Joe took her down a wide hall to a tiny elevator, paneled in some fancy, expensive wood. Inside, the lights shone: 1...2...3. Casey tried to remember what she'd seen of the house when she was there as a welcome dinner guest. Was there a tower somewhere? Or only an attic, with the servant's quarters? How many servants did he have and where were they?

The elevator opened into a pine-floored hallway with a skylight and a potted tree. She recognized it as a ficus, like the one on her balcony in Portland, like the one she'd had in Rochester. Joey probably bought them by the hundreds. As they walked by it, Casey brushed her hand through the slender ficus leaves; then lightly patted the slender trunk. It couldn't help belonging to a jerk.

Joey opened a nearby door, which led into a small, beautiful room, with a soft carpet, a lushly pillowed single bed with a deep blue duvet, and a high window, open to let in the evening breeze. Casey could hear ocean surf.

"Bathroom is here," he said, opening another door. "Towels, water glass, toothbrush. You'll be comfortable enough. I'll bring you some soup."

Like he was the host of her overnight stay. Or would she be here for weeks? Joey walked out and locked the door.

So he wasn't going to tell his servants that Casey was here. He would call Aunt Cill with his lunatic ransom demand. Even if her aunt wasn't worried yet, she would be furious about all the spoiled groceries. Aunt Cill and Dan—no, not Dan, he didn't care. But what would they do? They couldn't give Zora back the necklace. Or would Aunt Cill do it to get Casey back?

Casey couldn't think. Her head still ached. She drank two glasses of water; soaked a towel in cold water, placed it over the lump on her skull, and lay back on the pillows.

When she woke, it was dark. Turning on the bedside lamp, she discovered a covered bowl of minestrone soup and a slice of bread, which she ate hungrily. Joey hadn't taken her watch, probably because it wasn't smart or even digital—Casey preferred to tell time by shape, not by digital readouts. All her Rochester friends thought she was stupidly retro.

It was ten p.m. With her headache mostly gone, she decided to explore her comfy prison. In front of the high window was a small chest of drawers, which held a comb and brush, a box of tissues, and a small potted ivy plant.

She stared at the ivy. Then she climbed up on the chest to look out the window. Three stories down to the ocean, with its surrounding granite. The house was on a point. Ocean lay on three sides, edged by rock.

Casey considered the ivy again. Okay, it was impossible, but it would give her something to do. 'After all, she thought, I grew the oak branch by hugging the tree. But if I hug the ivy plant, I'll squash it. Maybe if I touch it, and think about how badly I need to get out of here. It's only a little plant. Does it want to be a jungle vine?'

"If it has enough time, ivy can take stone apart," said Annoying Voice

"Good idea," Casey told it. Annoying Voice wasn't so annoying now.

Putting both hands on the plant, she visualized long, thick vines, climbing everywhere, the same way she had imagined the cat-briar putting her whole concentration into the green stems, seeing them grow as if she were painting them.

*

Casey wasn't back for supper. Dan told himself that he should have been happy not to have to spend any more time with her chilly cheerfulness, but he was worried. Cill pretended not to be, but by seven o'clock, she asked him to try Casey's cell phone, using the landline. She didn't answer the cell phone.

"I'll go downtown and see if she's at the library," Dan said. "Her phone may be off."

"I'll come with you," said Cill. But before they were halfway to the door, her landline rang. Cill answered. Then she yelled in a way Dan had never heard her yell.

"You godforsaken bastard! What in all the holy hells do you think you're doing?" Her face turned so red; Dan was afraid she'd have a stroke. "Don't you dare hurt a hair on that child's head, do you hear me, Joseph Anthony Burnside?"

When she slammed down the phone, Dan was considering having a stroke himself. "He kidnapped Casey?" he shouted. "Call the police, for Chrissakes! What is he, the Mafia or something?"

Cill was pacing the floor. "Swearing won't help," she said. "Neither will calling the police. They all went to school with Joey. He gives money to their Benevolent Association. Benevolent my—" she glowered at Dan— "left hind foot. Besides, Priscilla will have to be missing twenty-four hours before any of those idiots will do anything." She paced around some more. Dan couldn't move.

"He said that if I sold him the south woods, he'd release Casey. Nothing about poor Zora. I always knew he was a mean little boy, but I never thought he'd grow up to be such a—" she stopped herself again, then said "nasty man."

Dan wondered what profane name she wanted to use for Burnside. He could provide Cill with a whole list, none of them fit for an old lady's ears.

"Okay," Cill said. "We need some poison ivy and a boat."

Dan knew they couldn't rescue Casey with a boat. Burnside probably had her at the top of the house in a windowless dungeon.

"What the hell we need those for?" he asked.

"The boat will take us around White's Point. Looking at that mansion, maybe we can figure out where that man has hidden Casey." Cill grinned evilly; a grin Dan had never seen. "If we're lucky, you'll find out why I need some poison ivy."

Cill collected her alcohol wipes, her long garden gloves, a trowel, a plant pot, a bottle of one of her potions, and a huge flashlight suitable for signaling ships at sea. Dan added a can of gasoline, in case they had to steal a boat, water bottles, granola bars, cheese sticks, and three jackets—one for each of them.

'We'll find Casey,' he told himself. 'We have to.'

Before they were at the end of Woodward Lane, Cill made Dan stop several times so she could get out, ferret around in the brush, and get back in again.

"Used to be some here," she'd mutter and climb back into the car. At the third stop, she said, "Hah!" jumped out of the car, and started digging.

'Great,' Dan thought, holding the plant pot and watching her. 'Nothing like a nice pot of shiny poison ivy to give your car a lived-in feel.' He was glad he had never been terribly susceptible, not that he went anywhere near the stuff. If he did, he washed himself with alcohol and strong soap.

What with gathering supplies and poison ivy, by the time they got to White's Point, the sun was beginning to set.

"We'll have to wait until dawn for a boat," Cill said. "Can't find anyone in the dark."

"Just get me on the grounds," Dan growled. "I'll find her."

"Joey may have armed guards, for all I know," Cill said. "Let's look around first."

They drove up the graveled driveway toward the Burnside mansion. Dan didn't think they could actually get up to the front door, and he was right. The driveway was guarded by a tall fence, black metal with sharp points, and a locked gate. Filigree lampposts lined the driveway on the other side of the gate, beginning to light up in the summer dusk. Cill got out of the car, took the potted poison ivy and a trowel, and began digging in the carefully tended grass along the fence.

Fierce barking made Dan jump. Three big dogs, two Rottweilers and a German Shepard, charged the gate like they meant to climb it. Cill kept digging as they howled and slobbered a foot from her head. Dan tried blinding the dogs with his flashlight, but the animals weren't fazed. They barked even louder. So he simply stood there, trying to look protective.

With the poison ivy neatly planted, Cill stripped off her gloves and held the stem between her fingers. The ivy grew quickly, twining up the fence, curling around the gate. It reminded him of Casey growing the cat-briar. Did Cill think it would pry the gate open?

Cill cleaned her hands with the alcohol wipes and some of her potion. "Jewelweed," she said. "Good against poison ivy."

Then headlights came gleaming around a bend in the driveway. Burnside in his Porsche. Probably heard his dogs barking. He stopped the car, got out, and spoke to the dogs, who sat down and panted cheerfully at Dan and Cill. Dan, at least, was not fooled by their doggy wiles.

Burnside came toward them, keeping the gate closed between them, and grinned.

"Thinking of breaking and entering?" he asked.

"You always were a mean little boy," Cill told him. "Used to tease the little Rosario girl every time she came into your uncle's store. Made her cry. I gave you a talking to at the time. Too bad your parents never did."

"You sell me the south woods and we might have something to talk about," Burnside said, coming closer to the gate.

"There's your poor old dad, stuck in a nursing home because his arthritis has crippled him. You have this mansion and servants, but you poke him in a dinky little room all by himself. Mean boy, mean man."

Burnside took another step toward them. "My dad was a lot meaner," he said. "I was never good enough for him. Besides, he's much better off in the nursing facility. We travel all the time." He put a hand on the metal bars of the gate. "We *would* travel, if you hadn't half killed my wife!"

A tendril of poison ivy curled around his shirt sleeve.

"Now how on earth do you think I did that?" asked Cill. "And why would I? What did she ever do to me?"

Without noticing the ivy on his sleeves, Burnside now put both hands on the gate.

"I can't wait for our lawyers to grind through this. Zora can't wait! You undo whatever you did to her, you sell me the south woods, and we'll talk about your darling niece."

He turned sharply and marched back to his car. The poison ivy snapped off and trailed behind him. Taking a chunk of it into the Porsche with him, he roared off.

Cill chuckled. "That boy used to get poison ivy rashes from stroking the cat," she said. "He's going to be very unhappy in the morning." She put the alcohol wipes back in her pocket. "Never gave me a rash, but better safe than sorry."

Petty vengeance was satisfying, but it didn't do anything for Casey. Through gritted teeth, Dan said so.

"By morning, they'll probably haul Joey off to the hospital," Cill told him. "Get him out of our way."

"You poisoned him." Dan couldn't decide whether she was evil or brilliant. He discovered that he didn't care if the answer was evil.

"He'd never learn how to identify poison ivy. Wanted to be working inside all the time, making money. Now he just tells old Tony Silva to be sure there isn't any around. Tony's his gardener." She stowed her trowel and gloves in the trunk. "Right at dawn, we get us a boat and see if we can rescue Priscilla. I'll call Manny; he'll know someone. Joey's not going to hurt her," she added as Dan opened his mouth. "She's his bargaining tool."

Dan had to go along with her plan. The waning light still reflected from the ocean, but it would be dark soon. Still, he didn't like it.

When Dan and Cill returned home, it was after ten p.m. Despite the late hour, Cill called Manny, who sent her to someone named George, who could take them out in his Boston Whaler first thing in the morning. She made up some tale about wanting to see the sunrise before it was too late for her.

'Too late?' thought Dan. 'This lady will live forever.'

"Time for bed," Cill told him. "We need to get some sleep."

But sleep didn't work for Dan. He gave up at about two a.m., tried to sketch, tried to read, finally went out and walked all around the house, on the edge of the woods where they met the lawn. Three times. Cursing himself for an idiot all the way. And brooding. He was an idiot about women. Always had been.

From the women of his family, Dan had learned to keep his mouth shut, to listen and nod, to go along to get along. He took that approach with him to his college girlfriends, and to Alix. Lately, however, he'd started thinking there had to be another way. A partnership. With Casey. Too late. She hated him now. She might die without ever knowing how he felt about her. They had to find her. He had to get her to talk to him. His thoughts went round and round.

Cill was up before sunrise. Finding Dan drinking coffee in the kitchen, she set about making oatmeal without comment. Well before the sun gleamed off the top of the eastern woods, they were on their way to the town wharf and George, who turned out to be a barrel-chested man in his forties with a thatch of graying brown hair. Cill gave him no explanations, and he didn't seem to want any, only pocketed the bills she gave him. She and Dan climbed into George's Boston Whaler.

"We need to go to White's Point," Cill said, as George cranked the engine.

A New Englanders like George wouldn't much care who owned the house today. It would be White's Point forever, even though no Whites had lived there for a hundred years.

Sunrise on the ocean is quite beautiful, but Dan was past caring about beauty. George circled the point with the Whaler, while Dan stared at the gray shingled walls of Burnside's house, trying to spot somewhere he might be keeping Casey. There were two turrets, one on the land side and one on the water side. Turrets were good places to imprison people. But so were dungeons. This house definitely had dungeons.

"Water side first," said Cill. "Since we have the Whaler."

George laconically headed along the point. Dan wanted to grab the tiller away from him and gun it.

The first thing they saw was a tree growing out of the roof next to one of the towers. Then they saw a rope coming down from the tower. A rope with leaves.

Cill clapped her hands softly. "She grew herself a rope. Looks like ivy. Grew the tree by accident."

"But where *is* she?" Dan demanded. She could have fallen on the rocks, rolled into the water and drowned. "Pull in here. Let me up there!"

"They'll be looking for her down here," Cill pointed out. "If they find us, we're stuck. Better not."

An ambulance wailed.

"They found her!" Dan yelled. "Dammit, why didn't we try to rescue her last night? She fell on those rocks! That ivy wouldn't hold a squirrel!"

"Bring us back 'round front, George," was all Cill said. "I think Joey has a bad case of poison ivy."

Dan kept protesting, but the Whaler chugged around the house and floated along the side of the yard. It was hard to see anything through the ornamental shrubbery, but they did see the ambulance, parked in front of the house. Then the EMTs brought out someone on a stretcher, followed by a woman in some kind of housekeeper's uniform.

Dan was sure the person on the stretcher was Casey. "Let me off this thing!" he yelled. But George ignored him, turning calmly to Cill for instructions.

"Nope, nope, nope," Cill told him. "Too big. Look at his stomach, look at his chest. It's Joey." She was actually grinning. "They'll fill him full of cortisone. That'll keep him out of trouble for quite some time."

"Where is Casey?" Dan said loudly.

Cill asked George to putter farther along the edge of the Burnside property. The rocks lining the ocean led to grass, first bordered by beach roses and boxwood, then, as the lawn widened out, by nothing. As the point curved away from the water, a small thicket of trees grew up.

"Will you look at that," Cill said, pointing to a heap of seaweed on a granite outcrop.

"It's seaweed!" Dan snapped.

"It don't pile up like that lest someone did it," said George.

Cill nodded. "She used it to keep those darned dogs away. Couldn't smell her through the kelp. All right, Riordan, you can get out now. Look for a trail where Priscilla went. Drape a little of that seaweed on you so those dogs won't smell you either."

He was out of the boat as soon as it touched the shore, tilting the Whaler until it rocked. George muttered something about damn stupid kids, but Dan didn't care. He was hunting for Casey.

And he found her trail. Broken weeds, snapped off branches, all the way to the road. Another pile of dried kelp. Casey had made it. She was somewhere on Blackwood Road. He began jogging.

But when he got to the spot where the harbor ran along the road, there were Cill and George in the boat.

"We need the car," Cill called to him.

"You get the car. She might have collapsed anywhere along here," Dan yelled back.

"I need you to drive," Cill said.

"George can drive!" Flinging away his seaweed cloak, he started jogging again. Then his phone rang.

TWENTY-SEVEN: FINDING SARAH

When she left Route 1 and found Blake Harbor, Rinne was feeling proud of herself. She found a little turnoff and called Val.

"I'm here," she said.

"I knew you could do it!" said Val.

"Now I just have to find Sarah."

"Good luck. Love you."

Rinne sent her love back, then drove through Blake Harbor. It was fancier than Wabanaki Port. Same touristy shops, set around a tidy green square complete with a white church and its tall steeple. Neither Jonesport nor Wabanaki Port had such a carefully manicured Common The road was lined with eighteenth century houses beautifully restored, making Rinne feel out of place in her clunky old car.

The actual harbor, however, felt like home. Chunky, grubby fishing boats and trawlers sat around at anchor, with a few fancy sailboats and yachts floating among them. Rinne's GPS told her to turn left at the harbor. Smaller houses gave way to larger ones, and then to carefully graveled driveways disappearing into well-groomed lawns. They reminded her of the "cottages" she took care of in Wabanaki Port. The third driveway led to the White's Point House, where the Burnsides lived.

But a tall black gate stood in the way. Rinne stopped her car and got out to reconnoiter. Beside the gate was a sign, "Ring for Entry," and a black button. Rinne pushed the button.

"Yes?" said a tinny voice. It came from a little speaker next to the button. Rinne leaned in to talk into the shiny grid.

"I'm Zora Burnside's sister. May I come in and see her?"

"Mrs. Burnside not here." The voice had a slight accent. Rinne couldn't place it. She didn't know anyone with a foreign accent.

"When will she be back?"

"Mrs. Burnside in hospital, very sick."

"What! Where is she?"

But another, louder voice broke into the background. After a muffled conversation, the loud voice said, "Mrs. Burnside is out of the country with her husband. I don't know when she will return." And the speaker clicked off.

Rinne punched the button a few times, but no one answered. Her head pounded with adrenaline. Sarah was sick? Or maybe she was having a child? Or did that make her sick? Could she truly be in Europe? No--the second voice was obviously lying. Getting back in the car, Rinne grabbed her phone. Hospital, there must be one nearby. Unless these people were so rich they'd taken her to Portland, or even Boston. Her fingers shook. Taking deep breaths, Rinne managed to stop shaking and key in "hospitals." There was one in a place called Greenville. It was worth a try. It was closer than Portland.

Greenville was thirty miles away over winding roads that made the distance seem even longer. By the time she finally drove into the hospital parking lot, Rinne had imagined every horrible possibility. She couldn't decide if she wanted to find Sarah here but dying, or not find Sarah at all. But she couldn't go to every hospital in Portland or Boston. She couldn't afford to stay in those cities. Or here. She'd planned to sleep in her car if she needed to be away for long.

"Hi, I'm here to visit Zora Burnside," Rinne told the white-haired lady at the reception desk, and waited for what felt like an hour while the lady consulted her computer screen.

"Third floor, room 421," the receptionist said. "Visiting hours are over at eight p.m."

She was here. Sarah was here. She wasn't dead. 'In a minute I'll see my sister,' Rinne thought, as she rode up in the elevator. 'I've found her,' she thought. 'I did it.' But would her sister be okay?

The only other time Rinne had been in an elevator was when she visited Helena at the hotel. This one made her feel seasick. Or maybe it was nerves. She'd never been seasick, even in the worst weather.

She'd never been in a hospital before. She passed a big desk with people working behind it, but no one questioned her. She looked at the doors. She found room 421. The door was open.

As Rinne entered, a nurse stood up. She was comfortably round, with a light brown face. She wore blue scrubs with kittens on them.

"May I help you?"

"Hi, I'm Zora's sister," Rinne said. She'd been working on this speech all the way up in the elevator, ever since she learned Sarah was actually here. "She's been estranged from our family." Rinne was proud of that word, estranged. "I only just heard she was in the hospital, so I came to see her."

"Oh dear," said the nurse. "I didn't even know she had family. Are you from Europe, too?"

"Um," said Rinne, trying to see past the nurse to the bed lying near a window full of flowers. How on earth did Sarah get herself to Europe? Why did the nurse think Sarah was *from* Europe? "What's wrong with her? She's always been so strong."

"I'm afraid the doctors don't know. She ate dinner at Miss Woodward's house, collapsed, seemed to be okay, but then fell into a coma. Well, not quite a coma. The doctors haven't figured it out. Yet," she added, after a look at Rinne's face. The nurse led the way to the hospital bed.

Sarah lay flat underneath the light blanket. Her eyes were closed, her face was thinner than Rinne remembered it, her blonde curls flat and lifeless. Blonde? They were supposed to be black, like Rinne's hair. Looking more closely, Rinne spotted the black roots, where the bleach had grown out.

The light hospital blanket rose and fell with Sarah's breath. An IV dripped fluid into her arm.

Rinne took her sister's hand. "It's Rinne," she said. "Sarah, it's Rinne." Sarah didn't respond. She wore a pink hospital gown that made her look even paler. The gold wind-worker necklace gleamed in the hollow of her throat.

"Who is this Miss Woodward?" Rinne asked.

TWENTY-EIGHT: IVY AGAIN

The ivy plant grew fast. After watering it three times, using the flowered ceramic cup she found in the bathroom, Casey hunted around for something larger to hold water. A tasteful array of those trendy, curly sticks decorated the only empty corner of the room. Investigation showed the fashionable twigs were arranged in an old chamber pot. Cute. She filled the pot with water and put the ivy inside, laying its two long tendrils out the window.

By the time the tendrils became ropes, Casey had to run her head under cold water, drink four cups of it, and lie down. Coaxing plants to grow was tiring, especially a little ivy plant that was never meant to become a jungle vine. But she couldn't rest. She must go down the ivy rope and get back to Aunt Cill before Burnside convinced her to give his wife back her necklace so Zora could destroy the rest of the south woods.

Winding one of the ivy ropes around her, Casey peered out the window at the other one, which snaked three stories down to lie on the rocks. Light from the lower floors showed a rock ledge, worn smooth by the sea but still able to break all her bones if she fell.

"No worse than climbing a tree," she told herself. But the comparison didn't cheer her up; Casey hadn't climbed a tree since she was thirteen. For Aunt Cill, she said to herself, but that only made her want to go back to bed.

"For the forest," she said out loud. It helped. She slid out the window, clutched the ivy rope, and started down.

Mentally thanking the hours she'd spent in the gym in Rochester, and the hours she'd spent hiking in Aunt Cill's woods, she braced her feet against the weathered shingles and walked her way down the side of the house, holding on to the ivy rope. At first, she resolutely did not think about rocks, only about climbing. Then her arms began to ache. Worse, they got shaky.

"Don't let go," she told them. "Rocks," she told them. She climbed down for what felt like hours.

When her feet finally hit rock instead of shingles, Casey curled up, breathed hard, and cried a little. The waves whooshed soothingly. The rocks smelled earthy and warm, with a tang of seaweed.

Just when she felt that she could actually get up, there was a huge crashing sound, like all the windows in the house had broken. Glass rained down. Diving for a cleft in the Rock, she buried her head in some slimy kelp.

When the tinkling of falling shards stopped, she peered around, ready to dive back into the kelp. Broken glass glittered all over the rocks. People were yelling in Portuguese. Casey hadn't planned on anyone waking up, or on anyone discovering she was gone until morning. Desperate to hide, she slid down into the water, the cold shocking her breathless. Half floating, feeling her way along the rocky ledge, she finally came to a place where she could risk looking up without being seen.

A tree was sticking out of the roof of the Burnside mansion. Its slender green leaves fluttered in the ocean breeze.

Casey had grown more than the poor little overworked ivy plant. The ficus tree in the hallway outside her prison room had come along for the ride, breaking through the skylight, reaching for the stars.

Where was Burnside? She couldn't wait around to find out. Besides, she couldn't feel her feet. The August temperature of the Maine ocean is about fifty degrees. Pulling herself along the rocky ledge until she was around to the side of the house, she felt safe enough to scramble out of the water, first onto the rocks, then onto the lawn. Figuring some speed would both warm her up and get her away faster, she ran. Her frozen feet felt like the rocks they were running on.

Then the dogs began barking.

How could she not have known that the jerk would have guard dogs? Casey scuttled back down toward the water, tripping on clefts in the granite, almost breaking her ankle on the slippery seaweed that lay stinking along the tide line. Stinking. What would it do to dog noses? Grabbing a handful of kelp, she draped it around her shoulders, then lay down in the rest of it. She couldn't get much grubbier. The dogs barked some more, scrabbling around on the rocks, their claws clicking and slipping. Casey held her breath, as much to avoid the seaweed smell as to keep the dogs from finding her. Before they gave up, Casey was shivering from her ocean dip. At last the dogs wandered back to the yard, looking for other intruders.

Wearing her seaweed cloak, Casey kept walking, this time staying on the edge of the water, among the seaweed. Now she could almost feel her feet, but her hands were frozen. Also, her arms and the back of her neck stung and burned from being scraped on the rocks and soaked in salt water. She would worry about it later.

Walking slowly in the dark, on rock ledges, with unexpected tide pools and patches of kelp trying to make her slip, worrying about the dogs, worrying that Burnside would appear in a motorboat, filled the rest of Casey's night. When she finally came to the fence—Burnside had run it as far down onto the rocks as possible—the sky had lightened enough for her to see the rails sticking up, black and pointed. At least she didn't have to climb the fence, because the tide was low enough for her to edge past the fence, keeping on the rocky, seaweed-slippery shoreline. Still listening for the dogs, she circled around, waded through some brushy woods and came to the road.

She'd been working so hard to escape, the ordinary road came as a surprise. For some time, her feet kept going, down Blackwood Road toward town, the rocky shore on her left, huge old mansions up the hill on the right. Then her knees gave way, and she crumpled up on the weedy strip next to the rocks.

Thirst woke her up, along with the sun in her eyes. Now what? She needed to call Aunt Cill, to call Dan, to have them come get her. But climbing the hill to one of the big houses, asking them to use their phone, felt too hard. And what if Burnside had called all his rich neighbors, told them to be on the lookout for a lanky redhead? Then she remembered. Another half-mile or so toward town there was a marshy spot with some smaller houses around it. Burnside wouldn't know such people. They'd let her use a phone.

Standing up wasn't easy, but she did it, and began stumbling along the road. She'd almost made it to the marsh when she heard a siren. Burnside had called his buddies at the police station. Casey dove into the reeds, adding the sulfur smell of marshy mud to the scent of rotting kelp.

A police car howled by, dopplered away, and turned right, down the road leading to White's Point. Had Burnside called the cops? Could they find her?

Up again. Walking toward town. Her feet grew blisters inside her salty sneakers, and her face itched from the marsh mud and the prickly reeds growing there. When the harbor joined the road again, she wanted to jump in and wash herself off, but was too exhausted to manage it. Besides, the water was too cold.

Close to falling down from exhaustion again, she saw the sign for Litchfield Road, which went uphill, back into the trees. Small, slightly rundown houses hunkered along it. No one who lived there would know Joe Burnside. More important, he wouldn't know, or care, about them.

The small uphill slope felt like a cliff. Fortunately, the first house Casey came to had someone in the yard. Perfect. She tottered up the walk. A youngish teenager sat on a towel, ear buds in, listening to music on her phone. Beside her, a baby babbled in its playpen.

"Hi," said Casey. Her voice felt scratchy. "I was in an accident, lost my phone. Can I use yours to call my family?"

The girl stared at her. Casey sat down on the grass because she couldn't stand up any longer. "Phone," she said to the girl, pointing at it.

The girl pulled out her ear buds. "What?" she said.

"I was in an accident, lost my phone. Can I use yours to call my family?"

"Was that what the ambulance was for?"

"No," Casey said. "It was something else. Could I use…"

"What happened to your phone?"

"He took it," said Casey.

Maybe the kid would imagine a cruel boyfriend. The girl thought for a moment, while Casey wondered about her. Surely no one would leave a disabled girl with a baby.

"Is it long distance? My mom says I use too many minutes."

"It's to my aunt, Priscilla Woodward, on Woodward Lane. It's not long distance."

After considering this, while twirling a lock of hair, the girl said, "What's the number?"

Casey told her; the girl punched it in and listened. "No one home," she said.

Aunt Cill was going to the hospital to wake up Zora. Zora would destroy the forest. Aunt Cill would die.

"Could you call my friend's cell number? It's not long distance either." Casey gave her Dan's number, then lay down on the cool grass.

"Hi," said the girl to her phone. "Someone wants to talk to you." And she handed it to Casey.

It was hard to hear Dan; it sounded like there was a loud motor nearby. Casey managed to get the words "Litchfield Road" through the noise. He yelled that he was on his way, and asked if she was okay. Casey said she was; anything else was too complicated.

She lay down in the grass, then remembered to hand the phone back. "Someone will pick me up soon," she told the girl, who began putting her ear buds in. "Wait," Casey said. "Could I have some water?"

Maybe the girl was hard of hearing; she stared at Casey for a moment, then said, "I can't leave Petey." Petey burbled something that might have been agreement.

Casey gave up and fell asleep.

TWENTY-NINE: RECOVERY

Dan leaped back into the Whaler, causing it to wobble and George to growl "trim the boat, dammit."

"She's somewhere on Litchfield Road," Dan yelled.

"We'll get there faster in the car," Cill said with annoying calm. "George, please takes us there."

It seemed to take forever to get back to the town wharf. When Dan complained, George said that it only took ten minutes and it shoulda been fifteen, he hoped he didn't lose his damn license. Cill and Dan ran for the car, jumped in, and raced at double the speed limit to Litchfield Road.

When they arrived, the little front yard seemed full of people. A mother was arguing with a young teenage girl, a younger boy was running around the yard with a plastic airplane making loud zooming noises, and a baby was howling in a playpen.

Cill got out of the car and stalked into the fray. "*Where* is my grand-niece?" she demanded.

Everyone shut up and stared at her, except the baby, who kept screaming.

"If you mean this woman who passed out on my lawn, you can have her," said the mother.

Casey was lying next to the playpen. The screaming baby hadn't woken her up. Her face was greenish pale. But she was breathing. Dan grabbed a water bottle, leaped out of the car, pulled off his T-shirt, dampened it, and washed the mud off Casey's face. Her hands were scraped raw, and there was blood on her shirt. He kept mopping. The blood seemed to be from her hands. At least he couldn't find any deep cuts. Finally, she stirred a little. Dan lifted her up and put the water bottle to her lips. She drank greedily; he had to stop her before it made her sick.

Behind him, the mother was arguing with Cill. "You must be one of those Oakley's," Aunt Cill announced loudly. "None of you with two brains to rub together. My grand-niece was kidnapped by Joe Burnside and escaped. Unlike the Oakley men, she does not drink to excess."

The woman was insulted, sputtering something. Dan ignored her. He picked Casey up, her long legs draping almost to the ground, and laid her down in the back seat of the car. Aunt Cill climbed in beside her niece.

"Give me another bottle of water," Aunt Cill ordered. "And your soggy T-shirt." Dan did so.

Mrs. Oakley was yelling something about drunken women and half-naked young men. Dan slammed the car into reverse and screeched out of the driveway. It made him feel better.

Cill fed sips of water to Casey all the way home. Maybe because it was still early in the morning, Dan broke the speed limit without anyone pulling him over.

Once they were back home, he stayed in the car with Casey while Cill fetched one of her brown bottles from the house, dashed the contents into a mug and made Casey drink it. The dose woke her up enough for them to get her into the house, one on each side, Casey stumbling between them. There was no way she could climb the stairs, so they made a nest of pillows and blankets on the big sofa and got her onto it. All her clothes were caked with salt. They peeled off as many as possible, cut off the rest, and bathed as much of her as they could reach, while Casey slept and muttered. Cill didn't seem to care how much water was spilled on the rug and the sofa. They also managed to get some more water past Casey's chapped lips.

"You did well, child," Aunt Cill told her. "Now rest."

*

Casey woke up on the sofa confused, especially when she smelled food cooking. The last thing she recalled; the sun had come up. Lying against the squashy sofa pillows, she gradually remembered her adventures. Joe. The ivy plant. The stupid girl.

She also discovered all her muscles hurt, and that she had a large collection of cuts and scrapes.

While Casey was still taking inventory, Aunt Cill appeared with a glass of water laced with one of her concoctions. Casey obediently drank it down, even though it made her tongue go to sleep. After a few minutes, she felt some of her aches slip away into the background. Her aunt gave her a faded chenille bathrobe that once was blue.

"Think you can get up the stairs?" Aunt Cill asked. "What you need is a hot bath. I'll get Dan to help you."

Casey did not want to climb the stairs with Dan's arm around her. "I'm okay," she said, wavering her way across the living room and into the hall. But the stairs looked like a mountain.

"I've got you," Dan said.

Where had he come from? He put an arm around her waist, took one of her arms and put it around his shoulders. It felt wonderful. They went up the curved staircase one step at a time. Fuzzily, Casey remembered climbing the stairs one step at a time years ago. She must have been about three years old. It had felt like an amazing feat. She'd had enough of amazing feats.

Having Dan's arm around her almost made her cry, but she bit her lip and staggered into the bathroom without weeping like a baby. There she balked. She was not taking off the faded blue bathrobe in front of him.

"That's right, shoo, shoo," Aunt Cill said. "We'll be fine." Dan left reluctantly. Casey could feel him hovering outside the closed bathroom door.

Leaning on Aunt Cill, she carefully stepped into the steaming tub. 'This woman might tell us she's a hundred and fifty years old,' Casey thought, letting the hot water soak away the aches. 'But I *feel* a hundred and fifty years old.'

Casey had never liked baths. They took too much time, and most of the places she'd lived only had showers, with bathtubs about three inches deep. Besides, washing your hair in a bathtub made it hard to get the soap out. However, after ten minutes in Aunt Cill's huge old tub, Casey decided she'd been wrong about bathtubs. In fact, she might remain in the tub for a week or two.

But Aunt Cill returned, bring a mug of tomato soup and a slice of bread and butter.

"I thought you drowned," her aunt said cheerfully. "You'll turn into a prune."

After drinking the soup and eating the bread, getting bread crumbs into the bath water, Casey hauled herself out. Back in the blue bathrobe, she accepted Dan's help into her room, where she fell into bed.

When Casey woke up again, she found one of Aunt Cill's potions on her bedside table, with a note in her aunt's spidery handwriting that said, "Dab into Cuts." A bunch of gauze lay under the potion bottle. The east window was dim with the twilight. She had no idea of the exact time; her phone had disappeared into Burnside's clutches and her watch hadn't survived its salt water bath. She smelled dinner cooking, which gave her a spaced out hungry feeling. The soup and bread seemed to have happened a week ago.

Many of the scrapes were in places hard to bandage—her back and one of her shoulders--so Casey dug out some old sweatpants and an equally ancient T-shirt that were soft on her abraded skin. Knowing the back stairs were too steep for her aching muscles, she tottered down the front stairs, clutching the banister like she was older than Aunt Cill.

In the kitchen, Dan was setting the kitchen table while Aunt Cill brought out large pot of macaroni and cheese.

Dan, who was idiotically cheerful, announced that they could never eat such a vat of food.

"It's not a vat," Aunt Cill told Dan. "It's a Dutch oven."

It didn't much matter to Casey what it was. The mac and cheese was wonderful, as were the apple pie, the iced tea, and the glasses of water Aunt Cill kept handing her. Finding herself almost asleep at the table, Casey refused Dan's help, climbing the stairs while he hovered behind her. Back in bed, she took a couple of aspirin, chased down with some of Aunt Cill's tonic, and conked out.

Over the next few days, Casey mostly slept and ate, feeling like she was recovering from an especially horrible flu. At one point, Dan came to her bedroom door to tell her the police had found her car in the grocery parking lot, and he and Cill had gone to pick it up.

"She actually drove your car," he said. "I didn't know she could drive. She only did about twenty-five miles an hour, but your car is back."

On the third day, she got down the stairs without clutching the banister. Dan came to meals as usual, but to avoid talking to him, she pretended that she felt worse than she did. He gave her some worried looks, but said nothing.

On the fourth day, Casey felt energetic enough to wander down to the south forest, where the saplings were now young trees, but the effort exhausted her, and she took another nap.

The next morning, she felt well enough to wake up worrying about Zora. Joey was clearly a textbook villain, but Casey still didn't want Zora to die. Knowing she was repeating herself, she said so anyway, over a breakfast of oatmeal and bacon, along with a glass of one of Aunt Cill's tonics and three cups of coffee. To her relief, Dan was out checking on the forest.

"If that Joey would come to us and admit what he did, maybe I'd worry about Miz Zora," snapped her aunt. "No, you are not going to that hospital again. Heaven only knows what would happen to you this time. Come sit out on the porch and draw your pictures while I shell the peas. Riordan is walking the north woods; you'll see him at lunch."

With unusual meekness, Casey fetched her sketchbook and pencils and followed Aunt Cill to the porch. She did not want to see Dan, and wondered if she could pretend to nap through lunch. Yesterday—or was it the day before?—had been brightly sunny, but today was softly cloudy. It suited her mood. She was collecting questions for Aunt Cill, but asking them felt like too much work. Sketching, however, helped her to forget her aches and worries.

Casey sketched a collection of pea pods, and was working on Aunt Cill's hands, when a car came roaring up the hill.

"Speak of the devil," said her aunt, as Casey jumped up.

But it wasn't Joe Burnside's Porsche; it was an old green Nissan. A woman jumped out, and yelled, "Priscilla Woodward!" and marched across the lawn to the porch steps, taking them two at a time, and slammed the screen door behind her. "Priscilla Woodward?" she asked.

Aunt Cill went on shelling peas. "I am Miss Woodward," she said.

"You poisoned my sister!"

THIRTY: RINNE'S STORY

When Dan returned from checking the north woods and saw the unfamiliar car, he wondered what was going on now. They'd had more visitors in the last week than in the whole three years he'd lived there. Not wanting to face Casey, who pretended he wasn't there every time they met, he slid into the back hall, then carefully peered into the kitchen.

And heard the yelling.

"Your sister wrecked our woods! Her husband kidnapped me!" shouted Casey. She sounded like she was out on the front porch.

"I don't care!" hollered an unfamiliar voice. "She's dying!"

Moving quietly through the living room and hall, Dan stopped inside the front door to check out the situation. A smallish woman, with pale skin, fierce dark eyes, and black hair standing up straight all over her head, stood nose-to-nose with Casey—which only worked because Casey was sitting down. Beside them, Cill sat calmly shelling peas.

Dan walked through the door.

The spiky-haired woman transferred her glare to him. "Who are you?" she demanded.

Cill stood up. "This is Rinne Gilley," she said calmly. "Rinne, this is Riordan Pelotte, who works for me. Rinne has been worried about her sister Sarah, and came to Blake Harbor looking for her. Sarah is the woman we know as Zora."

Dan had so many questions that he found himself speechless.

Cill continued. "That nurse woman told her Zora got sick here, and Rinne came to learn what happened."

"You took her necklace!" said Rinne. "She'll die without it. Give it back!"

"Go get the necklace," said Cill.

Both Casey and Dan said, "What?"

"Go and get it," Cill ordered. Casey frowned at her aunt, who frowned back.

"Are you sure?"

"Certainly."

Casey stood up, remained still for a moment, then sighed loudly, brushed past Dan, and stomped up the front stairs.

"Will you give it back?" asked the fierce woman. Dan felt the invisible spikes of her anger, which matched her spiky hair.

"If you can keep your sister from blowing down my woods," Cill said. The peas were shelled, but she carefully wrapped the pods in a newspaper while the Rinne woman fidgeted and Dan worried. Why had Cill told this stranger that they'd stolen Zora's necklace?

Casey returned, and handed the necklace to her aunt, who held it out toward Rinne, who stepped forward to examine it.

"That is my sister's necklace!" she said, snatching at it—and missing, because the necklace disappeared into Cill's apron pocket.

"It made me quite ill, having my woods destroyed," she said calmly, like she was chatting politely at a tea party. "Riordan and Priscilla had a copy of the necklace made and took the real one away. We're out of iced tea, and I have to take these pods to the compost." And Cill trotted past Dan, leaving Rinne staring at the south woods and Casey staring at Rinne.

"Those trees don't look right," Rinne said finally.

Dan decided it was time to intervene. "Because your sister blew them down, and Casey made them grow again."

"You have the Skill for growing trees?" Rinne asked. When she wasn't yelling, she seemed much smaller and quieter. And younger; she couldn't be much more than nineteen. Dan realized the girl yelled because she was scared.

"Skill," Casey said. "It's a good word for—whatever it is I can do. I seem to be able to re-grow trees, yes. Your sister has the Skill for blowing them down."

"She can stop the wind, too," said Rinne. "It's in our family."

"In your family?" asked Casey.

With a sharp exhale, Rinne crossed between Casey and Dan to sit in one of the wicker chairs. "My family lives on an Island near Jonesport. My father is a fisherman. He relies on our Skill to keep storms away from his fishing boat. It's the only way we can make enough money to live on. We don't have many wind-workers, mostly water-workers like me. My sister is a wind-worker. Wind-working is harder, and there's usually only one in a generation. Three years ago, she ran away. I've been looking for her ever since." She looked from Dan to Casey. "Why would she blow down your woods?"

"Her husband wants to build houses where those woods are," Casey said. "We made a copy of her necklace because the little charm thing had the same shape as the damage to our trees. We didn't know it would hurt her. But we don't dare give it back. Killing the trees will kill my aunt."

Dan had seen Casey re-grow plants and knew his sculptures warded off the strange wind, but he still couldn't believe they were having this conversation, like magic was nothing more than another kind of technology. 'Maybe it is,' he thought.

"I'd like to convince Sarah to come back to our Island," Rinne said.

"How did she decide to be Zora?"

"I don't know," said Rinne. "I don't know how she got to Europe, or why she's pretending to be from some other country." She considered Dan and Casey. "When my Gran hears what Sarah has done with the necklace, she'll take it away from her. Gran will know how to do it without hurting Sarah. Then she won't be able to blow down your trees. Will you help? Convince her to return to the Island? At least for a visit?"

"Absolutely," said Casey.

Dan couldn't imagine how they'd convince Zora to leave her mansion, but he nodded.

Then Cill appeared with iced tea. Rinne drank down a full glass, with two spoons of sugar.

"Now perhaps you will tell us how your sister came to leave your Island," said Cill.

"It's kind of a long story," Rinne said, finally. "I've only told it to one other person. But if you have the Skill to grow the trees, you won't think I'm crazy."

Cill poured her another glass of iced tea. "Dinner's on. Start at the beginning."

And Rinne did. It took her all the way through dinner and blueberry pie to tell the story.

*

The summer after Rinne turned twelve, a bad storm hit northern Maine, bringing with it the state's first-ever tornado warning. After that experience, Rinne said, Sarah had changed.

On the Island, their little village of three houses stood back from the ocean in a protected hollow. As soon as the weather reports came in, Rinne's uncles and father brought their fishing boats into the boathouse. But Mr. and Mrs. Bresky, owners of the big Seaview Cottage, hadn't paid attention to the weather reports.

As the storm gathered strength, Aunt Darina got a frantic phone call from Mrs. Bresky. Her husband and son were out on their small yacht, the *Fancy That*. They were struggling in the surf. They couldn't land. They would drown, said the panicked Mrs. Bresky. Could Brian and Neil bring their boats and rescue her boys?

"Not enough sense to pound sand down a rathole," Rinne's dad grumbled, after Aunt Cathy, Uncle Neil, Aunt Darina, and Uncle Bill all came over with the news, pulling off their dripping slickers in the back hall. Everyone gathered around Great Gran's chair in the front room, where they could see the waves pounding on the rocks.

"They go out without checking the weather, they can stay out there," Dad growled.

"You can't leave them out there, Brian," said Maris. Aunt Cathy nodded in agreement. Brian and Uncle Neil rolled their eyes at each other. Aunt Cathy and Maris put their hands on their hips and glared at their men.

Rinne and Sarah looked from the women to the men.

"Never seen one like this," said Great Gran. "You'll need all the help you can to land those rich idiots. Take the girls, too."

"I'm not bringing my girls out into that storm," Brian objected.

"You're gonna need the Sarah girl," Great Gran said. "T'other one can help out, too."

Rinne's mother could calm the waves, and Rinne had been practicing. Last winter, Sarah had slowed down a gale that threatened to blow down the henhouse, but she hadn't ever tried to deal with anything like this storm. Gran Aileen was a wind-worker, but Great Gran was the best wind-worker in several generations. However, Great Gran had weathered too many storms. Now she spent most of her time in a chair where she could watch the sky. From spring to fall, and on warm days in the winter, she kept the window open, so she could feel the wind and weather.

Aunt Darina and Uncle Bill, who were without Skill, said they'd hold down the fort and make some chowder to warm everyone up on their return.

After a little more arguing, Brian, Mavis, Aunt Cathy, Uncle Neil, Rinne, Sarah, and Gran Aileen, packed themselves into Uncle Neil's Jeep. Rinne sat on Aunt Cathy's lap in the back, while Sarah sat on Gran Aileen's lap. Brian, Mavis, and Uncle Neil sat in front. Getting across the Island to Seaview Cottage in ninety miles per hour winds took twice the usual time. Keeping the Jeep on the road took so much strength that the men changed drivers in Round Hollow, while the storm howled over their heads. As they bounced over the rocky terrain, Gran struggled to calm the wind enough so it wouldn't blow the Jeep into the ocean.

When they arrived at the cottage, Brian and Uncle Neil pretended to prepare the Bresky's Boston Whaler for an impossible rescue. Only a Coast Guard cutter could manage such a rescue, but in this storm, the Coast Guard had enough problems with boats farther out to sea. Mrs. Bresky paced the wide porch of the cottage, calling out useless instructions, which the wind blew away.

The women found a slightly sheltered spot in a grove of decorative cedar trees on the lawn--a lawn that Mr. Bresky kept endlessly re-planting when the salt killed it. There, they considered the huge waves, whipped to a froth by the gale.

"Can't touch those waves yet!" Maris yelled. "Mother, can't you calm the wind a little?"

Despite the chill the storm brought, sweat ran into Gran's wrinkles as she struggled to calm the wind. Slowly, the shrieking turned into a mere whooshing, and the cedar trees stopped leaning over. Then Sarah took Gran's hand. And the wind stopped, like turning off a fan. The sudden silence roared in their ears. Out toward the north, the gale still blew the tops off the waves. Here, however, it barely tickled the grass.

"Now we can flatten those waves," Maris shouted. She grabbed her sister Cathy, who grabbed Rinne's hand. Rinne had never tried to manage such a storm. It felt like lifting a Whaler over her head. It felt like running around the Island six times. Sweat rolled between her shoulder blades and into her eyes. Even with her mother and aunt's strength, the wind sucked her panting breath away.

Slowly, the waves calmed down until they could see the Bresky yacht. Brian had started the Whaler, but the yacht was already making way toward the dock.

"Boy, we sure lucked out there," said Mr. Bresky, as he and his son staggered off their yacht, salt crusting their faces and clothes. "Must have been the eye of the storm passing over us."

Dad and Uncle Neil rolled their eyes at each other again. Gran patted Sarah on the shoulder.

Mrs. Bresky stopped hugging her son long enough to invite everyone in for coffee. Not sure how long until the wind would return, Maris was about to decline politely, but a look at her mother changed her mind. Gran's lined face was greenish pale in the stormy light, and Sarah was holding her up.

Rinne had never been to Seaview Cottage in the summertime. She tried not to stare at the floating white curtains that would have to be washed every week, or at the softness of the rugs that would never stand the wet sandy boots of fishermen.

"We're starving!" Mr. Bresky announced. "No little tea cakes, Jessica. Bring out some sandwiches while we get cleaned up!"

After thick roast beef and cheese sandwiches, along with several cups of coffee, the grownups were as ready as they could be for the trip back. Gran no longer looked green. But they could all hear the wind returning. After Brian and Neil had shifted worriedly several times, Aunt Cathy stood up. They all thanked their hosts, and headed for the Jeep, bending low so the wind wouldn't blow them over. It howled as if to make up for its enforced pause. On the way home, the Jeep rocked until it almost turned over. Uncle Neil came up with some inventive cursing, but neither Maris nor Gran objected to his language.

Once everyone arrived safely, they all gathered in the Gilley house for chowder, bread, and more coffee.

"That Skill takes it out of you," Gran Aileen said, buttering another slice of bread.

"It does that," said Great Gran.

"Next storm, I'm going over to their little cottage to remind that Bresky character to stay ashore," Brian grumbled.

Everyone ignored him, too excited by Sarah's power to pay attention to anything else. "She's a very strong wind-worker, mother," said Gran Aileen to Great Gran. "As powerful as you ever were!"

"Bring her to me."

Sarah, still glowing with accomplishment, came to Great Gran's chair.

"Your gift brings responsibility," said Great Gran. "Do you accept this responsibility for the security of our houses?"

"I do," said Sarah.

After that day, Sarah ignored Rinne. Claiming she was exhausted from learning about wind-working, Sarah wouldn't talk things over with Rinne as they lay in their beds under the eaves. Gran and Great Gran were giving her lessons in focus, in dealing with wind from each direction of the compass, and in managing storms.

"I know you have a wonderful gift," Rinne said to her humbly. "But I'm still your sister. Why won't you talk to me?"

"I'm busy," Sarah said haughtily.

*

In the fall, Sarah went to school on the mainland, leaving Rinne with her two younger cousins. Liam often went fishing with the men, and Chloe was only eight. Even an eight-year-old would have been better than being alone all the time, but Chloe, the baby of the group, was a scaredy-cat.

"It's too *far*," Chloe whined, when Rinne wanted to go up to Lookout Ledge.

"It's a mile," Rinne said, exasperated.

"Let's stay home and make things," said Chloe. She loved to make clothes for her dolls. Her mother helped her, and was even teaching her to use the sewing machine, under careful supervision. Rinne thought sewing was the most boring and irritating task in the world. She'd rather clean the henhouse.

She went to Lookout Ledge alone. She missed Sarah. She sat in her favorite cranny, where the rocks kept her warm on chilly days. And she practiced. She learned to make the waves do fancy patterns. Then, one sunny fall day, while weeding the garden and picking the last of the squash, she found herself thinking about the well. That was water, too, very important water. The rocky Island's tiny spring provided fresh water for the three families.

Leaning over the stone wall rimming the precious well, Rinne stared down at the gleam of water at the bottom and concentrated. In a few minutes, the water curled up toward her. When she let it go, the water was higher. Her work had brought in more of the spring water. She practiced until time for supper.

"I pulled more water into the well," she told her mother, while she set the table.

"Did you weed the garden?" Maris asked, cutting up squash.

Rinne said she had. Clearly, her Skill was nothing useful. Maris could calm the ocean as well as Rinne could. She'd probably been keeping the well full of water, too.

Winter on the Island felt longer than usual. Snow squalls, ice storms, and pouring rain kept people indoors. Lessons continued, but without Gavin and Sarah to spur her on, Rinne's grades fell.

"What is wrong with you?" Aunt Darina asked. "You used to be so good at math!"

"If you don't do the reading, we can't talk about the book," said Aunt Cathy.

At least the science studies had something to do with reality. Habits of wild birds. How plants worked. What was happening to the world's oceans, which made Rinne long to go fix them all.

But then her aunts told Maris about Rinne's poor progress in reading and mathematics.

"If you don't study, they won't let you into the mainland school," said Maris.

Rinne said she didn't care.

"Well, your father and I care. No more wandering around the Island until your grades get better."

It was the worst winter of Rinne's life.

*

Two years crawled by. Gavin and Sarah had some kind of fight and didn't talk to each other. Sarah told Rinne that Gavin was just a dumb fisherman, and she had found a much better boyfriend. Rinne managed to focus on her schoolwork long enough to improve her grades, so she could attend the mainland school at Gorham Harbor. She joined Sarah and Gavin on the ferry, which chugged though the Islands, picking up schoolchildren and people who went to work on the mainland, and returning them every evening. If the weather looked bad, you stayed overnight with your old Aunt Edna and Uncle Bert and their three ancient cats.

Sarah loved staying overnight. Rinne hated it.

"Everything is so dusty," Rinne complained. "And covered with cat hair."

"Then don't stay here," Sarah said, heading out to see her latest boyfriend.

Soon, she had a standing invitation to stay at her friend Macy's house, an invitation that didn't include Rinne, who lacked Sarah's genius for making friends.

One day in April, when Sarah was a senior in high school and Rinne a sophomore, Great Gran got sick. Not sick, exactly, but she could no longer sit up in her chair. She lay in the bed where she was born, spending most of her time asleep. Until the day she woke up and asked for Sarah.

"She's at school, Gran," Maris said. "She'll be home on the late ferry."

"Tell her to hurry up," said Great Gran.

As soon as Sarah came in the door, supper was left to dry up in the oven while Gran Aileen, Brian, Maris, and Rinne joined Sarah in Great Gran's room. The old lady was so thin, she disappeared under the patchwork quilt--a quilt she'd made as a young wife. Now, Great Gran was only a fluff of white hair lying on the pillow.

"Help me with this," Great Gran said, fumbling at her neck.

"Mother, you can't give her your wind-worker necklace," Gran Aileen said. "She's too young."

"No she's not," said Great Gran, as Maris unfastened the necklace. "You know perfectly well she should have this."

Gran Aileen put her lips tightly together and stared down at the rag rug on the plank floor. Rinne felt sorry for her grandmother. She didn't like the feeling.

"Come here, girl," Great Gran said. "Sit."

Sarah sat on the quilt next to her grandmother.

"Wind-worker to wind-worker," Great Gran intoned. The wind chuckled around the corners of the house. "I give you the talisman of our craft. Use it well. Use it wisely."

With her shaky old hands, Great Gran held out the necklace. Sarah bent her head to receive it. Maris shut the clasp. The wind abruptly shrieked around the house like a winter storm, and just as quickly died down.

"That's done," said Great Gran, and fell asleep.

Out in the kitchen, no one spoke. Maris and Rinne put the codfish, potatoes, and the last pumpkin pie on the table. Sarah sat like a queen, straight up and very conscious of her new dignity. After the pumpkin pie, Maris said, "Homework," in a tone that sent Rinne and Sarah up to their room without protesting.

But halfway up the steep stairs, Rinne stopped and sat down without a word. In this spot, she knew, the narrow stairs funneled grown up talk perfectly.

"It was a bad idea," said Gran Aileen. "She should have given it to me years ago, so I could pass it on to Sarah when she's old enough."

"You aren't as strong as either of them," Maris said gently. "You've known that since we had that bad storm."

"I asked her to give it to me then," Gran said. "She wouldn't. I was never good enough for her."

"No one was," Brian said.

"Let's hope the child is up to the responsibility," said Gran. "Maris, I'll help you with the dishes."

Rinne stood and tiptoed up to the room she shared with her sister. In the years while Sarah attended the mainland school, her side of the room had sprouted a bulletin board covered with school banners, notes from her several boyfriends, and photos of her with her girlfriends, who had taken the selfies. She constantly pestered her parents for a cell phone. When the answer was no, asking her friends to print photos was the best she could do.

As Rinne entered, Sarah was rearranging the pictures on the bulletin board.

"Are you scared?" Rinne asked.

"Of what?"

"The responsibility. You'll have a lot to take care of when storms hit."

Sarah sat down on her bed. She had replaced the old quilt with a new one, in pink and black.

"I'll be fine," she said, and pulled out her math book.

THIRTY-ONE: THE HOSPITAL

By the end of Rinne's story, it was dark. The crickets and tree frogs were competing for who could be the loudest. Everyone was sitting around the dining room table, nibbling on cheese, crackers, and fresh peaches, drinking water and iced tea. Aunt Cill lit the candles, which always stood on the table. Oddly, for one so practical, she loved candlelight.

"I had no idea," Aunt Cill said at last. "Wind-workers and water-workers. Isn't that something."

"How come you don't have a necklace?" Dan asked Rinne.

"The Skill for water is pretty ordinary," Rinne said. "My mom has it; my Aunt Cathy has some. I think even Gavin has a little. But wind-workers are special. There is only one in each generation, and sometimes it skips a generation. It's harder to do than water-working. The necklace was created by our ancestor, Norris Halloran, to help focus his wind-working Skill. Each wind-worker puts his or her power into the necklace. The longer you wear it, the more it takes on your power."

Casey was glad they hadn't known that when they made the copy. After taking it from Sarah at the ill-fated party, she had stuffed the real necklace into an old enamel box on Aunt Cill's bureau. Now she almost wished it could have stayed there.

"Somehow, I need to get Sarah back to the Island." Rinne's dark eyes were shadowed with more than the candlelight, and she leaned her head on one hand. "If I can do that, Gran can cut her tie with the necklace safely. But Sarah will need the necklace back before we go."

"I don't trust her with it," Casey said.

"What I don't get," said Dan, "is why taking the necklace away put your sister in that coma thing? It's not like she was born with the darn thing."

"Once you've used your Skill with it often enough, the necklace connects you with its energy," Rinne explained. "So Great Gran didn't give it away until she knew she was dying. She'd used it for many years; she would have died sooner if she'd lost the necklace. Sarah must have used her Skill a lot in the years she's been gone."

"How can we let her have it back?" Casey asked. "How can we be sure she won't blow down our trees again?"

Rinne sighed. "I don't know. But having Gran break Sarah's tie with it is the best thing I can think of."

"We'll figure it out in the morning," Aunt Cill said. "It's way past my bedtime."

Aunt Cill put Rinne in the small bedroom that once belonged to the servants. Now it had a comfortable bed, an old chest of drawers with leaf-shaped pulls, a braided rug, and a view of the west woods.

"Thank you," Rinne said. "I'm sorry I was so angry."

"Of course you're angry," Cill said. "It's your sister. Sleep tight."

*

The next morning, Dan found Cill in the kitchen, baking applesauce bread and breaking eggs into a bowl.

"That child is too skinny," she said. "She needs feeding up."

Casey came down the back stairs to shower, went back up to change, and returned to help with breakfast. Dan was sure she was keeping as far away from him as possible. When he tried to help her set the table, she went back into the kitchen to cut the bread. If Cill asked them both a question, she waited for him to answer it. Dan fantasized about climbing through Casey's bedroom window one night, so he could force her to talk to him.

Rinne didn't come downstairs until almost nine o'clock. She was fully dressed. "I don't usually sleep so late," she apologized. "It was kind of a long drive to get here. I'm not used to Route 1 traffic."

Over scrambled eggs and applesauce bread, they took turns telling Rinne about Zora and Joe Burnside.

"Zora," said Rinne. "No wonder it took us so long to find her. Along with bleaching her hair, she changed her name. And she's pretending to come from somewhere in Europe."

"When we had lunch together, I asked her where she came from," Casey said. "She told me she came from Croatia. I had to go look it up."

"She's smart," said Dan. "My cousin went to Europe once, but only to Italy and France. Who knows anything about Croatia?"

"Her husband sounds like a jerk," Rinne said. "Don't you think he forced her to do this?"

"I think," Casey said carefully, "that she wants what he has. A big house, lots of money."

Rinne sighed. "You're right. She's always wanted those. But if I bring her back to the Island, my family will do everything to keep her there. They need her. Having wind-workers is how my dad and uncle do so well at lobstering and fishing. Without her, I don't know if the family can survive. My Gran is getting too old to go out with him, and my mom isn't a wind-worker." She thought a moment. "Once Sarah has the necklace and feels better, she'll want to get out of the hospital. I almost suffocated in there myself. For a wind-worker, it's awful. No real air. Even here, we're too far from the ocean for me. It should be easy to persuade her to leave the hospital. Then we can get her into my car. Somehow."

Dan cleared his throat. "How do you know she'll agree to return to your Island?" he asked. "I mean, she's married and everything. And if we try to bring her back there, what's to keep her from running away from us, necklace and all?"

"I'll talk to her. I'll tell her she can't blow down your woods because it will make Ms. Woodward sick."

Dan didn't think Zora would agree, but he kept quiet.

"It could work," said Casey. "Unless Joe objects."

"Joey has terrible poison ivy," Aunt Cill said, smugly. "He's in the hospital, too."

"If Sarah knows that he kidnapped Casey, maybe she won't want to stay with him," said Rinne.

"Do you really think so?" Aunt Cill asked.

Rinne stared at her. "I don't know," she said, finally. "I never understood Sarah. I didn't really understand why she wanted to leave until I started living on the mainland, with a job and—and some friends. Now I'm not sure I want to live on the Island again."

Dan knew the answer, but he figured he'd done enough, pointing out the problem that everyone else was ignoring.

But Casey said it for him. "She wants to be rich; have beautiful clothes, a big house. She changed everything about herself in order to get those things. We don't know what she told her husband. Does he genuinely think she's an exotic beauty from Croatia?"

"If we don't give her back the necklace, she'll die!" Rinne almost shouted.

Aunt Cill covered up the butter and piled up the dishes. "Casey simply put the necklace on your sister's forehead, and she woke up," she said. "If she doesn't behave, we take the necklace away."

"It's too hard to get on and off," Dan said. "When I exchanged those little pendants, when you were all asleep, I was terrified she'd wake up before I could get the darn necklace clasp undone."

"Help clear the table," Aunt Cill ordered. "We have to think."

But Rinne didn't move. "Where's the necklace?" she asked. "I still don't know if you have the real one."

Cill nodded, reached into a pocket of her slacks, and drew out the necklace. Rinne put out her hand. After a moment, Cill gave it to her. Casey stood up, opened her mouth to object, then sat down again. Dan stood up and moved to the balls of his feet, ready to grab the necklace if Rinne tried to run.

Holding the necklace up to the light, Rinne studied it reverently, as if it were a priceless gem instead of a small gold charm. Then she set it on her palm, holding it as gently as if it were a dragonfly or a butterfly.

Casey broke into Rinne's concentration. "So, is it the real one?"

Rinne nodded. "I never touched it before this," she said softly. "It always goes from wind-worker to wind-worker. It's warm," she added. "When I hold it, it's warm."

Dan looked at Casey, who shook her head. "I never noticed that," he said.

"Neither did I," she said. Aunt Cill nodded in agreement.

"It needs to touch human skin," Rinne said. "You really didn't feel it?"

"None of us would," said Aunt Cill. "It knows you, the way it knows your sister."

Dan decided things had become strange enough. He cleared away the dishes.

*

In the morning, yesterday's clouds came down to the ground, making a thick fog. It wrapped the road in silence and slowed their trip to a crawl. It didn't burn off until they were almost to Greenville.

Casey insisted on riding in the back seat with Rinne so she wouldn't have to talk to Dan. But the back of his head, where his long braid lay along his shirt, made her remember how it felt to kiss him, how they had made love in the growing forest. To keep from thinking about it, she asked Rinne questions, learning all about the Island and Wabanaki Port and Rinne's friend Val. Casey was glad when Dan and her aunt left them at the hospital. Being so close to him in the car was much too distracting.

"I hate this place," Rinne said, wrinkling her small nose as they walked toward the hospital elevator. "It smells like alcohol and sickness."

"Hospitals are for sick people," said Casey, who didn't like the place either, but wasn't going to admit it to Rinne.

When they arrived at Zora's room, a new nurse was on guard. He rose as they entered, greeting them with a neutral, "Hi."

"Hi," said Rinne. "Where's the other nurse?"

"She had a family emergency. I'm Brad Kellett. Can I help you?" He was tall, about Casey's age, with ruddy skin, straight light brown hair and bright blue eyes. His pale green scrubs couldn't hide his muscular shoulders.

"Is Nurse Deschanes okay?" asked Casey. "I met her when I visited Zora before. I liked her."

Nurse Kellett grinned. He had a great smile. "Her daughter in Portland had twins," he said. "First grandchildren for Dell. Her daughter panicked, called her mother to help."

"How are they?"

"All doing fine. Dell has already sent around a dozen pictures."

"This is Rinne Gilley, Zora's sister," Casey said. "I'm Casey Todd."

"Glad to meet you. Dell said you'd been by."

Rinne went over to see her sister. That was the first part of today's plan. Now Casey must distract the nurse. She found herself looking forward to it. The man was gorgeous.

"Did Mr. Burnside hire you?" she asked, staying in the doorway, keeping Nurse Kellett's back to the bed where Rinne was changing the fake necklace for the real one. Casey had found yet another gold chain for the real magical pendant—one with a heavy, easy-to-open clasp.

Brad—she liked thinking of him as Brad, not as Nurse Kellett—shook his head. "Mr. Burnside is down the hall; with the most awful case of poison ivy I ever saw. They have him doped up on cortisone and pain pills. I can't imagine how he got into any poison ivy. A rich man like him isn't going to cut down his own weeds. He's a mess, it looks like he rolled in the stuff. When they brought him to the emergency room, he was raving about someone poisoning him."

"That's awful," Casey said, trying not to giggle. When she had been too sick to avoid him, Dan had told her about Aunt Cill growing poison ivy for Joe.

Over Brad's wide shoulder, she could see Rinne having trouble with changing the necklace. A little flirting might help.

"Oh, I didn't explain. I live with my Aunt Priscilla Woodward over in Blake Harbor. Rinne is staying with us."

"Priscilla Woodward? My grandmother knew a Priscilla Woodward in Blake Harbor. Lived at the end of a two-mile lane into the woods. My grandfather used to deliver groceries there in the winter, on a snowmobile."

"That's the place," said Casey. "I've only been there a couple of months; I can imagine we'll need a snowmobile in the winter." Who were Aunt Cill's parents? Once again, Casey realized how little she knew about the Woodward family. No wonder her great aunt always called her "Priscilla." It must be a family name from way back.

Brad smiled again, giving Casey a small shiver. "I've heard about that place forever," he said. "I'd love to see it."

Zora stirred, and Casey shook herself. She'd been ready to invite this charming man to dinner. She must still be feeling the effects of her kidnapping.

"Rinne!" Zora's voice was raspy, but strong.

"Hi sis. How are you feeling?"

"What are you doing here? How did you—" but Rinne interrupted.

"I heard you were sick, so I came to see you."

Nurse Kellett took three long steps to the bed, and turned his smile on Zora. "You're awake!" he said, pulling out his stethoscope. "How do you feel?"

"Thirsty," Zora said.

The next few minutes involved giving her water, taking her vitals, and raising the head of her bed. Zora—Sarah—was glaring at her sister, but must have understood the benefit of keeping her mouth shut until she could figure out how Rinne had got hold of the real necklace. Meanwhile, Rinne kept smiling and patting her sister. Rinne was getting some revenge, thought Casey, being so sweet to the sister who'd made it so hard for their family.

Finally, Brad turned back to Casey. "This is quite amazing," he said. "Ms. Burnside has been nearly comatose for several weeks. I'll go down to the nurses' station and report this. The doctor will have to check her out."

Once he was gone, Rinne spoke to Sarah. "This is Casey, Priscilla Woodward's niece," she said. "When you blew down her woods, it made Priscilla sick. She's very old, and it could have killed her, losing the woods. To keep Ms. Woodward safe, Casey and a friend had a replica of your pendant made, so you couldn't hurt the woods. They didn't know what it would do to you."

"Joe made me do it," said Sarah. "I didn't know that old lady couldn't live without those woods. Joe didn't say anything about it."

"He probably didn't know," Casey said. "But he kidnapped me to make my aunt sell them."

"He wouldn't do such a thing!"

"You have a room on the third floor of your house, a sort of guest room. It has an old vase with curly sticks in it. There is—there was—a ficus tree in the hallway outside the room."

"How could you know...? Joe would never... why would he take you there? Have you seduced my husband!"

That was the silliest thing Casey had heard since she worked for Burnside Leathers. "Of course. Don't I look like a seducer?"

Rinne intervened. "Sarah, you can't possibly believe he'd prefer anyone to you."

"I'm so ugly now. You"—she pointed at Casey—"did this to me! I hate you!"

Casey snorted. Even thin and pale, Sarah was anything but ugly. "My Great Aunt Cill and—and a man who works for her—we planned how to exchange your pendant for a fake one. We all did it to you. To keep my great aunt safe. You'll have to spread your hate around."

Sarah turned over, showing her back to Casey. "Rinne," she said. "You gave me back my necklace. Thank God you're here."

"Come back with me," said Rinne. "We need you on the Island. Dad's business is falling apart without a strong wind-worker."

Sarah began to cry. "I can't go back," she said to Rinne. "We live like it's two hundred years ago. I hate it!"

"Marry Gavin; have some babies that will be wind-workers," Rinne said. "You can seduce him into living on the mainland in a nice house."

"I'm married already! And I hate Gavin. He smells like fish!"

This wasn't going to work, Casey thought. She reached out to unclasp the necklace.

"NO!" Sarah grabbed Casey's hand.

"Don't," said Rinne.

"If I have to choose between you and Aunt Cill, she will win," Casey said. "She's a pain in the ass, but she's my great aunt."

Sarah whimpered. However, before Casey could remove the necklace, Nurse Kellett came back with a doctor, shooed them out, and prepared to discover if Sarah was truly cured.

If she had to, Casey would take away the necklace—but not yet. Meanwhile, it was time for phase two of their plan.

*

The trip to the hospital had exhausted Casey.

"What is wrong with me?" she asked her aunt, who was feeding her yet another of her strange tonics. This one smelled, and tasted, like an impossible combination of pine needles, anise, and sage.

"You've regrown a whole forest, fixed the briar hedge, and turned a puny little ivy plant into a rope ladder," Aunt Cill said severely. "Not to mention falling into that frigid ocean. I'm surprised you're walking around at all. Drink up." Then she gave Casey a hot water bottle and sent her to bed.

"I don't need another nap," Casey objected. But she fell asleep almost immediately.

Sleeping so much, she couldn't ask Aunt Cill the hundreds of questions in her mind. But it also helped her to avoid Dan. Casey was not about to ask Aunt Cill if that bimbo had returned to the studio while Casey was at the hospital. It didn't matter, anyway. Jake's affair had shown her that she couldn't trust men. She had to keep telling herself men were unreliable, or she might just--but she wouldn't think about Dan.

Every day, Rinne visited her sister; every day the real necklace helped Sarah gain strength. The doctors pretended they weren't puzzled. Nurse Deschanes, back from looking after her daughter and the twins, believed families could do miracles.

"Seeing you made all the difference," the nurse told Rinne. "Families are magic."

When Casey finally started feeling human again, she celebrated by visiting the birch grove, lying in the spicy-sweet ferns, gazing up at the pale August sky through the slender white trunks and rustling green leaves. They had felt unhappy because they missed her. Right, maybe the kidnapping had softened her brain.

"No," she said, not waiting for Annoying Voice to say it. "I know how these trees feel. I'm not crazy."

She joined Rinne on the daily trips to the hospital, pretending to herself that she wasn't interested in Nurse Brad.

"If he asks, we could have dinner," she told herself. "It would help me to feel better about myself. Even if he's only another handsome guy who won't hang around long."

Rinne wanted to know how her sister got to Europe. They sent Nurse Deschanes for a well-earned break while Sarah told her story.

She and the boy she'd met in Bar Harbor—his name was Ethan—decided to go to Portland. There, she'd met Jared, a rich college boy, who invited her to travel with him to Europe for a month. Their relationship lasted until Vienna, but by then, Sarah had been ready for it to end. She had already met Joe Burnside in a café where, eager to impress this rich man, she had taken on her faintly European accent and a new name, Zora Marusic. Playing the mystery woman, she'd soon charmed him into a marriage proposal.

"Why not just be Sarah Gilley?" Rinne asked.

"You know nothing of men," said her sister. "Joseph wanted mystery."

"And someone who could blow down any inconvenient buildings or forests," snapped Casey.

"That," said Sarah, "is part of my mystery."

"It's destructive," Rinne said. "You aren't supposed to use the Skill for anyone but our family. It's not for making a lot of money."

"I only blew down abandoned buildings. Ugly, falling apart buildings. Then my Joe would build beautiful new apartments for people, in Boston, and Portland. He would build beautiful houses here, if only that old woman would let him. She has plenty of woods. People need houses; they don't need acres of poison ivy."

"She can't let him," Rinne said. "She needs the woods the way you need your necklace."

"That doesn't make sense," Sarah said. "Woods are nothing like my wind-workers' necklace."

To defuse the argument, Casey said, "Why doesn't Rinne have a necklace? She's a water-worker."

She knew the answer, but she didn't want Sarah to get angry and refuse to go back to the Island.

Sarah gave Casey a pitying look. "Wind-workers are special."

'Let her think so,' Casey thought. 'Until we can get her out of here.'

THIRTY-TWO: BRAD

Sarah had lost a lot of strength and was prescribed regular walks around the ward. Casey joined the sisters as they slowly rambled the hallways, because their plan required Casey to make friends with Sarah.

'Although,' Casey thought, 'Sarah didn't have friends. She only liked people who could be of use to her.'

On the third day of these walking tours, Nurse Brad joined them.

"Hello, Ms. Burnside. I'm glad to see you up and about." Brad spoke to Sarah, but smiled at Casey.

"I must work hard to get strong," Zora told him, fully in character as a mysterious foreigner. "Today we walk three times around the hallway."

"Good for you," Brad said. "Keep at it!"

The sisters walked slowly away, arm in arm. Before Casey could join them, she felt a warm hand on her shoulder, and a shiver down her spine.

"Everyone says her recovery is a miracle," the nurse said.

"Rinne has a strong will. I think she probably used it to help her sister," Casey said.

"You could be right. The doctors believe in science. Nurses sometimes know better." He glanced at Casey, seeming almost shy. "I'm going off shift now," he said. "Would you have coffee with me before I head home?"

"I'd like that," Casey said. He could at least help her to feel better about being deserted by two other men.

Casey told Rinne she'd be back soon, and Brad led Casey down to the cafeteria.

The place smelled like burned coffee and hamburgers, with an undertone of hospital antiseptics. Equal numbers of hospital staff and worried family members sat nibbling French fries. The coffee was better than Casey expected, although not at all up to the coffee Aunt Cill insisted on grinding fresh for each pot.

"How is Mr. Burnside?" Casey asked, once they had their coffee and found a Formica-topped table.

"He's well enough to be a pain in the neck, but not well enough to get around. They told him his wife was better—but she refuses to see him. The man threw quite a tantrum about it. He's used to getting what he wants."

'Good news and bad news,' thought Casey.

If Joe got better, he could screw up their plan. But both she and Rinne had explained to Sarah, many times, that blowing down the forest made Aunt Cill sick. The tenth time they explained it Sarah actually nodded. Maybe she understood that her necklace could be replaced with the fake while she was asleep. With luck, this would make her behave until they could get her back to the Island, and have their grandmother remove her magic connection with the necklace. But Sarah certainly wouldn't stay on the Island, no matter what Rinne hoped.

"Rinne has hinted that all is not well between the Burnsides," Casey said carefully.

Brad nodded. He had a tiny dimple on one side of his mouth. "From what I've seen of Mr. Burnside, he'd be hard to live with. He's rich, though. He could make it difficult for her to get a divorce."

"I hope not," Casey said. "I mean, if Zora wants one." She didn't tell him her Aunt Cill had talked with young Adams, as she called her lawyer, about how to release Sarah/Zora from her marriage. Time to change the subject.

"How did you decide to be a nurse?" she asked.

Brad came from a town south of Greenville. His mother was a nurse for a physician's office. His father had been a medic in the army, although now he owned a hardware store. Brad went to college in Maine, and then to nursing school in Massachusetts.

"Boston is *the* place for medicine," he told her. "I worked at Mass General for several years, but I missed Maine. Once a Maineiac, always a Maineiac!"

Casey had never heard the word before and made him repeat it. "It's been around forever," he said, with a grin. "It means you were born and grew up here."

"I don't know if I'm glad or sorry not to be a Maineiac," Casey teased.

"You're From Away, but you aren't what people call the tourists." When Casey raised questioning eyebrows, he said, "Summer Complaints!"

They laughed together. He was easy to talk to, with a gentleness Casey found appealing. She told him about her work in graphic design, and her decision to stay with her aunt while looking for a job. She did not tell him about working for Burnside's, or about her ability to make plants grow overnight.

"I hear the phrase all the time, but never understood what graphic design is," said Brad.

"I've mostly done advertising--the pictures, drawings, and typeface that you see in ads every day. Other graphic designers do that for brochures, or packaging, or even books."

"So you're an artist!"

"Not exactly," said Casey, reminded of the time Dan had told her the same thing.

Then Brad hesitantly ask her if she'd like to have dinner sometime. Thinking about Dan, Casey almost said no, then told herself that it would help her get over Dan and said, "That would be great!"

Back at Woodward Lane, Casey mentioned that she had a dinner date next Monday night.

"Not with those Burnsides, they're both in the hospital."

"I've got to know one of the nurses. His name is Brad Kellett."

Aunt Cill frowned and pursed her lips, making her look like an angry bulldog—if bulldogs had long noses.

"You know nothing about this man," she said. "Haven't you learned anything from your experience with Burnside?"

"I don't plan to work for him," said Casey. "He's sweet, he's kind, and he likes me."

"And Riordan?"

"He has a girlfriend. You met her, Aunt Cill."

"She's a dumb Dora. A what- you call it, a bimbo. She hates it out here."

"But she likes Dan. And he likes her."

"That remains to be seen," said Aunt Cill. "Don't you dare tell that nurse man about our plan." And she marched out to the kitchen.

'So much for our brief détente,' Casey thought. 'I'll never be what she wants me to be. Having this stupid, what did Rinne call it, Skill, isn't enough. I have to live Cill's way. I can only see people she approves of. She's like the rest of my family. I can't be successful like they are, but I can't live here and simply enjoy the forest. If I don't leave Woodward Lane, I'll be arguing with Aunt Cill all the time.'

Frustrated, Casey headed for the Rock, but it made her remember the best part of her childhood, now long gone. Instead, she crossed the top of the Rock, through its stubby cedars, and headed down into the north woods, to the dark stand of hemlock trees. They fit her mood better.

*

A few days later, Casey met Brad at a family restaurant between Greenville and Blake Harbor. Although it was decorated with the obligatory lighthouse curtains and photographs, the food was good, simple, and plentiful. Over hamburgers and coleslaw—the best coleslaw Casey had ever eaten—they talked. He told her about his love of nursing, about being a male in a crowd of female nurses, about how male patients asked for him. She told him about her newfound love of drawing, but did not tell him about her use of her painting skills to help the south woods to grow. He wanted to know all about her drawing.

"I don't know any artists," he said. "Probably because most of my family are in medicine. When I was in Boston, I went to a museum that had a garden in the middle of it. I like the garden, but none of the paintings made sense to me."

"The Isabella Stewart Gardner Museum! Yeah, some of the art is boring, but she has some wonderful impressionist stuff, and there's a Michelangelo that I love."

"Hey, I'm just a nurse--I have no idea what you're talking about!" His silly befuddled grin made Casey laugh.

"You're the first medical person I've ever known outside of a doctor's office," she said. "But nursing is an art, too. Like you said, science can't solve everything."

'Like re-growing a forest,' she thought. Magic, not science. She decided to change the subject.

"Tell me about being a Maineiac. I used to visit Aunt Cill when I was a kid, but I grew up in Brookline, Massachusetts." When he made a mock-disgusted face, she laughed again. "We lived in the part with trees and grass," she said. "But I went to college in Rochester, in upstate New York, and stayed there. It's a good-sized city. Living way out in the middle of nowhere with Aunt Cill is a new experience for me."

"Wait until winter. It snows and snows." He told her tales about shoveling snow as a kid. "We didn't get a snow-blower until I was already in nursing school. Dad bought it when my younger sister refused to shovel. Wish I'd been that smart! I loved Boston," he continued, "I really thought about staying there. But they don't need my help there as much as they do here."

A man whose whole life was about helping. How unusual. And he's easy to be with. And easy on the eyes. 'Just have fun,' Casey told herself. 'Don't trust him any further than that.'

She asked him about the garden outside the hospital—because it figured in their plans for Sarah. He laughed.

"It's run by the Greenville Garden Club. They can never agree on anything. The garden should have been larger, but then Mrs. Johnstone wanted to plant some kind of maple—silver maples, I think. All the other ladies hate those trees. How can you hate a tree?"

"Because they're messy, short-lived, and plant themselves everywhere," said Casey. Dan had told her that. She shut him out of her mind.

"Anyway," Brad continued, "Mrs. Johnstone asked her own gardener to put silver maples in, and the rest of the club refused to have anything to do with them. So part of the area planned for the garden is still an open field, with Mrs. Johnstone's maple trees in it. The rest of it is nice, though. Lots of us take our lunch out there."

Okay, so they needed to make sure their plan happened after lunch breaks.

Once the meal was over, Casey and Brad agreed to meet again for dinner sometime soon.

'He likes me,' Casey thought. 'He doesn't think I'm too tall, or too hard to talk to.'

Driving home, however, Annoying Voice showed up, telling Casey that Brad didn't make her feel the way Dan had—a combination of complete comfort and racing pulse. Not for the first time, she wished Annoying Voice would shut up.

THIRTY-THREE: MORE WIND

The next day, Rinne and Casey returned to the hospital. Sarah was healing quickly. But lying in bed made her cranky.

"I can't breathe in here," she complained. "Open the window."

The window was, of course, sealed tight, to keep sickness away from the rest of the population, to keep the air dry and warm, and to keep bugs and pollen out. Nurse Deschanes explained all this, but Sarah hated it.

"I need the world's winds," she announced. "Can't you break the window?"

Looking worried, Nurse Deschanes gently said she couldn't; it was against the rules.

"I do not care about rules!" Sarah said. "I am suffocating in here!"

Rinne frowned. "You've been here for weeks without suffocating. You can manage for another couple of weeks."

Casey put a hand on Rinne's arm. They exchanged a look. This was the perfect opportunity to begin the next part of their plan.

"Maybe we could take Zora outside one day in a wheelchair," Rinne suggested, carefully. "I think it might make her feel better."

The nurse said she'd ask the doctors. It took the doctors a week to decide.

"I cannot bear this place," Sarah kept saying.

"Then what do you want to do?" Rinne asked.

This Zora person was not her beloved sister Sarah, she was demanding and spoiled. Of course, Sarah had been spoiled, too.

"Get me out of here!" Sarah demanded. She was playing right into the plan, but a lot of things could still go wrong.

"I will, if you'll come back to the Island with me," Rinne said.

"I won't live there! It's disgusting and backward and horrible!"

"Come back, tell Mum and Dad you're married," said Rinne. "Then I'll bring you back here."

Sarah pouted. "Very well," she said, in her grand lady voice. "Just get me out of this place."

At last they had permission, and made arrangements. Nurse Deschanes wanted to come with them, but Rinne explained that Sarah might do better without reminders of the hospital.

"I'll put your number in my cell phone," she told the concerned nurse. "We can call if anything goes wrong. And we'll only go around that garden, the one at the back of the hospital."

Finally, the nurse agreed, brought a wheelchair to the room, and helped Sarah into it. Rinne put an embroidered shawl over her sister's shoulders.

The shawl had come from Aunt Cill.

When they were sitting in the Woodward House dining room planning this trip, Rinne worried about taking Sarah outside in her ugly, butt-baring hospital gown.

"She hates the awful rag—that's what she calls it—and for once I don't blame her," Rinne said. "It is awful. No one could get well wearing it."

"I have just the thing," Aunt Cill announced, and produced the beautiful shawl, made of heavy black silk embroidered with bright flowers. It smelled of lavender and mothballs. "Hang it up on the porch," Cill instructed. "It needs to be aired out. Been a long time since I wore it."

When Rinne brought it to Sarah, she loved it. "Where did you find this?" she asked. "It must have cost a lot!"

Rinne was about to explain where it came from, but Casey frowned her down. "It did," she said. For Sarah, money made everything beautiful. Sarah stroked the heavy silk reverently.

"Don't go far," said Nurse Deschanes. "Call me if she feels at all uncomfortable."

Casey promised—with her fingers crossed behind her back.

"Okay so far," Casey whispered to Rinne as they pushed Sarah out into the hall.

And there was Joe Burnside, swathed in gauze like the Invisible Man, but highly visible.

'Crap,' thought Casey, ducking back into Sarah's room. 'If he knows I'm part of this, he'll get suspicious.'

"Where are you taking my wife?" Joe asked loudly. "Who the hell are you?"

"I'm her sister," Rinne told him. "She needs some air. She doesn't like hospitals."

"Go later. I came to visit my wife."

Sarah sat up straight in her wheelchair like a queen dealing with an annoying subject.

"I do not wish to visit with you," she announced.

"I didn't know you were well again! I want to talk to you!"

Nurse Brad appeared at Joe's elbow. "Mr. Burnside, you can talk with your wife when she comes back. She won't be gone long. She's only going out for some air. You need to go back to bed now."

"I'll decide when I should be out of bed," Joe announced.

Nurse Deschanes turned to Rinne. "Perhaps we might wait," she said. "Mr. Burnside shouldn't upset himself."

"What about my sister?" Rinne snapped. "Should she upset herself?"

While the nurses considered this, Joe escaped from Nurse Brad's gentle restraint and leaned over Zora's wheelchair.

"We have to talk," he said urgently. "I need you, Zora. You know how much I need you."

Now fully in character as Zora, she gazed into Joe's eyes. "Oh Joseph," she said. "Let me have some air around me and then we will talk." She put her hand on his bandaged arm. He knelt down beside her, whispering in her ear.

Listening behind the door, Casey swore under her breath. 'She's a pushover for that man,' she thought. 'Or for his money.'

"Let him talk to his wife," said Nurse Deschanes.

"He can do that after she comes back from her airing," Brad countered.

With the nurses arguing, and the usual hospital background hum, only Casey heard the strange gulping noise. It sounded like the way the tide pushed into the rocks around the Burnside house. She peered out the door to see if Rinne had heard it, but Rinne was staring fixedly into the distance.

Water crept out from under the door in Zora's bathroom. Trying not to grin, Casey schooled her face into blandness, and stepped back into the hall. Joe was paying attention to his wife; he wouldn't see her yet.

"What's happening?" she asked, pointing at the growing puddle.

"Good heavens!" said Nurse Deschanes. The gushing sound echoed down the hall, as water poured out the door.

"The toilet is overflowing!" Brad yelled. "Get towels! Get maintenance!"

Both nurses leaped into action, grabbing towels and diapers to soak up the flood, hollering into the telephone for maintenance, trying to stem the tide.

Casey grabbed the wheelchair's handles and pushed Zora away from the chaos.

"Stop!" Joe yelled. "She's stealing my wife!"

By now, the hallway floor shone with water. Joe tried to grab Casey, slipped, and went down with a crash. Three more nurses converged on him, checking his pulse, looking for a concussion, yelling for a gurney. Casey kept going. Rinne ran after her.

They'd planned to take the visitor elevator, but Casey pushed by it, zipping around the corner to the elevator used for patient transfer. She hoped that any pursuers would use the visitor elevator.

"No!" Sarah shouted. "Joseph is hurt!"

"He hurt my aunt!" Casey snapped. "He used you. Shut up!"

"Don't yell at my sister!" Rinne yelled.

Miraculously, the elevator doors opened as soon as Casey pushed the button. Once inside, heading for the ground floor, she leaned over Sarah.

"I thought you understood how your husband used you to destroy my aunt," she hissed. "Now I don't care what you want. You're leaving here! Or I'm taking the necklace away from you! You can go back to the hospital in a coma!"

Sarah wept softly. Casey handed her a tissue and stood up, holding the handles of the wheelchair like a soldier on guard.

"Crying again?"

Sarah sniffled something incoherent.

Rinne took her sister's hand, holding it strongly.

"Don't listen to her," Sarah wept. "She doesn't understand."

"It's you who doesn't understand," said Casey. "Sarah, do you want to go outside, or shall we take you back?"

"How can you ask me that?"

"Blow your nose," Casey ordered. Sarah blew her nose, but continued to pout. She pouted beautifully, but it was wasted on Casey.

Outside, Casey wheeled her charge under the overhang that protected waiting patients and family from rain and snow, then rolled her along the sidewalk and into the little garden area created by the Greenville Garden Club. Plaques on rocks and benches honored the people who paid for them. Beds of multi-colored zinnias, bright red salvia, and white impatiens lined the walkway, shaded by maple and birch. One of the birch trees had grown too spindly. Casey stopped to feel the bark. Leaf miners. She focused on chasing them away. Rinne joined her.

"You don't have to be so mean," she said.

"I'm sorry, I know she's your sister, but she's a brat. A spoiled brat."

Rinne couldn't argue. All the time she spent hunting for Sarah, remembering only their happy childhood, she'd forgotten too much.

Sarah was taking deep breaths. As if on cue, a light breeze fluttered the green leaves and tall ornamental grasses. Opening her arms to the wind, she smiled, forgetting her tears.

The leaf miners died, and the birch tree hummed happily. Casey returned to Sarah, who was still soaking up the wind. While her sister was distracted by it, Rinne pushed the wheelchair through the garden and out toward the parking lot, where Dan waited in a blue Ford rental car. Aunt Cill had decided that they needed a car no one could easily trace. They'd rented it over in Augusta, and Aunt Cill's lawyer had signed for the rental.

Pushing the wheelchair up to the car, Rinne took her sister's arm and helped her out of the chair. But at the car door, Sarah stopped.

"Where are we going?" she asked.

"We talked about this," Rinne said. "Our parents need to know you are okay. Just come home with me for a little while."

"No," said Sarah.

Casey reached for the necklace. Before she could grab it, Sarah pulled the clasp to the front and wrapped her hand around it protectively.

"I hate you," she told Casey.

"It's only for a few days," said Rinne, moving between Casey and Sarah.

"I hate the Island! Everything there is ugly!"

Shoving her sister aside, Sarah ran into the little garden.

Rinne ran after her, calling, "Sarah!"

"Shit!" said Casey, and ran after Rinne.

The garden path continued through a small field of grass and weeds, edged by some spindly, newly planted saplings, the disputed silver maple trees. Sarah stood in the middle of the field, with a wind swirling around her; Rinne stood on the edge of the field.

"Stop it!" Rinne said. "You shouldn't use your Skill to hurt people."

"I'm not hurting anyone!"

Catching up to Rinne, Casey called, "You plan to stay in the middle of the field all night?"

"I'm not going back to that horrible Island!"

"Okay," said Rinne. "We'll take you back to the hospital."

"I don't trust you! You tried to kidnap me!"

"No I didn't! We talked about this! You said you'd like to see Mum and Dad!"

The wind grew stronger and blew toward Casey and Rinne.

"I don't want to go back to the hospital!" Sarah yelled. "It's suffocating me!"

"Okay, okay," Rinne said. "We don't have to go home yet. When you walk in on your own, the hospital will let you go. Then we can talk about going home."

"I am not going back in there!"

"Fine," Casey said. "Then stay here." She turned to leave, to go back through the little garden, hoping if Sarah were left alone, she'd get over herself.

But the wind became a small tornado. It blew Casey right off her feet. As she tried to get up, Rinne landed next to her with a hard thump. She shouted something, but the wind blew her words away. Even though they both lay flat, the tornado pulled at them, dragging them across the grass. Casey put her hands over her head and buried her face in the scratchy weeds.

This woman was flat out crazy. How long could she keep this up?

*

Meanwhile, Dan took time to park the rental car, figuring that Casey and Rinne could cope with lovely, loony Zora. Or Sarah. Whatever her name was. Car safely stowed; he walked down the path—until he heard a howling wind. Then he ran.

Sarah stood in the middle of a small field, arms out and draped with Cill's beautiful black shawl. Rinne and Casey were almost invisible under a baby tornado. Dan edged along the trees until he was out of Sarah's view, taking time to plan his attack. Then he dashed up beside her, grabbed the necklace, and yanked. Hard. Sarah shrieked in pain as the chain dug into her neck, and called up a wind that flattened Dan to the ground.

He rolled over, grabbed Sarah's bare legs, and brought them both crashing into the grass. He pinned her arms behind her and sat on her.

"Stop it!" he said. "Or I'll take the necklace away."

The wind blew harder. Dan reached down and unclasped the necklace from Sarah's lovely throat. Sarah shrieked. The wind stopped.

Sarah lay inert.

"Oh my God. Sarah!" Rinne, her short dark hair sticking up in all directions, dashed over to her sister, kneeling beside her, patting her face. "Put it back! You'll kill her!"

"It's a choice between your crazy sister and getting blown into little pieces." Dan hadn't felt this angry in years. If that woman couldn't get what she wanted by charm or by weeping, she didn't care who she hurt.

Rinne glared at him. "Give me the necklace. I'll put it on her."

Furious, without thinking, Dan threw the necklace toward the spindly trees. Rinne screamed and ran after it. He had never handled a woman so roughly. He had never been so angry in his whole, careful life.

Casey, her red curls straightened out by the wind, came over and considered the inert Sarah.

"Wow," she said. "Will she die?"

Rinne appeared from the edge of the garden. She had leaves in her hair.

"He hurt her! He tackled her like they were playing football! He threw the necklace away."

"I should've let the tornado flatten you," Dan said. "This isn't going to work. You'll never get her back to the Island of yours."

"I have to! If I go back without her, I can never see my parents again, or they'll make me marry Gavin. They'll turn me into a brood mare to make more wind-workers!"

"Instead of turning your sister into a brood mare?" Dan asked. "If she goes back with you, your family will have to find a way to get your sister to divorce her rich husband. Not gonna happen."

"Gran will take the necklace away from her!" Rinne shouted. She'd wrapped the necklace around her wrist.

They can't give the damned thing back to Sarah, Casey realized, not if she was going to use it to create tornadoes and hurricanes. Except Sarah might die.

Rinne paced the edge of the field, among the saplings.

"What do you want me to do? Give her back the necklace and let her go back to her mansion and blow all your trees down? I can't get her back to the Island if she calls up tornadoes all the way. Or should I keep the necklace and let her die? I'm not going to guard her all the time! I have a life!" She raised her fist at the sky. The necklace gleamed in the afternoon sun. "God dammit all!"

A wind howled through the baby trees, cracking several of them in half. Dan pulled Casey down on the ground. Dirt flew into their eyes.

As suddenly as it began, the wind stopped. Rinne was staring at the necklace as if it were a rattlesnake.

"That," said Dan, "was not Sarah."

"I'm not a wind-worker," Rinne whispered.

"Coulda fooled me," Casey said, blowing the dirt out of her nose with a tissue.

Dan pulled a collapsible water bottle out of his pocket so he and Casey could bathe their dust-reddened eyes. He always carried it. Casey had teased him about it when they were still talking to each other, but now she was grateful for the water.

Rinne stood nearby, holding out her necklaced hand like it didn't belong to her.

"You could try it again," Dan said, and swigged some water. "In case it was a fluke. Preferably without the dust."

Staring at the necklace, Rinne took a few steps away from them. Nothing happened. Then a little breeze came out of nowhere to ruffle their sweaty hair. It moved away from their hair and ran across the trees from left to right; then right to left, fluttering the leaves. Then it stopped.

"What about Sarah?" Rinne asked. "She needs the necklace! Great Gran gave it to her, not to me! She'll die!"

"You ready to go back to your Island and have babies?"

"Not with Gavin."

Before Casey could ask who she *did* want to have babies with, a moan floated up from the ground.

"I'm so thirsty!" Sarah whined.

At first, no one moved. Then Dan handed Sarah the water bottle. She drank, then smiled at him, flirtatiously.

"Thank you. I must have fallen asleep. Where are we?"

"In the hospital garden. Sort of."

Rinne walked slowly over to them, stopping several times as if she might change her mind about getting close to Sarah. Her sister smiled up at her fuzzily, like she'd woken up from a long nap.

"Will you take me home now? Can I stretch my legs first?" Sarah's skin wore a healthy flush. She stood up, easily, gracefully.

Then she saw the necklace on her sister's wrist, which Rinne still held away from her as if it might bite, or explode.

"You!" Sarah said, glaring at Dan. "You took it away from me! You hurt me!"

"You tried to kill us," Dan told her. "And you're perfectly fine without the necklace."

Impossible, thought Casey, but true.

Sarah glared at Dan, then turned to her sister. "Give it to me," she ordered.

Instead, the breeze popped up again, to further dishevel Sarah's blonde curls. Then it danced across the field, bouncing up and down like an excited puppy, before making a tiny dust devil.

"It's like playing with the waves," Rinne said, awed. "Only it's wind."

"You are not the wind-worker! I am the wind-worker!"

The dust devil grew larger and began to make figure eights.

"I'm not doing that," said Casey. "Are you doing that, Dan?"

"I'm not doing that," he said. "Are you doing that, Sarah?"

Sarah stamped her foot. "Give me the necklace! Great Gran gave it to me! *I* am the wind-worker!"

"No," Rinne said. "You used your Skill to hurt people. I'm keeping it."

"I didn't! I helped them! We built places for them to live! Give it to me!"

Sarah darted over to her sister, grabbing for the necklace. Holding her necklaced hand over her head, Rinne danced away. And the dust devil enveloped Sarah, making her cough.

"Stop it! You're hurting me!"

"You didn't care who you hurt. Why should I care about hurting you?" But Rinne moved the tiny tornado away from her sister. The spinning dust whirled quietly in a corner of the little field.

"How in all that's holy did this happen?" Casey asked. "How did the necklace transfer to you?"

Rinne laughed. "I have no idea," she said. "Maybe Gran can explain it."

"If you keep the necklace, Joe will divorce me," Sarah whimpered. "He only wants me because I can work the wind."

"You said he didn't know about your Skill when he married you."

"He didn't! But now he does!"

Rinne considered her sister, as if seeing her for the first time. "I don't remember you crying all the time when we were kids."

"I don't remember you being so mean!"

"How many forests did you destroy?"

"This was the only forest! I blew down old buildings. They would have fallen down any way. No one could live in them!! I'm not a killer!"

"You sure about that?" Dan asked.

Sarah turned to him, eyes wide and wet with tears. "I had to get away. Find someone to take care of me! I can't go back to that tiny Island, go out fishing every day to keep the storms away from the boat, dig in the dirt, smell like fish and fried potatoes, have hundreds of babies."

She buried her face in Dan's shoulder and wept. Rinne almost laughed at the look on Casey's face. Poor woman was torn between disgust and jealousy.

Dan held Sarah away from him. "Cill Woodward knows a good lawyer. Joe might divorce you, but you should end up with lots of money. Then you can go do what you want. No fish. No babies."

"Where will I live? I need Maria and Susannah to take care of me!"

"I thought you knew how to feed and dress yourself," Rinne said, glaring.

"*You* can go live on the Island and wear ugly clothes and work all the time! I've made a better life for myself, and I am going to keep it!"

"Do you love your husband?" Casey asked.

Sarah looked down at her dusty hospital slippers. "I don't know," she said, at last. "He's good to me."

"If you still had lots of money, would you miss him? If you had Maria and Susannah to take care of you?"

Rinne chose that difficult moment to laugh sarcastically. Casey wanted to smack her.

"Give me back the necklace!" Sarah yelled at her sister.

"Or what?" Rinne asked.

"Hey!" Dan roared. All the women looked at him. Casey didn't know he could sound so fierce.

"Sarah, if Joe only wants you because you have the Skill thing, Cill Woodward's lawyer can get you a divorce and you'll still have plenty of money. What's Joe going to say? I want to divorce my wife because she can no longer blow down whatever's in the way of my developments?"

"You have pictures of you and Joe at charity events," Rinne added. "You're a supportive wife. What can he really complain about?"

Dan said he would hunt down all of the pictures and give them to Cill's brilliant lawyer, young Adams. Casey kept quiet—Sarah was only paying attention to Dan, after all. She was that kind of woman.

"Joseph is still sick," Sarah said at last, "I can live at our house until he is well. Then we will see what happens. When I first met him, he had no idea I was a wind-worker. But he loved me anyway."

"You need to go back to the hospital," Casey said.

"NO!" And Sarah ran into the little field. "I will not go back there!"

Dan watched her go. He felt terrible about attacking her, and didn't want to do it again.

"Let's take her back to her mansion," said Rinne. "I'm tired of fighting with her."

Casey shook her head. "The hospital will be furious."

"What will they do, send the cops after us?" Rinne asked.

Dan nodded. "I don't want to wrestle her back into that wheelchair. Let the hospital complain." He took a few steps toward Sarah. "We'll take you home, promise. I'm sorry if I hurt you."

Sarah came to Dan and took his hand. "I'll go with you," she said sweetly.

They all walked sedately back to the parking lot as though nothing strange had happened. Rinne got in her green Nissan and headed happily to Val and home. She had found Sarah, and found the power of the necklace. For now, she didn't want to think about what to tell her parents. Val would help her decide how to manage them.

Dan and Casey dropped Sarah at the Burnside mansion.

"I will not hate you now," Sarah told them, back in her role as charming foreigner. "Wind-working is very tiring. It makes me look old. I will go to Carrie before Joseph returns, so I will be beautiful, and I will have Maria make his favorite dinner."

Dan and Casey drove back to Woodward Lane. He still felt strange after losing his temper so thoroughly, but he had to talk to Casey. Instead, the silence between them became thicker and thicker.

Finally, he said, "You think Burnside will divorce her?"

"I don't know," Casey responded, staring out the window.

"Casey," Dan said, before he could lose his nerve. "Alix and I broke up. She doesn't want to live out in the country, and I do."

"No one is stopping you."

"I never wanted to get serious about a woman. Because my mother was so unhappy in her marriage. I never wanted to do that to anyone. So I let women like Alix do what they wanted."

"Must be tough," Casey said. "Beautiful women crawling all over you."

"Not always beautiful. My girlfriend in college was an unhappy little thing. I wanted to help her."

"Cute little things and bimbos. Your taste in women sucks."

"I'm trying to tell you that! But I don't want them now!" He took a breath, and said more quietly, "I had no intention of falling for you, it happened before I knew it. But you're the—" he was going to say the best thing that ever happened to him, but Casey interrupted.

"It happened and it's over. Don't worry about it. Leave me at the end of the driveway please. I need some air."

"Casey," Dan said.

"Stop the car and let me out."

He did. He couldn't force her to stay. He'd have to try again, even though he hated to argue. He couldn't believe how furious he'd been with Sarah. He never wanted to feel that way again. Brooding, he drove to Augusta in order to return the rental car.

*

As she walked up the lane, Casey's phone chirped. She checked her messages. Just as she feared, the hospital had called. So had Brad. Several times.

"Where are you?" he said. "Where is Zora? Call me."

What could she tell him? She worried about it most of the way up Woodward Lane, coming up with several impossible tales. She wanted to put off talking to him. She certainly didn't want to talk to the hospital, so Brad would have to do. But Aunt Cill would want the whole story as soon as Casey returned, giving her no time to deal with Brad. Besides, this was close to the limit of cell phone coverage. Already it was difficult to place the call. She walked back the way she came, until her phone had more bars on it, and called Brad.

"It's a long story," she began once Brad finished telling her about the flood and Joe's concussion.

The concussion was mild, but Joe ranted and raved until all the nurses wanted to give him a heavy sedative, concussion or not. And no one could figure out why the toilet suddenly poured out water. And why did Casey take Zora away from the hospital?

"Joe was abusing Zora, not physically, but keeping her away from her family," Casey lied. "When her sister Rinne showed up, she and Zora planned to get her away, to bring her to their parents' house."

"She could have gone to a shelter," Brad said. "Or to the police."

"Joe owns the police. He went to school with half of them."

"If she'd told one of the nurses, we could have helped her. You should have said something to me."

"Joe is dangerous. He kidnapped me. Hit me on the head and locked me in. Then I—"

"How could that be? He's a respectable man. Where are you?" he added.

"I'm almost home. We just dropped Zora off at her mansion—her house."

"She should be in the hospital."

"She's fine now. She insisted on being taken home. She thinks she can get Joe to let her see her family." Lying is hard, Casey thought. I'm getting in deeper and deeper.

"You took it on yourself to take her home, without checking her out of the hospital?"

How the hell could she explain magical happenings to this nice ordinary man?

"Joe wanted her to stay in the hospital, where he could see her. Zora wanted to go home. She hated being inside the hospital. It's kind of a phobia." This can't possibly work out, Casey thought. What can I say? Brad, I have to help my aunt re-grow the south woods today, and take care of whatever ails the birch trees?

"Then she needed to explain that to the doctors."

"We couldn't convince her to return. Maybe you can. Try calling her. I'm sorry, the cell coverage is terrible here." And she kept walking until it was, and Brad's voice cut off abruptly.

Time to get on with her life. Alone. She couldn't possibly tell anyone, especially a man, about her Skill. Except—but she was not going to think about Dan.

THIRTY-FOUR: GOING HOME

Rinne was astonished at how much she had missed Val, even during all her adventures. They didn't talk much at first, but after their lovemaking, Rinne told Val everything that happened.

At first, Val found it hard to believe any of it. "You mean there are people who can make saplings turn into trees overnight?" she said. "Did you actually see it happen?"

"I saw a forest that looked like it had been in a tornado, tree trunks down everywhere, now all covered in new green leaves. It looked like spring, during the hottest part of the summer," Rinne said. "But yes, I asked Casey if she'd mind doing a demonstration. She took me to the wrecked forest, found a sapling, and put her hands on it. It grew three feet while I watched."

Val stared at her.

"Come on, you saw me calm the ocean. If you want, we could go out in the parking lot, and I can call up a wind."

Val laughed a little. "I'm good at databases, accounting, and electronic gear," she said. "I never had any use for those artsy-fartsy types in college. How did I get involved with all this magic?"

"Because I seduced you," Rinne said, and proceeded to do so again.

Afterwards, Val said lazily, "Now you're a double whammy. No, a triple whammy! Water, wind, and sex!"

The next day, Rinne worried about how she could explain what had happened in Blake Harbor to her family.

"They won't believe Sarah's Skill transferred to me," Rinne told Val. "If they do believe it, they'll find a way to keep me on the Island."

"What are they going to do, lock you in the cellar?"

"We don't have a cellar," Rinne said. "Only a crawl space. Too much rock."

Val rolled her eyes.

Rinne reminded Val about the way her father had evaded her question about whether or not he'd keep her on the Island.

"He didn't actually say he'd keep you there," Val said.

"He meant it. I know him. And I don't want to live on the Island now. But they deserve to know what happened to Sarah."

"How about talking to your Aunt Darina?" Val said.

Rinne had told Val all about her family, including how Aunt Darina and Uncle Bill didn't have any Skill to pass on to their children, and how they worked at Seaview Cottage, where they met a lot of different kinds of people.

Val had responded by saying, "No wonder she's your favorite aunt."

Figuring Aunt Darina would be more likely to believe her story, Rinne gave her a call.

"Is this really you?" Aunt Darina asked. "I'm so glad to hear your voice! How are things going? Brian says you have a job at some fancy store!"

Rinne said that she did, and explained about her job. Darina thought the name "the Puffin Feather" was the funniest thing she'd ever heard.

"I need your advice, Aunt Darina," Rinne said, when they stopped laughing. "It's kind of a long story."

"Let me get my knitting and I'm all yours," her aunt said. Darina loved to knit, making gloves, hats, and sweaters for everyone on the Island, as well as Mr. and Mrs. Bresky and all of their friends. She listened to Rinne explain how she became a wind-worker, only making exclamations now and then.

At the end of the tale, Darina said, "There's a story about a Halloran woman who could do both. We always thought it was only a story."

"How come I never heard it?"

"Your Great Gran told me the story once. I thought your mother knew about it, too. Someone must have told it to you."

"No one ever did. What happened to the woman?"

"The story didn't say. I always believed it was wishful thinking."

"Exactly," said Rinne. "It's what everyone wishes for. If I come back, they'll want to keep me there."

"And you don't want to stay here."

"I can come help a few days a week. But I have a job here, and—and friends."

For a moment, all Rinne heard was the far-off clicking of knitting needles. The sound reminded her of spending time with her aunt. It reminded her of home. But she had another home now.

"Okay," said Darina. "I'll get the gang together. If we're all there, no one's going to force you to do anything. Nola's working in Gorham Harbor, but visits on weekends. How about the weekend of September 7th?"

Rinne agreed. Ten days. Ten days to worry.

"Don't worry," Val said. "I'll come with you. I'll protect you!"

That made Rinne laugh, but her worry continued.

On September 7th, Rinne and Val drove to Gorham Harbor, where they could get the ferry to Halloran Island.

"Rinne Gilley!" said the ferry captain. "Haven't seen you in a coon's age! Can't Brian get away to give you a lift?"

Crossing her fingers against the lie, Rinne said he couldn't. Her insides were vibrating, and her hands shook. When Nola came down the dock, carrying a briefcase, Rinne forced herself to greet her cousin cheerfully.

"My mom told me quite a story about you," Nola said.

Rinne explained her plan to tell everyone the story all at once. She introduced Val, and then talked about her work at the Puffin Feather. The conversation took them part way across to Halloran Island. Then Val asked Nola what she was doing, and the rest of the way Nola told them about learning how to write computer code for her job with a building company.

At the Island dock, the ferry captain gave two long and three short blasts on his whistle, which meant the ferry carried both visitors and mail. It brought Maris, Aunt Darina, and little Chloe—not so little anymore—rushing down to the dock. Rinne stared at Chloe, who must have grown six inches in the time Rinne had been away.

"Oh my God, Rinne!" said Aunt Darina, and enveloped her niece in a hug.

Maris didn't say anything. She stared at Rinne as if she were a visitor from another planet. Which, Rinne thought, was pretty accurate.

Rinne introduced Val. Maris came out of her trance far enough to say, "Val Costa. I've heard of your family. Come up to the house. Darina has created quite a party for you." Maris didn't sound enthusiastic about that.

Darina had gathered everyone to hear Rinne's story: Maris, Brian, and Gran Aileen; Uncle Bill, Liam and Chloe; Aunt Cathy, Uncle Neil, Nola and Gavin. Liam and Gavin now worked on the Island fishing boats; Chloe was in school at Gorham Harbor.

"She's only ten," Rinne said to Darina. "We didn't go there to the mainland school until we were at least thirteen."

"She's eleven now. And she needs to be with other kids. You all had each other; Chloe is by herself."

"You have to *visit* me!" Chloe told Rinne. "I'm in the band; I play the drums! Do you like my shirt? I designed it myself!"

Rinne admired her cousin's pink shirt—which had flutter sleeves and a low neckline—and asked when the next band concert would be. Chloe had grown up a lot since Rinne last saw her. She wore fashionably slim jeans, along with her fancy shirt. They made the little girl Rinne remembered seem like a long time ago.

In the Gilley house, all the doors and windows stood open to catch whatever breezes they could find. Food covered the dining table: chowder and crackers, cucumbers and tomatoes, homemade bread, cookies, pies, and cakes. Rinne couldn't eat any of it.

"Now I know how you felt when you first met *my* whole fam damily," Val whispered, grinning. Rinne smiled back, although her chest felt tight, and her breathing didn't work very well.

Everyone listened quietly as Rinne told about hunting for Sarah, about finding her picture in a newspaper. Talking about her trip to Blake Harbor, she told them about her car.

"Can you *drive* it?" Gavin teased.

"All the way to Blake Harbor," Rinne retorted.

Everyone gasped when Rinne explained how Sarah came to be in the hospital.

"She wouldn't do such a thing," Maris said. "She wouldn't use her Skill to wreck anything."

"She admitted it," Rinne said. "Besides, I saw the trees. Blown down as if a hurricane had come through. Check the weather. No hurricanes this summer."

After Rinne told how the wind-worker necklace transferred from Sarah to her, and opened her shirt to show them the necklace, everyone was silent.

"That's quite a tale," Brian said at last.

"It was quite an experience," Rinne said.

"And we're supposed to believe that Sarah is fine, that losing the necklace didn't make her sick all over again?"

"I have pictures of her," Rinne said. "And of the forest she destroyed. I also have her telephone number. You can call her."

Gran Aileen spoke up. "We won't know if it's really Sarah on the phone."

Val opened her mouth, but Rinne responded first. "Then go visit her, if you don't trust me."

"I don't leave the Island," Gran said. "You know I don't."

"Then Dad can go. He sailed all down the coast looking for Sarah. Now he knows right where to find her."

"I have work to do," Brian said.

"Then you'll have to take my word for it." There was a suffocating silence. Rinne finally broke it. "As soon as I can find and train someone to work at the Puffin Feather, I can spend three or four days a week going out with you, Dad."

"That's very kind of you," he said. "What will you do for the rest of the week? Go out with those Costas?" He glowered at Val, who grinned at him. "Did you tell them all about the Skill?"

"No," Rinne said. "Only Val. Because I had to use it to save her brother."

Then she had to tell about how Carl foolishly took his trawler out when a storm was predicted, about his boat motor having trouble, and how Rinne had calmed the water so Carl could get home safely.

"You don't have the strength to do that," Maris said. "You aren't much of a water-worker."

"I was there," Val said. "I saw it happen."

More silence.

"I would never use my Skill with anyone else," Rinne said. "I know it's only for our family, only to make enough money to support us. I know that. Sarah didn't. Or she didn't care. She wanted to use her Skill to make lots of money."

Brian put down his pie and stood up. "We need you here," he said. "If you can work the wind, it's a bonus." He walked over to where Rinne stood and put a hand on her arm.

"I'm sorry Dad, Mum, I can't live here. I have a life in Wabanaki Port now."

Gavin came over and put his arm around Rinne's shoulders. "Come on, honey," he said. "We need you here."

Rinne sighed. "Don't do this," she said. "Please let me go."

"We aren't doing anything," Gavin said, grinning.

Val put down her coffee and stood up.

"You gonna fight me for your girlfriend?" Gavin asked.

"I dunno," said Val. "Why are you holding on to her like that?"

Maris stepped forward. "You have to stay here, Rinne. We need you here."

"I said I'd come help on the boat for several days each week."

"What if there's a storm?" Maris asked.

Val turned to her. "Don't you folks have accurate weather forecasting out here? Or do you go out in spite of them, like my stupid brother Carl?"

"I know all about you, Val Costa," said Gavin. "Uncle Brian, want to know what kind of friend your daughter has?"

"She's been a better friend to me than any of you have been," Rinne snapped.

"We're your *family*," Maris said, shocked.

Rinne was worried about her family learning about her relationship with Val, and didn't want it to confuse things. Her family had enough trouble believing what happened with the necklace. While telling her story, she had purposely placed herself with her back to the big window that looked out onto the Gilley back yard, with its garden, chicken house, and the well that provided water for everyone. Now she closed her eyes and concentrated.

Before Gavin could continue talking about Val, everyone heard a strange sucking noise. It sounded like the outgoing tide when it swept between the rocky clefts below Lookout Point. Darina, who was closest to the back door, ran over and peered through the screen.

"The hell is that?" asked Uncle Neil.

"I pulled the water out of the well," Rinne said. "I'll put it back when you let me leave."

"You'll put it back right now!" Brian said.

"Promise to let us leave in the morning when the ferry comes back, and I will."

"I don't give in to threats!"

"You're as bad as you say Sarah is, destroying things," Gavin said.

Rinne bit her lip. It was too horribly true. But her father and Gavin were scaring her.

"I'll put it back," said Maris.

"You can try," said Rinne.

Before the two could battle it out, Aunt Darina marched forward, getting between Brian and Maris.

"What is the *matter* with you people! Do you plan to shut your daughter up in the henhouse, or what? If you shut her up, do you really think she'll use her wind-working talent for you? Oh, maybe you plan to starve her until she does? This is ridiculous!"

Maris glared at her cousin. "You don't understand anything. You don't have the Skill. Stay out of this."

Rinne's dad dug his fingers into her arm. "Put the water back!" he snarled.

A small, fierce wind appeared at Gavin's feet, then twisted around him, pulling his shirt up over his flying hair. He yelled. So did everyone else.

"STOP IT!" Brian roared, jerking Rinne off her feet. But the wind found him, tumbling him head over heels.

"Rinne Gilley, you stop that right now!" yelled Maris.

Rinne stopped. Her father and Gavin thunked to the floor. A stunned silence, then everyone began yelling again.

Rinne turned and ran out the door. Val followed her. They ran past the garden, around the henhouse, and up the slope to the pine grove.

Behind them, they could hear pounding feet, and Gavin yelling, "They went this way!"

"Where can we hide?" Val asked.

Rinne shivered in the September heat. They had to hide. Hide from her family, from the people who were supposed to love her. Why did she run? She couldn't possibly hide from them on the small Island.

"Rinne!" Val shook her a little.

Gavin, and Brian, and Uncle Neil appeared at the top of the hill.

"I can't run away from this," Rinne whispered to Val, as the men joined them.

"We only want to talk, Rinne," said Brian.

"You have to put the water back in the well," said Gavin, and he took her by the arm again. Rinne stared at him, then at his hand on her arm. He didn't let go.

"What do you want to talk about, Dad?" Rinne asked.

"We need you here. You belong here," he said.

Rinne shook her head. She could see Maris, Darina, and Chloe coming up the hill. Running did no good. She should have known it wouldn't, but she'd panicked. Now everyone was here again.

Chloe arrived first. "Mum is so disgusted," she said to Rinne. "So is my dad. He'll take you back to Gorham Harbor in his boat. He's taking Nola and me back anyway."

"She's my daughter," said Maris, coming into the pine grove right after Chloe. "She's not Darina's daughter."

Gavin still held Rinne's arm. But she was suddenly so tired that standing up felt impossible. She sat down hard on the pine needles, taking Gavin with her. Val sat down on her other side.

"My goodness, this is one difficult climb," said Aunt Darina, staggering into view. "I'm not used to doing it at a dead run. Excuse me while I sweat." And she sat down too, mopping her face with a blue bandanna.

"Rinne is not your daughter," Maris announced.

Darina sighed. "Well, I just want to understand your idea, here. Rinne comes back to the Island offering you double Skill, and first you act like she made it all up, then you try to force her to stay here forever because you *don't* think she made it all up. It's not like she had to come back."

"But she's here," Gavin said, putting an arm around Rinne's shoulders.

Rinne felt like she was being tugged around like a boat in a rip tide.

"I did have to come back," she said. "I was worried, but I had to. And now I've used my Skill against my family. I lost my temper. I'm sorry."

"No wonder you did," said Darina. "What with those boys grabbing you. I can't imagine what on earth they expected."

"They expected her to tell the truth," Maris said. "She couldn't possibly have the necklace unless she did something to Sarah." She turned on Darina. "If you hadn't insisted that Sarah work at Seaview Cottage, none of this ever would have happened!"

Darina leaned against a pine tree trunk. "I don't recall insisting," she said. "As I remember it, Sarah insisted. You could have said no. But you never said no to her, did you? Did you really think you'd keep her here when she found a chance to leave? Or she'd ever come back, when she has a rich husband and a mansion to live in?"

"How do we know Sarah has a mansion?" asked Gavin. "If Rinne had taken the necklace from Sarah, that's what she would say."

"So why won't you check out her story?" Uncle Bill had appeared quietly. Now he leaned against the pine tree where his wife sat, and grinned at everyone. "I think the phrase is 'innocent until proven guilty,' isn't it?"

"She's guilty of one thing," Gavin said loudly. He let go of Rinne, much to her relief, and stood up. "Ask her what her relationship is with that Costa woman. Ask her!"

Everyone stared at Rinne. There was a terrible silence.

Darina put out a hand to her husband, who helped her up. "I figure it's like that nice Mr. Ferraro," she said, and smiled at Rinne. "He stayed at the Bresky house last summer. A good sailor and fisherman, wasn't he, Brian?"

Brian stared at her. "Yeah, so?"

Darina turned back to Rinne. "Your dad thought Mr. Ferraro was wonderful. Even took him out on the *Sary*. But we hated to tell him this, spoil his fun, so we didn't. Mr. Daniel, who also stayed with the Bresky's, who hated fishing? He was Mr. Ferraro's husband."

Val laughed.

Darina continued. "Ask the Bresky's if you don't believe me. Oh, I forgot. You don't want to check on anyone's stories, do you?"

Brian and Gavin gaped at her.

Darina took her husband's hand.

"Come on, Bill, let's take these girls home to the mainland." She put out her other hand to Rinne, who hesitated, looking at her parents. Neither of them would meet her eye.

"We'll protect you," Chloe said. "I'm going back with you. I stay with my friend Olivia during the school week."

Rinne made her feet move. Together, she and Val, with Chloe, Uncle Bill, and Aunt Darina, hiked back down the rocky hill toward the dock.

"How are you, hon?" Bill asked Rinne. "Don't worry, your folks will come around. I'd like to ask, though, if you'd fix the well. We need it too, you know."

"Mom can do it."

"You know how she is. She'll say that you did it, you can fix it. And we'll be without water for a week."

So Rinne detoured to her back yard—no, not *her* back yard anymore—and pulled the water back into the well, while Uncle Bill jogged ahead of them to get his boat, the *Dara*, ready to go. He didn't fish, but everyone on the Island needed a boat.

"Don't cry, Rinnlet," Val said. "I know it's hard, but they'll get over themselves."

Rinne scrubbed tears off her face, pulled out a tissue. "I am as bad as Sarah," she said. "I knocked my own father down with my wind because I was angry with him. At least Sarah believed she was fighting for her marriage."

"Sarah was fighting to be a rich kept woman," Val said. "And no, since you ask, I don't propose to turn you into a rich kept woman."

Rinne laughed in the middle of a sob; then choked. Val handed her a bottle of water. Rinne drank gratefully.

"When I didn't see them, my parents, I could pretend they cared about me," she said. "But they're like Joe Burnside. All they want is the Skill."

"They're scared," Val said. "It's gotta be hard, living out here the way they do. They need whatever edge they can get. You're their edge now." She pulled a bag of cookies out of her backpack. "You haven't eaten anything," she said, handing Rinne a cookie.

Rinne shook her head. She felt shaky. "It wasn't supposed to be like this," she said, and drank more water.

"Come on, let's not keep your Uncle Bill waiting," Val said. Hand in hand, they left the Gilley yard. Darina was waiting for them.

"Let's get going," she said. "The sooner you're gone, the better."

"Darina, I stole some of your cookies," Val said conversationally. "As soon as those two grabbed Rinne, I figured we might have to run, so I stocked up. Raisins, nuts, oatmeal, chocolate, every food group. You make one mean cookie."

"Thank you dear," said Aunt Darina. "I packed a lunch for us, too. Iced tea, sandwiches, more cookies."

"You're as bad as my mother," Val said. "I gain weight whenever I visit her." Both of them laughed. Rinne found herself actually smiling.

But when they reached the sandy hill above the dock, they could see Rinne's parents standing by Uncle Bill's boat, talking to Chloe. When she saw them, Rinne stopped so quickly that Darina stepped on her heel, dislodging Rinne's sneaker.

"What is this?" Rinne asked her aunt. "Is Gavin here, too?"

"I don't see him," Val said. From where they stood, they could easily spot anyone coming toward them. But Val leaned down and picked up a rock.

"I'll talk to them," said Aunt Darina. While Val and Rinne waited—and Rinne retied her sneaker—Darina went down the hill to the dock. Chloe went over to her father's boat, while her mother talked with Brian and Maris. Then she waved at Rinne.

"They only want to say goodbye," Darina called.

"Goodbye," Rinne muttered to herself, but once again, she made her feet move.

Her parents stood together, side by side. They never did that. They usually acted like they were only distant acquaintances.

"I'm sorry," Brian mumbled. "I'm worried about the business. If I can't sell lobster, we can't stay out here."

Maris nodded. "Without you, I can't get all my work done and still go out on the boat to help with the waves."

"You really want to live out here, don't you?" Val asked.

Both Gilleys stared at her. "Of course," said Maris. "We always have."

'They looked like children who had misbehaved badly and expected punishment,' thought Rinne. No one should have to see her parents like that.

"It's okay," Rinne said. "I can still come here a few days a week, like I said. I'll let you know."

Her father grabbed Rinne into a bear hug, let her go. "Take care of yourself," he said. Her mother's hug was more formal, and she said nothing.

"All aboard who's going aboard," Uncle Bill called.

As the boat chugged away, Darina made Rinne drink two more cups of water and another of iced tea, then left her with Val. Nola, who had avoided the family confrontation, stayed in the cabin, reading a book on computer programming. But Chloe came to sit with them.

"I used to go out to your place on Lookout Ledge, where you went when your folks argued. I missed you."

"I missed you, too," said Rinne. "I'll come visit you at school." She smiled at her young cousin. "You've grown up. And you look great. You inherited Aunt Darina's fashion sense."

"Thanks. All the other kids wear distressed jeans, but I've worn enough really distressed jeans that were covered with fish scales." She twirled to show herself off. "I'm going to be a fashion designer. We're all saving up to send me to a school where I can learn how."

The boat growled and muttered.

"You know," said Chloe, "when I was younger, I was jealous of you and Sarah, but now I'm glad I don't have any Skill."

Rinne wondered if she wanted to have two of them. One had been plenty.

Chloe went to get a piloting lesson from her father. The purring of the motor, the familiar smells of wet rope and salt water, put Rinne into a doze.

She half woke up to discover that her head was in Val's lap, and to hear Aunt Darina talking.

"...because Brian got more and more angry. Maris would do that to a saint, but if they'd ever cared about each other.... Welp, they never should have married. But Great Gran insisted. She'd do anything to keep her stupid Skill going. Brian and Maris are oil and water. Twenty-five years of that'd make anyone act crazy."

Nola murmured something, and Darina laughed. "They don't fight like Bill and I do," she said. "They only yell at each other. A good fight clears the air."

Val kissed Rinne's hair. "Guess we'll have to learn how to fight," she said.

THIRTY-FIVE: NOW WHAT?

As she walked up the hill to her aunt's house, Casey found herself thinking about a huge glass of iced tea, with mint leaves from the garden. She'd take it out on the porch and look at the new trees in the south forest. But Aunt Cill was on the porch, so before getting any iced tea, Casey would have to explain about trying to get Zora to go back to the Island, and how Rinne learned to be a wind-worker.

Aunt Cill listened carefully. Then she snorted. "Growing up with that sister, traveling all the way here, and that girl only *now* discovered she's a wind-worker?"

"Her grandmother gave Sarah the necklace and taught her about being a wind-worker. How would Rinne have discovered it any earlier?"

Aunt Cill pursed her lips. "At the hospital, she had the necklace in her hand. Why didn't she figure out her connection to the darn thing then? No gumption."

"Actually," Casey said, keeping her temper, "their great grandmother started it all. She gave Sarah the necklace when she was too young to understand or really take responsibility for it, no matter how much her grandmother taught her about it." And Casey pursed her lips too.

"Why couldn't Rinne have controlled that girl, with her blowing things around?"

"How would she have done it, exactly?"

"Don't use that tone of voice with me, young woman. You have time to check the west woods before supper. All this plotting has kept you and Riordan from your work."

Casey felt her temper rising. "May I have a glass of iced tea first? Being caught in one of Zora's tornadoes has made me thirsty."

"Take it with you," Aunt Cill said.

"Yes ma'am!" said Casey, saluting.

"Priscilla, I do not tolerate such behavior!"

"You won't have to tolerate it long." And Casey headed for the stairs to get her hiking boots.

'It's me,' she decided. 'Something I do, something I am, irritates people.'

"No," said Annoying Voice. You and Dan were gone so long that Cill got worried. She thought Dan would bring Sarah way up north to her Island home, and worried about that, too." Annoying Voice had a point, but Casey was too angry to care.

She changed from sneakers to hiking boots and filled a water bottle at the bathroom sink. Iced tea would have to wait. She clumped loudly down the stairs, across the porch, and down the porch stairs. Her childish stomping did not make her feel any better.

The west woods included the Rock, which sloped down into scrub oak and cedar trees before merging with spruce and hemlock to become the north woods. At the western edge of the Rock, you could look down on the trees of Thayer Park and out at the sunset. Sunset wouldn't happen until nine p.m., which was hours away.

After checking all the trees below the Rock, and discovering they were doing fine, Casey couldn't face returning to Aunt Cill's disapproval, or running into Dan when he came back from Augusta. She wasn't going to risk crossing the yard to check on the birch trees, either, no matter how much they usually calmed her frustration. Aunt Cill would just find something else she should do or hadn't done. The birch trees would survive another day. She drank more water, but wasn't hungry.

She climbed back up on the Rock and curled up in her favorite sunset-watching spot, a niche in the granite that provided a back rest, a comfortable patch of grass to sit on, and a fine view of treetops and silver-blue sky. This time, however, the Rock didn't help her to forget her problems. She could feel Aunt Cill's house looming behind her, with her aunt waiting to scold her for unnamed transgressions. The secret hideouts she and her sister once created no longer worked. There were no secret hideouts now; there was only finding a way to make impossible choices.

A small person stood next to her. Greenish gray fur, long yellow eyes.

"You again," said Casey, tiredly. "Find another Guardian. Aunt Cill doesn't want me around."

"She will die, and this ancient forest with her." The thing had a low, purring voice that couldn't possibly come out of its long snout. People, however small, do not have long snouts. This one did.

"It's been fine for at least three hundred years," Casey told the whatever it was.

"More years than three hundred. Quiet years. Others cared for it. They are gone. Your people drove them away. Now you must care for it. New threats appear each day."

"Go talk to Aunt Cill. Leave me alone." And Casey rolled over in her nest, turning her back on the small person.

Wings flapped all around her. Claws reached for her face.

"Go ahead," she said, not looking at the green-gray bird. "Claw away. Then I really won't be able to help you."

Only silence answered her.

Settling back into her nest, Casey returned to brooding about the choices that had led her here. She went over all her mistakes. Staying in Rochester after college. Staying because of Jake. Agreeing to start a company with him even though she had no real business experience. Not getting enough capital together to keep the company going until they could create a solid base of customers. Ignoring Jake's tantrums. Coming here to Aunt Cill instead of staying with her sister or brother until she found another job. Believing Joe Burnside. Falling for Dan. Not getting along with Aunt Cill.

Annoying Voice told her to get up and stop focusing on doom and gloom. Casey told it to go to hell.

She dozed on the warm granite. The sun slid down the sky.

THIRTY-SIX: CILL'S STORY

Looking over his shoulder all the time for a police car sent out by the hospital, Dan drove back to the car rental place in Augusta, picked up his own van, and returned to Blake Harbor.

As he drove, he wondered again where Cill's money came from. She was paying a lawyer. She'd rented this car without a word about the cost. Woodward House was well kept up, with fresh paint inside and out, repairs made whenever needed. But much of the furniture and rugs must be a hundred years old, and Cill's clothes dated from forty years ago. Still, something paid his salary. Maybe Cill's father had left her money. Maybe her mother had been wealthy.

He knew he was thinking about Cill's money to keep from thinking about Casey. Maybe only that magic Skill thing had brought them together. But just because he finally recognized that Alix would never want what he wanted, growing older together, growing gardens and forests, didn't mean he and Casey were meant to be.

She was the first woman he'd cared about who hadn't desperately needed him, like Ellie in college, or flirted and charmed her way into his heart, like Alix. Was he one of those jerks who wanted to be chased, so he fell for the first woman who ignored him? One of those stupid men who expected all women to throw themselves at him?

But he'd never met anyone like Casey. She loved the forest as much as he did. She didn't need saving. They could save each other.

Reflecting his racing thoughts, the Ford speedometer read eighty-five miles per hour. He tapped the brake, hoping a lurking police car hadn't noticed how fast he'd been going. The speed limit on Route 1 was fifty-five miles per hour. Drivers didn't always obey the limit, but Dan didn't need any contact with the police now.

The long twilight was fading into a moonlit night when Dan parked in Cill's driveway and staggered into the kitchen. He hadn't wanted to stop for a meal, only now discovering a hollow stomach and shaky legs.

Cill met him at the back door. "That girl has disappeared again," she said.

"What do you mean, *again*? Where did she go?"

"Into the northwest woods. I simply asked her to check on them, and she went into a kind of tantrum, stamping around like a child. Probably decided to stay on her Rock overnight. She and her sister always thought it was the most wonderful place in the world."

"She got back, when, at three? It's almost nine."

Dan opened the refrigerator. He needed to eat before hunting for Casey. She might have fallen, broken something. He grabbed a slab of cheese to eat on his way to find her.

"Don't do that. I've kept the soup hot." Cill handed him a bowl, which Dan, still standing, began to wolf down.

"Why didn't you eat on the way back? Sit down, for heaven's sake, you'll ruin your digestion." She put a plate of bread on the table.

Dan shook his head, but he sat down. "Had a lot on my mind. Couldn't face any fast food. Your cooking has spoiled me. Did Casey tell you what happened with the necklace? Did she tell you about the tornado?"

"I can't imagine why that Rinne girl cares about her sister. Seems to me that Sarah/Zora is much too spoiled. And I don't know why that Rinne didn't figure out her wind-working Skill any sooner. And Priscilla should have figured out how to get away from all that wind."

Dan put down his soup spoon. "What else did you say to her?"

"I asked her to check the north woods. What with all these goings on, no one has been checking anything."

Discovering his patience was still on vacation, Dan stood up. "Between the two of us, Casey has probably given up and run away."

"Her car is still here. She's only sulking."

For the second time in a day, Dan lost his temper. "You treat her like a bratty child!"

"I'm not the one with a bratty girlfriend," Cill pointed out.

"Yeah, well, between us, we haven't made Casey's life easy. But hey, don't worry if she goes back to Rochester, or decides to work in Boston.

You have me. I'll take care of your woods. Although I can't re-grow anything for you." Picking up a slice of bread and putting down his bowl, he walked away.

He was all the way out the back door when Cill grabbed his arm. "What nonsense are you spouting?" In the pale light, her face appeared ancient.

Dan didn't care. "You know how good she is. She re-grew an entire forest for fu—for heaven's sake. If you want someone to take care of your damn woods, don't treat her like scum!"

Cill sat down heavily on the wide granite step, which had probably been there since the house was built.

"Sorry," Dan said. "It's been a hard day, what with crazy women creating tornadoes." He considered the old woman. "You all right?"

"I've been alone too long," Cill said finally. "A lot of kids had that Skill thing with the woods, but they wanted to marry, have babies, go to law school. They forgot about my woods. Generations. Can't trust 'em anymore. Don't know how."

Dan sat down beside her. Generations?

"If I'd married," said Cill. "If I'd had children. Too obstinate. Too hard to get along with."

"Kind of like Casey," said Dan.

"She too much for you?"

He shook his head. "Not at all. Never. But I haven't treated her any better than you have."

"Find her," Cill said. "Bring her back. I'll tell you both the whole long story." Instead of pursing, her mouth turned down ruefully. "Maybe she'll stay for you, if not me. See what you can do."

"She's been avoiding me. We—she had every reason to think I... but then Alix... I did send Alix away. She hates the country, but I love it. I love your woods. I tried to explain all that to Casey, but she wouldn't listen. She's angry. She has a right to be angry." He stopped. "I care about her," he added softly.

"You might change your mind about staying here after you hear what I have to say." Cill climbed to her feet, drawing him with her. "I'll make cookies. Coffee. We'll need 'em." And she marched back into the kitchen.

Although a full moon slanted through the trees, Dan pulled a flashlight out of his car and headed for the Rock. Getting there was hazardous enough in daylight—hobblebush, stray stones, overhanging shadbush.

Up on the Rock, the moonlight was stronger, but it made shadows everywhere, shadows hiding Casey. Especially if she was hurt. By the time Dan finally saw the gleam of her hair under the flashlight, he'd convinced himself that something awful had happened to her, and the way she curled into the Rock made his heart pound with fear.

But when he touched her arm, saying her name, she stirred, blinked, and said, "Dan. What time is it?"

When the fear let go of him, his knees felt weak. He sat down beside her. "Almost nine-thirty."

"Oh my gosh. Is Aunt Cill furious?" She sat up. "Ow, I am stiff. Note to self: do not sleep on rocks." She stretched her arms and legs, then rolled her shoulders. "Yowch."

Dan found her water bottle where it had tumbled away and handed it to her. "We thought you might have run off. Neither of us has treated you very well."

"Don't worry about it." Casey was on her feet now. "It was the storm, or the magic or something. You have a girlfriend. I understand that."

"Alix is gone," he said. "I told her I wanted to stay out here. Then I ignored her pouting. She hates the woods like my mother hated the farm. She left." Dan considered explaining more about his life with Alix and why he thought he loved her, but thought better of it. Instead, he only said, "I was glad she left."

For a moment, Dan hoped she'd finally forgive him for Alix, but Casey turned her back on him, brushing off her clothes, drinking water.

"We need to get back. Aunt Cill is already angry at me. Missing supper will only make it worse."

"I told her to get over being angry, treating you like a naughty child. She wants to talk to us. Tell us the whole story, she said."

That brought her around to face him. "What whole story?"

They were standing close together, balancing on the uneven rock. He wanted to kiss her. He didn't. Her eyes gleamed in the shadows, with tears or anger, he couldn't decide.

"I don't know. She said it because I kind of yelled at her," he said. "Told her I wouldn't be surprised if you left, the way she treats you. The way I've..." He ran out of words.

She stared at him for what felt like five minutes, then said, "Okay, come over here where we can sit." She led him back to the little grassy area where she had been sleeping. "Tell me again how you ended up with Alix, and why you dumped her."

Dan had been thinking about this all the way back from Augusta.

"I grew up on a farm in New Hampshire. My mother hated it. I have no idea why she married my dad. She hated the time he spent in the fields and woods. But I loved it. Dad and I planted the fields, tapped maple trees, hunted for venison. Farming in New Hampshire doesn't make much money. We needed the meat.

"Thing was, my mom always wanted me to help fix things in the house, or weed the vegetable garden. It gave her a chance to complain about living on a farm. I learned not to argue," Dan said. "My older sister Cherie always sided with mom." He stopped for a moment. "The day Cherie married, mom left. Found a place near Cherie and her husband in Nashua. Dad was alone. One day, he went out into the Abenaki lodge I'd helped him make. He was very proud of our Native ancestors, so he made a lodge to honor them. He died there. We sold the farm. I took my share, quit my job in the carpentry shop, and took my stuff to craft fairs. Made my sculptures."

"Sculptures," said Casey. "They're your Skill." She put her hand on his arm, took it away again.

"I never wanted the kind of arguing that went on in my family," he explained. "As a result, I only had girlfriends who needed something from me, or flirted, like Alix did. I guess I was scared of having a marriage like my parents. Until I met you."

"Who didn't throw herself at you right away. What a shock it must have been."

"But you're yourself. You do what's important to you. You don't need a man to make you real."

She stared out at the dark sky, where a few stars blinked. "Maybe not to make me real. But something always comes along that's more important to me than he is. Men hate that."

"What if it's important to him, too?"

"Then he's too good to be true."

With a wry smile, Dan said, "That's not me. But I can learn."

Staring up at the moonlit sky, Casey was quiet for a moment.

"I have a lot to figure out, Dan. I have to get used to this thing Rinne calls the Skill. I have to discover if I can even live with my aunt. I can't be what she wants me to be. Whatever that is."

"I was pretty rude to her," Dan said. "Told her you'd probably leave in the morning, and she had only herself to blame. And me, I screwed up too, but I tried to explain—" He stopped, then started again. "I told Cill how badly she'd treated you. She might fire me for insubordination or something. If she does, she'll need you here."

"I won't leave until I find a job," Casey said, and laughed a little. Then she stood up. "Let's go face the old lady," she said, and led the way down the Rock.

They followed the flashlight beam along the path. Dan wanted to put an arm around Casey to make walking easier, but he didn't. She stayed in front of him all the way up the long porch stairs and into the living room, where the old lamp with the fringed shade brought out gleams of flowers on the faded Persian rug.

The smell of coffee and baking cookies made Casey stagger a little, brushing against Dan. "I didn't realize how hungry I am," she said, pulling away.

"There you are," said Cill, standing in the dark arch between the living and dining rooms. "Come into the kitchen. I have something to show you."

The kitchen table was set with the blue lusterware plates, cups and saucers, along with a platter of oatmeal raisin cookies, slices of cheddar cheese, and a pitcher of milk. Aunt Cill only used her old lusterware on what Casey's dad called "state and festival occasions," such as the formal tea party she'd held for her dad and mother when they first married. Casey's dad loved to tell the tale. "Scared to death I'd break one of those little cups," he'd say. "Never did get any tea."

Also on the table was the family Bible. It was immense, with an embossed cover and gold edging on the pages. Aunt Cill kept it in the drawer of a marble-topped table by the sofa. When Casey was about eleven, she'd begun to wonder what was in that drawer. One day, alone in the room, she'd opened it. The giant book with HOLY BIBLE on the front seemed to rebuke her for her curiosity. Hearing voices in the hall, Casey had shut the drawer carefully and never opened it again, or mentioned what she'd seen.

Aunt Cill poured coffee for each of them and handed Dan the pitcher of milk. Like Casey, Aunt Cill drank her coffee black.

"Before I tell my story, you each need to look at this," Aunt Cill told them. She set the Bible between Dan and Casey, opened at the first page. That page, and a few pages more, had originally been left blank, so the family genealogy could be recorded. And it was. At the top of the first page, in faded, spidery ink, Casey and Dan read:

Henry John Woodward b. 1849, d. 1949, m. Mary Thayer, 1870
Children:
Henry Woodward Jr. b. 1871, d. 1874
Priscilla Woodward, b. 1872
John Woodward, b. 1873, d. 1898
Katharine Woodward, b. 1879, m. George Oakes 1892, d. 1959.

"My poor father." Aunt Cill's bony finger rested on his name: Henry John Woodward. "He desperately wanted a son to carry on the Woodward name and tend his forest. But little Henry Junior died of some kind of fever. So many babies died before all the fancy drugs we have now. And my brother Jack died of what we called consumption. Tuberculosis, they called it later. But he didn't have that Skill thing. Only I had it. Sister Katherine didn't want it; she always wanted to marry and have dozens of children."

"Your *father?*" Casey asked, staring at the date. Henry John Woodward. Born 1849. Could his death date be wrong? No one in that generation lived to be one hundred.

And his child, Priscilla Woodward, born in 1872. With no death date. Impossible.

Aunt Cill nodded. "Stick with me a minute." She slid her finger down to the line below her sister Katherine and her husband George, to the list of their children: George, Mary, and Olive.

George Henry Oakes, b. 1893, d. 1938
Mary Elizabeth Oakes, b. 1895, d. 1915
Olive Katherine Oakes, b. 1901. m. Frederick Prichart, 1922. d. 1978.
Frederick Prichart, Jr, b. 1923, d. 1943
Elizabeth Katherine Prichart, b. 1930, d. 1999

"My sister Katharine had three children," Aunt Cill continued, looking at Casey. "One of them was your great grandmother Olive. She married a Prichart. Her son Fred was killed in that second big war. His sister was your grandmother Elizabeth. She married Jonny Bates."

That second big war must be World War II. A memory stirred in Casey. "My grandmother Lizzie told me about her brother. He was a hero. Died on Omaha Beach."

"That second big war," Aunt Cill agreed.

Casey stared at the handwriting. It hadn't changed in all those years. Did everyone write the same way? But on the next lines, she saw the names of her grandmother, her mother, and her aunt and uncle.

Elizabeth Katharine Prichart, b. 1930, m. Jonathan Bates 1955.

Mark Henry Bates, b. 1957

Priscilla Rose Bates, b. 1960, m. 2003, Eli Metzger.

Linda Susan Bates, b. 1965, m. 1987, Virgil John Todd

Casey put her finger on the name Elizabeth Katharine Prichart.

"That's Grandmother Lizzie. And there's my mom. Her name is Linda," she added, for Dan's benefit. "She was Linda Susan Bates before she was married. She took Dad's name, even though none of her friends took their husbands' name." She scanned the list of her ancestors. "My parents were never interested in genealogy. When some of the friends found theirs, and were all excited about it, Dad said 'It's who we are now that matters'." Casey grinned wryly. "He was wrong."

Aunt Cill sighed. "Both your mom and your Aunt Rose loved it here the same way you did when you were a little girl. But neither of them ever cared to learn about our family. And each one got married. Just like the rest of 'em."

Casey looked at the scratchy handwriting. There were her grandmother Lizzie and her children. There was Casey's Uncle Mark, who had married a man, although that marriage didn't make the Bible list. There was her mother, Linda. And her wonderful Aunt Rose.

Now she knew how her family was related to Aunt Cill. If she could believe any of this.

"All those children," said Aunt Cill. "All those years. I made sure that every single one of them visited me; let 'em play in the woods and on the

Rock. Had hopes for Olive's boy Harry, but he became a doctor. Then there was your aunt Priscilla Rose, your mother's sister."

"Aunt Rose was a Priscilla?" Casey asked, her finger on the name.

"Yup. When she was twelve, she decided to be Rose."

Feeling guilty about her own name change, Casey said, "Priscilla is a hard name for a kid these days. You get teased a lot."

"Well," Aunt Cill said, "your parents, and your Aunt Rose's parents, were hoping I'd give them my land. Sometimes I wonder if your father married Linda because he hoped I would. Like Joey, he wants to plant houses all over it."

Casey scanned for her father's name: *Linda Bates, m. 1987, Virgil John Todd.* Another impossible name for a child, so he was always called Jack. Aunt Cill had scrawled his name so furiously it was almost unreadable. She'd never liked him. Now Casey understood why.

Casey's name, however, was carefully printed underneath her parents' names. *Priscilla Moreen Todd b. 1995.* Printed, probably because Aunt Cill didn't want it to look like her own signature. Although Aunt Cill didn't seem to have a middle name.

"What happened with Aunt Rose?" asked Casey. Next to her sister T.J., Aunt Rose was her favorite relation. Too busy as a college professor of mathematics, Rose hadn't married until she was over forty.

"Same as you. She went to college, she went to work, she forgot the woods, she got married."

Casey wondered why she had wanted to marry Jake. He'd mocked her habit of sketching, called her Ms. Rembrandt or Picassette, until she stopped sketching. She had allowed him to stop her.

Dan never said things like that. She didn't look at him.

Dan put a finger on the name *Priscilla Woodward, b. 1872.*

"You're only a hundred and forty-five years old, not a hundred and fifty."

"If it's really you," Casey said. All this was interesting, but after her experience with Joe Burnside, Casey didn't want to believe anything unless it happened right before her eyes. Or under her fingers, when she was painting. Or growing a plant or a tree.

"Riordan, go get the picture album that's in the bottom drawer of the maple chest in my room," Aunt Cill said.

Once he was gone, she turned to Casey. "After everything you've been through, you can't believe one more unusual thing? You're certainly your father's daughter. All logic and accounting."

Ignoring the insult, Casey asked, "Does this mean I have to live forever?"

"My father only lived a hundred years."

"Was he the first in the family to take care of forests?"

"I think so. His father came here from Scotland to fish. My papa bought this land for the timber. But he couldn't stand to sell it. Every time a tree came down, he'd have to go to bed for three days. My poor mother thought he'd gone crazy. Eventually, he logged some of it himself, with a couple of hired men. It worked better if he could talk to the tree through its cutting."

"Good heavens," Casey said faintly.

"Father could pick out a birds-eye maple without even cutting into it, and those were like gold. And he sold off a whole patch of tall spruce trees for masts. But he was so careful, it took a long time to cut any of it, especially because he ended up in bed after every tree was down. Then he invested the money and lived by the interest, and by farming. He took care of the woods, too. Walked them every day until he was ninety-five years old. Re-grew the trees he had to cut down."

"Did he see green-gray animals or people? One looks like a coyote lizard, one like an owl. The first one I saw was a butterfly."

Her aunt stared at her in astonishment. "You saw them?"

"They're mad at me because I plan to leave here."

Aunt Cill suddenly looked every one of her impossible years. "I only saw one once, the owl, when I took over from my father. He only saw one once, too. The first time he cut down a tree. I think it was the coyote thing."

"Once is enough," Casey said. "They don't tell me anything useful. And that coyote thing wants to bite off my feet."

"But it didn't." And Aunt Cill actually smiled. "They never hurt you."

Dan returned, with a big old scrapbook. Turning pages, which wafted a scent of ancient mildewy paper, Aunt Cill showed them a sepia photograph of her family on the front porch, wearing old-fashioned clothes. Below the picture, in faded ink, it said: "Father, Mother, John, Priscilla, Katharine, 1893." Parents and three children; a teenage girl with her hair in a big ribbon, a very thin boy a few years older, and an older girl with her hair piled loosely up on her head. "Called a pompadour," Aunt Cill said, as Casey's finger traced the hair. "Very fashionable at the time. I was a very fashionable young woman."

The mother and younger son sat in wicker chairs that looked like the ones now on the porch, but couldn't be; wicker didn't last a hundred years. The father and two older children stood behind them. The older girl was long and lanky, like her father. She also had Aunt Cill's long nose.

On the next page was a photo of that older girl. She was gazing at a spray of leaves in her lap. Now her hair was loose, caught back with a big ribbon, curling frizzly. Like Aunt Cill's. Like Casey's. Casey turned the picture over. "Priscilla Woodward, 15 yrs" was written in faded brown.

"Red hair was unfashionable when I was young," said Aunt Cill. "I never figured out why. Now young women dye their hair red."

More pictures. The young woman that couldn't possibly have been Aunt Cill became older—and looked more and more like her. She posed with her sister Katherine's family, the girls in long dresses from about 1900. She posed with her niece Olive's family, the girls in low-waisted flapper dresses. And there was Casey's grandmother Lizzie as a young girl, sitting on the big front porch, in Aunt Cill's lap. Casey had seen that picture in her grandmother's house. Yes, it was definitely Aunt Cill's face. Casey had looked at the picture for many years, many visits to her grandmother, but had never realized that she was looking at Aunt Cill.

"Wow," said Dan, finally. "Didn't any of those nieces and nephews ever figure out how old you are?"

"I never thought about it," Casey said. "Maybe they didn't either. Part of the—" she stopped.

"Magic," Dan said.

Casey couldn't say anything. She had to believe it. Aunt Cill was born in 1872.

Aunt Cill snapped the book shut. "You're not eating your cookies."

Casey figured she'd already downed about ten of them, but took another. Here she was, plain Casey Todd, failure at everything she'd tried, now the last best hope of an ancient magic.

Dan was turning pages in the big Bible. "So none of these people, none of your relatives, had the—the Skill."

"A lot of 'em had it when they were young. But all of 'em forgot about it, gave it up, got married, went to work. I'd figured I'd be the last. So I asked young Adams to make me a will, putting some of the land into my mother's Thayer Park, giving the rest to the state of Maine."

"Thayer Park. West of the Rock ledge. Named for your mother," said Dan, in wonder. Aunt Cill nodded.

"That's why you didn't trust me," Casey said. "Even after I re-grew the south woods. You thought I was like all those others. I'd leave, get a job, get..." she stopped. She did not want to talk about getting married in front of Dan.

"Like I told Riordan, I've been alone too long," Aunt Cill said. "But if you'll stay, maybe this old dog can learn some new tricks."

Casey nodded. "Excuse me," she said. "Too much coffee." Besides, she needed time to think.

In the new bathroom with its shower and blue linoleum floor, she considered. She loved the woods. She hated the idea of returning to a nine-to-five job. No wonder those jobs never worked out. Did she really belong here?

Coming out of the bathroom, a breeze drew her to the screen door. Outside, tree frogs buzzed. And something was coming across the yard. She knew what it was even before she could see it clearly--the green-gray coyote thing.

Opening the door, she stepped out and sat on the big stone step. The thing came right up to her, tilted up its long head, and gave Casey a serious, yellow-eyed look.

"Whaddya think?" she asked it. "Shall I stay? Can I do this?"

The yellow eyes questioned her, and she answered the question. "I don't want to do it alone."

The thing smiled, licked her hand, then turned and flowed back across the yard. It disappeared even before the darkness swallowed it.

Annoying Voice cheered quietly. Not so annoying, Casey thought, mentally apologizing for calling it mean names.

"I'll always listen to you now," she told Annoying Voice.

As Casey returned to the kitchen, Aunt Cill looked up. Casey had never seen that look on her aunt's face, hope and fear together, as if Aunt Cill was a very young girl.

"I'll stay," Casey said, and put out her hand. Aunt Cill took it. Like business partners, they shook hands. Then Cill pulled Casey into a brief hug, and turned away.

"It's past my bedtime," the old lady said. "Don't forget to turn out the lights. Good night, dears."

And off she went, while Casey was still digesting being called her aunt's "dear."

"Well," said Dan. "I'll say good night too."

"Wait," Casey said, before she could lose her nerve. "I mean, it's not very late."

He said nothing for a moment—a horribly long moment—then he said, "Sure."

"There's some wine left," Casey said. "Not the poison kind."

He nodded and followed her into the dining room. She went to the sideboard for the old glasses—crystal with flowers etched on the sides—then pulled out the wine and poured them each a glass. They sat down at the table, Dan in the place he always took when reporting to Aunt Cill about her forest. Casey took Aunt Cill's place. She wanted to be able to see Dan's face, and sitting right next to him would have made it harder than it already was.

"So much has happened," Casey said lamely.

He nodded again, still serious. "It's a lot for you to take in."

"And you. I mean, I hope you don't feel--" She couldn't think of the right word. "That I've taken over your job."

"I don't think Cill will throw me out. She seems to have forgiven me for being so—straightforward."

"Of course she won't throw you out!" Casey hadn't even considered that. "The forest needs your sculptures." Deep breath. "But. I couldn't have managed any of this without you."

"You'll learn, though. You'll be fine."

"Well, I have a hundred years to learn how."

And, Casey thought, 'I'll be all alone like Aunt Cill, hoping maybe one of my nieces will grow up like me, only she won't, none of them will, and I'll have to wait a hundred years.'

"Hey," said Dan.

Casey swiped the tears away. "I guess I'm more tired than I thought," she said, standing up.

He stood up too, and took her into his arms. They stood there while Casey sniffled into his shoulder. After a few minutes, he said, conversationally, "I fall in love with this redheaded woman and then it turns out that she's a princess."

When Casey heard "fall in love," all the worried knots in her heart released. But then she leaned back to stare at him. "A what?"

"Heir to Cill's forests and magic. And me a farm boy turned starving artist."

"Who makes magic sculptures. Who kept Aunt Cill going until I got here, until I finally figured out what I was supposed to do and how to do it. Who kept me going while I did that. Who I can *talk* to."

He smiled. "You forgot the most important part," he said, and kissed her.

Out in the forest, a bird laughed. It sounded almost human.

END

www.ingramcontent.com/pod-product-compliance
Lightning Source LLC
LaVergne TN
LVHW090056161224
799166LV00006B/1195